The N

The Mistress

VIVIENNE LAFAY

Black Lace novels are sexual fantasies.
In real life, make sure you practise safe sex.

First published in 1996 by
Black Lace
332 Ladbroke Grove
London
W10 5AH

Copyright © Vivienne LaFay 1996

Typeset by CentraCet Limited, Cambridge
Printed and bound by Mackays of Chatham PLC

ISBN 0 352 33057 0

Chapter One

*E*mma Longmore was examining the photograph in her hand with a fond smile. She was in the drawing-room of her home, the 'Longmore Academy for Young Ladies', entertaining Sir James Northrop, a handsome man in his late forties.

'Your daughter is the perfect model of a blushing bride!' Emma exclaimed. 'How enchanting she looks. And the Marquis is such a charming young man. I am sure Henrietta will be very happy at Chateau Morville.'

'And here is the wedding group, yourself included.' Sir James handed her a second photograph, adding, 'You look quite ravishing, my dear. That elegant bonnet becomes you very well.'

Emma threw him a coquettish look. 'Thank you, Sir James. I was very pleased to be invited. Such a wonderful wedding.'

'I could not possibly have left you out, Mrs Longmore. It is all thanks to you that our dear Henrietta has been so satisfactorily matched. A father always has high hopes for his daughters, of course, especially when they are the apple of his eye. But French nobility! I would never have dared to set my sights so high.'

Emma put the photograph down on a small table nearby then faced the proud father with a smile. 'Hen-

1

rietta is a refined and beautiful young woman, Sir James, and will make a wonderful society hostess. Yet do not forget that it is a love match. Jules was completely besotted with her from the first time they met, and she was equally taken by him.'

'Ah, love!' Emma detected a twinkle in his warm brown eyes. 'When you get to my age I'm afraid the practicalities of life outweigh such matters.'

'Surely not, Sir James! A gentleman is never too old for romance!'

'Tell that to my wife, Mrs Longmore! Still, I am glad that my sweet Henrietta has a husband who is pleasing to her as well as titled. The fact that most of his fortune comes from the production of fine claret is a bonus, of course.'

He took Emma's hand and stared meaningfully into her eyes. 'Seriously, though, I am extremely grateful for all you have done for Henrietta. I can scarcely thank you enough.'

'It was my pleasure. But there is one small favour you might grant me, Sir James.'

'Anything, my dear!'

'Henrietta told me that you have a box at Covent Garden, and I do so love the opera. Alas, I have little opportunity to attend these days, and the best seats are so expensive . . .'

'I'd be honoured to escort you!' he boomed, beaming from ear to ear. 'They're doing something by that Italian chap. What's it called? La . . . something beginning with T.'

'La Traviata,' Emma said, stifling a giggle. It was clear that Sir James was no opera buff.

'That's the fellow. Are you free tomorrow night, Lady Longmore? I don't believe any of my wife's infernal relatives have booked the box until the weekend.'

'That would be perfect,' Emma smiled. 'It is so kind of you to invite me.'

'Not at all. Least I could do. Shall we say eight o'clock, then?'

He kissed her hand and departed, leaving Emma well pleased. Another of her young ladies married off most satisfactorily, and a treat for herself into the bargain. Since Sir James was clearly taken with her, and denied physical love by his strait-laced wife, Emma was confident that he'd be flirting and spooning shamelessly before the evening was over. How diverting!

Yet her thoughts moved rapidly on to the man who occupied the prime place in her heart. Long ago she and Daniel, Lord Merton, had decided not to live together permanently but to remain intermittent lovers. Emma had her Academy in London, while Daniel had Harfield Hall and his travels to occupy him. In the first glorious flush of their romance they had written many love letters when apart, but nowadays they seldom exchanged *billets doux*.

In some ways, however, they were fonder of each other than ever. When they did meet it was with renewed passion and a genuine interest in each other's life, particularly in their amorous adventures. Emma told herself that it was better that way. Yet she missed him most often when she was obliged to be in the company of lesser men, who lacked Daniel's wit, intelligence and breeding. Still, she thought with a sigh, examining the photographs once again, they made her appreciate Daniel even more when she did see him.

The Opera House at Covent Garden was full to bursting. From the excellent vantage point of Sir James Northrop's box, Emma could see many society figures in their jewelled finery, eagerly anticipating the performance by the young Italian tenor, Giacomo Venuti. As her glance swept over the faces of the crowd she recognised Charlotte Sayers, another ex-pupil of the Academy, sitting with her current lover, the wealthy and dashing Lord Cunningham.

Nearby was one of Emma's own former lovers, a brilliant surgeon. Her heart still leapt when she saw his handsome profile, but she had bowed out of his life discreetly when he married the woman who was now at his side. As she watched he glanced up and acknowledged her, with a nod and a slight smile, bringing a warm glow to her bosom.

Sir James handed her a pair of opera glasses. 'Are you quite comfortable, my dear?' he smiled, patting her hand.

'Yes, thank you Sir James! I am very happy.'

He bent towards her, murmuring in her ear as he looked down at her orchid corsage, 'Not half so happy as I am, Mrs Longmore. It is many years since I was sitting with such a beautiful woman as yourself and, I confess, I feel quite rejuvenated.'

This was most promising. Emma gave her escort an open smile and placed the glasses to her eyes, squeezing her bosom together with her upper arms to accentuate her cleavage. She knew that her companion would be making some kind of advance to her before long, and she was more than ready for it. The sight of so many distinguished and good-looking people was setting her heart racing and some dalliance with Sir James after the opera would round off the evening very nicely.

'My dear, this is very heaven!' he sighed, as the orchestra started up. When they lowered the house lights she felt his arm creep around her waist. Unprotesting, she moved her gilt and red plush chair a little closer to his.

The tragic tale of Violetta, the consumptive courtesan, began to unfold in glorious harmony, and Emma was caught up in the drama both on and off stage. She knew that she made an attractive picture, with the illumination from the stage brightening her dark-blonde curls, adding a warm patina to the naked skin of her arms and shoulders and highlighting the brilliant deep blue of her satin gown. She knew no man could resist her when she was on form, and tonight the tingling warmth in her veins must have been almost tangible, lending an enticing gleam to her eye and a subtle undertone to the jasmine and tuberose of her perfume.

In the interval, Sir James paraded her on his arm, evidently pleased to be seen with such a sophisticated and elegant lady. His wife was a dowdy soul, and the contrast between the two women was hinted at when a man of his acquaintance approached them in the foyer.

'Well, well, if it isn't Sir James Northrop!' said the young dandy, with a sneering smile. 'I hardly recognised you in such enchanting company. And how is your good lady wife?'

Once Emma would have felt snubbed and insulted, but she was long past fretting over such ill-mannered behaviour. Instead she stared straight at the man with an implacable smile. If his expression had not been so disagreeable he would have been decidedly handsome.

'May I present a business associate of mine, Stephen Landers?' Sir James said, turning to Emma. 'Stephen, this is Emma Longmore, the woman who has brought me the most happiness in the world!'

Emma was taken aback. What was he thinking of? She could see the young man's brows being raised so high that they almost disappeared into his hairline. After the shocked hiatus Sir James continued, 'She has turned my dear daughter Henrietta into such a fine lady that she has recently married into the French nobility.'

Bravo, Sir James! thought Emma, hiding a smile.

'Really?' Stephen shook her hand, his brown eyes glinting with new interest and a hint of respect. 'I suppose you do not practise matchmaking in reverse? I should not mind taking a French heiress to wife.'

Their laughter eased the somewhat tense atmosphere, and then Sir James sauntered off with Emma on his arm. She was beginning to enjoy the evening immensely!

As they returned to their box, Emma found herself reflecting on what had happened and mentally rehearsing how she would tell Daniel about it. This had become habitual with her. Every detail of her life apart from him was carefully filed away, like paper cut-outs in a scrapbook, to be brought out later for his entertainment.

Before the lights went down for the second act, Emma

glimpsed Stephen Landers near the front of the stalls, sitting between two men. Despite his rather rude manner Stephen was a handsome young beau. Intrigued, Emma watched him scan the crowd. He turned his head and surveyed the boxes on the other side of the theatre, then at last his eyes came to rest in her direction.

Now he was lifting the opera glasses to his eyes. Seeing him turn the focusing wheel, Emma was convinced that he was spying on her and Sir James and she felt an illicit thrill shudder through her. Leaning forward so that the deep cleft of her bosom could be seen more easily, she gave him a smile and a wink. Hurriedly Stephen put his glasses into his lap and faced the stage. *Touché*, she thought, with a little chuckle.

When the opera was ended, with the encores and applause still echoing round the auditorium, Sir James helped Emma on with her cloak and murmured, 'I should like to take you to supper, my dear, but I confess I do not know where to go. I am normally in town with my wife, and then we are obliged to stay with one of her numerous relatives.'

'I know the very place,' Emma smiled. 'Compton's Supper Rooms. It is just around the corner from here.'

It was an establishment that Emma knew well. She often entertained her lovers there, confident in the knowledge that they could later avail themselves of the private rooms upstairs. As they were on their way out, however, Emma saw Stephen Landers in the foyer. He looked embarrassed as she caught his eye, but she touched her escort's arm saying, 'Look, there is Mr Landers, by himself. Shall we ask him to dine with us this evening?'

Sir James looked quite put out, and she could guess why. He was hoping to have her all to himself that evening. 'I do not know the gentleman very well,' he hedged. 'We used to do quite a deal of business together, but I believe he has found other suppliers recently.'

'All the more reason for you to be civil to him,' she

smiled. 'Oh, do ask him, Sir James! We shall make a merry party, I'm sure.'

He still looked doubtful but was in no position to argue with her. Stephen looked surprised as the pair approached, and was even more amazed when the invitation was issued.

'You are alone this evening, Mr Landers, are you not?' Emma said innocently. He nodded, swallowing. 'Then you have no excuse. We are going to Compton's Supper Rooms, where there is always a congenial atmosphere. Do you know it?'

His blushing countenance said he did, although he made a vague denial. The three of them passed out of the palatial splendour and into the street, jostled along by the dispersing crowd until the bright portal of Comptons beckoned them in.

Although the head waiter knew Emma well he was, as ever, the soul of discretion. They were led to a curtained alcove where a table set for two was rapidly converted into one for three. Emma, seated at the end of the table with a gentleman on either side of her, felt her spirits rising like a barometer on a summer's day.

'Well, gentlemen, what shall we order?' she mused, surveying the menu. 'I believe the Whitby oysters are very good.'

She threw Stephen a mischievous glance and was gratified to see an answering gleam in his dark eyes. Something told her that he knew of the reputation of both Comptons and oysters. She was warming to him by the minute.

'Do you know that the French have the temerity to claim that our English oysters, the best in Europe, originally came from a bay in Brittany?' he said.

'Really?' Emma smiled.

'Not only that, but all their culinary skills have been stolen from the Italians, although they would never admit it.'

'Now just a minute, young man, I won't have a word said against the French in my presence! Not now my daughter has married one of 'em,' Sir James grumbled, but good-naturedly. 'Shall we have a dozen oysters each, then, and a bottle of champagne?'

Emma enjoyed watching the men taking a sensual delight in the consumption of the shellfish as they slid the live creatures slowly down their throats. She also made sure that each of them had a good view of her own technique. First she pursed her lips against the shell then languidly dropped the soft flesh onto her tongue, mouthing it a little with eyes closed in sensual appreciation of the texture and flavour, before washing it down with a sip of champagne. With both men's eyes upon her she felt an exhilarating sense of being in control, and her appetite was whetted for what would follow once they moved upstairs.

After they had dined on roast pheasant followed by lemon water ice, Charlotte Russe and cheese, the head waiter made his usual polite recommendation. 'May I suggest that you take your coffee and brandy upstairs, Madame, Gentlemen?'

Convinced that, by now, her two companions were aware of the agenda for the rest of the evening, Emma said, 'That will be most agreeable.'

The room that was Emma's favourite contained a large four-poster bed, chaise longue and several armchairs. Her companions took the chairs while she lounged on the sofa, her little feet freed at last from the high-heeled slippers. A waiter entered to serve coffee and Emma racked her brains to think of a way to bring the conversation round to erotic matters as quickly as possible. She seldom had to seduce two men at once, neither of whom she knew well. Although she could always fall back on the graphically illustrated volumes that were strewn on a side table, Emma regarded the situation as a challenge to her ingenuity and wished to manage without them if she possibly could.

A few moments' reflection was all it took to provide her with the perfect opening. Emma put down her cup, leaned back with a sigh and announced, 'I so much

8

enjoyed the opera this evening, but that story always leaves me feeling melancholy. I had the good fortune to see the great Sarah Bernhardt playing *La Dame Aux Camélias* on stage, but with Verdi's wonderful music the theme is rendered so much more plaintive. The very idea of a woman of pleasure sacrificing herself for her lover is touching, do you not find, gentlemen?'

'Perhaps she made a mistake in falling in love,' Sir James suggested, gruffly.

'Oh, I agree absolutely! But a woman cannot always control her feelings as well as a man. I believe it is easier for most men to distinguish between love and sex. It is one of the points I endeavour to impress upon the young ladies at my academy.'

Stephen looked surprised. 'You run an academy for young ladies, Mrs Longmore?'

'Please call me Emma. Yes, and it was there that I educated Sir James' daughter in the ways of the world.'

Stephen's brows made another swift ascent. 'Of the *world*? Surely you mean "polite society", Emma?'

She laughed. 'I meant what I said. Do you think that Henrietta Northrop would have landed such a fine catch as the Marquis of Morville if she had been a green girl with no expertise in matters of love?'

'So that's it!' Sir James chortled. 'I did wonder how the little madam managed it! Are you suggesting that my daughter seduced that Frenchie into marrying her?'

'I do not know exactly, of course. But my young ladies are instructed in certain ... techniques and approaches which are more or less guaranteed to win them the heart of any man they desire.'

'Extraordinary!' breathed Stephen, faintly.

After he had downed his glass of brandy, Sir James was looking very red-faced. From the fiery glint in his eye Emma could tell that he could hardly restrain himself, so when he lunged forward off his chair and knelt before her with his hand on her knee she was not in the least taken aback.

'Emma, dear lady!' he said, thickly. 'May I send my wife to your wonderful academy?'

She burst out laughing. 'Oh, Sir James! I am so sorry, but the places are reserved for the young and unmarried. Besides,' she took on a teasing tone, 'did you not tell me that at your age you have no time for such trivialities?'

'I thought that was the case, but you have shown me otherwise. My God, I'll tell you now before this gentleman here, I think you are the most ravishing woman I've ever set eyes upon!'

Emma reached out and stroked his balding head. He was in his cups and desperate for physical contact. With a low moan he placed his head in her satin-clad lap. She glanced at Stephen. The man was smiling in a sardonic manner, but evidently aroused himself judging by the ridge in his trousers.

'Arise, Sir James!' Emma laughed. 'Come, let me cradle you in my bosom. I can see you are sore in need of comfort.'

'Your bosom!'

With a cry half of anguish and half of rapture, James Northrop buried his face in the lace-trimmed corsage. His nose was practically caught in her cleavage.

Emma asked Stephen to pour her another glass of brandy. 'Then I suppose I must leave,' he retorted, sourly.

'Not at all,' she smiled. 'I need your help, Stephen. Sir James is obviously incapable of going anywhere tonight, so he must sleep here. I should be obliged if you would help me undress him.'

'Is it wise for you to remain, Emma? I am sure I can summon help . . .'

'Sir James would be most disappointed if I left, and so should I.' Emma took a sip from her brandy glass, pausing before she added, meaningfully, 'And so, I believe, would you.'

Stephen flushed as her words sunk in. 'You are quite right,' he murmured. 'I had not dared hope as much.'

'Come!' she said, briskly. 'Help me to remove his clothes.'

They soon had him naked on the bed. At once he collapsed onto the pillow and began snoring loudly. With Stephen's help Emma removed her dress and hung it in the wardrobe, then took the pins out of her hair. Before she could turn round, she felt eager fingers plunging into her long, thick locks and as she swung round found herself caught in the young man's embrace.

He kissed her boldly, thrusting his tongue into her mouth and working his lips against hers with a passion that first astounded and then delighted Emma. She had not expected him to be so enamoured of her, and his behaviour was already having a distinct effect. Not only was Emma's heart pounding and her pulse racing, but she could feel the familiar tingling in her breasts as her nipples swelled and the corresponding throb of her clitoris in its moist niche.

There came a sudden loud groan and Emma looked down to see Sir James sprawling naked on the bed and shaking his fist at them. 'What about me, you hussy?' he growled. 'I entertained you at the opera, I paid for your dinner, and now you're letting that damned upstart paw you. Curse the pair of you!'

Emma realised that he had recovered from his nap and was now subject to that intoxication of the spirit that roused the blood. She left her ardent lover and came to sit on the bed beside the irate Northrop. 'Dear James, I have plenty of kisses for both of you,' she smiled, tenderly caressing his brow. 'To tell the truth, I thought you were asleep.'

'Grrr! You mean to say you'd fornicate with that young whippersnapper while I slept?'

'Not at all! I am anxious to please you both but you have the prior claim, dear James. In fact, it would oblige me greatly if you were to undress me now and do with me what you will.'

His gaze brightened, and he put out a hand to stroke her bosom. 'Are you sure, m'dear?'

She nodded. 'Of course! Here, let me help you.'

Glancing at Stephen, who was looking quite put out, she smiled encouragement and hoped he had received the unspoken message that his time would also come. Clumsily Sir James fiddled with her ribbons and buttons and eventually she was able to remove all her under-clothes except her lace-trimmed cotton drawers. At once Sir James gathered her breasts in both hands and pressed each rearing nipple to his lips.

'Beautiful titties!' he crooned. 'I never saw such lus-cious lovelies. My wife has dry old dugs and I dare say an even drier old diddly, only she's not let me in for years.'

'Hush, James, just enjoy the moment,' she urged him. He spent a long time slobbering over her breasts, but although she kept a watchful eye on his tackle there was little sign of life in that quarter. Stephen was slouched in a chair observing the proceedings with a scowl, and Emma realised that she could not allow the situation to continue in that fashion for much longer. She gently moved his head away from her bosom and sat up.

'Come, Sir James, let us see if we can get your brave little manikin to stand up for himself.'

'He's a stubborn blighter!' Sir James announced. 'I doubt you'll succeed.'

Winking at Stephen, Emma said, 'I'll wager I will "suck seed" before the night is out!'

'I'll take you on, Emma!' Stephen murmured. 'Five guineas says you'll not get the old chap to shoot his load before morning.'

'You're on!' Emma giggled, bending her mouth to the member in question.

Emma was unused to having such a flaccid organ between her lips. Before long there was a definite stir-ring, although not enough to qualify as an erection. Although Sir James moaned and groaned, stroking her breasts as she tickled his balls and licked his shaft, when she was no nearer her goal after a good ten minutes of

12

constant stimulation it was clear that she was in danger of losing the wager.

'Why not admit defeat?' Stephen whispered in her ear. 'You would be better off diverting your attention to me. My organ is already rampant and eager to enter your exquisite body.'

'I shall not desert him,' she declared. 'But I confess that my own needs are being neglected while I strive to satisfy his. If you wish, you may enter me from behind.'

Stephen needed no second bidding. He stripped off his clothes and was soon kneeling on the bed behind her, penis poised at the ready. She felt the last bastion of her modesty being removed as her drawers were pulled down over her thighs and the plump cheeks of her behind exposed. Stephen gave a sigh of contentment as he placed his glans between her already wet lips and pushed slowly into her meltingly aroused quim. Although Emma, entirely focused upon the task in hand, was unable to raise her eyes to examine the other man's organ, it was evident from the satisfying fullness of her vagina that Stephen was particularly well-endowed.

The effect on Emma of having her pussy well serviced was to increase her enthusiasm for the prolonged fellatio and soon her energetic licking was bringing results. As Sir James became aware of what was happening, his libido was roused also. Eagerly he watched the young blade shafting away and, far from being jealous, was so heartened at the effect on his own, hitherto recalcitrant, organ that he began to shout encouragement.

'That's the ticket, give it to her good and proper Stephen! Ram it home, lad!'

The invigorating effect that Emma's ministrations and her own evident arousal had on Sir James was miraculous. His wrinkled little dick began to rise to the occasion and was soon of a very respectable size. Emma squashed her breasts together and put the penis between them, inviting Sir James to rub her 'boobies' against his tumid shaft and increase its girth still more.

All the while she could feel her own erotic tension

reaching fever pitch as the strong phallus made constant inroads into her hotly pulsating vagina. To her great satisfaction, Stephen had his hand over her mound with the tips of his fingers working her clitoris and thus proclaiming himself to be an experienced lover of sensually developed women like herself. She was soon on an unstoppable rise towards orgasm, wiggling her bottom and waggling her hips while she clenched his thick shaft with her inner walls. With an abandoned cry she gave herself up to the sudden onrush of her climax, her body responding violently to the pinching of her nipples and the rapid friction against her throbbing pleasure knob. At the same time she felt Stephen penetrate her more deeply as the peak of his own excitement approached.

They rode the wild waves of their joint consummation while Sir James added his vocal commentary. 'Oh, by Gad that's giving it to her good and proper! Make her come like a bitch on heat, you randy devil! Shoot your spunk into that sopping wet chasm, and thrill her to the core. Oh, but it does my heart good to watch you two young lechers go at it like rabbits!'

When she had recovered from her transports, Emma realised that Sir James still sported a sturdy erection. He placed her hand upon it and she felt the warm blood pulsing through the veins. 'I was afraid that having him tucked snugly between your lovely lollies would bring me off,' he whispered. 'But he's still raring to go, so now it is my turn. Fair's fair!'

'Of course, dear James.'

Emma lay back in his arms while he stroked her breasts with one hand and her thighs with the other. It wasn't long before she was ready to receive his impatient prick and he plunged into her without preamble since she was already fully aroused. Although he only lasted a few seconds before the convulsions overwhelmed him, he pronounced himself well satisfied.

'I never thought to enter a woman's blessed cunny again,' he confessed. 'Let alone one so sweet and welcoming as yours, my dear. Tonight you have made an old man very happy.'

'Old? Come, come Sir James,' she chided him, playfully. 'I think this night has proved that there is plenty of life in you yet!'

The same was true of her other lover for, although Sir James was soon snoring away, Stephen's sturdy organ was rearing its head ready to go again. Emma beckoned him over to the chaise longue, so that Sir James might sleep in peace, and lay with one leg raised along the back of the sofa while her other fell nonchalantly to the ground. The pose enabled her to open her pussy as wide as possible revealing all the rosy folds and contours of her sex which, in her experience, men loved to set their eyes upon before they feasted there with their other organs.

'Oh Emma, you are an extraordinary woman!' Stephen sighed as he gazed his fill, his erection growing stouter by the second. 'I confess I have never before encountered a courtesan with such a frank and open appetite for love.'

'I am no courtesan,' Emma smiled, indulgently. 'I am a woman of independent means who is beholden to no man. It is just that I have developed my taste for exotic pleasures over and above the average woman, and with no regard for the ridiculous strictures of our times.'

But Stephen was in no mood for debate. He was delicately probing her vulva with his fingertip, parting the outer lips to get a good look at her moist crevice and her sweet little rosebud, just venturing out once more from beneath its protective sheath. Then he bent his head and was soon savouring the womanly flavour of her, sighing and moaning as his tongue found her quim and penetrated as far as it could manage.

Now Emma was roused again, her veins on fire, and she whispered urgently, 'Let your fine prick come inside me, Stephen, I beg you!'

Emma shivered with pleasure as she viewed the full extent of his organ as it reared between her legs, the

15

purple glans enlarged almost to the size of a billiard ball and the veins outstanding down the shaft. She convulsed inwardly as she felt it nose its way in, deeper and deeper until its base was flush with her bulging clitoris. When he began to move in and out the most exquisite sensations ran through her and, as his lips hungrily sought the nipple that crested her right breast, she gave a guttural cry and clutched at his heaving buttocks.

Stephen's arousal was such that he could not hold out for long. 'Wonderful woman!' he cried, as the first spasms took him unawares and Emma felt the gushing fountain spray her insides. The sudden fierce thrusting against her engorged labia was enough to set off her own reactions. She bucked her hips and moaned in the extremity of her passion, wallowing in the seemingly endless rippling that spread through her body again and again, delivering thrill after thrill of pure, unadulterated pleasure until all was spent.

They kissed and embraced upon the chaise longue, then made their way back to the bed where Sir James was now slumbering soundly. Emma lay down between her two lovers and, secure in the knowledge that they were all three well satisfied, was soon asleep.

In the morning, Emma awoke to find herself alone in the bed. Puzzled, she washed herself at the marble washstand then dressed as best she could and went downstairs. At a table in the corner, drinking coffee, the two men were in deep discussion. From the scraps of conversation that wafted her way, Emma gathered that they were talking business. She silently left the restaurant, asking the doorman to hail her a cab and then make her farewells to the two gentlemen.

On the way home Emma reflected that, apart from sharing kin or a public school, there were few things that bound men so closely together as sharing the same woman, whether separately or simultaneously. It would not surprise her in the least if Sir James found a strong business ally in young Stephen Landers, after all.

Chapter Two

*E*mma was pleased to receive bouquets from both her lovers, but she doubted whether she would be seeing either of them again. Sweet as their encounter had been, it was one of those fleeting, unrepeatable experiences and she trusted that both men had the good sense to know this. Not only did the experience afford her many happy moments of recollection over the next few days, but her memories were tinged with that particular excitement and anticipation she always felt when contemplating how she would relate it to her dear Daniel.

Lost in such pleasant thoughts as she sat in her drawing-room in Brunswick Square, Emma was startled by a knock at the door. Louise, the parlour maid, announced a visitor. 'Mrs Kitty Belfort, Ma'am.'

'Oh, Kitty! How lovely to see you!' Emma exclaimed, as the young woman entered.

Kitty had once been her personal maid but she had married Emma's distant relative, a lawyer called Vincent Belfort, and now had a ten-year-old daughter. The girl had been christened Emily, but was known as 'Milly'. Kitty usually brought the child to see her godmother, but today she was alone. She also seemed in a state of distress.

'What on earth is the matter, my dear?' Emma cried,

seeing her friend's tear-streaked face. 'Louise, fetch us some tea will you? Right away.'

To Emma's dismay, Kitty flung herself into her arms and began sobbing. 'Oh, Emma!' she moaned. 'I cannot spend another day with him, let alone another night!'

Perturbed, Emma made her sit down while she brought some sal volatile from a drawer. 'Take a good sniff of this, my dear,' she advised. 'When you are more composed you must tell me exactly what is the nature of the trouble between you and Vincent.'

While Kitty was recovering the tea was brought. Emma sat reflecting on what might have upset her friend, and concluded that she was not altogether surprised. There had already been many indications that all was not well in the Belfort household.

After a few sips of tea Kitty was ready to talk. 'You know I have often complained that he hardly has time for me,' she began. 'He takes on more and more difficult cases, and lives only for his work.'

Emma sighed. 'I am sorry to say that many husbands neglect their wives after the first few years of marriage. Could you not find some consolation in charity work?'

'Charity work!' Kitty's blue eyes spat fire. 'I am surprised at you, Emma! You would not have suggested such a thing in the old days.'

'No,' she agreed, ruefully. 'Then I should have recommended that you took a lover. Well you still might, and have time for good works too. I only say that, Kitty dear, because I know what a kind and generous nature you have and how you love to do things for others.'

'You've always been so kind to me. And I have always been able to tell you anything. But the true cause of my present misery is so shameful I can hardly bring myself to speak of it.'

'Do try, my dear. I cannot help you if I do not know the cause of the problem.'

'Very well.' Kitty took a deep breath. Her forehead was furrowed with pain, and she looked older than her twenty-nine years, but she was still a pretty picture in her elegant rose-pink gown. 'Not to put too fine a point on it, Emma, my husband is a sodomite.'

'Oh, Kitty!'

'I only found out a few months ago, he kept it so well hidden from me. But it seems he has always had a penchant for boys.'

'That is often the case with men who have had a public school education.'

'But there is worse. After I had given birth to Milly, he told me we should not have any more children until he was well established at the Bar. I agreed, imagining that he would use one of the normal methods of prevention. But the way he chose to spare me the pain of another childbirth was . . . was. . .'

The tears began to flow again, but while Emma comforted her she guessed what Kitty had been hinting at. 'Do you mean to say he sodomised you, Kitty?' she asked, gently.

The other woman nodded, with downcast eyes. 'Oh Emma, I cannot bear it!'

'You should not have to. I believe there are some women who are not only accustomed to that form of intercourse but actually enjoy it. My own experience tells me that one finger is quite pleasant, but anything larger than that very unpleasant. No-one should be obliged to suffer in that way unless they desire it. Besides, your husband should know that it is against the law.'

'I would have no chance of suing him,' Kitty declared, grimly. 'His lawyer chums would certainly close ranks even if I had the money to bring a case against him. Besides, our marriage has become totally loveless. He does not pay Milly any attention either, and when he has been at the bottle he becomes so violent that I fear for my child's safety.'

'What about yourself – has he ever laid a hand on you, Kitty dear?'

She nodded, shamefaced. Emma put an arm around her shoulder. 'You cannot stay with him a moment longer. Bring Milly here, and stay as long as you wish. You are very welcome.'

'Oh Emma, I could not presume on our friendship!'

'Nonsense! What are friends for? I confess I feel responsible for you both. Not only is Vincent a relative of mine, but I am Milly's godmother. How could I pretend this is none of my concern? You must come here right away and if Vincent objects, leave him to me. I'll tell his mother the truth about him if need be. The threat of that will be enough to bring him to heel, I'm sure.'

'Oh Emma, thank you, thank you!'

Kitty began weeping again, but this time Emma knew they were tears of relief.

The prospect of the pair living under her roof, even for a short while, was a pleasant one. Although Emma had long been reconciled to the fact that she herself was sterile, she had grown very fond of her little god-daughter. It would be a simple matter to convert the attic into a pretty nursery, but it would take a while. Decorators would have to be called in, and there was furniture to buy.

Emma wanted to accommodate Kitty and Milly as soon as possible, believing them to be in danger every minute they were under Vincent Belfort's roof. Then the solution occurred to her. She would take them to Harfield Hall while their quarters were being prepared. Kitty was in agreement, so while she went home to pack, Emma sent a telegram to Daniel.

They travelled to Manchester by train next day taking luncheon in the dining car, much to young Milly's amusement. When they arrived in the late afternoon Daniel was awaiting them, resplendent in motoring cap and goggles, at the wheel of his splendid new automobile. The maroon coachwork was polished to a mirror-shine, and everything made of metal – from the spokes in the wheels to the magnificent trumpet-shaped horn – was equally sparkling.

'It is the very latest model,' he informed them, his brown eyes twinkling. His moustache brushed Emma's cheek as he kissed her, and her heart lifted as she scented his familiar cologne. 'The upholstery is of finest morocco with ivory buttons.'

'How splendid!' Emma ran a finger over a gleaming brass lamp. 'It looks marvellously comfortable, too.'

'I have brought you these,' he smiled, holding out two motoring veils. Emma and Kitty secured their bonnets then stepped onto the running-board. Emma sat next to Daniel while Kitty and Milly, open-mouthed with excitement, climbed up into the back seats. Once they had tucked the blankets around their knees, they were as comfortable as in any armchair.

They set out at a steady pace through the streets of Manchester, but when they were in open country, heading for the Yorkshire border, Daniel accelerated to a cracking pace. Emma gripped his arm as the motor car swayed alarmingly as they rounded a bend. 'Daniel! Do slow down, dear. I am sure you must be exceeding the legal limit!'

He gave a reckless laugh. 'But don't you just love the feel of the wind rushing past? Besides, if I kick up enough dust they can't make out my number!'

'Dreadful man! I think you are becoming one of that new species, the "road hog"!'

He turned towards her with a mischievous grin. 'Then if I should venture into the streets of Kensington I might be shot by that dastardly Marquis of Queensbury. His avowed intention is to take arms to defend himself against dangerous motorists!'

Emma could tell he was immensely proud of his new vehicle, and she was glad of it. Daniel still had an unquenchable thirst for adventure and when he grew bored with life in Yorkshire would take off abroad at a moment's notice, depriving her of his company for weeks on end. The more diversions he had to keep him at Harfield the better, as far as she was concerned.

As dusk closed in, the rather dour façade of Harfield Hall loomed through the mist. Although Daniel had improved the interior and grounds since he had increased his fortune, no amount of creeping ivy or trailing wisteria could disguise the fundamental coldness of the building that had once been a Cistercian abbey. There were rumours that the ghost of a monk still haunted the battlements.

'I have put you and the girl in the West Wing, Kitty,' he said, as the car drew to a halt in front of the house. 'I think you will be comfortable there.'

They dined together in the great hall at a small table that had been set up for them near the fire. Emma was both amused and touched by the way Daniel paid meticulous attention to her god-daughter's needs, answering the girl's questions with careful solemnity. She seldom saw him in the company of children. With Kitty he was courteous but distant, for Emma knew that he would not dare to flirt with her former maidservant in her presence. He had once shamelessly used Kitty to lure her mistress to him, but the two women had later conspired to wreak their revenge upon him in no uncertain manner.

Emma was relieved when the meal was over and the other two guests had retired to their rooms. She was finding it hard to restrain herself from touching her lover, so eager was she to resume physical contact with him. As soon as they were alone, and Daniel had dismissed the servants for the night, she flung herself into his arms.

'Oh, dearest! It seems so long since we were together, and I have so much to tell you!'

'Then let us sit here by the fire, and you may begin,' he smiled, kissing her tenderly.

He drew her close as they huddled on the sofa to one side of the marble fireplace. Emma untied the sash at her waist, removed her shoes and tucked her stockinged feet under her. She could smell the leather-and-spice scent of him, and her fingers toyed with his darkly flowing locks that were now just beginning to be streaked with grey. God, how I want this man! she told herself, feeling the first fluttering evidence of her lust for him awakening in

22

her lower regions. It never ceased to amaze her that, of all her lovers, he still managed to reign supreme.

'What naughty escapades have you been up to since I last saw you, my sweet?' he enquired.

'Mine is too good to tell first. I want to save it for later.'

He tapped her playfully on the nose. 'Minx! I suppose you wish to hear mine, then?'

'Of course. One of them, at least.'

'I'll tell you what, we shall toss for it!'

Emma laughed. 'Any excuse for a gamble, is that it? Well I made a wager with a young gentleman that I won hands down – I won't say down where!'

'And did he pay up?'

'Come to think of it, I don't believe so. Though I was well recompensed in other ways!'

'I am sure you were. Now, declare: heads or tails?'

Emma won the toss so Daniel had to tell his tale first. He settled back with his arm around her, his face glowing ruddily from the fire and a secretive smile on his lips. 'My story concerns a charmingly naive young woman who had got it into her pretty, empty noddle that she wished to become a nun.'

'Oh! Was she a novice at the Sacred Heart convent?'

'Yes, but a recent one, hardly indoctrinated by the Sisters, so I knew there was a chance of saving her. The girl's name was Ellen, and she had the most wonderful face and figure even though she was no more than five feet tall. A veritable "pocket Venus" one might say.'

'But how did you get her alone, never mind manage to seduce her?'

'Aha! I confess it was a challenge, but the kind my wits thrive upon. You probably remember that my factory supplies the nuns with their shifts and drawers?'

Emma nodded, smiling. She'd always found it amusingly incongruous to think that her reprobate lover was responsible for the plain and serviceable underwear of the Sisters as well as the enticingly frivolous corsetry of society belles.

'When I heard that they had ordered a batch of drawers I gave orders that only half should be sent, with the message that we had been let down by our suppliers. I asked them to send one of the novices to the factory in three days to collect the rest.'

'Wicked man! But they had no suspicions?'

'Of course not. I am the very soul of an upright gentleman, as far as the Mother Superior is concerned. I keep the old dame sweet with a box of cigars every so often.'

'Cigars!'

'Yes. Smoking is her secret vice. She creeps down into the crypt for a quick puff, where no-one can smell the stench. At least, I assume she smokes them! She prefers large Havanas, such as the King is partial to. But I digress. Fresh as a daisy on Thursday morning, along comes young Ellen to my factory. She is all bright-eyed at having such an important mission to fulfil, and readily accepts the invitation to wait in my office until the garments are packed.'

'In your office! I can just imagine how her eyes widened as she looked about her!'

Emma knew that Daniel kept miniature samples of his latest styles displayed on figurines. He also had many pictures of naked and semi-nude women on his walls. All in good taste, of course, and designed to influence the buyers who put in large orders for the big stores.

'Quite so. And I lost no opportunity to comment on the difference between the goods she was about to carry back to the convent and the latest fashions in corsetry. What a shame, I told her, that dedicating oneself to God involved giving up all the pleasures of the flesh. For if God had made our bodies, how could the enjoyment of his gifts be seen as sinful?'

'Did she swallow that? Surely not!'

'Not at first. I got the usual guff about self-sacrifice and choosing to follow the chaste example of the Blessed Virgin. But once I got down to showing her one of our latest creations, a model called "Daphne" trimmed with

24

the most exquisite Brussels lace, I saw that the little fish was nuzzling at the bait. I said didn't she regret having to give up wearing fine clothes and jewels, and she confessed that she did, a little. So then I said that as she was still a novice and under no binding vows, she could feel free to try on said garment if she so desired. And I directed her to the changing cubicle in the corner.'

'She must still have been nervous, with you in the room.'

'Oh, I took care of that. I said I must go and see how the packers were getting on and would she mind being left alone for ten minutes.'

'And you knew she couldn't resist trying it on the minute your back was turned!'

'Precisely. I left the room and waited until I heard the curtain of the changing cubicle being closed, then I crept back in. She had left the curtain open a little and I could see her reflected in the long mirror. Already her nun's habit was removed and she was standing half naked, admiring the corselette. It is one of the lightweight, more flexible kind that moulds without distorting. I shall make you a present of one before you leave.'

'Thank you, dearest! And I've no doubt that every time I wear it my enjoyment will be increased by remembering this seduction scene of yours!'

Daniel kissed her avidly, raising her heartbeat and whetting her appetite for the treats to come. Then he continued. 'At last she removed her shift and I had a clear view of her breasts. And such breasts! She had the most beautiful pair I have seen in a long while. Not huge, but perfectly round and in proportion, the colour of marble and with a deep pink tinge to her nipples which had contracted on exposure to the air and were pert as can be. I admit that by now my organ was straining at the leash and making me feel decidedly uncomfortable.'

'Poor, dear organ!' Emma chuckled, touching his lap. Not surprisingly she found it distended beneath the cloth of his trousers. Her own secret places felt hot and swollen too, so that she wriggled against the cushion on which she was seated to ease the itch a little.

'Well, I waited until the girl had pulled "Daphne" over those shapely globes and slim hips. Then I made a great show of opening and closing the door, as if I had just returned. I told her not to worry if she was trying on the undergarment because I was quite used to fitting women of all ages and sizes and would not be embarrassed.'

'You said *you* would not be embarrassed!' Emma giggled at his sheer nerve.

Daniel let his hand drop onto the smooth skin of her upper breasts. He continued to stroke there softly as his tale unfolded. 'I opened the curtain just a few inches and spoke with my eyes averted. I said that the order would be a while yet, and asked what she thought of my latest creation. She said that it was very comfortable to wear.'

'No word about how it enhanced her figure, then?'

'Of course not. But I then launched into my standard lecture on how not wearing a foundation garment could ruin a woman's figure. She countered by saying that nuns had no need of such, but I said what if she changed her mind, deciding not to take her vows after all?'

'Clever!' Emma unbuttoned her blouse and revealed her own uncorseted bosom, the still-firm contours giving the lie to his lecturing. She undid the ribbons of her camisole and revealed the swell of her breasts, letting his fingers dabble in the sensitive cleft between them. She gave a languid sigh and stretched one foot across his lap, her big toe freely toying with his erection.

'I gave her to understand that if she wore the shapeless and unsupportive underwear that the Sisters insisted upon she might ruin her charms for good. "No young man wants a wife who has let her breasts sag and her hips spread," I told her. She blushed a little at my frank talk, and I could tell she was aroused by my being so close to her semi-naked body.'

Emma pulled her camisole down over her left breast to allow him access to her nipple which, by now, was tingling urgently and in need of stimulation. Daniel continued, 'I said it was a shame to spoil the fine dowry nature had given her, whether she was to become a nun or no. She smiled shyly at me, and I said I could see that she was blessed with a perfect figure. Any man would be proud to have her as his wife, I added. She mouthed some platitude about being a bride of Christ, but I ignored it. Then I decided it was time to act. I told her that the corset had not been properly put on, but if she wished I would adjust it for her.'

'Impious man! Oh, that feels good – do that again!'

He scratched her nipple lightly with his nails once more. 'Like this? Well, the little creature was mesmerised by now. Her eyes were quite glazed and she was swaying a little. I doubt she had ever felt such keen longing before. I entered the cubicle and drew the curtain behind us, then fiddled with the lace that covered her sweet breasts. She was growing eager for she knew not what, but I brushed against her tender parts so very lightly, stroking beneath the cups to make sure her bosom filled them and the nipples were properly lodged in their satiny points. She stood there passive and dazed, her face flushed and her maidenly body trembling all over.'

'Like a fallow deer kept at bay by hounds, I dare say.'

'Take off this infernal garment if you please, Emma, so I can treat your two beauties equally. That's better. Now, where was I? Ah, the remembrance of it fills my veins with fire! I could detect the first traces of a natural wantonness in the girl as I let my hands drop to her narrow waist and felt her hips wriggle in response. Her bosom was heaving now and her breathing more rapid. I patted her neat little bottom and told her how trim she looked.'

Daniel lifted the hem of Emma's skirt and delved beneath her petticoat to find her gartered thigh. His fingers reached up and as he found her nether lips she shuddered, saying, 'You managed to get her into one of your corsets, but how did you get her out of it again?'

'I did not need to. She still had her drawers on but it was a simple matter to persuade her to roll them down a little so that I could pull the corselette more snugly over her hips. I confess I nearly gave the game away once I glimpsed the top few hairs on her mound of Venus. I could scarcely resist plunging my fingers down into her bush. Instead I told her that the corselette was now a perfect fit and she should admire herself in the mirror.'

'And did she obey?'

'She did indeed, preening and twisting this way and that, fancying herself like a high-class whore. Then I said she should divest herself of the garment because it was, after all, not the sort of underwear that she would have any further use for. She was utterly crestfallen!'

Emma could no longer endure the torment of his teasing fingers. She pulled his hand up to her damp crevice and sighed as he wormed his way in. 'But she took off the corset, did she? Oh, at last! That is so much better, Daniel dear! Please do not go away from there, will you?'

'Not yet awhile, I promise. How wonderfully damp you are, my sweet. But this is just too distracting. Your pussy is blurring my memory . . . Oh, I think I have the thread again. Yes, I stepped outside of the cubicle for a few seconds. Long enough for her to take off the under-garment but not long enough for her to have put on her own underclothes again. It was very finely judged, I recall, for I managed to pull back the curtain at the very moment when she stood almost naked. I had another corset in my hand by way of an excuse, but it was soon obvious that I needed nothing but my tempting presence in order to gain my objective.'

'Why was that?' Emma asked, faintly. He was now rhythmically caressing the hard nub of her love-bud while momentarily pressing his lips to her erect nipple, and she found his actions, combined with his lascivious account, increasing her arousal to an almost unbearable pitch. Reaching out, she began to unbutton his fly.

'She turned to me with a cry of pure longing, her twin glories immodestly exposed and her drawers about her loins, showing the whole of her delicious delta, carpeted with light brown hair. I knew at once that my delicate manipulations of her body within the corset and my soft words of encouragement had done their work. She was ready for me, and I for her. But I had to be quite sure of her desire. I pretended that the undergarment in my hand, the "Figurefit" model, might be more to her liking, but she put her hands beneath her breasts and held them up to me with a smile, somewhat nervous but quite charming, as if offering them to me. "Do you really think I have a good figure?" she asked me. Well, what could I say to that? Nothing at all! I reached out and let my hands take the place of hers.'

'You boldly caressed her breasts?'

'I did. And kissed her yielding lips until she scarcely knew where she was. By the time I dared probe between her thighs and found my way into her honeyed quim she was swooning with feelings she'd never felt before, and ready for whatever I wished to do with her.'

Emma pulled out Daniel's penis, whose erection she had been nurturing within his trousers all the while. 'But you did not enter her straight away?'

'Do you take me for a brute? No, it was the girl's first time and I let her relish it. She hung back a little at first, but then I said, "If you are to renounce the world, the flesh and the devil, you may at least know what it is you are missing!"'

'And did she fall for that?'

'Hook, line and sinker! Naturally I kept the fellow you're fondling well hidden, so she should not be frightened by its unfamiliar dimensions, but I soon had her naked and lying stretched out on the couch in my office where I could caress and mouth her pretty parts to her heart's content – and mine.'

'And did you make her come before you entered her, just as you are about to do to . . . Ah! Oh, my God!'

Emma's whole body filled with golden warmth as the

shuddering ecstasy winged its way through her veins. While she languished in the throes of her extreme pleasure Daniel kissed her tenderly on the breast, magnifying her sensual gratification so that she almost swooned with the intensity of her feelings. He knew her so well, knew just how to time his caresses, when to touch here or how hard to press there, that their lovemaking was always pure perfection and none other could match it.

For a while he held her quietly while her bodily functions returned to normal, but soon as her breathing was regular and her heat dispersed she was eager for more detail. 'Tell me how long it took the girl to experience her first orgasm,' she whispered, stroking his organ so that it stood up straight and proud from his fly.

'Not as long as I had expected. In fact, when the crisis was upon her, brought on by the expert manipulations of my tongue, I suspected that she might not have been the total *ingénue* that I took her for.'

'What are you suggesting, Daniel?'

'Only that she might have performed a few experiments upon herself. I would not dream of suggesting that the good sisters had had any hand in her debauchery.'

'Of course not! So how did she appear when in her climax? Was it violent and thrashing, or soft and sweet?'

'Oh, I think "deliciously voluptuous" would be the phrase. It was a pleasure to watch her pale breasts flushing deep pink, like the heart of a newly-opened rose, and her long lashes fluttering like captive birds as she gave herself up to the sweet pulsations.'

'But still you held back? How could you bear it?'

'With difficulty, I must admit. But you can imagine my surprise when dear, innocent Ellen came straight out of her transport and seized my stout fellow with eager hands. You would think she knew exactly what to do with it, although I am ready to swear she did not.'

'Did she handle him well, then?' Emma asked, her

own hands deftly bringing his penis to the very peak of its arousal.

'Well enough, for a beginner. But she soon convinced me that her aim was to have him inside her, for she opened her legs wide and practically pulled him in. I had to move quickly to make sure I was not injured, I can tell you that.'

'Eager for it was she? The hussy!' Emma felt a twinge of jealousy, just enough to enliven her own appetite once again. She guided him towards her still throbbing vulva and felt his glans lodge just inside her opening. This was a moment to savour. She was in no hurry to have him thrust inside, so she lay quite still and waited for the resumption of his narrative.

'Well she had a tight little quim, that I can say, although there was no great obstruction as I pushed my way into it. Her hymen had been loosened, probably by bicycle riding. I wonder if it crosses the minds of doting parents that such a vehicle can effectively deflower a young girl if ridden in the modern way, rather than side-saddle? But I digress.'

Daniel pushed a little farther into Emma's soft and willing flesh, making her moan with longing. She clasped him eagerly with her inner lips, feeling the sharp contact with her clitoris and the subsequent acceleration of her desire. Unable to help herself, she thrust her pelvis and enclosed the length of him completely, making him utter a reciprocal sigh. 'Now you are completely inside the girl,' Emma whispered. 'Show me how you pleasured her to the full.'

'Slowly at first, so that I could accustom those virginal walls to my form. It was not long before she was clasping me as I slid in and out, squeezing every ounce of sensation from my movements and becoming so wet and aroused herself that I slipped deeper and deeper inside her until she was accommodating me entirely. How she loved it! I can see her rapt face now, and hear her little moans and cries spurring me on towards our mutual consummation.'

31

Emma felt her inner and outer flesh throbbing with one accord. 'It was mutual, then?'

'Yes. I paced myself to her, you see. Soon she was urging me with her hips to go faster, she wanted to feel the powerful male organ driving hard inside her tender body. It seemed I could not be too rapid for her. She kept up with me and still begged for more, until I was going like a steam hammer. Then I saw her face flush and her eyes widen in amazement as she reached the brink. I joined her in the electric spasms of her climax as she clutched at me with her hungry little quim.'

Emma's own orgasm was very close now. She began to move her pelvis in the circular motion that she knew would bring her on. 'Oh, how wonderful! How she must have felt! I can imagine ... no, I can do more than imagine. Faster, dearest, I want you deeper, yes! Ah!'

As she gave herself up to the swirling sensations that racked through her she was aware of Daniel giving half a dozen rapid lunges in order to join her. They swooned together, mouths meeting in a final salutation before they sank back into each other's arms on the couch.

When he had her in his arms and was gently kissing her brow, Daniel ended his story.

'Ellen returned to the good Sisters and told them she had changed her mind about joining them,' he said. 'Naturally, I felt somewhat responsible, so I found her a position as a lady's maid. I sometimes hear news of her, and I believe she is very content with her new life.'

'All's well that ends well, then,' Emma smiled, sleepily.

'Now it is your turn, my sweet. I am eager to hear of your adventures in London.'

'Would you mind if I saved it until tomorrow night?' she asked. 'I am tired after travelling.'

'Forgive me, my angel,' Daniel whispered. 'A pleasure deferred is a pleasure doubled!'

Lifting her into his arms, he carried her out of the hall and up to bed.

Chapter Three

'Shall there be swing boats at the fair, Uncle Daniel? That would be such a lark. I do so love swing boats!'

Emma listened to her god-daughter's excited voice, watched her animated face, and felt a strange anxiety within. She was unused to seeing Daniel with children and it awakened long-buried instincts in her, a poignant wish that she could have shared with a husband the ordinary pleasures of family life. She had thought Daniel immune from paternal feelings, but now he was proving that he certainly knew how to please females of all ages. His proposal to drive them over to the Wakes Week Fair at Oldham had filled young Milly with joy.

They arrived in style in the splendid motor car, but as the day was hot Emma and Kitty soon sought the shelter of the tea tent while Daniel escorted Milly to the swing boats. Afterwards they strolled beneath their parasols through the rowdy crowd, admiring the various stalls and amusements. Emma had been to the Wakes at various cotton towns but Kitty had never seen such a colourful and noisy pageant before. She was wide-eyed as they passed the side-shows, rubbing shoulders with the mill workers, itinerant vendors and occasional gentry.

Suddenly, in a corner of the field, they came upon a

crowd gathered round a rostrum on which four earnest young women were standing beneath two banners. One was white with a purple border, and 'Women's Social and Political Union' embroidered on it in green; the other proclaimed, 'Votes for Women'. Next door, on a packing case, stood a disgruntled-looking quack brandishing a bottle of his panacea and haranguing the few onlookers who were still paying him some attention. Most of his audience had defected to the women, and were thoroughly enjoying the heckling.

The chief speaker was an attractive young woman in her mid-twenties, with a calm manner and serious eyes. Her voice was educated, low and melodic, and carried well over the heads of the crowd to where Emma and Kitty were standing.

'In Australia and New Zealand women already have the vote,' she was saying. 'Yet in the very country that they look to as their land of origin, where the Palace of Westminster houses the Mother of Parliaments, women are still denied the franchise. Is this not a scandal?'

'Petticoat government would be the scandal!' some wag retorted, delighting the crowd.

'Ay, let women stay where they belong – under men!' another jeered.

Undaunted, the young woman continued with her reasoned argument. 'We are not fighting only for the educated woman, or for titled ladies or even just for married women. We want the vote for all members of the female sex. Why? Because it is women who have to manage on the wages men bring home, women who rear future generations, women who become war widows, or who work in sweated labour. The laws that men pass affect the women and children of this country even more than they do the men. For, in the end, it is women who are the home-makers, the keepers of the domestic purse and the educators of the young.'

Emma glanced at Kitty. She was staring at the speaker with rapt attention, her cheeks glowing pink and her blue eyes bright with inspiration. At last she turned with a smile.

'Oh Emma, isn't this *wonderful*! I have never heard such things said in public before, and yet I have thought them so often.'

As the speaker went on to talk of social justice, and then of the way that some men abused their wives, Emma knew she had no hope of tearing her friend away before the meeting had ended. Kitty began to edge forward, away from the heckling men and towards the gang of mill girls at the front. Before she slipped away entirely, Emma caught her by the sleeve.

'I shall go back to the tea tent,' she announced. 'Someone must be there for when Daniel returns with Milly, or he will wonder where we are.'

Kitty nodded but paid her scant attention, and soon her bonnet was bobbing amidst the crowd of eager young women with their plaid shawls and Lancashire clogs.

Emma returned to the tent and, barely a minute later, Daniel appeared with an exuberant Milly. The little girl's cheeks were flushed and she was clasping her 'Uncle's' hand. There was a black smut on her cheek that Daniel had neglected to clean off, so Emma took out her lace-edged handkerchief, and gave the girl's face a wipe.

'Did you have a splendid ride, Milly?' Emma enquired.

'Oh yes, Aunty Em! We went very high up in the sky. Uncle Daniel held me fast all the while in case I should fall out.'

'I should hope so!'

Emma laughingly looked into Daniel's eyes, but she could not fathom what she saw there. A kind of wistfulness, perhaps. They went to have tea, with lemonade for Milly, and soon after Kitty returned still agog with excitement.

'Oh, Emma, I have discovered the name of that wonderful speaker! She is Miss Christabel Pankhurst, and her mother and sister are also in the Women's Suffrage

Movement. A girl called Annie told me. She is a mill hand, and she started work at the age of ten, imagine! Now she says she will devote her whole life to the Cause...'

'By Jove, Emma, I believe we have another convert here!' Daniel chaffed.

But Emma felt suddenly irritated. 'Well I hope these wonderful women are not neglecting their other obligations while they stampede around the country preaching at the crowd.'

Kitty looked suddenly contrite, putting her arm around her child. 'Oh, I am sorry. I did not mean to leave Milly with you for so long.'

'Well you may resume your maternal duties now,' Daniel told her, offering Emma his arm. 'We shall take a stroll around the fairground, my dear. There is much to see.'

They left mother and child in the shade of the tent and went to enjoy the fun of the fair. As usual Emma was half fascinated and half revolted by what she saw. The Freak Show was quite horrible, with the rolls of blubber wobbling all over the Fat Lady who sat outside, and Emma had no desire to enter the tent and see the even more grotesque sights within. She did have three unsuccessful tries at the coconut shy, however, and then stood watching as the gaudy horses of the carrousel spun round accompanied by raucous organ music.

'Shall we take a ride, my dear?' Daniel suggested.

Soon they were seated on their golden steed, Emma sitting side-saddle with her navy serge skirt spread and her rose taffeta underskirt rustling beneath, while Daniel was perched behind, his strong arm around her waist. She squealed with alarm as the ride began with a sudden jolt, and the wooden horse broke into its feigned gallop to the strains of 'The Liberty Bell'. The horse's swooping motion, when combined with the spinning, was very exhilarating and the rousing music stirred her blood further. The grinning faces in the crowd grew blurred as the whirligig gained speed.

'What a wonderfully smooth ride,' Daniel murmured into her ear, his hand moving up to encompass the curve of her breast. 'I have never contemplated making love on horseback. The thought of being thrown while in the throes is most unpleasant. However, I can well imagine making merry on a merry-go-round. What a shame you are obliged to ride side-saddle, Emma. Shall we creep back when all the folk are gone and ride by moonlight to our heart's content?'

Emma giggled, enjoying the fantasy immensely. It was not hard to imagine Daniel plunging into her from the rear as their steed whisked them up and down. She already felt quite ecstatic, and as her lover's fingers crept round the side of her breast and unerringly located her nipple she felt the familiar tingling between her thighs intensify. If only she could sit astride! The long twisted pole might afford her clitoris the necessary friction while Daniel probed her cunny from behind. She could picture them riding together, stark naked, to the tune of 'Trottin' to the Fair' and, ludicrous as the image was, it proved enough to stimulate her almost to the point of climax.

When the roundabout finally slowed to a halt and Daniel helped her down from her high horse, Emma felt her knees crumple under her. She was weak with desire, as well as from the giddying motion, and as Daniel half carried her from the platform she begged him to find her somewhere to sit down.

'We shall do better than that,' he promised her. 'Can you walk a few yards at least, Emma?' She nodded. 'Good. Then we shall make for the Fortune Teller's tent over there.'

The gypsy woman was doing brisk business but she allowed Emma to sit on one of the stools at the entrance to her tent until she had recovered her strength. Daniel brought her a drink of ginger beer, which Emma sipped gratefully. Soon the gypsy reappeared, her black eyes bright beneath her red patterned headscarf. 'Tell your fortune, lady? You have a lucky face, m'dear.'

'Oh, all right. Here's your fee!' Daniel said, good-naturedly.

They followed the woman into the tent where a table was spread with a black cloth embroidered with moons and stars. On it were some curiously illustrated cards. The gypsy shuffled them with expert ease and placed the pack on the table, face down. 'Pick three cards, dearie, any ones,' she urged Emma.

The three chosen cards were laid out in a row, still face down. Emma waited in slight apprehension for the scrying to begin. The gypsy seemed to be concentrating very hard as she turned them over, one by one. 'This card, the Female Pope, speaks to me of the past,' she said, revealing a picture of a robed woman with a three-tiered crown. The next card showed an itinerant man with a dog at his heels. 'And this tells me about the present influences around you.' The third card was turned, and the illustration was of a man behind a trestle table like a pedlar displaying his wares. 'Your future,' the dark-skinned woman said, bluntly.

'But what does it all mean?' Daniel broke in.

'Patience, sir. All will be revealed in good time. I must allow the Sight to come upon me.'

Paradoxically, she closed her eyes. Emma clung to Daniel's arm, somewhat afraid although she didn't really know why. What could there possibly be in these play-things to trouble her?

The gypsy opened her eyes. Staring at the first card, she began to interpret it. 'You have sought to experience the feminine mysteries, to explore secrets which other women have been taught to fear. Much strength and wisdom have you gained from this.'

Daniel gave Emma a smile of complicity. But then the seer continued, 'In the past you have been fortunate, and now you continue along the same path. You see life as a great adventure and seldom look before you leap, trusting to your instincts. But lady, beware! Sometimes our animal instincts may lead us astray. You may be living in a Fool's Paradise.'

38

Daniel muttered, 'Humbug!' then said to the woman, 'Have you nothing better to offer? No news of health, good or bad, of fortunes gained or lost? Some fortune-teller you are!'

'Mock all you like, sir!' the woman answered tartly. 'But I'll wager my words mean something to the lady in question.'

Curious to know what else she would say, Emma nodded. 'Yes, I think I understand what you mean. But can you tell me what this one signifies?'

Emma pointed to the third card. The gypsy nodded. 'You will need to learn self-control for the trials which lie ahead of you. Diplomacy in friendship and skill in dealing with situations, for the coming years will not be easy. But if you can find your true power, my dear, then you may attain inner peace in your riper years.'

Daniel remained unconvinced. 'Why tell her what "may" happen? She wants to know what *will* happen.'

The canny jet eyes of the gypsy were fastened keenly on him now. 'We all have the power to change our fate, sir. Perhaps you would like to know what possibilities lie in store for yourself?'

'Oh yes, Daniel!' Emma laughed. 'Do try the cards. You might find yourself less inclined to scoff then.'

'I doubt it, but if it provides you with some entertainment, Emma dear, I shall cross this charlatan's palm with silver once again.'

With a show of disdain, Daniel picked up the top three cards from the shuffled pack and threw them down onto the table. The gypsy set them out neatly in a row then revealed the first. This time she changed her procedure, interpreting each card as it was turned. The card that stood for the past was labelled 'Death' and brought a gasp from Emma as she saw the grisly portrayal of the Grim Reaper.

'Through the death of a relative you have gained an opportunity, and your life has gone in a different direction from that which was expected.'

Daniel raised his brows at Emma. She knew he was

thinking of the way his elder brother had died prematurely, making him heir to the family estate. Well, he could not fault that interpretation, at least!

The gypsy turned the second card: 'The Pope', male equivalent of Emma's 'past' card. 'You are thinking about forming an alliance – perhaps marriage?'

Daniel muttered, 'Tosh!' and the woman continued more hesitantly, aware that she might be on the wrong track. 'Or perhaps a bond of friendship is being strengthened, but it is a personal relationship I see here, not a business one.'

Daniel smiled at Emma, who felt reassured. The final card, depicting Daniel's future, also looked promising. It was called 'The World' and showed a woman dancing within a laurel wreath with the apocalyptic beasts at the corners.

Emma thought, 'She will say something about him travelling around the world now!'

But the words that came out were very different. Even the tone of the gypsy became more confident. 'This is both an end and a beginning, the completion of one cycle and the start of the next. The arrival of a son and heir will continue your line and establish your position more firmly within society.'

Daniel gave a scornful laugh. 'My position is firmly *without* society, and long may it remain so!'

The gypsy woman shrugged, gathering up the cards with a resigned air. Yet Emma remained in a state of mild shock. The idea of Daniel marrying and producing a son had struck a chill into her, but she put it down to disturbing echoes of her own history. After her marriage to Sir Henry Longmore was annulled, Emma had heard that his second wife had borne him two strapping sons and one daughter. Although her own inability to bear children had been no great disappointment, it sometimes irked her that matrons who produced offspring seemed more valued by society than spinsters or childless women. Emma regarded her own calling, as an enlightened educator of young women, as every bit as useful as that of a mere brood mare.

While they walked from the gypsy's tent, Emma vowed to put the prophecies out of her head. At least no outright disasters had been predicted. When they returned to the tea tent, however, there was no sign of Kitty and her daughter.

'I think I know where she may be,' Emma said. They returned to the spot where the women's suffrage meeting had been held and, as Emma had divined without benefit of Tarot cards, there was Kitty! She was talking earnestly with two of the women while some others piled their banners and makeshift rostrum into a horse-drawn cart.

Milly spotted her godmother straight away and tugged at her mother's skirt, but Kitty was oblivious until Emma joined her. 'Oh, Emma, you have found me! I did not mean to stay so long. May I present to you Miss Annie Kenney and Miss Billington, who is a schoolmistress.'

She seemed proud of her new acquaintances but Emma shook their hands somewhat coolly, uncertain what to make of these forthright young women with their proud bearing and determined expressions.

'We shall be holding a meeting in Manchester next week,' Miss Billington said, giving Emma a handbill. 'Your friend already has a copy of "Votes for Women". I do hope you both will read it.'

They had to leave then, so Kitty bade them a warm farewell, announcing that they had 'made her day'. She was still bubbling with excitement as she made her way with the others to Daniel's waiting automobile but Emma did not wish to encourage her friend and responded to her enthusiasm with monosyllables. Something about the unseemly zeal of those women had disturbed her.

All in all a rather disquieting afternoon, she thought, as she adjusted her veil and settled back into the padded leather seat for the journey back to Harfield. And tomorrow there would be a disagreeable task for Kitty to perform. She must write to her rotter of a husband and tell him that they would be living apart from now on. Emma would help her with the letter, but it must be done. She sighed, thinking of poor little Milly. Somehow she and Kitty must contrive to make sure the girl wanted for nothing as she grew to maturity. Well, between them they would manage somehow.

They were all fatigued from the heat and excitement of the fair. When they arrived at Harfield, Daniel suggested that after the nursery distractions of tea and bath Milly should be put to bed and the women should take a nap before dinner at eight. When the three adults finally assembled in the great hall for their evening meal, Daniel at once resurrected the topic of the Women's Vote, much to Emma's displeasure. She did not want to encourage Kitty in what she considered to be a rather dangerous new interest.

'So, Kitty, you found those strident women quite splendid this afternoon, did you?' Daniel began, teasingly. 'I must say they seemed more entertaining than the Sally Army bunch, but I cannot say more than that. Did you find their arguments convincing?'

Kitty looked him firmly in the eye. 'Very much so, and completely in accord with my own views. I found it most heartening to hear my own thoughts on the subject expressed so eloquently.'

'So you believe this country would be a better place if women were given the vote, do you?'

'I don't know about that. But I do find it an injustice that we are denied a say in government when it is we women who often suffer most from unjust laws.'

'I can understand your feelings, Kitty dear,' Emma broke in. 'That wretch of a husband of yours, lawyer though he be, should not have the law on his side when it comes to mistreating his wife. But I believe there are many men who would be as anxious as you to reform the law, without recourse to a woman's vote.'

Daniel turned to her with a smile. 'Do I take it, Emma,

that you are not a sympathiser with the Women's Cause? I cannot believe that!'

'A sympathiser, yes, but I think we should proceed carefully. Of course we women deserve the vote, but we do our cause no good by stridently proclaiming it at a country fair. Why, that puts women on the same level as tooth-drawers and mountebanks!'

'But where else are they to preach women's suffrage to the women who really need it?' Kitty's voice rose as she became inflamed. 'They are spreading the word in the Lancashire towns now, but one day they will be marching on London, believe me!'

'I've no doubt you are right,' Daniel said, attacking with gusto the trout that had been caught on his estate and was now served up with caper sauce. 'But London has weathered many an assault and will no doubt survive this one.'

The discussion petered out as Kitty realised she could get nowhere with Daniel present. But Emma had the distinct feeling that she had not heard the last of it yet.

After dinner Kitty went off to her room while Emma and Daniel remained drinking wine by the fire. He took her in his arms as soon as they were alone and gave her a kiss, but there was a mischievous look in his eye. 'You are up to something, Dan, I know it!' Emma grinned. 'You have something up your sleeve. Come, admit it!'

'How well you know me, Emma dearest! Yes, I do have a surprise for you but we must go into the drawing room to see it. I've asked Burgess to lay a fire in there.'

'Then what are we waiting for?' Emma leapt up, smoothing down her green taffeta skirt.

Daniel chuckled, pulling her back. 'Not so fast, my sweet! I wanted to talk first of our ride on the carrousel this afternoon. Was it not enjoyable?'

'Thrilling! Quite disgracefully so, as a matter of fact, due to your indecent remarks.'

'I thought as much. You could scarcely walk afterwards you wanted me so. Admit it!'

She laughed, her face close to his. 'You always know how to rouse me, wicked man!'

He kissed her passionately on the mouth before they both got to their feet and went through to the drawing-room. As Daniel switched on the newly-installed electric light, Emma gasped. For there, standing in pride of place in the middle of the floor, was a magnificent red and white rocking horse.

'I had Burgess bring him down from the attic. Told him I wanted to give the girl a ride in the morning. Isn't he splendid? He was mine, you know, when I was a boy.'

Emma walked forward and set the toy swaying back and forth on its long rockers. She grasped the horse's mane to still it again. 'Real horsehair, of course,' Daniel smiled. 'Want to mount him?'

She nodded, beginning to understand the nature of her lover's 'surprise'. Deciding to play along she said, 'I had better remove my dress first, so it won't get spoiled.'

'Of course. Here, let me help unfasten those hooks and eyes.'

When she was down to her shift, Emma climbed up onto the hard wooden back and sat astride the red leather saddle. 'You have a fine seat on a horse,' Daniel declared. 'I should not be ashamed to parade with you in Rotten Row. Shall I come up behind you so we can take a ride together? Dobbin is a sturdy fellow. I think he can take us both.'

Emma smiled, confident of the sport to come. She hitched her cambric chemise halfway up her thighs so that the beribboned lace of her French knickers was provocatively revealed. Daniel, like most men, loved to be teased by the sight of frills and furbelows.

Soon she could feel his naked thighs brushing her own, his hands seeking out the roundness of her breasts beneath the thin shift. She heard his soft, 'Gee up!' and felt the swaying motion of the wooden steed beneath her buttocks. Remembering the exhilaration she had felt on the fairground horse Emma's desire increased, aided by

44

the gentle pinching of her already stiff nipples. She could feel her tender labia swelling, opening like buds after rain, and knew that when her lover did decide to penetrate her she would be more than ready for him.

The speed of the horse increased, aided by Daniel's powerful thighs, and the rough edge of the saddle began to press against Emma's protruding clitoris, making her want him even more.

'Hold tight!' he whispered, lifting up the skirt of her chemise and caressing her naked behind with one hand. She squirmed then rose up in the saddle like an experienced horsewoman, and his finger found its way into her streaming cunny. Emma groaned, plunging down on him and feeling her vagina clasp the invading digit eagerly.

Soon their headlong dash slowed and then Daniel was lifting her bottom with both hands, the head of his sturdy organ nudging its way through her distended outer lips and into the warm burrow of her cunny. She gave an 'Aah!' of satisfaction as the puny dimension of his finger was replaced by the ample girth of his penis. His lips mouthed the skin of her neck as they began the rocking motion again and one hand crept to her breast, heightening Emma's pleasure as it rubbed and squeezed the solid mound of flesh beneath the thin cloth.

'A slow trot will suffice for now,' Emma gasped, finding it difficult to keep her balance as the delicious, dizzying feelings overtook her.

'Of course my sweet. But we shall have you at full gallop before we are done!'

After a while Emma managed to synchronise her movements with those of Daniel and 'Dobbin' so that she was able to gain maximum benefit from the dual motion. It was extremely exciting. Unlike the fairground ride, she knew that it would not come to a sudden end, and Daniel would speed up the horse or slow it down at her whim. Soon she was using her riding skills to good effect, rising up in the stirrups to feel the tip of his prick against her sensitised clitoris, then sliding down the shaft again to grind her engorged love-bud against the hard pommel. Every time it happened she felt herself propelled a little further towards the brink.

Emma wiggled her buttocks sensually against his thighs as she sat down in the saddle again, eliciting a groan of lust from her co-rider. For a while she sat tight, squeezing him with her insides as he increased the pace of their ride, her vulva pressing hard against the tough leather. If she needed to be reminded of why she and Daniel were still ardent lovers after ten years then this one instance would suffice: he would stop at nothing to invent new ways to titillate and satisfy her, using his imagination and resources to the full in order to keep their love life vital and stimulating.

She heard him whisper in her ear, 'Remember Florence, and the Jockey Club?' At once the memory of their early days returned to her, and she felt a warm rejoicing at the way they had remained such enthusiastic lovers over the years. Little had she realised, when he subtly paid court to her all those years ago, arousing her covertly and filling her with a desperate, though only half admitted, desire for him, that the fires of their love would remain burning for so long.

Daniel lifted the shift over her head and threw it down so that her whole body was exposed to his touch. Emma gasped as his roving hands caressed her stomach, breasts and thighs, taking her to new heights of glorious sensation. He began to probe her faster, filling her up with his hot, thick presence, making her juices run and her clitoris throb with accelerated longing. Powerfully he thrust into her, heedless as a headstrong horse, and soon she felt the inevitable rush of energy begin to swirl around in her, gathering momentum until it burst into a wild, spasmodic dance of pleasure, taking her into its shuddering embrace and beyond. Her body continued to rise and fall in time with the bucking horse but she was floating above it all, on a cloud of pure sensuality, and it wasn't until she felt the surging movement of the horse slow down that she came back to herself.

Exhausted she flopped forward, clutching onto the wooden neck as the dizzying sensations faded and she became aware of Daniel crooning affectionately into her ear,

> 'Trottin' to the Fair, Me and Moll Maloney,
> Seated I declare, on a single pony . . .'

The pleasant sojourn at Harfield Hall had to come to an end. Daniel had pressing business in London to attend to and offered to accompany the women on the train from Manchester. Although Emma was pleased that she would have his company in London for a while, she was also feeling apprehensive about asking him if he would mind Kitty and Milly moving in with her. She now realised that mother and child might have to stay more than the couple of months that she first envisaged, for after talking to Kitty it was obvious that she had no money of her own and would either have to find some sort of employment or live on Emma's charity.

The situation was a delicate one. Daniel had allowed his mistress to treat his Bloomsbury mansion as her own up to now, and had never tried to interfere in her domestic arrangements. But he had a perfect right to refuse to give house room to Emma's former maid and her child if he so desired.

To her relief, he proved sympathetic. 'Of course Kitty and the child may stay with you, Emma, if it is what you wish,' he smiled. She kissed his cheek gratefully. Then his expression grew stern. 'But on one condition.'

'Oh? What is that?'

'Simply that you shall not join those strident women that Kitty seems so struck on.'

Emma laughed. 'There is no danger of that, I can assure you. I am all for moderation in political matters.'

'I am relieved to hear it. Heaven knows, Emma, I would give the women the vote tomorrow if it were in my power to do so, but I heartily disapprove of ranting women on the rampage. It is an offence against nature!'

When they arrived at Daniel's London home Emma

47

and Kitty went straight up to inspect the new quarters. The attic room had been turned into a pretty nursery with a Mother Goose frieze around the walls, flower-sprigged curtains and matching bedspread. Sitting perkily in a child-sized chair was a splendid American teddy bear, which Emma had asked Mrs Perkins, the housekeeper, to order from Harrods while they were up north.

'Oh! May I hold him Aunty Em?' Milly pleaded.

Emma gave the girl a brief hug. 'He is yours, my dear. A present to welcome you to your new home.'

Overjoyed, the girl picked up the yellow plush bear and cuddled him. 'I shall call him "Danny", after Uncle Daniel!'

It was rare for Daniel to spend much time in London, and Emma was determined to make the most of it. Yet his 'business' occupied him fully during the first week, and he spent most nights away from home. After the enthusiastic love-making they had shared at Harfield it was both disappointing and worrying. On his country estate Emma had little competition, but here in London there were so many society belles, voluptuous embodiments of the 'Gibson Girl' and pretty actresses to divert him that she feared his taste for novelty must eclipse his more sentimental feelings for her.

Emma had her own circle of friends and acquaintances, mostly consisting of grateful parents of girls who had married well, and just lately she had begun to mix in more artistic circles. Perhaps, she decided, it was time to show Daniel that she also had her admirers. Maybe he was taking her too much for granted. On one of his fleeting visits she managed to get him to agree to a dinner party.

'Provided you arrange it all, Emma,' he insisted.

She smiled to herself. Of course she would arrange it all, and very much to her own advantage!

Chapter Four

*H*aving received Daniel's permission to hold a dinner-party at Brunswick Place, Emma found herself with cold feet. Yet she knew she could count on help from the Hon. Miss Sybil Mountjoy, one of Emma's former pupils. She had become the mistress of Paul Stevens, an up-and-coming young architect, and had brought many interesting guests to the 'artistic evenings' that Emma had begun to hold once a month for the benefit of her young ladies.

'I am anxious to send out invitations immediately,' she began, as they sat taking tea together. 'The date that Daniel and I have agreed is Saturday, July the fifteenth.'

Sybil looked thoughtful. 'Henley will be over by then, but there is still the cricket at Lord's. However, I am sure that enough people will be in town. If we are fortunate Mr John, Paul's artist friend, will attend. Would you believe, he keeps a *ménage à trois* with his wife and mistress! He also likes to play the gypsy, and writes his love letters in the Romany tongue.'

'We need as many diverting characters as possible,' Emma smiled. 'I think twelve would be the right number, but since that will include Daniel, Kitty and ourselves then we need only find eight more.' She affected a casual air. 'Oh, that budding painter I met at

Paul's house would be welcome. What was his name? Ah yes, Rupert!'

Sybil agreed to place him on the guest list with a knowing smile. She was aware of Emma's attraction to the handsome, rather diffident young man but she was too well-mannered to mention it. Although the two women had become friends, Sybil had never lost respect for her former teacher.

As the date for the dinner party approached, Emma grew increasingly nervous. She knew she was playing a dangerous game, but she would do anything to retain Daniel's interest in her. They had made love only twice since returning to London, once in bed and once in the drawing-room at tea-time. The latter had been a rushed affair, after which Daniel had gone out on the town and spent the night at his club. Although Emma could have amused herself elsewhere, she would prefer to rekindle her lover's desire for her. They had been through cool patches before but always their ardour had been revived, like a fire that could be damped down and then brought back into roaring life at will.

Meanwhile, Kitty and Milly seemed well settled, and so far there had been no interference from Vincent. He had not replied to Kitty's letter but neither had he taken any steps to recover his wife and child. Emma comforted herself with the thought that if he were planning any legal action it would take months to come to court, during which time alternative plans could be made. Emma was quite prepared to send the pair abroad, if necessary, to save them from that dreadful man's clutches.

July the fifteenth dawned bright and sunny. A good omen, Emma decided, as she drank her tea in bed. The house had been cleaned from top to bottom by the two housemaids and Mrs Perkins was busy organising the kitchen and dealing with the various tradesmen. As the Academy was in summer recess, Emma could give all her attention to the preparations.

In the late afternoon Alice, Emma's personal maid,

went to her mistress's bedroom for the long preparation. First Emma was immersed in the steaming, scented water, while gentle hands titillated her breasts and thighs with their soapy caresses. Then came the donning of her underwear. Over her ivory silk chemise went the low-necked corset, one of Daniel's models, that pushed up her bust into a pleasing *décolletage* and cinched her waist in to a respectable twenty-two inches without unduly straining her abdomen. There were matching knickers, with pale cream bows and ruffles, then silk stockings to be drawn on with the utmost care and fastened with suspenders to the corset. Emma's petticoat was of tiered valenciennes lace protected by an under-flounce and topped with an amethyst underskirt in chiffon taffeta that rustled beautifully as she moved.

'Blimey, ma'am, you look a real picture!' Alice declared. 'I reckon you could go to dinner in your underthings, and no-one 'ud notice!'

Emma laughed. 'I believe in tantalising a man with a hint of lace, a glimpse of ruffle, before a woman permits her figure to be revealed in the full glory of its underpinnings!'

Alice took the brush and began to stroke her mistress's long hair with it. 'How should I do your hair, ma'am?'

'I think swept into a chignon at the back with perhaps a topknot? I have a cluster of "Devonshire curls" that might do the trick.'

'Right you are. Like you wore for that Ambassador's Ball?'

'Exactly. But with one or two side-curls dangling fetchingly about my ears, I think.'

Alice performed her transforming magic with the aid of the supplementary hairpiece and myriad invisible pins, then studded the finished work with tortoiseshell stars and crescents studded with *diamanté*. 'Perfect!' Emma announced, seeing herself in the glass. 'Now my gown, please dear. Carefully over my coiffure!'

The magnificent robe of Liberty silk, figured in exotic, jewel-bright colours, brought forth fresh gasps of admir-

51

ation from Alice. The low neck revealed the creamy depth of Emma's cleavage to perfection, and the soft folds lent an air of mystery to the curves and boundaries of her figure. On her feet she wore dainty black velvet slippers with *diamanté* clasps, and a glittering collar of diamonds and amethysts was placed around her neck. Before she had even glanced at herself in the wardrobe mirror Emma knew she looked utterly irresistible.

'Some of this Attar of Roses, please,' Emma smiled, handing Alice the spray of Atkinson's perfume that reinforced the subtle aroma of her corsage. Soon she was enveloped in the essence of a June garden, and her spirits rose in harmony with the scent.

'Now off you go, Alice, and help Kitty.'

When she was alone, Emma practised a few coquettish looks over her fan. She was determined to enjoy the evening to the full. Already she could hear the carriages and automobiles drawing up outside, with Stanton opening the door and murmuring a welcome. She knew that Daniel was in his dressing room, and soon they must descend to the drawing-room and greet their guests. Strangely enough she felt nervous at the prospect, although they had played host together many times. But this evening had to be a success – and on her terms – or she could see her lover and closest friend slowly slipping away from her.

When Kitty appeared, Emma complimented her sincerely. She was looking her best in a peach silk gown with a ruched lace bodice and silver brocade overskirt. Her eyes sparkled in the self-same blue as her dainty sapphire pendant and matching earrings. One of the guests, a young man called Arthur Kingsley, had been invited specifically with Kitty in mind. If the young poet had any true poetry in his soul, Emma thought, then his eyes would not stray from her friend all evening.

When Emma went to find Daniel her heart lifted, seeing him in his evening dress suit with the stiffened white piqué shirt and embroidered silk waistcoat, his moustache trimmed and scented with citrusy Eau de

Portugal. By the end of the evening he would reek of tobacco, but for now she relished the freshness of his cologne.

'Well, my dear, you look even more ravishing than usual in that gorgeous gown,' he smiled, as they reached the hall. 'And Kitty too.' He offered her his other arm with a rakish grin. 'Now to make every damn fellow in the place green with envy!'

As they entered, the small crowd in the drawing-room rose to be presented. Emma recognised the man that Sybil called 'Gus' straight away. He had magnetic eyes, an unruly beard and hair that reached below his collar. Although he had donned a shabby dress suit for the evening Emma was startled to see that he wore a red cravat and a single gold earring, Romany style. Emma had met the other guests before: 'arty' Vanessa Stephen and her escort, Mr Clive Bell; chirpy Daisy Lorrimer and witty Arthur Kingsley, both literary friends of Sybil's; a pretty Italian art student called Francesca, brought along by Gus John, and of course blonde, beautiful Rupert Heaven, nicknamed 'Angel' by his friends.

'How very nice to see you again, Rupert,' Emma murmured, taking his arm as they walked in to dinner. She had never heeded the rules of precedence so her dinner parties were free and easy affairs, as befitted her bohemian guests. Seeing Daniel accompanying the fiery Italian girl produced mixed feelings in her. It was not often that Emma had a chance to see him flirting with another woman, and although a part of her ached at the sight she nevertheless admired his seduction technique as her lover leant close to the pretty girl, talking slowly in Italian.

Mrs Perkins had done her proud with the table, which was set with the best silver, linen, crystal and china, with small bowls of flowers down the centre according to Emma's instructions. She knew it was the habit of some society hostesses to arrange tall floral displays on their tables so that she could hide the guests who were abhorrent to her behind the floral barrier. However, since

Emma refused to have anyone she disliked in the house such tactics were unnecessary. As she looked around the table at the animated, charming faces of her guests, Emma knew her dinner party was going to be a success. She had placed Rupert directly opposite herself, with Gus on her right hand and Paul on her left.

It was Vanessa who claimed her attention first, however. As soon as the soup was served she said, 'I understand that you are involved with the education of young women, Emma. From what Sybil tells me, your views are very advanced. I should like to know more.'

All eyes were on the hostess. 'It is true that I have a somewhat unusual curriculum for the Academy. I do not shy from teaching my girls what I feel they should know about life, and that includes many topics that even their own mothers are too bashful to discuss with them.'

Gus gave a hearty laugh. 'Don't say you tell 'em about the birds and the bees, Emma!'

She turned to him with a smile. 'Oh yes, indeed I do. The study of nature is high on my list of priorities – human nature, perhaps I should say.'

'But don't you think that's for a man to teach a woman? You'll be doing us men out of one of the greatest pleasures in life if you tell 'em all our secrets.'

'If all men were accomplished in matters of love there would be no problem. But one cannot count on it. Indeed, since most of my young ladies have been brought up to expect marriage into the upper class they are unlikely to encounter men of the world such as yourself. An education at Eton followed by Oxford is doubtless most useful for most aspects of life, but I can assure you it is almost a guarantee of ignorance so far as the fair sex are concerned.'

'In that case,' Gus retorted, 'perhaps you should open an academy for young gentlemen!'

There was general laughter, but as Emma caught Rupert's eye she saw his pale cheek flush with pink. She knew he made no secret of his total virginity, but almost boasted that he had never so much as kissed a woman.

54

At Sybil's house she had seen some of his paintings – studies of ethereal women with androgynous bodies beneath diaphanous robes – and she suspected that he had not even seen a female body in the nude, despite his claims to be an artist. He did not attend college but lived on an allowance from his rich parents and had apparently lived a sheltered life. Emma found the challenge he presented irresistible. She longed to initiate him into the mysteries of sex, but knew she must tread carefully.

While the second course was being served, and the company began to debate the interesting topic of whether the arts had a morally improving effect on mankind, Emma contented herself with throwing smiles and fond looks in Rupert's direction. He responded shyly, sometimes with a brief upturn of his red, sensual lips, sometimes with a fleeting glance that hinted at hidden passions but dared not reveal them nakedly. Emma found herself becoming roused with subtle excitement. The wine was making her bold, and she knew that Daniel was regarding her from his place at the other end of the table with lustful eyes. She fancied that the other men present were not entirely immune to her charms either. Every remark she made was listened to attentively and applauded so that she was encouraged to show off her wit and intellect, sparring with the other sharp minds present.

'So, Emma, you consider that nudity in art is an education in itself, is that so?' Clive said.

Emma nodded, aware that everyone's eyes were focused upon her. 'I do indeed. We live in such prudish times that there is no other way for a young man or woman to compare their own developing anatomy with that of the rest of the human race, or to become even superficially acquainted with that of the opposite gender. If you had heard the stories that some of my poor young ladies tell of how they were kept in dire ignorance of the changes that came upon them in puberty, you would find it shameful.'

'And what of love, Emma?' Paul enquired, with a sly wink at Sybil. 'Can the arts educate us there also?'

'Of course. What more sublime introduction to the finer feelings can there be than to read a Shakespearean sonnet or hear a Chopin nocturne?'

The discussion occupied them to the end of the meal. Then, instead of banishing the women while the men smoked and drank port, Emma suggested that they should adjourn to the drawing-room for some home-spun entertainment. Gus at once volunteered to sing, and Sybil was persuaded to perform upon the piano, while Francesca shyly agreed to recite a Petrarchan sonnet in the Italian tongue for everyone's ears to feast upon the musical vowels.

Emma was pleased to find that Gus had a rich and sonorous voice. He chose a bawdy troubadour ballad and then a gypsy song which sounded perfectly respect-able until, after rendering it in Romany, he gave them a rough translation! Sybil played one of the pieces she knew by heart, but then Emma recalled a Chopin noc-turne that she had once heard her play to perfection. 'Can you perform that for us now, Sybil?' she asked.

The girl shook her head with a regretful smile. 'Not without the music I fear, Emma. It was Miss Dawson's copy that I used to play from.'

'Miss Dawson's!' Emma started at the name of the music teacher who used to give lessons at her Academy until she went north to nurse a sick relative. 'I believe we still have a trunk full of her belongings here. Maybe that music is amongst them.'

Sybil's face lit up. 'Oh, that would be marvellous!'

'I shall go and search directly, while you play another of those Mendelssohn pieces,' Emma declared. Then inspiration struck. Turning casually to Rupert, who was sitting nearby, she said, 'I may need help to move some heavy trunks. Would you oblige me please, Rupert?'

He rose with alacrity, and the pair left the others to their entertainment and went upstairs. The trunk room was a small loft beside the attic nursery and access was by means of a rather rickety wooden ladder. Emma asked Rupert to hold it steady while she ascended and made sure she held up her skirt and petticoats high enough for him to have a good view of her legs. When she was in the loft she bent down and offered him her hand, knowing full well that her gaping neckline was showing off her bosom to perfection. By the time the young man scrambled into the dusty loft he was looking decidedly abashed. Emma closed the trapdoor after him and the loft was plunged into semi-darkness, lit only by the full moon that peered down at them through the murky skylight.

'It is so dark and dingy up here, and I am afraid of spiders!' Emma sighed. 'Can you find a candle for us? I believe there is one somewhere.'

Rupert soon located the candle and old-fashioned tinder box. He managed to light it and at once the place was bathed in a rosy glow that Emma knew would be flattering to her complexion. She arranged herself decorously on the lid of an empty trunk and proceeded to direct operations. 'Try that brass-bound trunk over there, Rupert. It has the initials SMD on the side and is definitely Sarah Dawson's trunk. Let us hope it is not locked.'

Emma knew it was not, for there was nothing of value inside. Below the layers of embroidered mats, books and photograph albums Rupert found the sheet music they were looking for and drew it out in triumph. 'Here it is: Twelve Nocturnes, Frédéric Chopin.'

Emma rose and approached him, putting her hand on his arm. 'Oh, well done! Sybil will be pleased. And, if she plays them as well as she used to do and is not too lacking in practice, our guests will be entranced.'

As if to show her gratitude she gave his cheek a gentle kiss and at once saw it catch fire. Pretending to be intrigued by his response she added, quietly, 'Oh Rupert, forgive me for being so forward. Is that the first time you have been kissed by a woman?' He nodded in silent confusion. Emma took the music from him and placed it on the lid of the trunk, then turned to face him. In the flickering candlelight his cheek seemed as pallid as a moth's wing.

She took his hand and addressed him earnestly. 'You know, there is nothing wrong in having ... feelings, Rupert. All young men have them, and young women too.'

'I know.' He was staring resolutely at his boots but suddenly he raised his head and looked straight into her eyes, saying, 'But oh, Emma, if you knew how much I long for some tender contact with womankind! I have gazed so long upon portraits of beautiful women. When I have the time I go to the galleries and feast my eyes, or just sit in some park and watch the ladies pass by. Sometimes I am sure that if I could just approach a young lady at a ball and ask her to dance she would be sure to accept me, but I never have the courage of my convictions.'

'Poor Rupert! It must be painful to be so shy, especially when there is no need. You are a good-looking young man with a sensitive temperament and an honest heart. The kind of man any girl would be happy to be courted by.'

His blue eyes grew eager. 'Are you sure, Emma? Oh if only you *did* have an academy for young gentlemen so that I could learn what to say and how to behave! There is so much of which I am ignorant, and I am so afraid of making a fool of myself and being ridiculed. If any pretty woman should laugh at me I would die, Emma! I am sure of that.'

'You poor boy!' She smiled, smothering a giggle. 'But although I have no "gentleman's academy" I am not averse to giving you some private tutoring, if you really desire it.'

She could tell that he was becoming even more heated by her proximity and her own body was responding in a similar fashion so that, beneath the layers of her skirts, her thighs were becoming quite clammy and the secret folds of her sex were opening up like petals to the sun.

58

Rupert's embarrassment increased. 'I do not know if my allowance would stretch to such instruction. What would be your fees?'

'Well, I should be most happy if you would paint my portrait in lieu of remuneration,' she told him with a smile.

'Really?' His face beamed at her, incredulously. 'You would teach me how to talk to young ladies and ... all that sort of thing.'

'Yes, indeed.' Emma drew him down onto the lid of a trunk beside her and clasped his hot hand between both of hers. 'And, if you wish, I could begin to instruct you right away. For example, there is an art in kissing a lady's hand, you know. Lift mine to your lips and press them softly against the back of my hand. You may linger a little. Yes, that is about right.'

He looked up at her, his blue eyes shining, and Emma felt a thrill pass through her. It was a long time since she had seduced such a complete innocent, and she revelled in the heady sense of power it gave her. 'Was that correct, Emma?' he asked, doubtfully.

'Perfect! I felt your delicate lips caress my skin so sweetly. A woman prefers a tender approach in the early stages, Rupert, when she is still somewhat unsure of her lover's integrity. Later, when her passion is roused, a different technique may be called for but we shall deal with that on another occasion.'

'Oh Emma, you do not know how happy you have made me!'

'I think I do. Would you care to press your lips to my cheek now, with a more lingering and slightly more forceful touch?'

He obliged willingly. Emma felt the flesh at the back of her neck tingle with anticipation as his soft mouth met her equally soft cheek and pressed into it with barely subdued passion.

'You are an excellent pupil. Just to complete this lesson in the art of the osculation I shall allow you to kiss me fully on the lips.'

She let the lips in question part slightly in readiness as Rupert's cherubic mouth pursed itself into a cupid's bow. Soon he was eagerly kissing her, blindly following where his instincts led him, his arm held tight about her waist and his thighs shifting restlessly against her skirt. Emma could not resist teasing him a little with her tongue, making little forays into his sweet mouth and stroking his warm cheek all the while.

When they finally broke apart, Rupert sighed. 'That was even more wonderful than I imagined in my dreams! Now I see why kisses are of such importance in courtship. They are not to be given away lightly, as I believe some flighty young girls will do. I am very glad that I waited to give my first real kiss to you, Emma, for you are being so kind to me.'

'Tell me what you felt while we kissed,' Emma said, encouragingly. 'Were you aware of any rousing feelings, any stirrings in parts of your body?'

Rupert blushed. 'I believe so.'

'You mean, down here I dare say.' Boldly Emma reached out and touched his fly, where the solid bulge of his erection was clearly detectable beneath the stiff cloth. 'Ah yes, I think your reaction is very normal Rupert, very normal indeed.'

'Really?' He stared at her with relief. 'I thought I was somehow different from other men. At school they taught us that we should never touch ourselves when we were in that state or we should be defiled. They said it was against Natural Law and God's Ordinance. But I seem to get into that state so very frequently.'

Emma smothered a laugh and instead addressed him gravely. 'How can what is natural be wrong, Rupert? That fine organ of yours was made to give women pleasure and receive pleasure in return. That is the only Law of Nature that I believe in.'

Rupert seized her hand and brought it spontaneously to his lips. 'I am so glad I have met you, dear Emma! You have given me such courage already.'

'Then kiss my mouth again, and show me what you have learnt this evening.'

Their second mouth-to-mouth encounter was more passionate than the first, not least because as Rupert's tongue entwined lustily with hers Emma fondled the ridge of serge between his legs, her experienced fingers accurately assessing the hidden dimensions. It was soon obvious that the young artist had a well-proportioned tool, long and thick with a head that rubbed itself eagerly against her palm and told her that he had undoubtedly indulged in the occasional, guilt-ridden episode of self-abuse. To free him from his self-recrimination and shame would not be easy, but it was a task that she had set herself before, with other unfortunate young men, and the outcome had always been most successful.

Aware that her guests were downstairs, however, Emma knew she could not go much farther on this occasion. Slowly, and with some reluctance on both sides, the luscious kiss drew to its end. But before Emma could even rise a voice assailed her from the other side of the trapdoor. 'Emma! Are you up there?'

It was Daniel. Filled with confusion, she asked Rupert to push the board aside and soon her lover's head was thrust up through the hole. 'Ah, I see you have found the music!' he said, in an ironic tone. 'Sybil is waiting to play it, so I suggest you allow me to help you down.'

Emma could hardly hide her erotic excitement from the man who knew her so well. As he held the ladder for his mistress to descend, her somewhat dishevelled appearance and the heated flush that was coursing through her entire body could easily be discerned.

'It took a while to find the Chopin,' she said, breathlessly.

'Yes, and I dare say you found one or two interesting diversions along the way.'

Emma was disturbed by his tone, detecting a note of disapproval beneath the irony. She took his arm and together they descended the stairs, leaving Rupert to follow with the music. In the drawing-room the guests were engaged in animated conversation and Emma was intrigued to see Kitty in private discussion with Vanessa Stephen. She caught the tail end of the latter's words before the room fell to a hush. 'My sister and I would like to discuss this further with you. We are at home every Thursday evening, at 46 Gordon Square.'

The party soon settled again, eager to listen to the exquisite music on the tinkling pianoforte. During the rest of the evening Emma often noticed Rupert staring at her with an expression of adoration on his angelic features. But she was also aware of Daniel's eyes upon them both, watching hawk-like whenever they exchanged a look or a word. Had she succeeded in her goal and made her lover jealous? It certainly looked as if she had, but instead of the triumphant feelings that should have filled her breast Emma only felt apprehensive.

When the last of the guests had left, full of compliments and good cheer, Emma faced Daniel in the deserted drawing-room. 'Well, I think the evening was a great success, don't you agree Dan? A most entertaining mix of company. In my experience one can always count on the artistic fraternity to provide good looks, charm and witty conversation.'

'A frivolous bunch, in my opinion. What do they know of industry or commerce, Emma, or the daily grind that most people have to endure?'

'Good Lord, you are talking like a Fabian now!'

'And you, Emma, have been behaving like a trollop!'

She stared at him incredulously. 'What do you mean, Dan?'

'You know very well. Seducing a young man under my roof while I, and your other guests, wait impatiently for your reappearance. Shame on you!'

'I thought you'd be amused,' she pouted. 'You know you enjoy hearing about my exploits.'

'Only when you have been discreet, Emma. Did it not occur to you that if anyone present had suspected what was happening upstairs they would have regarded me with contempt, as some kind of cuckold?'

'I am sorry. I did not think of that. But surely none of our guests . . .'

'From what I could gather, several of those present are not received in polite society.'

Emma's incredulity grew. 'When has that ever troubled you, Daniel?'

'I am in town to pursue my business interests. Whatever you or I may do in private is of no concern, but I cannot permit this address to gain the reputation of a house of ill repute. I even had doubts about the wisdom of allowing you to hold your Academy here, but I trusted to your discretion. Now I fear I may have made a mistake.'

Emma jumped up from her chair and paced the room, seeing her whole future suddenly plunged into jeopardy. 'Daniel, this is ridiculous! One small indiscretion . . .'

'Deserves punishment, do you not agree?' Daniel broke in, his eyes gleaming lasciviously.

Suddenly Emma felt relief and excitement wash over her in equal quantities. Of course, he was teasing her! This was a game they had played many times, but she had not recognised his opening gambit. Lowering her eyes she answered demurely, 'Whatever you say, Sir. I confess that I have been indiscreet, and indulged in lewd behaviour with an innocent young man. I deserve whatever punishment Your Lordship cares to visit upon me.'

'Then come, bend over the arm of this chaise longue.' Emma's heart was beating rapidly as she complied. 'Now lift up your skirt, wicked woman, and lower your petticoats. I want to see those cheeky round buttocks of yours blush in shame at your outrageous behaviour!'

Carefully Emma draped the lacy, billowing folds around her waist and waited for Daniel to lower her ivory silk knickers. She could feel her pleasure knob hardening against the velvet-covered arm of the sofa, sending hot ripples of desire throughout her nether regions. Her lover's palm began caressing the smooth globes of her rear beneath the silky cloth, preparing her for the harsher stimulation to come.

His voice crooned, softly, 'What an impudent little *derrière* you have, Miss. So pert and prominent, as if butter wouldn't melt between its cheeks. I shall teach it to know who is master round here. It is a naughty little posterior, and must be chastised for its own good.'

Daniel drew down her knickers until they were held at the top of her thighs beneath the taut suspenders with her fundament nakedly exposed beneath the corset. She heard him take up the riding crop that always stood in its niche by the fireplace and test it in the air a few times. Hearing the familiar swish her body stiffened, both dreading and desiring it. When the first stinging blow was inflicted on one side of her helpless behind she winced with the sudden pain, but knowing that it was a prelude to greater pleasure she willingly endured it. The leather came down again on her soft flesh, this time on the other side, making her shudder with the acute sensation.

'Importunate hussy!' Daniel whispered in her ear, leaning forward and pinching her left buttock hard between finger and thumb. 'Did you debauch that effete young whipper-snapper in the loft, amongst the dust and cobwebs?'

'We did nothing but kiss, Sir, I can promise you that.'

'Ah, but you intended more did you not? Confess it, or I shall beat it out of you! Had I not arrived in time I'll wager you would have had him right there on the rafters with his pecker out, crowing like a cock in a barnyard!'

'That was never my intention, Sir.'

'Well my intention is to punish you further, since you are still unrepentant and will not admit your guilt. Spread your legs wide, you wicked woman, and brace yourself for some more lashes!'

Emma did as she was told, her excitement growing. A few more swipes with the crop followed, making her bottom smart with tingling heat, but then she felt Daniel's rough fingers groping at her entrance and soon they came right into her vagina, filling her up deliciously. She wriggled against him, closing over the bunched fingers and wallowing in the richly pleasurable sensations that more than compensated for her pain.

'If you want to be prodded, choose a proper man not a beardless boy!' Daniel grunted, pulling out his hand and summarily replacing it with his stout member. Emma gasped as the thick penis plunged into her wet and ready cunt, thrilling her to the core of her being. She felt her inner flesh yield utterly to the bold invader, melting in its own juices as he began the vigorous thrusting that gave her hungry clitoris the friction it craved.

Soon her lover's hand was thrust into the front of her bodice, pushing the flimsy lace aside until his fingers could grasp the erect button that adorned her breast. She gasped as he pinched her nipple, sending immediate shock-waves through her highly charged nervous system, making her tremble like a taut wire that has been lightly touched. The throbbing in her vulva intensified, blurred her mind, took her to the limit of her capacity for sensual pleasure and held her there, challenging her to go further.

With three more thrusts of Daniel's lusty prick and a couple of tweaks upon her tingling nipple for good measure, Emma found the last vestiges of her self-control dissolving into a blissful release. As she wallowed in the waves of warm sensation she was dimly aware of Daniel reaching his own groaning climax, and her satisfaction deepened. At last she collapsed forward, onto the seat of the chaise longue, with her lover sprawled over her back.

'God, Emma, you are still the horniest little madam this side of the English Channel!' Daniel declared, as he levered himself up and then staggered round to flop onto the sofa with Emma's head in his lap. She kissed his half-flaccid penis affectionately then reached up to draw herself into his arms. They lay there motionless for some time, each dreaming contentedly of the other, until the chill of the night sent them reluctantly to their bed.

Chapter Five

*E*mma was disappointed to learn that Daniel was going off on his travels a few days later. They had enjoyed a brief renaissance of their love, but as he bade her farewell Daniel's brow was furrowed. He warned her not to have too much to do with her 'arty' friends. 'Particularly that young no-good dauber that I found you with in the loft. You are wasting your time with him, Emma. I would prefer it if that creature and his ilk did not come into my house again.'

Emma knew it was useless to argue with Daniel when his mind was made up, but as he drove away she was puzzled by his attitude. It was the first time he had ever attempted to interfere in her social life, and she regarded it as an unhealthy precedent. Yet she was aware that, at the end of the day, the Bloomsbury house belonged to him and she was only his tenant.

Instead, she would visit the aspiring young artist at his lodgings where she could sit for him as his model. 'Angel' intrigued her, and the thought of being alone with him filled her with thrilling anticipation. He was all white and gold, truly like some angelic being in a painting by Sir Edward Burne-Jones or Sir John Millais. Indeed, she could picture Rupert as a child, with his golden curls and innocent expression, as a model for 'Bubbles', the famous advertisement for Pears' soap.

He lived in a first-floor flat in the same square as the Stephen sisters, so an arrangement was made for Emma and Kitty to travel there together on a Thursday evening, Kitty to enjoy some intellectual conversation and Emma to indulge in more physical pleasures. The two women set out full of excitement one warm summer evening, walking the short distance through leafy Russell Square until they reached their destination.

'I shall call for you at eleven, since Rupert has kindly agreed to escort us both home,' Kitty smiled, then made her way towards number forty-six.

Rupert was clearly quite beside himself with joy to see Emma again. He proudly led her into his studio, and offered her some coffee. While they waited for the drinks to be brought, they began to talk about art and Emma asked him what his favourite painting was.

'*La Belle Dame Sans Merci*, by Sir Frank Dicksee,' he replied, without hesitation. 'I saw it exhibited at the Royal Academy three years ago, and it has haunted me ever since.'

'Ah! So "La Belle Dame Sans Merci hath thee in thrall!"' Emma smiled. 'Describe the picture to me, Rupert.'

The artist's face grew animated, shining with the vision that had etched itself into his memory. 'It shows a beautiful woman with long, flowing red hair seated upon a horse. At her side, a knight in armour walks with his hand on the horse's bridle. His helmet hangs from the saddle, adorned with the lady's favour. But what impressed itself upon me most was the expression on the man's face. He walks with arms outspread, like a somnambulist, and he is gazing up at the lady as if entranced. She looks down on him intently, bending from the horse, and their lips are but inches away, yet I have the feeling that they will never meet, and therein lies her power over him.'

Rupert blushed and his eyes grew dark, opaque. For a

moment, Emma had the feeling that she was looking into the depths of his soul. The coffee arrived, breaking the spell, but some subtle communication had definitely passed between them.

'Perhaps you would care to look at some sketches I have made,' Rupert said as she sipped her coffee, thrusting a portfolio nervously onto the small table beside her. Emma thumbed through the collection. The subjects were almost entirely women. Some showed promise, although all were clumsily executed and there were no nude studies.

'You know, the place for you to study is Paris,' she told him, with a smile. 'You would find inspiration there, and guidance too. The Montmartre district is brimming over with young artists, and the models are more than willing to pose for the price of a bottle of wine.'

'You have been to Paris, Emma? How I should love to see it!'

'Well, perhaps you should study a little more here in London before you attempt to go overseas. Now Rupert, answer me plainly please. Have you ever set eyes upon a woman's naked body before?' He blushed and averted his gaze, shaking his head. 'I thought as much. Well I pride myself on the fact that I have looked after my figure, and I think you will find that I make an acceptable artist's model. So, if you are in agreement, I shall undress here in front of the fire and then you may set me to pose any way you want me.'

'You mean, you will sit for me in the ... altogether?'

Rupert's periwinkle blue eyes were opened wide with astonishment at the prospect, but Emma remembered that she must refrain from laughing at him at all costs. She turned away, on the pretext of unbuttoning her blouse, so he could not see her trembling lips. 'Of course. There is no other way that your artist's eye might become accustomed to female anatomy. Help me with my stays, if you please. They are rather tightly laced.'

Emma could feel his tremulous fingers fumbling at her back, and the heat of his breath on her bare neck.

Tonight she would further his education in both the Art of Portraiture and the Art of Love. 'Now, Rupert, if you would help to remove my stockings.'

'Gladly, Emma. But there is just one thing . . .'

'What is that, dear boy?'

'I should like it very much if you would call me "Angel". It is what all my friends call me, my surname being "Heaven". It began as a kind of joke, but now I prefer it. Only mater and pater call me Rupert now.'

Emma bent forward and kissed his forehead, letting his nose linger in the perfumed precinct of her bosom and savour the perfume she had mixed herself, a *pot pourri* of cottage garden flowers. He knelt before her, adoringly, and unclipped the suspenders with a kind of reverence, then rolled the silken sheath down her leg.

'Now my petticoats please, Angel.'

When she was completely naked, the young artist simply could not take his eyes off her. Never had Emma been perused with such intent curiosity, such avid attention to detail. She watched his eyes move from her round stomach to her equally rounded bosom, the nipples just starting to change from their soft, relaxed state to full erection on exposure to the air. Angel took in the curvature of her breasts with an incredulous gaze and she knew he was longing to take them in his hands and press them to his eager mouth, like fruit fresh plucked from the tree. Well, there would be time enough for that later.

His eyes dropped to her plump thighs and the brown patch between them, a tangle of tightly-furled curls that she knew had taken him by surprise. He had no idea what was hidden behind her pubic mound, of course. If she were to open her legs wide and give him a good view of her vulva he would no doubt recoil in horror, so she must be decorous for the time being. Everything must be done in easy stages with this *ingénu* or, like a wild animal being tamed, he would take fright and bolt.

'I should like you to sit on this chair that I have covered with draperies,' he said at last, leading her to an armchair swathed with fringed Paisley silk. She arranged her limbs for his approval and he seemed very pleased with the effect. 'I shall first make some sketches in charcoal. Then I should like to try a water-colour, with your permission.'

'Of course, dear boy. I am quite comfortable. Do as you like with me!'

Emma watched him snatch up his drawing-board and begin to set down his vision of her with manic haste. Whatever demon was inspiring him made his fingers fly over the page, his eye fixing her momentarily with its steely gaze then recording some detail with his hand in a manner that seemed almost automatic. Emma, remembering the lazy brushmanship of the Parisian artists who sat all day in bars making sketches which they would exchange for the price of a glass of absinthe, found this hectic inspiration quite breathtaking to observe.

'There, I have done!' Angel announced, signing his name with a flourish. 'Look, Emma, what do you think?'

He held up his first sketch for her to see. The lines were bold and flowing, quite different from any of his other work. Although her face was sketched in so vaguely that there was no point in judging its likeness, her body was displayed in all its sensual splendour, every familiar curve and line lovingly depicted.

'Why, that is marvellous!' Emma exclaimed, sincerely. 'Angel, I do believe that my sitting for you has been an inspiration.'

'It has, it has! Oh you have no idea, my sweet Emma. When I first saw that heavenly body of yours I just knew that I could render it faithfully, to the life.'

'Would you like me to change my pose a little for your second sketch?'

Emma raised her left knee onto the seat so that the closed lips of her sex were just visible beneath her hairy vee. She wanted to introduce Angel slowly to the secrets that lay concealed between her thighs and this seemed an appropriate way. Although he gave no sign of having noticed when he first set to work, Emma knew that the artist would be bound to examine her very closely when he came to draw that part of her.

He began with a general outline, spending a while on her breasts and stomach before his gaze dropped to her pudendum. Under his intense inspection Emma could feel her dark outer lips moistening and softly opening, no doubt revealing the pink lining within. She felt a tingling there, as if his eyes could stimulate her at a distance, and her clitoris was soon throbbing so insistently that she longed to squeeze her thighs together or rub herself but she dared not.

At last Angel had finished and Emma was able to see his work. This time he had surpassed himself, putting in more detail and drawing with a finer line. She was pleased to note that he had faithfully reproduced the folds and contours of her genitalia with meticulous accuracy.

'You see, dear Emma, you are the perfect model for me!' Angel murmured, boldly putting his arm around her naked waist and kissing her cheek.

She turned and let him take her fully in his arms, relishing the feel of his warm hands upon her hips. 'Kiss me again!' she smiled, offering him her mouth this time.

He obeyed without hesitation, and soon she could feel his hands caressing her ample buttocks and the backs of her thighs as their tongues met in passionate accord. A nagging voice told her that the art lesson was not yet over, that he had a third sketch to make, but the tide of feeling that was beginning to overwhelm her took no heed of artistic endeavour.

Neither, it seemed, did the artist himself. His vision now was taking quite a different form as his hands grew bolder, passing between their heated bodies to stroke the swell of her stomach and clutch at the fullness of her breasts. When he found her erect nipples Emma gave a loud moan of desire that seemed to fuel him further. He pressed her back towards the armchair so that she sank into it, and then proceeded to let his lips roam with wild

71

abandon over every part of her nude body that he could reach.

Soon Emma was too far gone in her arousal to call a halt. After his preliminary reticence, the eagerness with which her naive young lover was now exploring her body was immensely gratifying and made her long for a swift conclusion. Yet she was mindful of the need for caution. Too forward an approach and she might frighten him off, but she knew that he was in need of some guidance.

'My sweet Angel, will you not permit me to undress you so that we may enjoy each other's bodies unencumbered?' she murmured, as her lips strayed to his ear.

He gave a grunt, too preoccupied with the enticing curve of her right breast to stay his mouth and hands. Emma did her best to unbutton him wherever she could, easing the shirt off his back and undoing his waistband, but only when his trousers were about his knees did he break off his amorous endeavours and allow her to finish the task of undressing him.

Now it was Emma's turn to subject the Angelic Body to scrutiny. His chest was hairless, though quite well moulded, and his small brown nipples stood out against the pallid hue of his skin. Travelling down from his navel was a column of sparse fair hair that spread out into a mass of blonde fuzz at the base of his belly. Of far more interest to Emma, however, was the sturdy pillar that rose in eager anticipation of joys to come. It was not the longest she had seen but it was certainly one of the thickest, pale as cream with a shiny pink head.

'Oh, Angel! What a magnificent member you possess, my dear!' she cooed, eager to bolster his pride for she knew, from experience, that a man could only give of his best when he felt perfectly confident.

'Do you really think so?'

Angel looked almost comical as he peered down at his tackle and the eye of his rosy helmet seemed to stare back at him. Emma decided it was time for deeds, not words. She led him over to the couch, swathed in gaudy

72

Indian cotton and scattered with cushions that stood against the far wall, and arranged her body upon it so that she was reclining with all the sensual majesty of Manet's *Olympia*. Then she held out her arms to him.

'Come, Angel, don't be shy. This couch is wide enough for us both.'

Emma knew he couldn't resist her. The flames burning in the centre of his dark pupils spoke of hidden passions, secret dreams, of desires scarcely admitted but nonetheless powerful for that. Well, she would enjoy ascertaining the exact nature of his predilections!

To her surprise, instead of falling into her arms he fell to his knees. 'Oh Emma, I am not worthy to touch your beautiful form!'

'What nonsense is this? Did you not enjoy caressing my breasts just now?' He lowered his eyes, but not before she had seen his shame in their depths. Emma remembered his fascination with the image of fatal, ruthless beauty but she divined that asceticism was not his bent. Much as he would love to adore some woman from afar he also needed physical satisfaction.

Suddenly she saw clearly what was occurring within the poor lad's psyche. He wanted so much to taste the forbidden fruit, but he could not overcome his guilt. What he needed, more than anything, was for her to take all the responsibility, to make him act according to her command rather than of his own free will. It was a familiar characteristic of men reared by an authoritarian nanny.

She drew herself up into a more severe attitude and said, in the voice of authority, 'Well, wretched boy, if you wish to receive the special privileges that only I can bestow upon you, then you must earn them. Get down on all fours, like a lap dog, and show me the utmost obedience. Bring me the silk scarf that I have left on that small table over there. You may carry it in your mouth like a well-trained hound.'

From the way he scurried eagerly over to the table Emma knew she had hit upon the right approach. It was not the first time she had commanded men who were completely fulfilled only by sexual servitude, but it promised to be the sweetest. All the gentlemen she had played this game with hitherto had been well aware of their bent, but Angel was a total novice and she found the prospect of initiating him very appealing. He knelt patiently by the sofa with the scarf hanging from his mouth, staring up at her with his soulful eyes so like a faithful retriever that she actually began to laugh but changed it at once to a cough.

'Good boy! Now let me have it.'

Emma took the silk from his mouth and used it to bind his arms behind his back. Angel was staring at her with an inscrutable expression but she could almost feel the sexual heat emanating from his pores. She suspected that he found his sudden helplessness very gratifying, although he would not know why. There was something very satisfying in knowing a man's secret desires more explicitly than the man himself, a feeling of power that Emma had often enjoyed. She kept him there in suspense for a while then asked him to fetch her an artistic journal from the other side of the room in the same manner as before. He had some difficulty getting there on his knees alone, and even more in manoeuvring the paper into his mouth, but eventually he managed to bring it back to her and she removed it from his mouth with a curt, 'Now, STAY!'

Casually she stretched out on the sofa and opened the illustrated journal, apparently oblivious of her devoted slave. Although she would not regard him directly she was aware of the continuing state of his erection and knew that in his extremely aroused state anything she did, anything at all, would provide him with the most exquisite satisfaction. Although she was determined not to abuse her influence over him it was most pleasing to have a young man entirely at her beck and call. After the way Daniel had imposed his will on her, making her acutely aware that her very presence in the Brunswick

Square house was dependent on his favour, she could not help but enjoy this sudden reversal of power.

For quite some time Emma continued to flick through the pages, making Angel remain upright on his knees in an uncomfortable position which would soon be quite agonising. Whenever she glanced at him out of the corner of her eye, however, his expression was entranced, beatific almost, as befitted his nickname.

One of the photographs reproduced in *Art and Architecture* was of Donatello's *David*. Looking at it Emma was reminded not only of Angel's slim form but also of a trip to Florence, long ago, when she was pursued by Daniel incognito, to startling effect and a very satisfying conclusion, and she felt a sharp rise in her libido. Many men were aroused by the sight of a woman pleasuring herself, and she suspected that Angel would be no exception. One hand strayed to her breast, her nipple swelling and stiffening at her touch and evoking a corresponding surge of longing down below, making her throb and tingle.

Emma was about to let her other hand delve between her thighs, to feel her wet labia open and yield the hardened nub of her desire to her nimble fingers, when she thought better of it. Instead of forcing Angel to be a mere spectator in the display of female eroticism that was about to unfold, why not let him be a participant? Thoughts of all she could make him do sent new thrills speeding through her veins, filling her with delicious heat and making her wriggle seductively against the soft folds that surrounded her.

'Now, come here!' she commanded. Obediently he shuffled forward, obviously relieved to be allowed to change position. Emma opened her thighs. She saw his involuntary glance down at her wide open vulva, noticed the quivering jerk of his penis as lust caught him helplessly in thrall. Smiling she trailed a finger between her outer lips then held it, glistening, to his nose.

'That is the scent of woman, boy! But you shall also taste my female essence. Consider it your reward for

75

good service but be warned, if you do not perform well I shall punish you!'

She swivelled round until her glistening folds were within reach of his Cupid's bow lips, shuddering a little in anticipation of the pleasure she would derive from training his untutored mouth. Carefully she parted her outer labia with her fingers, revealing the pink inner ridges with their twin, carefully-guarded treasures: the precious pearl and the opening to the secret cave, both bathed with sweet liquid.

'Put your mouth to my lower mouth and lick me!' she commanded. He looked startled but soon leaned close, his lips hovering over her thighs. 'Be slow and gentle at first,' she cautioned him. 'If you hurt me I may beat you.'

Angel raised his frightened eyes, in which excitement also lurked. Emma watched him put out his red tongue and poke tentatively at her vulva, bliss-waves spiralling through her at the sensual melding of their wet flesh. She moved rhythmically against the flat of his tongue, subtly instructing him, and he soon caught on. He began to savour the taste of her pussy, licking and sucking with regular movements, now poking the pointed tip just inside her quim, now bathing her rampant clitoris with his saliva. The resulting sensations were keen and had her poised on the rim of ecstasy, ready to demonstrate that women, be they whore or goddess, could give themselves up to the passionate throes of Eros just as well as men.

Yet a part of Emma remained fully in control, mindful of the fact that her lover was experiencing his first intimate contact with female flesh. Somehow she sensed that Angel was not able to 'perform' in the normal sense of the word, that he could not do, only be done to. It was in his nature to be passive as far as the act of sex was concerned, to act on orders rather than his own initiative. How could she introduce him, however fleetingly, to the mysteries of the orgasm?

Suddenly she called, in a peremptory tone, 'Stop!'

The artist stilled his tongue and slowly raised his head, his eyes dazed and distant. Emma could tell, from the flush in his cheeks, that he had found his first taste of cunnilingus extremely exciting. 'Now lie on your back on the floor!'

He heaved himself awkwardly off the sofa and fell with a thud onto the carpet. As Emma rose he rolled over until he was staring up at her, helpless, an uncanny light in his blue eyes as if he really were possessed by the spirit of that poetic knight, 'alone and palely loitering'. There was something abject about him that almost revolted her, but she knelt down and began to caress his still erect penis, stroking it as if it were some furry pet animal. Angel lay tense with anticipation, fearing that her soft approach might be the prelude to some cruel trick.

Emma could feel her cunt aching to be filled, with the fleshy bead just above it also clamouring for fulfilment. She knelt astride his slender thighs, took hold of his solid shaft and placed the head within the oiled groove of her pussy. She sighed with contentment as she made contact with the tingling nub of her desire, then let the bulbous glans lodge in her entrance for a few seconds, squeezing it with her inner muscles so the thrilling feelings redoubled, taking her near the edge again. Once she felt Angel give an involuntary thrust, however, she swiftly returned his organ to her clitoris and stimulated herself there again.

This pattern was repeated for several minutes until both Emma and her supine lover were stretched to the limit of their continence. When she was sure neither could bear it any longer, Emma engaged the head of his prick in her cunny and sank down hard upon it, eliciting a loud groan from Angel. She then proceeded to work up and down rapidly, extracting the maximum sensation from the slippery contact between his hard tool and her soft inner walls while her finger worked rapidly upon her external trigger. Soon a strong upsurge of energy caught her in its vortex and she was only briefly aware of Angel's first spasms before succumbing herself, riding on the exquisite ebb and flow of her orgasm with voluptuous joy. She felt a weak jet rise within, was aware of the gradual diminishing of his erection, and then her own climax slowly subsided into the familiar warm glow, tinged with regret that it was over.

Reaching out to Angel's wrists Emma untied his bonds, led him gently back up onto the sofa and let him rest curled in her arms with his head on her bosom. She knew the experience had been overwhelming for him and now he needed less a stern mistress, more a comforting nurse. Gently she stroked the matted strands of his hair, feeling his breathing and heartbeat become more regular as his eyes closed in a total relaxation that verged on slumber.

After about ten minutes, Emma carefully dislodged herself and rose to her feet. The night sky, with its scattered points of light, was filling the undraped window and she knew that soon Kitty would be arriving. Swiftly she dressed, tidied her hair as best she could, and was just putting the finishing touches to her coiffure when the doorbell rang.

Angel started from his sleep, eyes wide awake but his brain still fuzzy. 'Who is that?'

Emma gave him a reassuring hug. 'Do not fret, my dear, it is only my friend Kitty.'

'Oh, I promised to accompany you home. Oh, oh! Where are my clothes?'

'Angel, don't lose your head! Your clothes are here, and while you dress I shall go and greet Kitty. Then you may meet us in the hall.'

Kitty had been let in by a servant and was waiting on a hall chair. Emma took the one beside her and the two women were soon chatting away.

'Oh Emma, I had such a marvellous evening!' Kitty began, excitedly. 'I can't tell you how fascinating those two sisters and their friends are. All such excellent conversationalists.'

'What did you talk about?'

'Everything under the sun – well, almost! We talked of women's suffrage and I was able to tell them what I had seen and heard at Oldham. They were most impressed!'

'I am glad, Kitty dear. It will do you good to be in company again.'

She looked at Emma from below her lashes, bashfully. 'Maybe more good than you imagine. I met a gentleman there who seemed quite taken with me. His name is Charles.'

Emma had been disappointed that nothing had come of introducing Kitty to Arthur Kingsley. Her delight now was genuine. 'My dear, I am so pleased. If I could see you become some kind man's mistress, or even his wife if you could get Vincent to divorce you, then I should be the happiest woman alive!'

Kitty bent forward to give her benefactor a spontaneous kiss. 'You are so good to me, Em. And I do not want to be a burden on you any longer than I have to.'

'That is not what I meant at all!' Emma frowned. 'I would sooner we grew to be old maids together than see you chained to another rum bugger like Vincent.'

Kitty laughed, but just then Angel appeared, fully dressed but looking somewhat the worse for wear, and the two women rose to be escorted out into the night air.

Chapter Six

Within a few weeks Emma had Angel well trained, and he was turning out to be a very obedient and satisfactory slave. Respecting Daniel's wishes, she did not entertain him at the Brunswick Square address but only visited him in his own apartment, during which time she behaved exactly as if she were the mistress of the house. It wasn't long before she had devised a suitable uniform for him: a leather collar and matching wristlets, with a loincloth that could be easily removed when necessary.

It was not often necessary, however. Angel preferred to service his mistress with his lips and hands, finding the act of intercourse too anxiety-provoking. He soon became an expert in foreplay, pleasuring Emma in whatever manner she desired and adoring her unconditionally, whether she behaved kindly or cruelly towards him. He also acquired a taste for the whip, his taut, boyish buttocks relishing the sting of his mistress's expert caresses every bit as much as his penis enjoyed the occasional brush of her lips. For Emma he was proving to be a useful diversion, especially while Daniel was away on his travels and she had no other suitor.

Both Kitty and Milly had begun to blossom under Emma's care. The child had her own governess now, and loved to show off to her godmother in the evenings, performing upon the pianoforte or reciting a poem she had learnt. Her mother was occupied with her new lover, and Emma soon became curious about him. She questioned Kitty when they took tea together one dull afternoon in August, when all of London Society seemed to have followed the Prince of Wales to Cowes for the regatta, or migrated to the Scottish grouse moors.

'Tell me about this Charles,' she began, pouring two cups of Earl Grey. 'I can see that he is making you happy, my dear. What does he do for a living – or does he have private means?'

Kitty obviously welcomed the chance to talk about her new beau. 'He is an art dealer. He began in Paris, but now has a shop in Chelsea. Naturally he mixes with all the up-and-coming artists in London. He knows Clive Bell of course, and Gus John and Duncan Grant and . . . Oh, just about everybody who is anybody in artistic circles!'

'I should like to meet him.'

'Oh you shall, and sooner than you think. He is calling for me at six o'clock today, to attend a private viewing of a new exhibition. I am so excited!'

Despite herself, Emma felt a little as if her nose had been put out of joint. Before Kitty came to live with her the bohemian world of artists and intellectuals had been her domain, and now it seemed as if her protégée were invading it. Not that she needed to feel excluded, of course. She could attend any soirée that might be held, ask Angel to introduce her to anyone she fancied, but since Daniel had expressed disapproval of such people she felt reluctant to consort with them. Angel Heaven, with his loving dependence on her, was the only one of her old acquaintances that she still saw regularly. Although she was annoyed with herself for giving in to Daniel's unreasonable demands, she was too afraid of losing him to risk being seen in such circles again.

Promptly at six the doorbell rang and Kitty's lover was shown into the drawing-room, where the two women were chatting. Emma rose with a smile but, as her eyes met those of the gentleman caller, her smile turned to a rictus. She felt her heart beating rapidly and was afraid she would faint, but somehow she regained control of herself and allowed the introduction to be made even though it was unnecessary. For she knew Charles Purchase of old.

He came forward and stiffly shook her hand, his eyes glinting in recognition. 'Lady Longmore,' he said, giving her title slight emphasis, 'I am delighted to make your acquaintance.'

Emma had an absurd urge to laugh, but Kitty's nonchalant attitude puzzled her. Didn't she remember how they had met in Paris, ten years or so ago, when Charles had been the willing victim of Emma's charms? It seemed like only yesterday, and yet she could plainly see the effects of the passage of time on his features. The innocent, youthful look was gone and in its place was the knowing sophistication of one who was familiar with the *demi-monde* of two of the greatest capital cities in the world.

'Kitty tells me you deal in art treasures, Mr Purchase,' Emma said, striving to appear composed. 'What a fascinating occupation.'

'Indeed. I began ten years ago when I was studying at the Sorbonne,' he said, pointedly.

'Ah yes! I know it well. Paris is a city where a young man may complete his education in a number of interesting fields.'

'I believe my time there was wisely spent,' he continued, a hint of amusement in his eye. 'But I owe a lot to my good fortune. I was introduced by a lady friend to the artistic quarter of Montmartre, and there I bought sketches and paintings from a number of struggling young artists who have since gained renown.'

'Tell us more!' Kitty enthused. 'Whose paintings did you buy in the beginning, Charles?'

'I was a student so I could not afford the work of anyone established. There was a young nobleman who painted dancers and ladies of the night. His name was Henri de Toulouse-Lautrec. He was a semi-cripple, poor man, but his talent was prodigious. When I knew him he was willing to sell me some of his work in exchange for the price of a glass of absinthe. I bought several lithographs and poster designs which have now become quite sought after.'

'Yes, I have seen some of his sketches,' Emma said dryly, remembering scenes from a brothel. She couldn't help wondering if Charles and Henri had shared the same whores.

'Another artist I was fortunate enough to encounter was a Spaniard called Picasso. He had just moved to Paris and was producing the most exquisite paintings in shades of blue and pink. I bought some of his Harlequin studies and resold them recently for a great deal more than I paid for them.'

'And are you buying up the works of our English painters, too?'

'Of course.' He gave Emma an ironic smile then turned to Kitty. 'Are you quite ready, my dear? If we want to catch the opening we should leave now.'

'Charles, may we invite Emma along? I know she is interested in art and far more knowledgeable than I am.'

But before Charles could answer either way, Emma interjected. 'Thank you for thinking of me, Kitty, but I must decline. I have made other arrangements for this evening.'

'Oh.' Kitty looked genuinely disappointed and Emma was satisfied that, incredible as it seemed, she really did not remember Charles from their time in Paris. 'Another time, perhaps.'

'Perhaps,' Emma smiled, but without conviction. She could never lower herself to play 'gooseberry' to her ex-lover and former maidservant.

When the pair had gone, Emma recalled how she had seduced that young man, fresh from Oxford and in a foreign city, free from his mother's stifling influence. As far as she could remember Kitty had remained discreetly in the background most of the time, so perhaps it was not surprising that she had not recognised him in a different context. After all, he had changed from a gauche youth into a confident and rather portly man approaching his thirties.

It piqued her to see them together, nevertheless, even after all this time. She had always harboured fond memories of Charles Purchase, who had been only the second young innocent that she had initiated into the joys of sex, and the thought of him sporting with Kitty was upsetting. It revived other disturbing memories, such as the time when Emma had believed that Daniel had seduced her maid, although it had turned out that he'd only been using the girl to get at her mistress.

Along with that degrading emotion which she recognised as jealousy, she was eaten up with curiosity. What had happened to the youthful Charles after she'd left him in the capable hands of her friend, Lily Merchant? Had he recognised Kitty when he met her recently? Had he even begun courting the maid to gain access to the mistress? These and a dozen other questions plagued Emma's mind until she resolved that she simply must get to see Charles alone, in order to have at least some of them answered.

Before Emma could make any such arrangements herself, however, she was in her sitting-room one afternoon around five o'clock when Mrs Perkins appeared with a card on a silver salver. 'Gentleman left this, ma'am,' she announced dubiously. 'Says he would like a few words, if convenient, otherwise please may he call again.'

Emma took one glance at the name printed with an italic flourish and nodded. 'Show him in please, Perkins. I shall see him now.'

Charles entered smiling broadly. He came straight up to Emma and kissed her hand with just a hint of the boyish enthusiasm that had endeared him to her so long ago. 'My dearest Emma, I just had to see you alone. Forgive me if I am intruding.'

His entrance had lifted her spirits and she found herself dangerously pleased to see him. 'Not at all. As you see I am quite alone. Daniel is out of town and Kitty has gone to some meeting or other.'

'The Kensington Suffragists, to discuss the recruitment of the East End women to The Cause. She told me all about it.'

Charles had spoken ironically. 'You know about Kitty's political involvement, then.'

'You might say it was what brought us together. When we first met at Gordon Square she spoke with such passionate fire about votes for women that I instantly desired her, even though I knew perfectly well who she was. I also realised that she had no idea who I was.'

'So you took advantage of her!'

'I believe not. She was clearly enamoured of me, and at first I had no idea that she was living with you. But when I found out I knew that fate had taken a hand. I questioned her about you – discreetly of course – and when I discovered that your lover was presently out of town my joy knew no bounds.' Charles seized her hand again, staring into her eyes with intense longing. 'Oh Emma, just to see you, to talk with you again, fills my heart with rapture!'

Although it was flattering to find that Charles still harboured tender thoughts of her after all those years, Emma was still uncertain how to proceed. She offered him a glass of Madeira, since she was in sore need of some fortification herself. They sipped the strong wine sitting near the window, with the late afternoon sun gilding their faces, and Emma felt a corresponding warm glow inside as Charles recalled their Parisian idyll.

'Do tell me about Lily Merchant,' she said, remembering her old friend affectionately. 'When you last heard of her, was she still mistress of that Russian archduke and living in that wonderful apartment?'

To her surprise, he shook his head. 'I believe she was no longer under his protection. The last address I had for her was off Boulevard de Clichy I believe.'

Emma was shocked. Although only a few streets away from her former prestigious address it sounded as if Lily had moved into the red light district that surrounded the famous cabaret of the Moulin Rouge. Still, she recalled her friend saying that she felt as much at home amongst the whores and showgirls as in the salons of the aristocracy.

'I lost touch with her after I returned to England. Did she look after you as she promised?'

'Oh yes. It was she who introduced me to the artists in Montmartre, enabling me to start on my present career. Mama, you know, wanted me to go into the diplomatic service, but she passed away before I returned from France and then I was free to do as I wished.'

'And did that include marriage, by any chance?'

His eyes levelled with hers, sending a warm thrill of response down Emma's spine. 'No. I have never found a woman to equal you, my dear, and until I do I shall remain a bachelor.'

'You alarm me, Charles. Now I feel responsible for spoiling your marital prospects.'

'Nonsense! I dare say I shall wed when the time is right. Until then, however, I am fancy free and intend to make the most of it.'

He came over and put his arm around Emma, pulling her to her feet. She felt helpless to resist, feeling the powerful tug of their old attraction as well as the intriguing new feelings induced by Charles' mature personality. To see the innocent youth developed into a man of the world, and to know that she had played a substantial part in the metamorphosis, gave Emma an irresistible thrill.

Nevertheless, she felt it prudent to break away from him. 'What if Kitty should return? What would she think if she saw me in your arms?'

Charles gave a knowing smile, his face bright and seductive. 'After the political meeting she is invited to dine with Miss Sylvia Pankhurst and her friends. I think she will be away for some time yet.'

He tightened his embrace and Emma felt her will to resist melt in the heat of his passion. His lips were near enough for her to feel his warm breath on her face and a voice in her head said, 'Why not?' She had been the first woman Charles had loved, and it seemed that he still cared for her. If she had been looking for someone to play second fiddle to Daniel, someone she could run to if the worst happened and she were discarded by her lover like a worn glove, then Charles Purchase would be a far more suitable candidate than Rupert Heaven.

Besides it was enormously exciting to have him overpower her. Only Daniel had been so forceful with her before. As his mouth crushed her lips with merciless abandon she felt her insides swoop with keen desire and knew that she must have him, now or whenever, regardless of any loyalty she might feel to Kitty.

'Oh, Emma!' she heard him mutter, in a guttural tone, when their tongues had locked in mutual play for some minutes. 'Shall we stay here or go upstairs?'

'Perhaps we had better go upstairs.'

Emma could feel her heart racing as she led the way to her bedroom, cautioning Charles to tread quietly upon the stairs. She'd not felt so excited since her encounter with Daniel upon the rocking-horse. Almost as soon as the bedroom door had closed behind them Charles fell upon her like a ravening beast, doing his best to find his way through the maze of buttons and tapes to the naked flesh beneath. Emma helped him as best she could and soon her breasts were burgeoning out of their confines, her nipples peeping shyly out from their nest of lace and frills to be eagerly seized upon by Charles' fingers.

'Oh, you have lost none of your charms!' he exclaimed, taking one rosy teat in his mouth and pulling the other out between finger and thumb, tweaking it unmercifully.

The urgency of his need was apparent as his thigh pressed against hers, letting Emma feel the rigidity of his erection. She let her hand enclose the tweed-clad ridge, feeling it grow in her grasp, and her own desire quickened, making her gasp as the warm flurries of energy flushed through her veins. Soon Charles was tearing the shirt off his own back, pressing his manly chest against her half-naked breasts so that their racing hearts could beat as one.

'Help me out of my dress,' she beseeched him.

His fingers fumbled with the last fastenings until her silk tea-gown fell to the floor, exposing her pretty underwear. Charles' eyes lighted at once on the vee of her sex between the frilled suspenders, still concealed by a layer of lace-trimmed cotton. His hand reached up and his finger slipped in through the leg of her knickers to touch her swollen vulva. Emma groaned and fell back onto her bed as he made contact with the shuddering button of flesh through her nether lips. So aroused was she that the minute her lover began to rub her there with his fingertip she knew it would not be long before she reached the point of no return.

Charles' eyes glinted feverishly at her, overcoming any lingering scruples with their mesmeric intensity, and Emma soon felt her climax building with relentless speed, like a gathering storm. Her body grew rigid against the bed where she was lying, her breasts thrusting eagerly out of her corset with their red nipples throbbing almost as wildly as her clitoris. His wet lips bathed each with cool saliva, but the juices flooding her vulva were her own, seeping from the ripe fruit of her cunny and making his fingers slip all over the delicate folds and ridges of her sex. The lubricated friction continued apace until Emma felt the first trembling onset of her orgasm and gave a loud moan of relief. Fiercely the spasms racked her, causing such acute pleasure that it bordered on pain, and making Charles tear at her underclothes in his desperate lust to get inside her while she was still hot and wet.

Emma felt him thrust in through the torn lace, finding his way straight into her quim and filling her up completely. She lay inert, incapable of more, as he made the four or five jabbing movements necessary to bring himself on. As he groaned his way through his coming

Emma kissed him fervently on the neck, feeling her own libido revive a little before exhaustion caused them both to collapse, senseless, on the bed.

'God, Emma!' was all he could mutter, his lips moving feebly against her bosom. They lay embracing for a while, Emma remembering how she had first led him on, step by step, into her enchanted garden. Now he needed no encouragement but how many lovers had he enjoyed in between, as many as she? With a warm glow of anticipation Emma began to dream of exchanging erotic histories with him, of catching up on the wealth of sexual experience that he must have accrued since she'd left him in Paris, no longer an innocent but not yet a fully-fledged libertine.

She felt Charles stir against her, and began to caress him. The years of good living had filled out his chest, arms and stomach to solid proportions, but she could still recognise the old schoolboy lurking in those candid blue eyes and hovering around his sensual lips. Recalling how he loved a good spanking she began to envisage treating him to a sample of one of the supple canes she kept for disciplining her Angel. It would be wonderful to have him round on her afterwards and make her submit to his summary penetration by way of revenge!

Pleasant as her day-dreams were, Emma's ears were still attuned to the faint noises that told her what was going on in the rest of the house. She heard the front doorbell ring, followed by familiar voices in the hall, and was suddenly wide awake.

'Dear God, I think that must be Kitty!' she gasped in a hoarse whisper, sitting bolt upright.

Charles opened his sleepy eyes and regarded her with lazy indulgence. 'Nonsense! She won't be back for ages yet.'

'No, Charles, I am sure it was her! Please stay here while I go downstairs.'

She pulled on her robe and went to the door, but quick footsteps were already approaching along the landing. No sooner was the bedroom door opened than Kitty appeared and, before Emma could stop her she was being pulled back into her own room by her excited friend.

'Oh Emma, I have had such a wonderful evening! I must tell you all about – '

Kitty's outburst ended abruptly as she spied Charles lying naked on the bed. Her face turned white then pink, by turns. With a look of horror on his face, Charles made a vain attempt to pull the counterpane over his privates but it was a futile gesture.

'How *could* you!' Kitty exclaimed at last, tears springing from her eyes. She glanced from one to the other of the guilty pair, unsure which to blame the more.

Emma tried to take her arm but was abruptly shrugged off. 'Kitty, dear, Charles and I are old friends. I thought you would have recognised him.'

'Friends?' She looked dazed. 'Lovers, I think you mean. Oh, why did you not tell me before, Emma? You've allowed me to make a fool of myself. I can never forgive you for that.'

She turned to leave, but Emma tried to restrain her and this time succeeded. She led Kitty, evidently still in a state of shock, to an armchair and made her sit down. Then she found a bottle of smelling salts in the drawer of her dressing table and waved them under her nose.

'I am sorry you had to find out like this,' she said. 'I didn't intend this to happen. But Charles called here and we fell to chatting about old times and, well, one thing led to another.'

'I remember now!' Kitty exclaimed, her voice shrill and almost hysterical. 'On the boat to France, the young student. It was you, Charles, wasn't it?'

Shamefaced, he nodded. 'I should have reminded you, Kitty. I don't know why I didn't.'

Kitty stared at him, her fists and jaw clenched tightly. 'Because you hoped I'd lead you to Emma, presumably. All your kisses were to sweeten me, to trick me into letting you come here. I see it all now!' Her fury rose as she turned on Emma. 'And you thought you had a God-given right to him, I dare say. Just because you'd been the first to debauch him, the way you've done with dozens of others. My feelings don't matter, of course. I'm supposed to be grateful, aren't I? Taken in like some poor relation. Well, I was taken in all right!'

Her voice broke on a sob and she rose rapidly from the chair, pushing it aside as she dashed from the room. Emma called after her, but Charles said, 'Let her go, Emma. She will calm down in time. It has been a shock to her, that's all.'

'I never wanted to hurt her. I didn't think . . .'

'Neither of us did. We were overcome by passion. I think I had better leave now. I shall call again another day, if I may?'

'Of course. But let me deal with Kitty. I should not attempt to contact her until I have managed to calm her down.'

While Charles finished dressing himself Emma said, 'I should be obliged if you could let me have that address for Lily, Charles. I should like to write to her.'

'Certainly. I shall look it out and let you have it next time we meet.'

His last words were caught by Kitty, who had suddenly appeared in the doorway, her face still ashen but composed. 'So you are already planning to see each other again?'

'Kitty . . .' Emma rose with a gesture of conciliation, but she was stopped in her tracks.

'It is all right, I am over my distress. I was foolish to react as I did. But that doesn't excuse your behaviour, Charles. I think you deserve to be punished, don't you agree Emma?'

There was something in her friend's manner that struck a chord with Emma. She nodded, with a faint smile. 'Yes. If you say so.'

'I'm glad you agree. Perhaps we may chastise him together. You have the means, do you not?'

Emma looked at her friend first with surprise, then

with admiration. 'Of course. I shall give you the choice of instrument, Kitty. Wait, I will fetch them now.'

As she hurried into her dressing-room, where she kept her assortment of whips, canes and other devices, Emma felt her heart pounding with joyful relief. So Kitty meant to make some sport of it – good for her! She selected half a dozen whips and canes then returned to the bedroom to find Charles already kneeling on the floor with his arms on the bed, presenting his chubby posterior to view.

'You will help me administer this penalty, Emma?' Kitty asked as she tried out the various instruments by whipping and slashing through the air.

Emma nodded, selecting her own favourite; a supple and lightweight cane. The two women stood on either side of their victim. 'You take the left buttock, and I the right,' Kitty suggested. 'We shall give alternate strokes. Half a dozen each should suffice, I think.'

Kitty evidently believed that being the wronged party gave her the right to take charge of the proceedings, and Emma tacitly agreed. After the first stinging contact had been made, followed by a sharp intake of breath from Charles, the two women struck up a steady rhythm and Emma began to pant with the exertion. She found the spectacle of his pale skin reddening quite arousing, and began to contemplate making love in a threesome. Could that be the solution to their current dilemma?

The correction was over all too soon, and the two women helped Charles to lie face down on the bed and recover from his pain. When Emma suggested soothing his raw behind with cold cream Kitty readily agreed. They each rubbed the rose-scented salve gently into the buttock they had been lambasting, only seconds before, but after it was done no move was made to take it any further despite Charles' sensual moans and groans.

He turned over at last and surveyed the two disciplinarians with a wan smile. 'I am duly chastened, ladies.'

'But you are not the only wrong-doer,' Kitty said, with

a sly smile. 'I consider that you have betrayed me too, Emma, and deserve to pay a similar penalty.'

'What?' Emma laughed incredulously, sure that she must be teasing. 'You surely cannot be serious. I admit that I allowed Charles to make love to me, but. . .'

'Aha! So you confess your guilt.' Kitty's eyes were filled with a strange light, making Emma feel decidedly nervous. 'Charles, will you assist me in administering the chastisement?'

'This is preposterous!' Emma exclaimed, but the pair of them had already seized her arms. They forced her to kneel upon the carpet and pulled up her robe, exposing her plump and rosy behind to full view. She struggled, but firm hands held her down while other hands wielded the whips and prepared to strike.

Even when the first strokes fell upon her tender flesh Emma could hardly believe this was really happening to her. Only Daniel had ever been allowed to lay his hand upon her in such a manner before, and when she reflected upon the fact that one of her tormentors was her former maidservant she was overcome with shame and humiliation. Was this how she was to be rewarded for all her kindness in taking that ingrate and her child into her household? The stinging strokes went almost unnoticed as Emma fumed inwardly, vowing to take revenge on the woman.

The smarting blows stopped abruptly and Emma found herself lying prone on the bed while the pair rubbed cream into her sore buttocks. She relaxed and allowed their fingers to slip into her twin cracks: one into her arse and the other passing between her thighs to caress her between the labia. So that was their game! Pretending to sleep, she lay luxuriating in the sensual feelings that were flooding through her. Arching her back she raised her bottom slightly to allow whoever was stimulating her in front to reach the hard bulb of her clitoris and heighten her arousal. From the delicate way in which those fingers pressed and probed she guessed they belonged to Kitty, who must already be feeling remorseful and wanted to make up for the pain she had caused her with a corresponding degree of pleasure.

With her lower regions still hot and throbbing from their beating, it didn't take long for Emma's body to make the transition from agony to ecstasy. Soon pleasurable feelings had overtaken the unpleasant, and she found herself on another rapid rise towards orgasm. She cupped her breasts with her hands, fingered her squashed nipples and was soon thrashing wildly in total abandon while her two lovers kissed and caressed her, cooing encouragement all the while. Sweet feelings continued to course through her, long after the keener sensations had diminished, and as her body gently thrilled to the voluptuous after-effects she slowly became aware that the pair had slipped out of the room and she was alone in her own bed.

Chapter Seven

*E*mma had a letter from Daniel saying that he had returned to Harfield Hall and would be pleased if she paid him a visit. She was very relieved. There had been a certain frostiness in the air before his departure from London and, as usual, she had heard nothing from him while he was on his travels. Added to which, since her brief fling with Charles Purchase had gone so disastrously wrong, relations had been strained between her and Kitty so she would be glad to get away for a while.

When she mentioned it to Kitty, however, she was surprised by her response. 'I should like to travel to Manchester with you,' she said at once. 'Christabel has invited me several times to stay in her mother's house in Nelson Street, so that I may attend the rallies and help out. But I need to ask you a favour.'

Emma disliked Kitty's tone, which seemed to suggest that she was owed some kind of recompense. They had been civil, rather than friendly, with each other ever since Charles had decided to back out of the complicated situation he had found himself in. Emma did feel somewhat guilty about the sorry affair. Nevertheless she replied, coolly, 'What might that be?'

'Would you take Milly to Harfield for me? She had such a wonderful time there before, and I fear that the

95

London air is not good for her lungs. A few weeks in the country would do her a great deal of good, I am sure.'

This was a favour that Emma was only too pleased to grant. She could never have too much of her young god-daughter's company.

So it was arranged. On a warm day in late August they travelled to Manchester by train accompanied by Jane Bates, the Nanny, and Emma's maid, Alice. They were met at the station by Christabel Pankhurst, who whisked Kitty off as soon as she had said goodbye to her daughter.

'When will you be returning?' Emma called after her retreating figure.

Kitty's answer was a shrug and a broad smile, which Emma found somewhat irritating since she was going to be responsible for young Milly. The girl looked quite woebegone, but her face lit up at once when Daniel suddenly appeared, full of apologies.

'Sorry, Emma dear, ran out of water on the way. Hullo, young Silly Billy! Have you come to frighten the geese again?'

'My name is not Silly Billy!' the little girl said, indignantly. 'It is Milly.'

Daniel chucked her under the chin. 'All sounds the same to me. Anyway, when they heard you were coming, the geese flapped their wings and flew to Lapland.'

Emma laughed along with her god-daughter, but there was something poignant to her about the way Daniel bantered with the girl and she couldn't help feeling oddly out of place. She shrugged off her melancholy for Milly's sake, and enthused about the prospect of another ride in the splendid motor car.

Worn out by the long journey, the girl was fast asleep by the time they reached Harfield. Emma left her in Jane's capable hands and went to her room. Daniel had given her a free hand in its decoration, two years ago, so that it was very much a 'home from home'. Yet now, mindful of the way Daniel had disapproved of her

London friends, Emma couldn't help reflecting on how much she relied on his generosity. Her very livelihood depended on the Longmore Academy being accommodated in his Bloomsbury house. Without that she would have nowhere to live and no means of support.

Mentally scolding herself for her morbid thoughts, Emma washed in the lavender scented water and rang for Alice, who helped her to dress and did her hair. When she was looking her best, in a loose-fitting gown of midnight blue velvet trimmed with lace, she went downstairs to find Daniel in his study. He was leafing through one of his books on anthropology.

'Ah, how very lovely you look tonight Emma!' He beckoned her over and, when she was near, gave her a warm and lingering kiss on the mouth. Then he turned back to the volume on the table. 'I thought you might be interested in the defloration ceremonies carried out on this remote South Sea island. There is a full description and some illustrations.'

Emma sat on his knee and read the account while he stroked her bare arms and kissed her neck. It seemed that the native girls were deprived of their virginity by the tribal chief as soon as they reached puberty – sometimes as many as a dozen in one night.

'What a very virile man the chief must be!' Emma commented, wryly.

'Yes. That is the chief qualification for being head of the tribe. He has to have a large member, too.'

'What happens if the girls become pregnant?'

'It is no problem there, for the babies are reared communally. They do not set much store by the family, it seems, but everyone puts the good of the tribe first.'

'How fascinating. Quite the reverse of the way it is here.'

Daniel was kissing her neck with abandon now, his hand slipping down the front of her dress to feel the soft swell of her breasts, and she was almost beside herself with longing.

'I had some cold meats and salad sent in here, since it

is cook's night off,' he murmured. 'I hope you don't mind, Emma. I thought we could be quite cosy in here together, by the fire.'

Emma didn't mind a bit. She soon joined him on the leather sofa, spread with cushions, where he fed her titbits of fish, chicken and game washed down with wine. While they feasted on their indoor picnic, Daniel told her about the adventures he'd had whilst travelling. It seemed he had been all over the British Isles with his catalogue of latest fashions in ladies' underwear.

'And which did you like best, the women of Dublin, Cardiff or Edinburgh?' Emma asked him, mischievously.

'Hard to say, since they all have their good points. The Irish girls have marvellous clear skin and merry eyes, but they are very shy and religious so seduction is somewhat tedious and often ends in a slap across one's face.'

'Poor creature!'

'Mm. The Welsh girls are rather more lively, but their manners leave much to be desired and their habits can be dirty. I actually took one of them in a pigsty, would you believe!'

Emma laughed. 'Yes I would, actually. Was the pig in residence at the time?'

'No, but his odour remained. My clothes stank so badly after that little escapade that I was obliged to throw them on the bonfire.'

'And the girls of Edinburgh? How did you fare with them, Sir?'

'Very well. They are no-nonsense types, and if they like a man they will let him know in a straightforward fashion. Ah, dear little Molly McGregor! She let me know how she liked it, and no mistake!'

Emma settled back comfortably into his arms and allowed him to loosen her dress without protest. While he spoke his hands strayed into her corset, bringing out her two round trophies to be gently toyed with. 'It was on a mountain walk that I first met Molly. She was the daughter of a Highland doctor, a comely lass with big firm breasts and a backside to match, and I had her down for a forward piece from the start. But you know, Em, there is a certain light that appears in a woman's eye when she has developed a taste for you-know-what and is determined to have her share. Once a man has learned to spot them the signs are unmistakable.'

'So how did she manage to seduce you?'

'By getting us well and truly lost! We strayed from the footpath on a walk with some friends of hers and she pretended to strain her ankle. I told the others to go on and get help, but she persuaded me to carry her into a wayside hut where she had her wicked way with me.'

Emma sighed as his fingers tweaked her nipples into firm, rosy perfection. 'Come Daniel, the details, the details!'

'Very well. We found a tartan rug inside the hut and laid it on the floor . . .'

'It reminds me of the time Kitty and I spent the night in an Alpine chalet . . . Oh!'

Emma squealed as Daniel gave her nipple a hard pinch. 'That's for interrupting, my sweet. Let me tell the story straight through, so the naughty images conjured up may work upon my libido. You shall benefit in the end, I promise you.'

'Then why not close your eyes and pretend I am that lascivious Molly while you enjoy me?' Emma pouted.

Her words had been intended ironically but Daniel agreed it was an excellent idea, lifted up her dress and began to stroke her thighs while he continued.

'As I was saying, we lay down together on the rug and it was obvious at once that Molly's ankle was not hurt and it had been a ruse to get me alone in that remote spot. She loosened her stays and let me pull out one of her lovely fat breasts to suckle. I let her set the pace, sensing that she had done this at least a dozen times before and knew exactly how to proceed. After a while her fingers began fumbling with my buttons and soon she pulled out my organ which, as you can guess, was rearing up straight as a flagstaff by then.'

Sensing her cue, Emma did likewise and found his member in a satisfactorily tumid state as she had expected.

'To my amazement she instantly bent her head to my dick and began to suck away,' Daniel continued. 'By Jove, she paid me excellent lip-service, I can tell you that. A true mistress of the fellatory arts! She sucked my balls too, drawing them in and out of her mouth while she rubbed my rod until I was sure I could hold out no longer. But then, as I was on the verge, she suddenly lifted up her skirts and showed me her bare behind. There she was, kneeling on the rug with her great buttocks stuck in the air and her fingers parting her cheeks to display her puckered arse-hole. It took me a while to grasp what the hussy wanted.'

'You mean – sodomy?' Emma couldn't help interjecting. 'Ow!'

Daniel's hand had already found its way inside her knickers and now he jabbed his finger into her own back passage to make his point.

'The very same. Well I was so worked up by now that if she'd wanted me to shaft her ear-hole I'd have been happy to oblige. There being no other lubrication to hand, I licked my finger and made her ready for my entrance as best I could, then in went my glans. "Oh!" she cried, then another "Oh!" as I moved in another half inch, then "Oh! Oh! Oh!" every thrust of the way until I was all the way into her snug little anus.'

He broke off to give Emma's breasts a thorough licking while he fingered her below. She squeezed his solid penis in the hollow of her hand, making him groan, and wondered if either of them would have the self-control to wait until the end of Daniel's story before sating their lust on each other.

After a few minutes, however, Daniel lifted his head, kissed her briefly on the lips, and went on with his tale. 'As she knelt there, Molly's big breasts had come adrift from her stays and were hanging down beneath her like great speckled udders. I seized them with both hands and began to squeeze and pull, but she turned her head and gave me a grin, saying, 'Och, will ye no pull one pump after the other, and give a braw lass a bonny treat?'

Emma couldn't help giggling at Daniel's appalling Scots accent. He frowned and tweaked her nipple again before continuing. 'Well, that was the gist of what she said. So I obliged her, of course, and was soon pulling away at a fine pace, for all the world as if I were milking a cow. I got up a fine rhythm, too, between my hands and my prick – pull on the left, squeeze and thrust, pull on the right, squeeze and thrust – until I had her bucking and whinnying like a bronco in the Wild West. She almost threw me off, but I hung in there like a "dang cowpoke" and soon she began to scream so loud I knew she was coming. So I pulled out and gave myself a few tugs, not wanting to spurt into her fundament. My seed shot clear across that old log cabin, I can tell you that.'

'And was that the end of it?'

'Sadly, yes. We heard our "rescue party" hollering, and had to show ourselves. But I shan't forget young Molly McGregor in a hurry.'

'Well I've no such adventures to relate,' Emma sighed, unwilling to tell him about Angel or Charles. 'It's been a dull summer in London. I could not wait to see you again, Daniel.'

'Let us not waste time then. I have a fancy to watch you pleasure yourself, Emma. You know how I love to come straight into you while you are still hot and streaming. Lie down on the rug, there's a good girl, and show me your sweet fanny.'

Obediently Emma lay down in front of the fire and pulled down her drawers. The heat of the coals was wonderfully relaxing and she was soon playing lazily with herself, pulling her labia apart to give Daniel a good view while he toyed gently with his still-strong erection. Every so often she would raise one hand to her breasts, shining golden in the firelight, and caress the smooth skin or tease the turgid nipple with her fingertips to bring on a rush of tingling excitement. While she masturbated she watched her lover's intent gaze, knowing that soon he would be plunging into her with all his strength, and the anticipation fed her lust. She could see his purple-headed prong standing up ready to pleasure her and a sudden spasm caught her unawares, catapulting her into a maelstrom of dizzying force that made her gasp and cry out. She lay back, succumbing to what she could no longer control, wallowing in the sheer bliss of her extended climax.

Dimly Emma was aware of Daniel coming to kneel on the mat between her thighs and then she felt him, hot and solid, between her softened outer lips. One long, strong thrust and he was right inside her, filling the still-pulsating length of her vagina with his hard flesh. She moaned softly as he rode her with unfettered vigour and soon, incredibly, she felt the dying embers of her own orgasm ignite once more. Daniel arched over her, his mouth bending to her nipple, and the rich sensations poured through her, this time triggering a similar response in her lover. She could feel him pulse within her, feel the energy with which his seed entered her and met hers, like two cross-currents in mid-ocean. How many times, she wondered faintly, had the two of them shared that familiar yet always new, experience? Somehow the thought saddened her, so that when the last shudderings faded she lay there wet-eyed.

'What's this?' Daniel asked softly. '*Post coitum triste*?'

'Something like that,' she sniffed. In her heart, she knew there was more to it but she didn't wish to explore her most hidden feelings right then.

The following morning she was in a brighter mood, relieved that good relations had been restored with her lover. Young Milly did much to cheer them up as Daniel took them on a tour of his land, pointing out everything he'd had done recently. But when he began to ask Emma's advice on whether he should let out this field or do up that cottage she grew bored.

'Really, Daniel, there is no use asking me these things,'

she sighed. 'I know nothing of how an estate should be managed.'

'But I thought you would at least be interested.'

'Why should I? Long ago, when I was married, I had to endure the petty chit-chat of country life but now I would far rather be in town. And I am surprised that you take so much interest, Daniel, after travelling all over Europe and enjoying the pleasures of many capital cities. You have Brown to manage your affairs for you. Why not leave it all to him?'

'I thought you understood me better, Emma. It's true that I never expected to inherit this place. My elder brother was the heir, and I was the 'spare'. When he died my world was turned upside down, and for many years I neglected my duty to Harfield. But now I realise I was wrong.'

Emma laughed. 'Don't tell me you're going to settle down and play the part of a landed gentleman at last!'

She watched with alarm as her lover's face showed signs of anger. 'Both the factory and the estate deserve more attention than I have given them to date. I want to modernise them, to bring them into the twentieth century.' He grasped her hand and she saw the burning zeal in his eyes. 'We have seen such wonders invented in our day, Emma – electricity, the telephone, the internal combustion engine. I want to ensure that Harfield takes full advantage of them all.'

So saying he changed gear and began to race around the bend at such speed that Milly began to scream in panic and Emma clasped her charge tightly, begging him to slow down. When he finally returned to a sedate pace she was furious with him and asked to be let out. While he mocked her with his laughter she made Milly climb out of the car and they began the long walk back to the house. Despite her efforts to point out the wild flowers to her god-daughter and appear unconcerned, Emma was seething all the way.

At luncheon she confronted Daniel again. 'I will not have you take reckless chances with that girl's health and safety,' she began, as soon as they were alone in the dining-room.

'There was no risk,' he said, coldly. 'Motoring is a perfectly safe sport and the brakes on my automobile are excellent. Emma, you're becoming stuck in your ways. Even Kitty is more forward-looking than you.'

'What?' Emma stared at him in astonishment. 'How can you say that when I am engaged in teaching young women what no-one else dares to teach them?'

'You talk as if what men and women do in bed is the be-all and end-all of their existence. There is more to life than a good fuck, you know.'

She stared at him, affronted. 'I never thought to hear you, of all people, say such things!'

'But it is the truth, and you know it. I intend to spend far more time here in future. I have built up markets for my goods in six countries. Now is the time to increase my productivity. My wealth has been frittered away in superficial pleasures these past few years, but there will be an end to all that. I shall make Harfield Hall one of the most splendid residences in the north, and you shall help me, Emma dear. I need your advice about how to decorate the rooms, what furniture to buy, and so forth.'

Emma moved towards the buffet and took a plate to serve herself. She hardly knew what to say. Daniel was in danger of treating her more like a wife than a mistress and it was a rôle she had no desire to play.

She tried to show interest as he spoke enthusiastically of his plan to install a telephone system and new machinery in the corset factory. He also intended to take on a secretary who would be both typist and steno-grapher. While he rambled on Emma realised that he was intending to spend far more time at Harfield than ever before and if she wanted his company she would have to stay there more often too.

It was a sobering thought. Her Academy kept her in London for most of the year and she'd always relied on Daniel visiting her there, either when he wished to take advantage of the opportunities in the capital or when he was departing for or returning from Europe. The future that he was describing seemed to hold little place for a mistress who was based two hundred miles away from Yorkshire.

Nevertheless she put a brave face on it and responded eagerly to the invitation to join Daniel at a dinner party. It was to be held at Moorfield, home of his neighbour Sir Edward Banks, who owned a biscuit factory in Leeds and a couple of bakeries in Manchester. He suggested they should travel to town and buy Emma a new gown for the occasion.

The following Saturday night, Alice helped Emma to look her best in the shimmering robe of blue-grey taffeta with the cream lace insert in the bodice. In her hair she wore the sapphire and diamond comb that Daniel had given her years ago, while long sapphire earrings, a matching choker and bracelet completed her parure. She was rewarded by an appreciative gleam in her lover's eye as she made her way downstairs to the waiting motor car.

'You look superb, Emma,' he murmured, as she took his arm.

How many times have I heard him say that? she wondered, with a faint sigh. Despite her determination to enjoy herself Emma had to fight off a melancholy mood that had overtaken her when she lay down to rest that afternoon. If only she didn't have that strange foreboding that her being at Harfield was somehow the end of an era. Shrugging off such morbid thoughts she climbed into the seat, allowed Daniel to arrange the wrap around her shoulders, and braced herself for the drive.

They did not often venture out together, being more inclined to enjoy each other's company in private, so the visit was filled with a sense of occasion. They were greeted by Sir Edward, his mousy wife Helena and their nineteen-year-old daughter Caroline. Over the years, Emma had acquired a great deal of experience in assessing the characters of young women and her immediate impression of Caroline was not favourable. Although the girl was endowed with a pretty face and good figure, she had a vacant look in her eye and a voice that was too high and soft to sound intelligent. She was, however, exactly the type that men doted on and Emma was surprised to find a girl of her sort not only still single but apparently unattached.

Emma's worst fears about country life were confirmed over dinner, when she was obliged to listen to tedious discussion of farming matters, provincial gossip and endless talk about food. There was, however, some entertainment to look forward to afterwards. It being a fine warm night the Bankses had arranged for dancing on the terrace, and Emma spent much of the meal deciding which potential partners she would encourage and which she would do her best to avoid. The best of the bunch seemed to be a young doctor, Jeremy Lewis, and she managed by dint of much eye contact to ensure his interest.

When the music finally struck up Emma was gratified to see him make a bee-line for her.

'Mrs Longmore, would you care to join me in a waltz?' he invited, with a slight bow.

She smiled into his soft brown eyes, seeing the fire ignited there, and knew that if she played her cards right there might be the opportunity for more than just a dance with this personable young man. She was in the mood for a flirtation, a spot of illicit love, and if she could amuse Daniel by relating her adventures afterwards so much the better.

Like many other couples they soon waltzed right off the terrace and onto the smoothly manicured lawn. As she whirled around, Emma caught sight of Daniel with the daughter of the house and tried to catch his eye but he was wholly engaged with his partner. Perhaps he, too, would have a story to relate by the end of the evening!

Emma could tell that Jeremy was attracted to her, and she encouraged him with smiles and subtle pressure on his hand while they danced. At last, pretending to be out of breath, she suggested a stroll in the grounds by moonlight and he readily agreed. Soon she was chatting away in a low voice describing life in London, which he had never visited.

'Emma, you are quite a woman!' he smiled, leading her down a pebbly path into the shrubbery. 'There are many girls half your age who would be gasping still after such exercise.'

'Really, Jeremy! It is not polite to mention a lady's age, as well you know. I shall not put up with your provincial manners.'

'I beg your pardon.' He bent to kiss her hand, sending wild shivers of anticipation down her spine. 'I confess I have never met such a woman as you. The normal rules of etiquette hardly seem to apply.'

They had reached a rosy bower surrounded by a thick laurel hedge. Emma suggested they should sit together on the stone bench. She knew Jeremy's blood was roused and soon they would be embracing. Pretending to feel chilly, she let him put his arm around her and pull her close. She rested her head on his shoulder and soon his hand crept to caress her hair, inducing a languid mood in her. At last Emma lifted her face and their lips met in a long, slow kiss that filled her veins with a delicious voluptuousness and a promise of more delights to come. Her lips opened, inviting him in, and as their tongues met in sensual abandon Jeremy began to caress the curve of her breast.

Suddenly Emma's erotic reverie was interrupted by faint giggling from the other side of the hedge. Then a young woman's voice could be plainly heard, whispering, 'Are you quite sure we shall not be discovered here?'

Emma drew back from Jeremy, indicating the hedge, but he just winked and began to plant feather-light kisses on her bare neck, making her shiver. 'Cold, my dear?' he whispered.

She shook her head and his eager lips traversed her

shoulders then plunged into the deep ravine of her bosom. Feeling herself beginning to melt within, Emma was ready to abandon herself completely to their love-making when she heard more noises from behind the hedge, the same female voice sighing and moaning. At first she tried to ignore the sounds, but when her lover's name was mentioned her ears were instantly alert.

'Oh Daniel!' came the disembodied voice which Emma now recognised as belonging to Caroline Banks. 'I do so want us to belong to each other completely. How much longer do we have to wait?'

Emma could not resist a smile. If she knew Daniel, he would press home his advantage right away. Just as Jeremy was now doing with her, she reflected, as his hand went below her skirt to find the smooth skin of her thigh. But then she was distracted once more, this time by Daniel's answer. 'Not long, my sweet. I must break the news to a certain person, then we can announce our engagement.'

Emma felt her blood chill. Caroline said, 'You mean that woman you came with tonight, don't you Daniel? She is your mistress, do not deny it. Oh God, I am so jealous of her! Promise me that once we are wed you shall have nothing more to do with her.'

'Of course not, my dear. With you as my lovely wife, what more could I want?'

From the escalation of her girlish moans Emma knew that he was pleasuring her with his lips and hands, just as Jeremy was doing to her, but the knowledge filled her with dismay. Somehow she could not dismiss his words, as she might have done in the past, as the casual lies of a seducer. There had been a sincerity in his tone, a terrible inevitability about his words, that had shaken her to the core.

Suddenly she could bear no more of Jeremy's passion-ate advances. She rose from the seat in panic, brushing him aside, and began to stumble back along the path to the lawn. He followed, full of concern. 'Emma, what is it? Have I upset you? If so, I apologise. I thought I was behaving as you wished me to.'

'It is not your fault, Jeremy,' she assured him, tears blurring her vision as she stepped onto the springy turf. 'I am feeling somewhat queasy, that is all.'

'Shall I fetch you a glass of water? Would you like me to examine you? I am a doctor, after all.'

'There is one thing you can do for me,' she said as he caught hold of her arm and helped her up the steps to the terrace. 'You can take me back to Harfield. I regret that I cannot stay here any longer.'

The obliging young doctor drove her back in his own pony and trap. He would have done more, but Emma assured him that she was merely over-tired and would be fine in the morning.

'Then I shall return to Moorfield and tell Lord Merton that I have brought you home.'

'Thank you. But please tell him not to leave the party on my account.'

It was only when she was alone in her bedroom that Emma was able to give in to the welcome release of tears. She knew that once she confronted her lover she would be filled with self-righteous indignation, and would probably say things that she would later regret. But, for the time being, she found a perverse consolation in letting self-pity overwhelm her.

Chapter Eight

'*I*s it true, Daniel? Are you really planning to marry that girl?'

Emma confronted her lover at the breakfast table next morning. She was determined to remain in control of herself, but it was very difficult. Just looking at him made her heart ache horribly and she could hardly stop herself from throwing herself at his feet, pleading with him in a way that would have destroyed her dignity and self-respect. So she refrained from looking him in the eye.

'I meant to tell you myself, Emma. I'm sorry you had to find out by eavesdropping on us.'

'Eavesdropping! I could not help but overhear what that hussy was saying. And when you told her I meant nothing to you . . .' She turned away, half choking, and soon felt Daniel's hand on her shoulder. Angrily she shrugged it off.

'Emma, I know how you must be feeling. But I tried to involve you in my plans and you wanted nothing to do with this house, the estate or the business. I need a woman who can be with me here, to entertain my guests and run the household. In short, I need . . . a wife.'

'Yes, I see that now,' she said, bitterly. Framed in the long window was the distant row of oak trees that

Daniel had recently had planted. Obviously he was looking to the future, to the generations to come. He wanted a family, a son to inherit Harfield, but that was the one thing she could never give him.

Emma had faced that painful situation before, and now it seemed that fate was laughing at her once again. She had believed Daniel was different, that he lived for the moment not for tomorrow, but she'd been wrong. He was like all other men, wanting to leave something of himself for posterity. Well, let him take that simpering little fool as a wife. He would soon tire of her and look elsewhere, but Emma would no longer be there for him.

'My dearest, please don't think badly of me. If I marry Caroline it does not have to mean the end of our relationship. I can still see you in London.'

'Ha! You want to have your cake and eat it, do you Lord Merton?' Emma sneered, her wrath giving her the courage to stare scornfully into his eyes. 'Well you shall not. If you have no more need of me, then I have no more need of you!'

'I did not mean to abandon you, Emma. I said it only to reassure Caroline. You may stay on in Brunswick Square, my dear, until the end of your days. I owe you that, at least.'

Emma was about to throw it back in his face when she realised that would be foolish. She did not have enough behind her to build up her Academy again in rented premises. 'Yes, you do owe me that,' she said, calmly. 'I have given you the best years of my life and if you throw me out on the street now I shall make sure that the whole of London society knows it.'

Daniel's expression grew cold. 'You need not threaten me. I gave you my word. But I think perhaps it would be best if you went back to London as soon as possible, don't you?'

'So that you may make your wedding preparations, you mean?' He threw her one last appealing look but she hardened herself against him. 'Very well, I shall ask Alice to pack straight away and we shall take the

111

afternoon train. Be so good as to inform Kitty at once by telegraph, please. You have her address in Manchester. Tell her to meet us at the station at two o'clock if she wishes to return with me and Milly.'

The next few hours were an ordeal for Emma, but she busied herself with getting herself and her god-daughter ready for the journey and tried not to think of what she was leaving behind. There would be plenty of time to reflect on that later.

Daniel drove them to Manchester but Alice took the front seat while Emma sat in the back with Jane and Milly. The young girl's childish chatter took her mind off the parting that she must soon endure. Would she ever see Daniel Forbes again? That question was one of many that she thrust to the back of her mind as the countryside flashed by.

To Emma's surprise, and mild annoyance, no Kitty awaited them at the station.

'Perhaps she was not at home to receive the telegram,' Daniel suggested. 'I am sure you will hear from her soon, my dear.'

I am not your 'dear' any more, Emma thought, but dared not say it in front of the servants.

The great steam train was puffing out white clouds and the guard was blowing his whistle, but still there was no sign of Kitty. The two women took Milly into the nearest free compartment and Emma began to climb the step, but Daniel seized her arm. His eyes looked heart-rendingly sincere as they met hers, and Emma found a lump forming in her throat as she choked back tears.

'Emma, dearest, I shall never forget what we meant to each other, and I hope you will not either. I shall write to you soon, I promise.'

'You know where to find me,' she snapped as she hovered there, not wanting to close the door entirely on him, with the guard's whistle sounding increasingly shrill.

Daniel closed the door and Emma turned her back on him to join the others. As she sat down she glanced through the window but there was no sign of Daniel, who must have hurried off at once, unable to bear the farewell scene any longer.

It was an interminable journey. Emma let the two women amuse Milly while she pretended to doze, but she was full of unpleasant thoughts and ugly emotions. She knew there was no point in being angry with Caroline Banks, who must have been putty in the hands of a past master of seduction like Lord Merton.

No, it was Daniel himself who bore the brunt of all Emma's ill-feeling. The deceptive manner in which he had courted Caroline behind her back had wounded her sorely. They had always shared their deepest, most secret, feelings with each other but this time he had chosen to exclude her and that was what had hurt most of all.

'Aunty Em, will you read me the story about the girl who went down the rabbit hole?'

Emma opened her eyes at the gentle tug on her arm and smiled down at her god-daughter. At least she now had Milly to brighten her days.

There was no word from Kitty awaiting them in Brunswick Square and Emma was slightly anxious, but she told Jane to see that Milly settled quickly into her usual routine. Meanwhile Emma had to prepare for the reopening of her Academy in mid-September. She had to send out reminders to parents of former pupils who were returning and place advertisements in the London journals to attract new clients. Many came through word-of-mouth recommendation, but Emma believed it did her no harm to keep the name of her establishment in the public eye.

Two days after her return from Yorkshire Emma received a letter from Kitty, saying that she had been asked to stay on by the Pankhursts and would be much obliged if Emma would look after Milly while she remained in Manchester for a while. Emma read the letter in a sober mood. She could see that Kitty was becoming more involved with the Women's Social and

Political Union than she had imagined. Motherhood already seemed to sit lightly on her shoulders, as if the ties between her and Milly were being loosened along with those of her marriage. It was obviously best that her daughter remained in a stable household, yet Emma could not help the feelings of resentment that were welling up at having surrogate motherhood thrust upon her.

Still, she vowed that under no circumstances would she take her sour feelings out on Milly. On the contrary she began to plan little treats and outings for the girl: educational visits to museums, shopping trips to Marshall and Snelgroves or Swan and Edgars, expeditions to Rotten Row where she might learn to ride, or to skate at Prince's rink, followed by tea at Lyons' Corner House. The more accomplishments a young woman acquired the more successful she might be in the marriage stakes, and there was no-one better suited than Emma, Lady Longmore, to be Milly's 'social godmother'.

It was not long before Angel called to leave his card, and Emma was thankful to resume her relationship with him since it took her mind off what she imagined Daniel might be doing at Harfield Hall. Often they would meet at some artistic gathering, sending signals to each other with their eyes across crowded drawing-rooms, and then Emma would make her discreet way to Angel's apartment, following him on foot or in a cab depending on the weather, until she found him awaiting her dressed in his 'uniform' of dicky-bow and bridle, jockstrap and reins, or clad in a tight 'Little Lord Fauntleroy' suit of Prussian blue velvet with a flap behind that could be lowered to expose his bare buttocks.

Sometimes Angel would draw or paint his mistress as she lay reclining on a chaise longue, but more usually Emma would require him to perform a range of services for her, some very personal. He would carry them out punctiliously until, at some point in the evening, he would slyly commit some misdemeanour that required punishment. Although the programme remained much the same, both Emma and Angel revelled in introducing subtle new twists and variations to spice up their routine.

Even so, Angel's strange foibles began to pall after a while and Emma found herself longing for Daniel more and more. It was not just the love-making she missed, although she had reached heights of passion with him that she had never achieved with any other man. No, it was just as much his conversation, his companionship, the thrill she felt in sharing her amorous adventures with him and hearing of his in return. With a new 'Lady Merton' installed in Harfield, things could never be the same between them. Her only hope was that when he tired of young Caroline, as he surely would, he might return for solace from his old mistress on his occasional visits to London.

Yet the weeks went by and still Daniel kept away. Emma received two letters from him, brief and unsatisfying missives, the second giving December the twenty-fourth as the date of his marriage. Needless to say, Emma was not invited.

She also heard from Kitty, who finally reappeared at the end of October in a state of exhaustion. When she had rested and spent some time with her daughter, Emma questioned her about her time in Manchester.

'Emma, you will not believe how strong the resolve is amongst the women of the Union,' Kitty began, her eyes shining. 'Many are working-class girls who realise that they cannot count on men to improve their conditions in the factory or at home.'

'And are you still making a spectacle of yourself at the Wakes, Kitty?'

Kitty frowned. 'We spread our gospel wherever we can. Soon we shall be in London, and then the men of Westminster had better look out! They have already had a taste of us, after the Liberal meeting at the Free Trade Hall two weeks ago.'

'What happened then?'

'We caused a hullabaloo, that's what! The candidate

115

for Oldham, a Mr Winston Churchill, was addressing the meeting but when we asked him if he would give us his support if elected he would not answer 'yea' or 'nay'. A band of us began to cry, "The question! Answer the question!" and we were shown the door, but we held a meeting outside and dear Christabel and Annie were arrested.'

'Oh my God! Kitty, you did not clash with the law?'

'Not I, although I should have been proud to spend time with them in Strangeways.'

Emma gasped. 'In *prison*?'

'Yes. Annie told me it was not so bad. She said Chrissie looked very pretty in her prison cap. But do you know what that Churchill fellow had the cheek to say? He said he "would not be henpecked on a subject of such grave importance". *Henpecked*, I ask you!'

Emma went over to Kitty's chair and, kneeling beside her, put her arms around her friend. 'Please, Kitty, promise me that you will not get into that kind of trouble. Remember you are a mother and think of little Milly, I beg you.'

She could see that her entreaties were falling on deaf ears. Kitty's mouth was set firm in an obstinate pout. 'There are more important things in life than mother-hood, Emma. We are fighting for the rights of all our daughters, and our grand-daughters.'

'I fear for you, Kitty . . .'

'Do not worry, my dear. I know my friends will never let me down. But you have been a good friend to me too. I do not know what I should have done without you.'

'Then heed my advice, please. Milly needs you, and you should think of the future.'

'But I have been thinking of the future, of a future where women shall have a say in shaping this nation's destiny as well as men!'

Emma knew it was useless to prolong the conversation. Kitty's heart, mind and soul had been given over to the Cause and rational argument was impossible. Still, she must face up to her responsibilities. In return for board and lodging Emma asked for her help in running the Academy. She soon devised a plan that would keep Kitty's mind off 'that insufferable suffrage nonsense' as she privately dubbed it. She set her to learn on a new-fangled model of typewriter and Kitty quickly became so adept at it that the busy tip-tap of the machine soon became a familiar noise, issuing from the small office near the front door. Emma felt it gave her Academy an aura of business-like efficiency. And if some of the letters went off to Manchester, instead of to fashionable London addresses, she was prepared to turn a blind eye.

Christmas was an ordeal. Although Emma did her best to make it a happy occasion for Kitty and Milly, her heart was heavy throughout the festive season at the thought of those other celebrations that would be taking place in far-off Yorkshire. She had sent a card to Daniel, a formal greeting bordered with holly, but had received nothing in return and she began to fear the worst. The dreary weather of January did not help to lift her spirits, and she was growing tired of the endless games with Angel, games that seemed no longer to have any point to them.

Then, one wintry afternoon, Emma was surprised and pleased to receive a call from Sybil Mountjoy. She came bustling into the house in her fur tippet and Emma at once ordered tea and crumpets to be brought into the sitting-room.

'Sybil, how good to see you again!' she smiled, kissing her friend's ice-cold cheek. 'It has been so long since that dinner-party I gave in the summer. How is your architect friend?'

At once Sybil's pretty face darkened. 'Oh Emma, disaster looms! You cannot imagine how worried I have been, and I have no-one to turn to. That is why I have come here. You have always been so wise and under-standing in these matters.'

'My dear girl, whatever can you mean?' She paused while Alice brought in the tea, then resumed. 'Tell me at once, Sybil. And if I can help in any way be assured I shall do my best.'

'I do not believe there is anything you can do, Emma. I think poor dear Paul and I will be obliged to take the consequences. But if I can at least unburden myself to you, that will be something. You see, we have received a threat of blackmail.'

'Blackmail? But why? Surely Paul is doing well as an architect, is he not?'

'Very well, but that is the trouble. He has come under the wing of Edwin Lutyens, who is letting him help with some of his commissions, and others are jealous of his success.'

'But how can they possibly *blackmail* him? What does he have to hide? Has he committed some kind of indiscretion?'

Emma was astonished to see a blush creep over Sybil's pale complexion. 'I am afraid it concerns his affair with me. Not that anyone would take notice in the ordinary way. We move in circles where brows are seldom raised about affairs of the heart.'

'Then what is the matter? Don't beat about the bush dear, please.'

'Very well.' Sybil pulled a letter out of her bag and handed it to Emma. 'This will tell you all you need to know. It is the only item of our correspondence I still possess. The other letters have been stolen.'

'Stolen?' Frowning, Emma unfolded the pale lilac paper that still smelt of violets. She saw a neat but unfamiliar hand, and guessed it must be Paul's. Curiously she began to read:

My Beloved Mistress,

I never dreamed that servitude could be such a sweet thing as it has proved to be with you. When you place me in shackles and require me to perform whatever menial task your whim directs my joy knows no bounds and I am happy to lick your boots or any part of your anatomy, most beautiful goddess,

118

until you are fully satisfied. Last Sunday, when you bade me clean out the toilet bowl and then scrub my hands and nails until they were raw and bleeding, I obeyed gladly, believing your commands to be my sole reward and your service my only desire. But then you compounded my rapture by requiring me to lick out your secret temples through both the front and back doors, completing my worship of your celestial form and affording me more exquisite gratification than it is within my power to express. Believe me, dearly beloved, if you should order me to roll naked upon a bed of broken glass I should perform it with the greatest pleasure. Or if you wish me to wallow in dung, or eat platefuls of ordure, I should willingly obey. I speak not in metaphors but as a matter of fact, to which I am sure my previous service will stand as testimony. The reason is that you are the Goddess whom I worship, the Mistress whose very existence I give eternal thanks for and whose wonderful ways I daily praise. If you can think of any new task, however low or degrading, bestial or painful, that it is your pleasure to set me when we next meet I shall be in seventh heaven. I remain, your utterly faithful, adoring and obedient servant,

Paul.

Emma folded the letter gravely and handed it back to her. 'I see.'

'Do you?' Sybil raised tormented eyes as she put the letter back in her bag. 'There are many more like this, some even more explicit. They were stolen from my bedroom, Emma, by some ruffian who is now threatening to send copies to all of Mr Lutyens' current clients, telling them that this is the sort of person who is helping to design their houses. Can you imagine what a scandal that would cause? Paul would never be able to work for respectable people again. His reputation and career would be ruined.'

'Has he any idea who is behind this threat?'

'Yes. He is certain it is a chap who was at college with him, and who has not prospered as Paul has. His name is Farlow, William Farlow. He had all the advantages in life, coming from a wealthy family and going to Harrow instead of a local grammar like Paul.'

'So he went to Harrow, did he? Leave it to me, my dear. I shall find out as much as I can about William Farlow, Esquire. With luck I shall get back to you in a few days.'

'We only have until the end of January,' Sybil said, her lip trembling. 'Oh Emma, will the day ever come when the private life of a man or woman shall remain just that, and not be a target for low-minded individuals to ridicule and condemn what they do not understand?'

When Sybil had gone Emma sent a note round to Charles Purchase's address. It was the first time in months that she had contacted him, not wishing to antagonise Kitty again, but this time she was acting out of a desire to help another friend. Fortunately Charles was at home and responded to the note of urgency in her message by calling on her at once.

'Dear Emma!' he smiled, as he entered her drawing-room just after nine o'clock. 'I was so glad to hear from you again. I thought you had cut me off completely after that unfortunate episode with Kitty.'

'Let us not speak of that. I wanted to see you on an entirely different matter. Will you take some port wine?'

Emma waited until they were seated opposite each other, sipping glasses of the sweet liquor. Then she asked him if the name of William Farlow were familiar to him. 'Farlow?' he frowned. 'It does seem to ring a bell. Long time ago though.'

'In your schooldays, perhaps?'

'Farlow, Farlow . . . yes! There was a chap used to fag for a pervert called Haynes when we were in the Remove. I'm pretty sure his name was William. We used to call him something else though. Ah – "Slicker", short for "arse-licker". That was it.'

'What kind of a "pervert" was this Haynes, then?'

'Oh, he was a real rum bugger. Liked to dress up in women's clothes and be screwed in the arse. That Farlow

120

fellow was of the same bent, as far as I can recall. Heard about him at an Old Harrovians cricket match a few years back. Rumour had it that he makes a dishonest living out of luring men into compromising positions, photographing them with a hidden camera then blackmailing them.'

Emma jumped up and gave him a kiss on the lips. 'Charles, thank you! That is exactly the sort of thing I was hoping to hear.'

Thanks to her detective work, Emma and Sybil were able to devise an anonymous letter addressed to 'Slicker' Farlow. They told him that unless he returned the letters intact he would be prosecuted, and seven of his previous victims would have no hesitation in testifying against him. It was all bluff, since Charles had not approached the unfortunate seven directly but had relied on hearsay to identify them.

Amazingly, the ruse worked. Within a day of sending the threatening letter Sybil came home to find the stolen bundle of love-letters on her dressing-table, tied up in the same blue velvet ribbon. It seemed miraculous to Emma when she heard about it.

'I don't know how I can ever repay you!' Sybil declared, kissing her benefactor on the cheek. Then she hung her head and sighed. 'But it is all over between me and Paul. He cannot risk such a scandal again. But, oh, I shall miss him!'

'And his strange predilections?'

Sybil gave a bashful smile. 'You know Emma, when you told us – years ago – that some men love to be dominated by a beautiful woman, it struck a deep chord in me. The idea of ruling a man completely, of him worshipping the ground I walked on, was most appealing.'

'But does not every woman feel the same?'

'Not to the same degree. I wanted absolute power over my lover, to make him do whatever I wanted him to. Even then I realised that with power comes responsibility. I knew just how far to take Paul, just how much he could stand of humiliation and pain, and I believed I never once overstepped the boundaries.'

'It sounds as if you have become an expert dominatrix,' Emma said, admiringly. 'I could never enter into the rôle quite so completely as you have appeared to do. In fact, I have an affair of that nature at the moment which is proving very taxing. How would you feel, Sybil, about helping me out?'

Her face lit up. 'I should be delighted! Do you intend us to work with the gentleman separately, or in tandem?'

'Oh, together at first I think. If he is in raptures about one woman ordering him around surely he will be in seventh heaven if two of us take the reins! We shall see how you get on with him. You know him already, of course.'

'I do? Not Charles, surely?'

'No. I gave you a clue you know, Sybil, when I said he would be in "seventh heaven"!'

'Oh, you mean *Angel*!' she laughed. 'I am not surprised. I always thought he was the sort although I never knew for sure. Well, if you will arrange a time and place maybe between us we can make that angel fly!'

Emma smiled, but couldn't help hoping that she might make her Angel fly *away*, off into the arms of his new and demanding mistress, leaving her free to move on to pastures new.

Sybil did not take long to learn how to put Angel through his paces. The two women had several joint sessions with him during which Emma was astonished by the enthusiasm and ingenuity that her friend brought to the task. She invited Emma to employ his naked back as a footstool while he knelt on all fours or, most amusingly, would make use of his arse-crack to hold a magazine. Poor Angel would have to kneel there for hours with his buttocks clenched but he seemed to adore being used in that way.

Another favourite diversion was what Sybil called 'toilet training'. She would make him kneel holding a chamber pot at chest level and then she and Emma would piss into it with their skirts held high, giving him a good view of their privates and often splashing his face in the process. Angel took it all unflinchingly.

In her gratitude for getting Paul out of trouble, Sybil made sure that Emma was fully pleasured by her lover as well. On the first occasion it didn't take Emma long to realise that she had by no means been taking full advantage of the young man's talents. Sybil told him to build up the fire with logs and coals, then to fill a hip-bath with hot water. She ordered him to remove Emma's clothes, giving him detailed instructions on how to undo all the fastenings. As she was revealed in her full nakedness his penis grew aroused and sprung up so quickly that both women laughed and he blushed terribly, increasing their ridicule even more.

Once Emma was seated in the warm water Angel was under orders to soap her all over, starting with her feet. Emma lay back and relaxed, knowing that she would be bathed from head to foot with a meticulous devotion that none of her personal maids, not even Kitty, had ever shown. His gentle hands moved all over her with quiet reverence while Sybil directed him in discreet murmurs.

'Soap the undersides of her breasts just with your fingertips, smoothing round and round. You may use your palms on the sides ... Now put some of the froth onto her nipples and rub them very, very gently between your fingers and thumbs. That's right. See how hard and shiny they are becoming, like pink pearls.'

Emma found this running commentary almost as arousing as the actions themselves. When Angel was at last instructed to insert a soapy finger between her lower lips and thoroughly cleanse all the folds and crevices of her sex, Emma was already throbbing deliciously with sensual enjoyment. His light touch upon the hard projection of her clitoris caused her to elicit soft moans that gave Sybil her cue.

'So, you have found the lady's prize jewel! Continue to polish it with your fingertip in a circular motion while you place your other finger, well smeared with soap, into the treasure cave and work it slowly in and out.'

Angel's ardent ministrations, together with Sybil's encouraging and picturesque remarks, soon succeeded in filling Emma with paroxysms of voluptuousness. She threw back her head and her breasts heaved with passion while she bucked and thrashed in the shallow bath, throwing water over the sides onto the towels that Angel had laid down all around.

Afterwards, he was required to oil and powder his mistress with equal care. The heavy rose scent and delicate touch of his fingers on her dry skin soon had Emma in a state of utter bliss once more. This time Sybil bade him work with a firmer touch, rubbing the oil well into her erect nipples and kneading her tumid breasts with greater pressure of his palms. He dusted a fluffy swansdown puff with talcum powder and tickled her sensitive breasts with it, making the lower half of her body shudder with longing.

'Oil your fingers well with the rose unguent, then use them to lubricate those delicate pink petals,' came the order at long last. Emma lay back and wallowed in sweet anticipation. In less than a minute Angel succeeded, with his swift strokings of her pleasure bud, in bringing her to a second magnificent climax. The erotic energy pulsated and cavorted through her body with complete abandon until she was thoroughly satiated.

She rested awhile, content to let Angel brush her hair with soothing strokes while the heat within her dwindled to a warm glow. Then, when she had returned to normality, she sat up and was dressed in her silk robe.

'Now, Sybil, it is your turn!' Emma declared. 'You may be sure, my dear, that I shall direct Angel to your complete satisfaction!'

Sybil pulled up her petticoats and pulled down her knickers with a grateful sigh as Emma took over command and made Angel kneel between her outspread thighs. Watching Angel give Emma such a complete servicing must have aroused her almost to the limit of endurance.

'Part her love-lips with your fingers, carefully now, and let your tongue slide all over the delicate parts within,' Emma began, feeling her own nascent desire begin to throb again between her thighs. 'When you find her little topknot, let your tongue flick back and forth rapidly over it while you slowly insert the tip of your forefinger into her wet opening. With your other hand, stroke her bottom cheeks and, if you find her rear entrance is open and ready to welcome you in then you may proceed, but with caution. Be guided by the surrounding flesh: if it is slack continue to probe, but if it should tighten up then withdraw immediately.'

It was not long before Sybil began to groan and wriggle her hips in eagerness to hasten her approaching climax. Emma watched, fascinated, as her pale throat tightened and flushed a deep pink, then a great gushing sigh issued from her parted lips as the full force of her orgasm swept her into semi-oblivion. She continued to moan and thrash for some time, but at last she sank into rest with a pleased smile on her lips.

Amidst all the excitement of her friend's coming Emma had failed to notice that Angel, too, had succumbed to an overwhelming urge to ejaculate. Now the unmistakable signs of his intemperance were spattered all over Sybil's thighs and petticoats.

'Disgraceful fellow!' Emma boomed, noting the sly look that came over his features as he anticipated having to pay the penalty for his misdemeanour. 'You have ruined poor Sybil's pretty undergarments with your disgusting effluent. You must be severely punished.'

'Yes, indeed!' Sybil growled, rising unsteadily. 'He has offended both of us with his undisciplined behaviour. Six strokes of the cane I think, Emma, followed by several more with the slipper. Which would you prefer to administer?'

'The cane, I think,' Emma smiled, opening the cabinet where the assorted instruments of chastisement were housed. She took out a well-sprung withy, that she knew would perform the task to perfection. Sybil took out the leather-soled slipper that had also been used many times to good effect. Then the women took it in turns to thrash their secretly enraptured victim.

Chapter Nine

The advent of Sybil had taken the game to new heights of daring and excitement and for a while Emma was content to remain in the threesome, allowing her friend to take the lead in the proceedings. In other ways, though, she was less happy. Daniel was becoming a distant memory for, as Emma ruefully reflected, he had not contacted her for months. And she no longer saw Charles, since she was anxious not to upset Kitty who had become touchy of late.

Emma soon heard that the WSPU members, 'suffragettes' as they had now been dubbed by the *Daily Mail*, had finally arrived in London and had begun to campaign amongst the women of the East End. Not surprisingly, Kitty was often absent from home. She'd become convinced that Emma did not support the Cause, and when questioned would only mutter scornful remarks or reiterate dogma.

In fact, Emma was in accord with their aims. She firmly believed women should have the vote, but she thought it should be won in a ladylike manner. The spectacle of respectable middle-class women parading with banners in the streets and barracking at public meetings would surely do their cause no good at all.

Yet she could not blame her friend for taking a militant

stance. The way she'd been treated by her husband had led her to regard most men as blackguards, and Kitty seemed to have lost interest in finding a new husband or lover. Perhaps she had found solace in the arms of a fellow suffragette. Emma smiled to recall the time, so long ago, when she had taken it upon herself to introduce her shy young maidservant to the pleasures of the flesh. The possibility that Kitty had now turned to her own sex could not be ruled out. But while Emma shuddered at reports in the newspapers of demonstrations at the statue of Boadicea, marches on Westminster and rowdy meetings at Caxton Hall, often culminating in arrest and imprisonment for the ring-leaders, she refrained from asking questions. Kitty was a grown woman and must lead her own life now.

Instead of fretting about her, Emma made it her duty to see that Milly was well cared for. The girl was eleven years old, on the verge of puberty, and had the kind of shy charm that her mother had possessed when Emma first knew her. Judging from the raised voices that sometimes issued from the nursery, the girl could be strong-willed and defiant, but Emma had never found her anything but sweet and affectionate. She tried to fit in as much contact with Milly as her timetable would allow since she feared she might not enjoy her god-daughter's company for much longer. What had begun as a temporary arrangement had already lasted almost a year and Kitty might have other plans for her daughter.

The 'Longmore Academy for Young Ladies' was proving a great success that season. News had spread throughout the lower echelons of London society that if you wanted your daughter to marry a rich industrialist, a foreign ambassador or even an Earl, the Longmore Academy was the place for her to complete her education. Emma had even been obliged to open a waiting list.

Now there were four classes of ten girls each and Emma employed a staff of eight plus some part-time tutors. She herself only taught the few that she had personally selected. Over the years she had come to recognise these special young women with a kind of sixth sense. They had certain qualities of intelligence, poise, confidence and an underlying sensuality that she knew would enable them to benefit from the special instruction she gave.

In their turn, the young ladies were honoured to belong to this élite. They would learn secrets that their own mothers never knew, and enjoy pleasures far beyond those experienced by other women. By virtue of their specialised knowledge and skills they would have greater power over men than other women too, and be more in control of their own destinies.

One afternoon in May, Emma was talking to a group of six girls in the garden of the Brunswick Square house. She had decided to take advantage of the glorious spring sunshine to talk about 'Young Men's Fancies', one of her favourite topics. They were decorously arranged in a circle under the shade of a chestnut tree so as not to spoil their complexions, and out of earshot of the house so Emma felt free to speak openly.

'Now, ladies, you may recall the words of Alfred, Lord Tennyson: "In the Spring a young man's fancy lightly turns to thoughts of love". Perhaps you think you know what this means. You might imagine that they lie mooning over a pretty face, or sighing for a sweetheart, but I can tell you that most red-blooded males fancy something a good deal more down-to-earth than mere romance.'

'Are you saying men are not romantic?' asked flighty, raven-haired Dora.

'Not at all. What I am saying is that men have a different idea of romance from women. While a girl may dream of a pleasant walk on her beloved's arm, a fellow will be wondering just what her body looks and feels like under all those billowing petticoats and constricting corsets. While she longs to be given roses, he desires the sweetest rose of all – her virginity. And while she thinks of sweet nothings murmured in her ear, he wants to hear only one word from his true love's lips, opening the key to unimaginable pleasures, the word – Yes!'

'You mean, that she'll consent to marry him?' Dora persisted, a wicked glint in her eye.

'Marriage is not generally regarded as an end in itself amongst young men, the way it is by many young women. For most men it is more a matter of the price they have to pay. If they could have sexual pleasure with the woman they love without benefit of marriage lines they would do so. Yet conventional morality demands that they be 'respectable' in order to remain within polite society. So they suppress their feelings and marry girls to whom they are probably quite unsuited physically and temperamentally.'

'I am not sure what you are telling us, Lady Longmore,' said Julia, of the sparkling blue eyes. 'Are you saying we should indulge this instinct in our suitors? Surely we'll then have no chance of marrying them, for they'll regard us as soiled goods and look elsewhere for a bride.'

Emma sighed. She had heard this argument so many times before. 'That is only true if the experience is a meaningless or disagreeable one. Sex with an ignorant or unskilled girl is bound to be a disappointment to a young man. You must learn to enthral your lovers, to make them want you more than anything else in the world and then, when you at last grant them the ultimate favour, they must find it the most wonderful event of their entire lives. They will want to repeat it over and over again, and marriage will no longer seem a burden but a joy.'

'Will you be teaching us how to achieve that?' Dora asked, breathlessly.

'Of course,' Emma smiled. 'The lessons I have given you so far have helped you to understand how your own bodies function. You have all practised self-pleasuring until you are familiar with the range of delectable sensations produced. But desire is generated not in the genitals, but in the mind, and over the next few weeks I am going to introduce you to some of the ways that you may stimulate and excite a man's mind as well as his body . . .'

The faces of the girls sitting opposite suddenly became animated as they looked over Emma's shoulder, and she heard a soft footfall on the grass. She turned and was unable to stop herself from gasping with surprise. For there, framed against the standard roses and doused in bright sunshine, was the dark figure of her own long-lost lover.

'Daniel!' she exclaimed, her heart thudding so wildly that she feared she might suffer a seizure. The sight of him standing there with his familiar straight-backed posture, an ironic smile forming beneath his moustache, and his dark eyes surveying her with calm assurance, made Emma almost faint with joy.

'Lady Longmore,' he began, with a stagy bow. 'I wonder if you'd be so kind as to grant me a few minutes of your time – when you have finished with these lovely ladies, of course.'

'Oh yes, of course.'

Emma turned back to her charges feeling flustered and uncomfortably aware of the pink that must be showing in her cheeks. None of the girls had seen Daniel before, and now they were giggling and nudging and whispering in a most unseemly manner.

'Ladies! Remember your manners, please!' she commanded them. Then, turning back to Daniel she said coolly, 'If you would care to wait in the drawing room I shall join you in ten minutes, Lord Merton.'

He inclined his head, still with the faintly mocking smile, and began to stroll back to the house across the lawns, watched by six pairs of curious eyes. Emma did her best to continue the lesson but her pupils were restless and started to whisper amongst themselves.

'Dora! What were you saying to Julia?' she snapped at last.

'I'm sorry, Lady Longmore. I was just wondering who that gentleman was.'

Deciding it would be better to satisfy their curiosity than encourage speculation Emma said, in as matter-of-fact a tone as she could muster, 'That was Daniel Forbes, Lord Merton. He owns the house occupied by this Academy.'

'Is he married?' Julia asked, and they all giggled.

'Yes.'

'But maybe he would like to take a mistress!' Dora put in, evoking more laughter.

Emma frowned, then decided that they were in no mood to take her lesson seriously. 'Well, I think we shall leave it there for today. Girls, you are dismissed.'

As she made her way back across the lawn Emma found herself shaking with excitement at the prospect of seeing Daniel again. She went upstairs, where she washed her face and hands, powdered her cheeks, adjusted her hair and dabbed some scent behind her ears and into her cleavage. All the time her mind was racing: what could have occasioned this unexpected visit? If he was simply in town on business, with no particular desire to see her, Emma knew that she would feel hurt and humiliated. She also knew that she could not afford to show it. Steeling herself for the interview, she began to descend the stairs.

'Emma my dear! How charming you look.'

Daniel's first words were encouraging, and as he held his arms out to her she felt her heart leap with suppressed hope. He embraced her and kissed both cheeks tenderly, but then he drew back and bade her sit down. They faced each other, sitting on separate chairs, and Emma's volatile spirits began to sink again as their meeting took on the tenor of a formal visit.

'I had some business in town,' Daniel began, fuelling her fears. 'So I thought I should remain a while. If it is inconvenient for me to stay here I could put up at my club.'

'Oh no, your room is always kept ready for you here,' Emma said, a shade too eagerly.

He smiled, and she basked in the warmth of his brown

eyes. 'I was thinking more of your feelings, Emma. I have no wish to impose my presence on you if it would be unwelcome.'

'This is your house, Daniel, and I hope you will always feel free to come and go as you please,' she answered, primly.

'It is your home too, Emma, and I have no wish to upset you. I realise that things can never be quite the same between us now that I am married.'

Emma stiffened, then braced herself to say, 'Forgive me, Daniel, I have not enquired about your wife. How rude of me. Is she well?'

'As well as any woman can be when she is with child.'

'So soon?'

The words had slipped out in a vain attempt to disguise the turmoil that his words had thrown Emma into. All her old insecurities returned with a vengeance. A child would set the seal on their marriage and Daniel would no longer have any interest in her.

He gave a low chuckle, stirring Emma's loins against her will. 'It seems that I am fertile as well as virile! But now that I stand to gain an heir for Harfield I feel my business there is done, for the time being. I have laid plans for the refurbishment of the house and the modernising of the factory. My orders are being carried out throughout the summer and I confess that I've no desire to return until the autumn.'

Emma could not prevent the surge of optimism she felt at hearing his words. Neither could she resist asking, slyly, 'But what of your wife, Lady Caroline? Does she not need you?'

Daniel waved his hand dismissively. 'She has a host of relations around her. Every week some distant aunt or cousin arrives for a prolonged visit. The house is brimming over with dreadful women and I can stand no more of it.'

Emma laughed. 'Lord Merton, the henpecked husband! I never thought to see the day.'

'Neither did I!' he grinned, ruefully. Then his dark

133

eyes filled with passionate fire. 'Dear God, how I have missed you Emma! I confess I nearly funked the wedding. It was only the thought of my duty to Harfield and a stiff tot of brandy that got me through.'

'You did not write,' she said, reproachfully.

'How could I? If I had revealed my true feelings you would have regarded my letter as a preposterous piece of cheek, but if I had concealed them I would have been able to find nothing truthful to say.'

'Is that why you are here now, to tell me the truth?'

'I am not sure that my truth is what you would want to hear, Emma. I know how wounded you were by my marriage, and no doubt you have found yourself another lover by now. The last thing I would want is to make you unhappy again.'

Emma got up and walked to the window, where she could see the trees in the square breaking into new leaf and some children playing under the watchful eye of their nanny. She spoke without looking round, afraid that if she looked Daniel in the eye she would falter in her resolve to make him understand how she truly felt.

'I have been doing my best to forget you, these last few months,' she told him, hesitantly. 'But it has not been easy. I do have a lover, but he is nothing like you and sometimes I feel I would rather be celibate than accept second best. Perhaps, now that I am in my thirties, I should accept that my days of passion are over and begin to grow old gracefully.'

By way of reply Daniel came up behind her and kissed her on the nape of her neck, sending immediate shivers of desire down her spine. 'Really Lord Merton, this is so sudden!' Emma mocked him shrilly, turning with a reproving frown, her surprised eyes meeting his laughing ones.

'Don't play the bashful chambermaid with me, Emma. Hardly appropriate after all we've been through, you must agree. The question is, are we to continue where we left off?'

Emma knew, in that instant, that the fulfilment of all

her most heartfelt desires was within her grasp, yet still she hesitated. Daniel had hurt her once: would he do so again? Her pride would not let her give in straight away. Instead she walked over to the sofa and sat down, patting the place beside her. 'Come here, Dan, and we shall discuss this further.'

He gave a casual shrug of his broad shoulders. 'What on earth is there to discuss? You want me or you do not, and there's an end to it.'

'Of course I want you. I shall want you as long as I live, and you know it. But sometimes there are more important things in life than carnal desires. You're a married man now, and your first loyalty must be to your wife. How would Caroline feel if she knew you'd returned to your old mistress? I had the impression, last time I was in Harfield, that she didn't care for me much.'

'Caroline does not care for anyone much, including me. She is spoilt, vain and empty-headed. When I married her it was with the good of Harfield in mind, not my own welfare. Emma, I beg of you, please don't make me sacrifice my happiness on the altar of Harfield.'

She had never seen him so distressed, so patently miserable, and her heart went out to him. Despite her odd sense of history repeating itself, she opened her arms to him and let his head nestle in her bosom. Once she had shunned the man who was closest to her because he had looked elsewhere for an heir. She would not do the same again.

'Poor Dan,' she murmured, stroking his greying locks and relishing the memory of how they felt to her fingers. 'I cannot bear to see you so unhappy.'

'Then you will have me back?'

His face looked up eagerly, the brown eyes vulnerable, the sensual mouth pleading. She smiled and bent to kiss his lips. They felt soft and luscious, opening to her gentle pressure, and she let the tip of her tongue run along between them. Her breasts were tingling and, down below, her secret parts began to swell and moisten, all the complex machinery of love becoming oiled and geared up for the action to follow.

Yet, somehow, Emma found the strength to interrupt the process. She was determined not to give in too easily to her lover's demands. She terminated the kiss and drew away from him, holding him at arm's length. His breathing was irregular and his eyes burnt with a bright, slow fuse. In their depths she saw a flicker of uncertainty and she felt an answering thrill of triumph. He was still just as much in thrall to her as she was to him!

'I think we should celebrate our reunion with a toast,' she smiled, ringing the bell for Mrs Perkins to bring up a bottle of Napoleon brandy from the cellar.

'To the future!' Emma proposed, as they held their glasses high.

'To *our* future!' Daniel corrected her.

After a few sips of the warming liquid Emma felt her defences begin to fall and she was soon embracing her lover on the sofa. When his lips fell to her breasts, however, and her feelings were beginning to spiral out of control, she decided to make him wait a little longer.

'Tell me, Dan, what happened on your wedding night? I am dying to hear all the details.'

He looked up and, for a breathless moment, she feared he might rebuff her. But then his face broke into the old, wicked smile and he sat up with one arm around her and the other lightly stroking the exposed tops of her breasts.

'I was very drunk, as you can imagine. Had been all day, as a matter of fact. Then I started to worry about whether I could actually get the old rascal up on the night. I mean, Caroline isn't the most alluring of females. She has a pretty enough face, when she isn't scowling, and a good figure, when she isn't slouching. But she lacks a certain something – a kind of chemical magnetism, perhaps – that you possess in abundance, my dear.'

'Enough flattery. To the point, you old devil! Did she play the shy, retiring bride, or what?'

'She was already a *demi–vierge*. Well, can you imagine

136

me not trying my luck beforehand? No chance of anticipating marriage entirely, with Mamma always hovering
around, but I did manage to get a finger up her tight
little cunny. She seemed to endure it rather than enjoy it.
Wouldn't go near my tackle, of course. Acted as if it was
the devil incarnate. She liked having her soft little titties
licked, though.'

'Your wedding night,' Emma insisted. 'What
happened?'

'Ah, yes. Well we were in the master bedroom at
Harfield, kitted out for the occasion with garlands round
the four-poster, all that nonsense. I'd never seen her
completely in the nude so I started to undress her by
candlelight, but she wanted me to blow them out. I flatly
refused and made her strip before me. She didn't like it,
but I thought the sight of her nakedness might rouse my
flagging prick. No such luck!'

'Didn't you like her body?'

'It was nice enough, slim and dainty, but not voluptuously rounded like yours, Emma.' He gave her breast a
squeeze, making her nipple yearn so achingly to be
tweaked that she struggled out of the top half of her
clothes and sighed with relief as his eager fingers found
it. 'Anyway, she wanted to put on this special nightgown that her sister had embroidered for her, but I made
her leave it off so she went into a sulk. I said she could
put it on afterwards, but it would be easier to consummate our marriage if we were both nude.'

'It sounds as if there was an awful lot of talk between
you!'

'Well there was, I suppose. It was as if we were both
wanting to stave off the moment when we would meet
in our nakedness. I confess I felt a strange kind of
nervousness, almost as if I were a virgin doing it for the
first time.'

Emma laughed merrily at the thought. 'Did you enjoy
the feeling?'

'No. I just wanted to get it all over with as soon as
possible. I took off my clothes and doused the candle, as

137

Caroline had asked. We lay in each other's arms for a while, kissing and cuddling, but I knew she was frightened, which didn't help. I stroked her breasts and then put my hand down to feel if she was wet. She wasn't, of course. She started shivering and I asked the silly bitch if she were cold, but I knew she was trembling with trepidation.'

'Did you succeed in calming her?'

'No, quite the contrary. She was obviously not going to relax, no matter how many kisses and cuddles I delivered. That's what first alerted me to the fact that she hadn't married me out of love but solely because she wanted the social clout of being Lady Merton. Anyway I gave a few tugs on the old tadger, just to bring him up to scratch, then decided to press ahead. I straddled her and probed the dry little ditch with my penis but when I began to thrust she screamed, "Oh, you are not going to put that horrid big thing into my little wee hole!"'

'What else did she expect? Surely she had been told the facts of life?'

'Apparently not. The dim-witted girl believed that conception occurred when a man's organ entered a woman's mouth. That's what her married sister had been told, apparently, as an inducement to perform fellatio upon her husband while preventing further pregnancies, and the fable had been passed on.'

'I don't believe it!' Emma giggled. 'She really thought that?'

'I had no time to explain in detail. I knew if I hesitated too long my penis would shrink. And at that moment, dearest, I must admit that I was thinking of you.'

'Of *me*?'

'Yes. It was the only way I could maintain my erection through what was proving to be an ordeal. I closed my eyes and blocked my ears and pretended that I was thrusting into your sweet cunny as I did that time in Florence, when I pretended to be an immoral priest.'

'Oh Daniel!'

'If I loved the woman I should be feeling guilty, but I

138

do not and never have done and never will do. You are the only woman I have ever loved, please believe that Emma.'

So saying he gathered up both her breasts in his hands and kissed each nipple reverently. Emma felt a great swoop of longing within and knew she had to have him right then, with no more ado. She lifted up her petticoats and heard him gasp with joy as his fingers found the smooth expanse of thigh beneath the cotton frills. Lying back on the sofa with her breasts bulging out of her loose-fitting corset she sighed with equal pleasure as eager hands tore down her knickers and found the slit pouch of her sex already laden with love-dew. His lips moved in to suckle there, noisily relishing the juices that began to flow more rapidly the more he drank them in, and she opened her legs wider to let his tongue probe between her inner lips.

'Emma my love, I must find sanctuary, I must find peace!' she heard him moan as he unbuttoned himself and pushed down his trousers. Looking down she had just one brief glimpse of his pale organ before it delved straight inside her, to the utmost delight of them both. To be filled to the brim with keen sensation, to feel his lusty thrusting again in the place that had been bereft for so long, gave Emma a deep satisfaction.

Somehow all the hundreds of previous occasions on which they had made love, in so many different ways, gave weight to that longed-for consummation. Having deprived themselves of each other for so long, they were now making up for lost time. Emma felt the first tense quiverings begin immediately and soon was in the throes of a mind-shattering climax that strengthened as Daniel quickened his pace, striving towards his own. Waves of pulsating heat engulfed her, caught him up in the vortex and turned her solo performance into a double act, wedding the pair more completely than any mere form of words or piece of paper could do.

Afterwards, lying in his arms, Emma found the temerity to say, 'You know, I feel sorry for Caroline. I'm sure she can never know you as I do, never share what we have shared.'

Daniel kissed her on the tip of her nose. 'Cheeky cherub! You are right, of course. And I have often wondered why certain things are possible with some women but not with others. Is it breeding or upbringing that makes the difference? I cannot say. All I know is that I can tell at once if a woman is sensual and pleasure-loving or cold and puritanical.'

Emma glanced at the marble and ormolu clock on the mantelpiece. 'Well, this pleasure-loving woman has one or two duties to perform right now, I am sorry to say. But perhaps we may dine together later?'

Daniel kissed the fingers of her right hand, punctuating his words with them one by one. 'Of – course – we – shall – dearest.'

Emma reluctantly drew away from him and stood up, fastening her clothes. She saw Daniel's eyes rove all over her and knew she looked as radiant as she felt inside. It was as if, during the past months of exile, she had withered inside and now she was blossoming again like a tree in spring.

'I have some business to attend to myself,' Daniel told her, with a twinkle in his eye. 'But I shall return for eight.'

They bade each other a long, passionate farewell then Emma went to tidy up so that she could face her girls again. After finishing class she went to bathe and dress in her finest new gown. As the long-case clock in the hall chimed eight she descended to meet Daniel in the dining-room and her heart almost burst with joy when she found him already there awaiting her, with a red rose and an envelope in his hand, a look of fond anticipation in his eye.

'Emma, this is for you,' he smiled, handing her the two items. She breathed in the heady scent of the crimson rose with a sigh, then opened the envelope. Inside were two tickets for the boat train to Paris, dated for a week's time. 'You will come with me, won't you Emma?' he pleaded. 'I have so longed for us to return to the city where I first set eyes on you, so that we may enjoy its pleasures together.'

Emma's eyes began to mist as she recalled those far-off days. Although their romance had, in a sense, begun in Paris they had only viewed each other from afar. Now, in this renewed spring of their love, a trip to France with Daniel would be truly wonderful. 'Yes!' she smiled, embracing him warmly. 'Of course I shall come!'

Chapter Ten

*P*aris seemed even more beautiful and exciting to Emma than the last time she was there, perhaps because she was visiting it with Daniel. In addition to the familiar old monuments there were some new ones: the elegant Grand and Petit Palaces and the gilded splendour of the Alexander III bridge, all built for the great Universal Exhibition of 1900. Emma noticed far more automobiles in the streets, and evidence of the métro was everywhere, with people milling through its wrought-iron entrances made in the fashionable Art Nouveau style.

They stayed at the Hotel des Tuileries on the Champs Elysées, a luxurious palace of gilt and marble. She had the impression that Daniel was trying to make up for betraying her, or perhaps he was showing his gratitude for her forgiveness. Either way, she had no complaints. Their first night there was as perfect as any honeymoon.

Surrounded by exquisite pink and gold furniture, great urns filled with roses and lilies and as much champagne and caviar as they could consume, Emma and her lover frolicked on a four-poster bed swathed in satin brocade drapes. On that first, rapturous night in Paris they took their time over their love-making. First Emma lay, face down, relishing the cool smoothness of the silken sheets against her naked skin, while Daniel made his way up from her feet to her neck with tiny, whispering kisses that made her tingle all over. By the time he came to use his hands on her she was quivering with anticipation and half melting inside, but still she lay with her back and buttocks exposed, silently inviting him to caress her. She knew that her self-control now would yield a rich harvest of sensation later.

'Keep your eyes closed,' he murmured. 'And tell me what this is.'

She felt a delicate coolness on the warm skin of her buttocks. It drifted up her spine, soft and frilly as butterfly wings, and then she smelt its faint but familiar fragrance. 'A rose!' she whispered.

'Mm.'

He brushed the petals across her neck, tickling the backs of her ears, then down her back again to swirl around the mounds of her bottom. When he drew the flower gently down the insides of her thighs Emma shivered with the peculiar sensuousness that tickled her skin, awakening the desire for more novel stimulation.

It came soon in the form of a hand, his own hand, but clad in a mysterious material that felt as warm and smooth as her own skin, yet with a subtly different texture. Being stroked all over with this mitten was very soothing, and Emma didn't want to disturb her mood by puzzling over it. He let her wallow in relaxation for a while, then whispered, 'What is it?'

'I don't know,' she answered, lazily. 'But it feels wonderful.'

She turned her head and opened her eyes. There on Daniel's hand was one of his silk socks. He smiled, tweaked her nose with it, then bade her lie down again and close her eyes.

Next time she had some clues about the source of the stimulus before it occurred. She heard the glugging sound of liquid being shaken in a bottle but before she could respond there was a hissing, fizzing noise and a cascade of foam hit her shoulders, the cold liquid splash-

143

ing her like a shower and running down her spine. A sharp, grapey scent filled the air and she felt Daniel's mouth in the hollow of her back, sucking up the bubbles with noisy abandon, licking the drops from her flesh. His hands kneaded her buttocks and soon he was probing with his tongue into the crack between them where the wine was dribbling down. Emma wriggled in erotic abandon, feeling the surface of her back cooling rapidly where it had grown sticky with champagne and saliva.

She heard him pour the rest of the bottle into two glasses. 'Turn over!' he said, huskily.

Emma rolled over languidly, her breasts pointing in pert expectation to the ceiling, their nipples puckering into hard pink studs. For a second she saw Daniel kneeling over her, a wide glass of effervescent liquid in each hand. Her mouth watered in anticipation of drinking more of the delicious champagne. But then, before she had time to register his intention, he suddenly lunged at her and inverted the glasses over her breasts.

Emma screamed with the shock as her nipples were submerged in ice-cold liquid. Daniel chuckled as the wine began to flow down the divide between her breasts, some gathering in a pool round her navel the rest flowing on to swamp her pubic hair.

'I wanted to see if it was true that champagne glasses were modelled on Marie-Antoinette's breasts,' he explained, dabbling his fingers in the accumulated wine and sucking them appreciatively. 'If it *is* true then she had far smaller breasts than yours, my sweet.'

'Daniel! You are ... you are ...' Emma spluttered, unable to find a suitable adjective, but soon she was wriggling and giggling as Daniel's lips were going everywhere, licking and sucking at her wet breasts and stomach with orgiastic glee. His tongue eventually found its way, like the wine, into the folds and crevices of her pussy where his enthusiasm grew for the game. Soon he was catching every last drop of the liquid that filtered through the curly hair above, oozed over the promontory

144

of her clitoris then seeped into the cleft between her labia.

Emma picked up the two glasses where they had fallen by the side and drained them of any lingering dregs. Daniel looked up at her and smiled. 'Don't worry, there's another bottle in the ice bucket.'

'Later!' she sighed contentedly. 'Don't stop what you are doing now, I beg of you.'

The champagne was taking effect, her head reeling giddily and her body reacting to the varied assault upon her senses with renewed appetite, all her nerve-endings vibrantly alive. Daniel was giving her tumid love-lips some serious attention, running the tip of his tongue along them and dipping down between them, probing from time to time where the sticky residue had gathered, like a bee foraging for nectar.

Soon his insistent lapping at her pussy tipped her over the edge and into a whirling heaven of deeply rewarding sensation. Emma gasped out her pleasure as she surrendered to the powerful throbbings that had her squirming with sensual hunger against his mouth, heightening and prolonging the delicious sensations to the utmost, focusing her entire being, mind, body and soul on the fire that raged through her. She remained suspended in that voluptuous otherworld of erotic bliss until at last her pelvis sank, her thighs lay still, her breasts heaved with dwindling force as her breathing returned to normal.

Faintly she could feel Daniel's hard flesh nudging at her cunny and knew that he was about to make his entrance while she was still dewy soft and fully open to him. For a while Emma just lay there, incapable of movement, while he slowly rode her, caressing her inner walls with his warm, velvety member. Then she was aware of slight stirrings, deep within, and knew that the long, slow rise towards her second climax had begun.

Daniel sensed it too, and quickened his movements, alternating long sweeps with shorter stabs, the way she liked it. Her hips began rotating almost of their own accord in a sinuous dance that brought her clitoris into closer contact with the base of his shaft as he wove in and out of her awakening quim. She could feel the nub of her desire harden in response to the friction, and felt the gathering wave of her orgasm lift her up onto the next plane of ecstasy.

'Oh, Dan!' she murmured. 'No-one else has ever made love to me like you.'

'Nor ever will,' he smiled down at her. Then his expression changed, his eyes narrowing and his mouth curving into a secretive smile. He reached down behind the bed and drew up another bottle of champagne which he had craftily concealed there while Emma was recovering from her first climax. Now he was shafting her with the lusty, vigorous strokes that he knew would bring her on, and himself at the same time.

Emma felt the new urge to come take over her will, driving her on towards her second consummation with inexorable speed. Then, just as the quivering onset began, Daniel gave a loud groan, and with his thumb, eased the cork off the champagne bottle. It popped over her head and the foam burst out all over her once more, intensifying her shudders as every nerve in her body seemed to experience a miniature orgasm of its own. She could feel her lover fountaining up inside her cunny until she was awash with white foam, inside and out, wallowing in the watery embrace while she thrashed her way through the acute spasms of this new ecstasy that was even more fulfilling than the last.

'Sweetheart,' she heard Daniel murmur when, eventually, she regained consciousness. She was lying in his arms draped in sodden sheets that reeked of wine.

'Oh, you wicked man!' she laughed. 'Spoiling best champagne like that!'

'Spoiling?' he frowned. 'I can't think of anything better to do with it. Apart from drinking it, of course.'

So saying he handed over the glass that he had already poured for her. Emma sat up a little and sipped the delicious fizz, eyes closed. 'I shall never be able to sip champagne again without thinking of this night!' she declared.

'Good!' Daniel nuzzled up with his head on her shoulder, like an affectionate pet. 'I want to give you as many happy memories as possible, my dearest.'

Suddenly Emma was gripped by dark, corrosive doubt. 'Why, are you planning to desert me again?'

The words had slipped out before she knew what she was saying. When she glanced at her lover his smile was gone. 'No, Emma, but we cannot be together all the time, more's the pity. And yet I have often thought that that is the reason we have stayed together all these years. You know what they say about absence.'

'Hm. If only all other men did not pale by comparison with you, Dan!'

'Let us not talk in this morbid fashion any longer, Emma. Life is for living and here we are in the liveliest city in the world. Let us make the most of it.' He rose from the bed and went over to the window, where he threw open the shutters. 'Come, take a look at Paris by night!'

It was indeed a beautiful sight, the lovely buildings lit by a thousand street lamps whose reflections shimmered in the waters of the Seine, mirroring the stars above. The night air was cool, but Emma had wrapped a sheet around her and Daniel's warm hands were already feeling beneath it, squeezing her breasts, slipping a finger into her still-juicy vulva. He began to kiss her and she felt his organ rearing insistently against her naked thigh, stiffening again.

Soon it was slipping easily inside her and she gasped as Daniel held her against the wooden blind, flung back against the wall, and made love to her in a standing position. His strong hands helped her to remain upright while he drove in and out, the bunched sheet providing a buffer between her and the hard surface at her back. Emma gazed out into the lush Parisian darkness and the dancing points of light becoming blurred as her eyes ceased to focus.

Emma thought of all the melancholy night-life going on out there: the leggy dancers in their plumes and spangles desperately hoping to attract some new admirer as they went through their routines; the jaded prostitutes plying their trade, still believing that one day the man of their dreams would rescue them from the street; the old men lusting hopelessly after pretty boys; the women tied to men they no longer loved; the men yearning for women they could never have. Then she thought of her own life and rejoiced in the reassuring familiarity of her lover's body joined with hers. How grateful she was to Daniel for rescuing her from a similar fate! As her thighs trembled and her heart raced in anticipation of another taste of sweet oblivion Emma vowed that she would not allow any more morbid thoughts to spoil the rest of their time in Paris.

They awoke late next day and, after breakfasting in the hotel, strolled out into the spring sunshine to do some sight-seeing. Emma had not ventured up the Eiffel Tower on her last visit, so Daniel insisted that she should now go, and she found that the view from the top was truly worth all the anxiety of the ascent.

They lunched at Chez Maxim, their happy faces reflected in oval mirrors framed with the sinuous lines of the new style and festooned with flowers. Afterwards Daniel took her to the Paris branch of Tiffany and Company, where he bought her an exquisite brooch by René Lalique of gold leaves and gemstones in autumnal colours: topaz, amber and ruby. Emma was sure she had never been so happy. The cloud that had hung over her briefly last night had been completely dissipated.

After a brief visit to the Louvre in the afternoon, the pair returned to the hotel for a 'rest', although it took them a while to get around to it. Their love-making was free-ranging and joyful, taking place now on the velour and gilt of a chaise longue, now in the large bath situated in the adjoining bathroom, with its wonderfully efficient plumbing system and overhead shower, now on a zebra-skin rug before the fire. Only after an hour or so of such frolics did Emma slip between the satin sheets and rest her head upon Daniel's embracing arm.

They were awoken at five by a polite knock at the door. Daniel put on his robe and took the tea-tray from the boy then Emma joined him at the small table. 'What shall we do this evening?' she asked, languidly sipping her tea.

'Oh, I have something rather special in mind,' he grinned. 'But there is a small operation that must be performed first.'

'Operation? That sounds alarming.'

'Not at all. It is you who will perform it upon me, Emma dear, and I have the utmost faith in the steadiness of your hand.'

'Dan! You are alarming me even more. Stop teasing, and tell me what you mean.'

But, despite all her entreaties, he would not. Only when they had finished their tea did he place one of the chairs in the centre of the floor then disappear into the bathroom. He returned with a bowl of warm water, a couple of hand towels and his shaving kit. 'Oh, you want me to be your barber!' Emma giggled. 'Well, this should be interesting.'

'Yes, indeed, for I require you to shave my moustache right off.'

'Shave your moustache? But why, for heaven's sake? I like it. You wouldn't be you without it, Dan.'

'That is more or less the idea.' He placed the bowl on the table, took the razor out and gave it a few brisk scrapes on his strop, took out his shaving cream and his bottle of *Eau de Portugal*, placed a towel around his shoulders and sat down. 'I'm all yours, my dear!'

'No, really I can't.'

'Of course you can. Just take it slowly, a little at a time, and you will do splendidly.'

'But your entire moustache – are you sure?'

'Quite sure,' he answered, resolutely. 'Do not fret,

Emma. It will grow again in a month or so. Besides, you might prefer me clean shaven, you never know.'

Seeing that his mind was made up, Emma took a blob of the shaving cream and smeared it all around his mouth. It smelt pleasantly of lavender. Then she took the razor and, very tentatively, made the first small shave at the end of his moustache. Half a dozen dark hairs, speckled with grey, fell onto the white towel.

'That's the ticket!' he said, encouragingly. 'Now nerve yourself, girl, and finish it off.'

It was strange seeing the familiar swathe of hair slowly disappear from his upper lip, revealing the smooth skin beneath. When the moustache was all gone Emma splashed the orange flower water around his jowls, making him wince, then stepped back to survey her handiwork. The new Daniel smiled up at her, cheeky as an overgrown schoolboy. Emma had the strangest sensation that she was about to fall in love with him all over again.

She giggled. 'It has taken years off you Dan! You look quite the "beardless youth" now.'

'Just the effect I was after. Well done, young woman. Now I think you deserve an outing to somewhere rather special. Let me choose the gown for tonight while you fetch my dinner suit and a white shirt.'

'Shall I ring for the hotel maid and valet, to help us dress?'

'Er, no my dear. Let us help each other. I would prefer it if we remained private.'

So they went to each other's wardrobes and laid the clothes they had chosen on the bed. Emma was surprised that Daniel had picked out one of her high-necked dresses. He usually liked her to show off her cleavage when they went out together in the evening. However, the gown he had chosen was certainly elegant, in a deep green taffeta with full sleeves narrowing to the wrist and a triangular panel over the bosom of cream Nottingham lace.

'I shall shower first, if you don't mind,' Emma smiled.

'It will take me longer to get ready than you. Are you sure we should not call the servants?'

'Perfectly sure!'

Emma went into the bathroom and wound a towel around her head, turban fashion, then turned on the shower, enjoying the novel sensation of having water pour down on her from above. She felt inordinately excited at the thought of stepping out that evening with Daniel. Bereft of his facial hair he appeared quite a new man. The difference was as great as when a young girl put up her hair for the first time.

Fresh and gleaming from her shower, Emma went back into the bedroom. At first she thought she'd made a dreadful mistake and gone through some hitherto unnoticed communicating door into a different apartment. A woman stood with her back to her, fixing pins in her hair, but after a few seconds Emma realised the gown she was wearing was *hers*!

'Excuse me . . .' she began, but the words faltered as the 'woman' turned around.

'Daniel!' Emma exclaimed, almost fainting with shock.

His slow smile widened as she took in the astonishing picture. Daniel had managed to get into her dress by leaving the buttons undone at the waist and covering the gap with a satin cummerbund. The loose sleeves hid his brawny biceps from view, although the buttons at the wrist had to be left unfastened, and the flowing skirt covered pretty much everything else. With his own dark locks concealed beneath some of Emma's false ringlets and hairpieces his 'coiffure' looked most convincing.

'I need some help,' he said, matter-of-factly. 'Do you have some padding for my front? And some ornaments for my hair. Oh, and some of your nice perfume would help.'

'Daniel Forbes, would you mind telling me what this is all about?' Emma demanded, hands on hips, as she made an incredulous tour of inspection.

'Not yet, you'll find out. Now do be quick, dear, and help me put the finishing touches to my appearance. A little powder and paint would be a good idea too, don't you think?'

Exasperated by his coolly evasive manner, but equally seduced by the extraordinary picture he made, Emma went to do his bidding. As she fiddled with his hair and powdered his newly-shaven cheeks she assessed the effectiveness of his disguise. With a couple of silk scarves thrust into place in the bodice of the dress and a hint of rouge on his lips Daniel made a remarkably convincing woman despite his stature. 'Matronly' was the word, she decided.

'Do I pass inspection?' he asked, coyly.

'Move around a little. I want to see you walk. No, not like that, take smaller steps. That's much better. Pity you can't get into my shoes but if you cover your boots with that underskirt no-one will notice. Oh, I've just remembered! I have some detachable lace cuffs that I think will cover your wrists and make your hands look a little more dainty.'

When he was all ready Emma placed a wide-brimmed hat on his head and gave him a last, critical viewing. If you didn't look too closely and he was standing still or sitting he would pass muster, she decided, especially in a dim light. It gave her a weird thrill to think of that masculine body beneath all those feminine frills. She had seen transvestites a few times before and always been fascinated by them, but she had never known any of them intimately.

'Now, Emma, it is your turn to get dressed.'

Daniel took her hand and led her to the bed where she had laid out his own clothes. When the truth dawned on her she gave a little cry. 'Oh no!'

'Oh, yes!' he said, firmly, removing her wrap. His hands clasped her breasts. 'First we must find something to bind these with. Do you have a large silk scarf, or something similar?'

'Daniel, you are being quite impossible!' she protested. 'What is the point of all this?'

'You'll see,' he repeated, calmly, rummaging in a

drawer. He brought out a shawl of Indian silk. 'This will do well. Arms up, my dear, and let me do the honours.'

Meekly Emma submitted to the ritual of being dressed in his clothes. Inside, she was fluttery with excitement but apprehensive too. She stepped into the strangely rough trousers, feeling them encase her legs, and pulled the waistband halfway up her chest. 'Far too large!' she crowed.

'Never mind, we'll manage. If I can get into your clothes you can surely get into mine.'

Daniel contrived to turn down the waistband and tie it with another cummerbund into which he tucked the long tails of his shirt. Emma hated the beastly stiff collar she was obliged to wear. It made her neck itch and was terribly hot. 'I don't know how you men can stand to wear such awful garments,' she complained.

'It can't be as bad as lacing oneself into a tight unyielding corset – the sort *other* manufacturers produce!' he said, with a wry smile.

When Daniel had finished dressing her, with a tie and smart waistcoat, double-breasted jacket and glacé kid shoes with paper stuffed in to make a fit, there remained the problem of her hair. It was long and thick but he slicked it down with macassar oil, much to Emma's disgust, parted it on one side then pinned it up discreetly at the back, hidden by a dashing black Homburg hat.

'That will do,' he declared at last. 'One last finishing touch.'

He made her sit down in the chair where she had shaved him then brushed above her mouth with something sticky. Before she could protest he had produced a thick blonde moustache and was pasting it onto her.

Emma made her muffled protest. 'Daniel! For heaven's sake!'

But it was too late, the offending facial hair was fixed with theatrical adhesive. Glancing at herself in the mirror, Emma burst out laughing. Daniel came to stand beside her and took her arm. 'Don't we look a rum pair?'

She giggled. 'It's a good job we are only dressing up like this in private!'

'But not for long! As soon as I've chosen my cloak we shall go downstairs and you can hail us a cab.'

'What?' Emma stared at him, dumbfounded, but he had found her blue velvet cloak lined with white silk and was fastening it around his shoulders. 'You are surely not serious?'

'Indeed I am. Don't worry, Emma – oh, we need new names. I shall be ... let me see, "Danielle", and you can be "Clem", an abbreviated form of Clement. Then if I forget and call you Emma with luck no-one will notice.'

'Daniel, you are not suggesting that we should pass ourselves off as the opposite sex in *company*, surely?'

'It will be very special company, I can assure you. Now, shall we go?'

Half an hour later the pair were entering the same club that Emma had once visited, years before: L'Hermaphrodite. The cellar bar was already crowded but as Emma entered the darkened interior with Daniel on her arm she felt more at home. The journey there had been an ordeal, with people staring at them oddly. Here no-one would find them strange. There were people dressed in the most extraordinary clothes. A man wearing a shirt and tie with a flouncey skirt gave her a wink, and a woman with her hair in a bun wore trousers with braces. A band on the stage played frantic ragtime tunes for dancing, and the air was thick with smoke.

They sat at a table where a waiter with green hair brought them drinks. Soon they were joined by another couple who introduced themselves as 'Jo and Joe'. They were both exotically camouflaged, the one posing as a male having cropped dark hair and a loose-fitting suit, while the 'female' wore an extravagant wig and a low-necked, tight-fitting gown of pink and silver. Emma couldn't help staring in fascination at the appearance of a cleavage. How had he managed that? she wondered. She saw that the upper arms were very muscular and thought that he had probably been exercising with weights to increase his pectoral muscles. What lengths these bizarre folk will go to, she thought.

'Shall we dance?' Emma was startled by the request issuing from Jo's mouth but, since Daniel was already mincing towards the dance floor holding Joe's hand she smilingly agreed.

They danced wildly, frenetically, as if the world were coming to an end tomorrow. Most of the dancers seemed to be inebriated and, together with their weird costumes and ambivalent faces they provided an unsettling spectacle. Emma wondered what was going on beneath Jo's tight skirt. How could he conceal his erection, if he had one? Were his parts bound up as tightly as Emma's breasts? She was already finding it difficult to breathe and the smoke and exertion were adding to her discomfort.

At last she had to sit out. They returned to their table and Emma enjoyed watching Daniel in her dress making a determined effort to act ladylike.

'You are new to this, are you not?' Jo enquired, in a faint accent, taking Emma's hand and looking deep into her eyes through long, dark lashes. 'What you think – you like this?'

'It's very . . . interesting.'

'But not for you, eh?'

Emma smiled ruefully. 'I must say I feel awfully uncomfortable in this get-up.'

'That is because it is his clothes, yes?' She nodded. 'We who have made this our way of life, we do not wear the clothes of others. We have our own *tailleurs* and *couturiers*.'

'Really?'

'Yes. We hold our own fashion displays in the spring and autumn. Sadly you have just missed the first of this year. I am wearing a gown by Fifi Lamont, one of the most famous designers.'

'Fascinating! I had not realised that there was so much provided for . . . you people.'

Beneath her nervousness, Emma was feeling a raw

tide of sexual excitement. She tried to imagine herself kissing Jo on the lips, taking the initiative in their love-making, but when it came to undressing her imagination failed her.

'Ah, *cherie*, it was very brave of you to do this experiment tonight. But I have to tell you that unless the desire is in your soul you will never be one of us.'

'I think you are right.'

They danced again, this time in a waltz, and Emma found the courage to hold Jo close. Suddenly all the lights went out and before she knew it Jo's mouth had met hers, and they were kissing with a semblance of passion. In the dark it felt like being kissed by a man, and yet she could feel the skirt brushing against her own trousered legs, touch the hair that was swept up in an elaborate coiffure and smell the sweet odour of lilac. At the same time she could feel the muscular contours of those bare arms, smell the unmistakable odour of male perspiration issuing from those armpits that no amount of perfume could mask completely, and sense the foreign power that was hiding beneath that skirt. The effect was most disconcerting.

When the lights went on again Jo gave her a rather sad smile. 'Thank you, Clem. It has been nice meeting you.'

As Jo walked off and joined a party near the bar, Emma felt herself begin to panic. She was not used to being left alone in a strange milieu, and Daniel was nowhere in sight. The people near her were regarding her with curiosity and she found herself putting a hand up to her hair to see if it were still secure at the back. Someone laughed, and she was sure they were laughing at her. She walked through the crowd in increasing desperation. Everyone seemed to be mocking her with their smiles. She did not fit in, and suddenly she felt like an upstart in society trying, unsuccessfully, to become accepted.

Then she felt a tap on her shoulder. She turned with a sinking heart, but to her great relief it was Daniel. 'I think I want to leave!' she said impulsively, forgetting to put on a deep voice.

He gave a high-pitched laugh and took her arm, saying in a falsetto, 'Certainly, dear. Will you get us a cab?'

Emma was only slightly reassured by his presence, since he insisted on keeping up his rôle. As they moved towards the door a man in a ball gown gave her a mocking glance that said, as plainly as words, 'Amateurs! You don't belong here!'

By the time they returned to the hotel Emma was feeling relieved and her earlier disturbed feelings were dwindling. But as she prepared to take off her alien clothes Daniel came up, batting his eyelashes coquettishly at her. 'Clem, you are not going to be so ungallant as to undress in front of a lady, surely?'

'Oh Dan, for heaven's sake! Can't we stop all this now?'

'Why so uncomfortable? I'm enjoying exploring the hidden side of myself. Why can't you?'

He held her hand and led her over to the bed, where he lay back seductively, looking up at her. Emma had to admit to herself that he made a handsome woman and, as she sat there leaning over him, his mouth seemed very alluring. She bent and kissed him, letting her tongue pass between those reddened lips, with her hands on his sculpted arms. It was strange kissing him without a moustache. She had grown so used to that brush of hair against her face, and now its absence increased the impression that she was, indeed, embracing a rather masculine type of woman.

'Oh, so wonderful!' she heard him breathe, in a high whisper. 'Love me, my darling!'

Beginning to enjoy herself, Emma lifted up the skirt and felt his hard thighs beneath the petticoats. There was a powerful urge in her groin and to have him lying there open to her, his virility concealed beneath the layers, was strangely erotic. She felt beneath the frills and lace of her own knickers and found that his arousal equalled hers. Slowly she stripped him of his disguise and the sight of his organ rearing manfully amidst all that feminine finery was wonderfully incongruous. Emma giggled, but soon bent her lips to kiss the bulbous head of his penis while she wallowed in the surrounding ribbons and lace.

'Oh yes, yes!' she heard him cry, still in his falsetto. 'Love me now!'

Swiftly Emma took off the cummerbund and let the oversize trousers fall below her knees. She struggled at first but managed to position herself so that she could sit astride him and was soon sliding down onto his strong erection, exulting in the caress of the silk and cotton as it brushed against her naked thighs. As she thrust herself down on him, feeling powerfully in control, it was just possible to imagine that his organ was hers and that their gender truly was reversed. He lay there passively letting her do all the work and she felt hard and strong, forcing herself down upon him and, in her imagination, into his body. There was at first a mild confusion in her mind but then, as her climax neared, a kind of fusion happened and her conscious awareness seemed to flip over so that she could experience love-making from the other side.

Suddenly all that was feminine was viewed from another, more objective, angle and Emma realised at some subliminal level just how little of her true identity was bound up with her clothes, or even her body. She had taken on a part of Daniel's consciousness, could peep into his mind and soul, could feel what he felt when he made love to her. She summoned up the energy to move faster, more aggressively, became aware of the piston-like movement of her hips as she rocked back and forth and the power behind them. The movements became mechanical, dulling her mind to all but the hot, fierce sensations that were engulfing her from the waist down. She heard Daniel begin to moan and gasp but felt that it was *her* ejaculation approaching, with all the inexorable force of a steam engine in full throttle.

At last the pent-up energy burst from her, wet and

pulsating, all her pulses tuned in to that one magnificent throbbing rhythm as it tore through her body. She roared out her ecstasy, felt the guts half ripped out of her, was turned inside out by the exultant force of her coming. Gathering up handfuls of cotton frills she gasped out the dying throes of her orgasm then sank, utterly exhausted, with her face in a sea of silk and satin.

Chapter Eleven

*F*or two more days Emma basked in the warmth of Daniel's love, in the city dedicated to lovers. They took a boat trip on the Seine, visited the glittering *boîtes de nuit* in Montmartre where risqué cabarets of all kinds took place, promenaded in the Bois de Boulogne, attended the Opéra and the Folies Bergère. Yet whatever they did Emma was always glad to have him all to herself in their hotel bedroom at the end of the day and renew the seemingly eternal flame of their romance with kisses and caresses.

Then, just when Emma was feeling secure again, and happier than she had felt for over a year, Daniel dropped a bombshell in her lap. 'I have some business to do,' he announced over breakfast, with studied casualness. 'Don't you have an old friend here in Paris? Perhaps you could stay with her for a night or two.'

Emma stared at him in horror. 'You mean you are going to abandon me?'

'Don't be silly, Emma. You know I must combine business with pleasure on my trips abroad.'

She was near to tears, but would not let him see it. Daniel hated 'scenes' and she didn't want to spoil the perfect rapport they had seemed to achieve over the past few days. With an effort of will she quashed the jealous suspicions that were crowding her mind and said, brightly, 'Well, I am sure I could manage here alone, although I would rather see Lily if I can. I have often thought about her. I have an address for her in my diary.'

'That's the spirit! I'll leave you some francs, to spend as you wish. And when we meet again we'll be all the more pleased to see each other. Remember, absence makes the heart . . .'

'Please do not keep saying that, Daniel,' she broke in. 'That saying is quite false, as far as I am concerned. When we were apart for so long, I confess I came near to hating you.'

But he only chuckled and kissed her on the forehead, making her feel annoyingly like a wayward child.

Mid-morning, they set out for Montmartre together. Charles had told Emma that the last time he'd seen Lily she was living in Rue Lepic, near the Moulin Rouge. The apartment block was a dismal-looking building and when Daniel rang the bell a suspicious concierge grunted at them through a grille before he would open the door. He led the way through a warren of corridors and up an iron staircase to a door on the first floor. 'She never gets up before noon,' he said with a shrug, when she failed to answer the bell.

'Please try again,' Emma begged him. 'I have come a long way to see her.'

At last there were sounds of stirring inside and a voice called, '*Qui est là?*'

Beating the surly doorman to it Emma replied at once, 'It's your old friend Emma Longmore, from England. Remember me?'

There was a shuffling of bolts and the door suddenly opened to reveal a middle-aged woman with her hair half hidden by a black lace mantilla and a red shawl around her shoulders. She gazed incredulously at Emma then quickly embraced her.

'Emma! Of course I remember you, even after all these years. What a wonderful surprise!' Becoming aware of

161

Daniel, she grew suddenly flustered. 'I am sorry, *Monsieur*, I did not know she was not alone.'

Daniel gave his most charming smile and introduced himself. They shook hands, but just as Lily was about to invite them in he said, 'Please excuse me, Madame Merchant, but I have some business to attend to.' He took Emma in his arms and, as they embraced, whispered, 'I shall see you at the hotel on Friday morning. Be good, now.'

He left Emma to face a flurry of questions and compliments. 'What are you doing in Paris, my dear? Oh, you look so elegant! Was that a new lover of yours, or a long-standing one? What an exquisite brooch! It looks like Lalique . . . It *is* Lalique! Well, well.'

While she satisfied Lily's bubbling curiosity as best she could, Emma looked about her. The room was dimly lit, with the shutters closed, but there was little of the splendour she remembered from that other apartment near the Boulevard des Italiens. She recognised a bronze lamp and some graceful statuettes of nude women, but the flat was shabbily furnished and the treasures looked out of place amongst dingy walls and threadbare carpets.

'I have come down in the world, haven't I?' Lily said, suddenly. Emma realised that her wandering eyes had been noticed and she began to apologise but her friend bade her sit down in a comfortable armchair with faded upholstery while she sat opposite.

'Five years ago my protector decided he needed a newer, more fashionable model so my time was up. Dear Sergei was generous, I'll give him that. He still pays me a small pension that keeps me off the streets.'

'It seems so unfair, Lily. You gave him the best years of your life, after all.'

'If your face is your fortune you can hardly complain if it is worth less when it deteriorates!' Lily chuckled. 'And I am certainly not complaining. My life is a very pleasant one compared to many others in my profession. But how rude of me, I have offered you no refreshment!

162

I am accustomed to taking a little brandy in the mornings. Will you join me?'

Emma was shocked, since she never drank spirits before noon except as medicine. However, she hid her disapproval and agreed to keep Lily company. She began to tell Lily about her Academy in London, then about her affair with Daniel. As their conversation became more intimate they began swapping stories about Charles, their mutual friend. Lily recounted how she had got him a job as a nude model for some artists in Montmartre.

'He was still so green!' she giggled. 'And very much addicted to *le vice anglais!* When I told my friends Jaco and Louis they played a good trick on him. They asked him to pose tied up to a plaster column they used as a prop for their photography. Said they were doing a "classical study of Samson". Anyway, he fell for it. When they had him trussed in the nude Louis said he'd changed his mind and was going to do a study for the "Flaying of Marsyas"!'

'What happened?'

'They blindfolded him and then the fun started. He became the whipping boy all right, but the artists had smuggled in two pretty women, whores who did modelling too, and it was they who gave him the birching. When Louis took off his blindfold Charles' eyes nearly fell from his head when he saw the two naked beauties still with the whips in their hands.'

'I dare say he was pleased.'

'He could hardly hide his pleasure, not with his stalk standing to attention for all to see! Anyway, they untied him and said they were sorry for playing such a mean trick on him. They promised to make it up to him and . . . well, you can imagine the rest.'

Emma sipped the last of her brandy, already in nostalgic mood. 'Dear Charles! I have had many other lovers since him you know, but no-one else could hold a candle to my Dan.'

'Tell me more about him,' Lily smiled. 'Why you are not with him now, for instance.'

Emma's face dropped and, to her dismay, she suddenly burst into tears. Feeling Lily's comforting arms around her she controlled herself and took the proffered handkerchief. 'I am so sorry, that took me quite by surprise.'

'It is good to weep, my dear. Holding in one's emotions only leads to illness. Would you like some camomile tea? I find it very calming.'

When she had recovered, Emma continued her story. 'I thought everything was very good between us. I had my Academy and he had his factory and home in Yorkshire. We met not as frequently as I would have liked, but often enough to remain passionately in love – or so I believed. But last Christmas something I had never imagined happened: he married!'

Lily laughed then, seeing Emma's puzzled distress, squeezed her hand. 'Forgive me, dear, but your story is very familiar. So many mistresses live in cloud-cuckoo land! Most men want a wife and children for the sake of society, but a mistress on the side as well, for their own gratification. If you cannot accept that, then perhaps you had better marry yourself, Emma.'

'I believe I have accepted it now. After all, he brought me here to Paris leaving his wife at home. She is expecting their first child.'

'And probably not responding to his advances.' Emma's face fell again. 'Excuse me, I am just a cynical old woman.'

'Old? You are not yet old, Lily. I am sure that when you are dressed up . . .'

'With powder and paint to cover the cracks? Yes, you are right. I can still pass for bedworthy in the circles I move in. Don't look so shocked. You are looking splendid yourself, my dear, truly. I would not say that if I did not mean it.'

'If only I could be sure of Daniel!' Emma sighed.

'Nonsense. If you were completely sure of him you'd

be bored, and begin to despise him. It is good that he keeps you on your mettle. But you must do the same to him. Don't let him think that you live only for his looks or he will abuse you. Men cannot help it, they need the thrill of the chase.'

'Oh, it is so good to hear you talk!' Emma exclaimed, kissing her soft cheek. 'There is no-one else I can be so frank with.'

'Sometimes one needs a friend to keep up one's morale. Being a mistress can be a lonely business. I think you are very wise, Emma, to have another occupation. Your Academy sounds marvellous. Women are beginning to demand their rights, and the right to sexual pleasure is surely fundamental.'

Emma grimaced. 'Don't talk to me of women's rights! You remember my maid, Kitty? She has become a suffragette and has her head filled with their dogma.'

'Do I take it that you don't approve?'

'I am all for women having the vote and equality with men, but I do not like the way they are going about it.'

'You don't think the end justifies the means, then?'

'Not if it means a mother leaving her child with me to go marching in the streets!'

'Personally, I admire those women greatly. If I were living in England I am sure I should be one of them. France is so reactionary. I believe that even Finland is in the process of granting women the vote.'

'Well, it is more for future generations than for us, I suppose,' Emma sighed. 'Sometimes I envy the young girls who attend my Academy. They take so much for granted these days and have so much more freedom.'

'My goodness, you are talking like an old maid!'

'Sometimes I feel like one!'

'So do I, but this will never do. We need to prove to ourselves that we are still capable of having fun and attracting new lovers, Emma. Let us go out on the town tonight, just the two of us, and see how much fun we can have together. Are you game?'

'Of course!' Emma laughed. 'What a marvellous idea.

Shall we go shopping first and see what fripperies we can find to doll ourselves up with?'

As they giggled and ogled their way around the Paris stores Emma felt her old *joie de vivre* returning. It was marvellous what a rejuvenating effect Lily was having on her. Then, just as they were about to ascend the central staircase at Galeries Lafayette that swirled out sinuously like an elegant corrugated skirt, Emma heard a woman call her name.

'Emma, Lady Longmore! Can it really be you?' She turned to see a pretty young woman, dressed in a loose jacket of brown silk with ecru lace motifs and matching striped taffeta skirt, regarding her quizzically. 'It is Henrietta, one of your former pupils.'

After a few seconds Emma gave a gasp of recognition. 'Hetty! But I would not have recognised you, my dear. You look so . . . sophisticated!'

'And you look just as lovely as ever. How we girls admired you, Emma. You were always the perfect model of a society beauty for us.'

After she had been introduced to Lily, the three women ascended the stairs together. It seemed that Hetty was only in Paris for another hour before returning to her chateau near Bordeaux, but she was reluctant to part from her old teacher so soon. 'Why don't you come and visit us, Emma? I should love to show you my beautiful home. Come soon and stay as long as you like – please say you will!'

'It is very kind of you to invite me. I am only here for a few days more but I suppose I could come, just for one night.'

The more she thought about it, the more Emma liked the idea. She was very fond of Hetty, whom she had regarded as one of her star pupils, and if she went off to Bordeaux by herself it would show Daniel that she still had that independence of spirit that he so admired. By the time they parted Hetty had told her which train to catch, promising that someone would be there to meet her at the station.

Before then, however, she and Lily were determined to have some sport. After taking tea at the Grand Café the pair went back to the apartment in Rue Lepic to rest before getting ready for the evening. Lily proved an expert coiffeuse, decorating Emma's hair with the butterfly ornaments she had bought only that afternoon. Then she helped her into the pretty low-necked gown of shell-pink silk with lace scallops, purchased with some of Daniel's generous allowance.

'I love it!' Lily declared, adding mischievously, 'It makes you look so young and innocent! I shall dress likewise, Emma. We might be taken for two virgin *ingénues*, out on a spree!'

Unlikely as it seemed, they really did look the part when they surveyed each other, side by side, in the mirror. Lily had chosen a simple dress of white muslin with garlands of flowers embroidered around the neck, sleeves and hem. Her hair was lifted back from her face and tied up with a large bow, allowing full rein to her large, expressive eyes. They looked gleefully at Emma as she said, 'Now, to the bar of the "Folies"! If we cannot find two handsome young escorts there we are not worth our salt as *demi-mondaines*!'

The bar was crowded by the time they arrived, the air full of champagne bubbles and the scent of Havanas. The two women sat down at a corner table to survey the crowd and select their victims. All around were men of distinction and society belles, many known to Lily who dished the dirt on them behind her hand.

'See that woman in the turquoise dress with the peacock feathers? That is "La Belle Otéro", who was once a circus performer. She possesses a priceless collection of jewels, for she has been the mistress of Kings and Princes, including you-know-who! He still comes to Paris every spring, you know, under the pseudonym of "The Duke of Lancaster". But now La Belle Otéro is being wooed by Vanderbilt, the millionaire. The French authoress, Colette, has described her as having the classic profile of a Greek statue and breasts like elongated lemons, would you believe!'

'She is certainly very lovely,' Emma commented, enviously.

'And over there, see that little man with his black locks falling over his darting eyes and a red scarf around his neck? That is Pablo Picasso, the artist, with his mistress Fernande. And that young man nearby is Maurice Chevalier. Mistinguett, the cabaret queen, believes he will go far in the Folies for he is a gifted singer and dancer.'

'You seem to know everything about everyone,' Emma murmured.

Lily sighed. 'Perhaps that is because I am no longer in the swim of things, as I used to be. Gossip is, after all, the last refuge of the socially *passé*.'

'Come, Lily, I shall not allow you to become morbid!' Emma declared, taking her friend's arm. 'Let us promenade a little, and view our prospects more closely.'

They wandered amongst the crowd until Emma suddenly spotted a conspicuous pair hovering at the door. They were twins, dressed identically in stiff suits and Windsor collars, their only concession to individuality being that one wore a cerise tie and matching waistcoat with gold buttons, while the other boy wore saxe blue with silver buttons. Each had a clean-shaven face, fair hair smarmed down and parted at the side, and shy grey eyes that clearly showed they felt all at sea amongst the assembled *glitterati*.

'Look, over there!' she gave Lily a nudge. 'Those two young lads seem to need some help!'

'I think you are right,' Lily smiled. 'Leave this to me!'

Boldly she strode forward and dropped one of her white gloves quite deliberately at the boys' feet. Emma smiled to see one of them pick it up while the other attracted her attention. Lily turned with a vague expression that turned into one of gushing gratitude. She immediately engaged them in conversation and, in less than a minute, was beckoning Emma to join her.

'Emma, my dear, may I introduce Michel and Antoine Davigny? These two charming young men have invited us to dine with them!' she said, much to Emma's astonishment.

'How kind!'

'They are newly arrived in Paris from Provence,' Lily explained, with a meaningful look as if to say, 'Here are two innocent country bumpkins, for sure!'

'Yes, we know hardly anyone here in Paris,' Michel admitted, blushing fiercely as if he had confessed to some carnal sin.

'Except Monsieur Le Duc, our Uncle,' Antoine added. 'He is our only relative but he is very old and, alas, bedridden.'

Lily gave Emma a wink saying, 'Since these gentlemen are new to the city I have taken the liberty of suggesting that we dine at Duval's.'

Emma smiled. That was one of the brasseries frequented by the whores and 'models' of Montmartre, with rooms available above. Furthermore, it was in Place Lepic, not far from Lily's apartment. She suspected it was not the first time her friend had made use of the place.

Soon all four of them were walking the short distance to Duval's with Lily chatting animatedly to the two boys. Emma couldn't help admiring the way she put them at their ease, making them laugh although they were obviously tongue-tied. By the time they were sitting at one of the cordoned-off tables in a dark corner there was an air of expectation and sexual excitement about the pair that was almost tangible.

'Correct me if I am wrong,' she heard Lily say, 'but I believe you two gentlemen are not used to dining with ladies, am I right?'

'Oh, have we done something wrong?' Michel enquired, anxiously.

'Not at all, you are behaving impeccably! It is just an instinct of mine.'

'Your instinct is correct, Madame,' Antoine said,

gravely. 'In fact this is the very first time we have dined alone with two such charming ladies as yourselves. You see, our dear, late Mamma was very strict . . .'

'Quite right too!' Lily said, sternly. 'You might have got into bad company. But now that you are old enough to make your own decisions we are flattered that you have chosen to spend the evening with us. Now then, the menu!'

Although Emma contributed the occasional remark to make the conversation flow, she had to concede that Lily reigned supreme, complimenting them on their looks, their table manners, their choice of wine and food in almost perfect French. Smiling and giggling like a cocotte she quoted romantic poetry, praised their manly appearance and refilled their glasses without them noticing until, what with flattering words, admiring glances and copious amounts of wine, their heads were almost visibly swelling and spinning on their shoulders.

When the meal was over and the two lads were flushed and eager for whatever was to come, Lily suggested they should go upstairs for 'Le Cabaret'.

'Oh, is there a show here too?' Antoine enquired, innocently.

Winking at Emma, Lily led the way up the dark staircase to the room that she had already booked with the waiter. It was all red plush and thick carpets, the bed discreetly curtained off and a table and chairs set out in case clients preferred to dine there in complete privacy.

'Now, you two, sit there while Emma and I decide how to entertain you both,' Lily smiled.

The women retired behind the curtain that concealed the large, four-poster bed. 'I think a classical theme would do well for these two darlings,' Lily whispered. 'I shall set the scene and, when you are ready, I shall pull aside the curtain to reveal you in a *tableau vivant*. Venus rising from the foam will fill the bill, I think. Just the briefest of veils to cover your modesty, dear. You know what is required. There is a phonograph to supply the music, I believe.'

'Very well,' Emma murmured, hoarsely, 'But please undo me at the back first!'

While she swiftly undressed, Emma could hear the commentary that Lily was making to the background music of Debussy's 'La Mer'.

'We are about to witness the miraculous Birth of Venus, Goddess of Love. Picture, if you will, those deep blue waters, gilded with sunshine, gently wafting towards the shores of the Island of Cyprus. A giant shell is bobbing on the waves and on it stands the most beautiful woman you have ever set eyes upon. Nearer and nearer she comes and we see she is almost naked but surrounded by roses, whose sweet perfume wafts towards us on the breeze . . .'

As the music reached a crescendo, Emma heard Lily's voice whisper, 'Are you ready?'

'Yes!'

The curtain was slowly drawn back to reveal Emma standing on her flounced petticoats, to suggest a scallop shell, with her right hand drawing a wisp of lace across her breasts and her left hand shielding her pubis. The men gasped and murmured in tones of such awe that Emma almost believed she had a divine aura. She remained perfectly still, in the manner of the nudes at the Folies Bergère, and soon her audience was applauding loudly: '*Bravo! Quelle spectacle!*'

'Which one of you will be bold enough to divest Venus of her last garment?' Lily asked.

Both rose eagerly, almost knocking each other over in their haste to be first at Emma's side. Snatching the veil from her fingers they stood there ogling her shapely breasts.

'She is no statue made of marble,' Lily told them as she stood nearby, gently encouraging. 'Put out your hands and touch her warm flesh. Then, if you are lucky, she may come to life!'

The brothers reached out and touched her with tentative fingers. Emma's nipples responded by tightening and swelling, making her bosom appear even more ripe

171

and rounded. She gently caressed each of them on the cheek in return. 'You see? She likes you both!' Lily laughed. 'You may kiss her hands, if you wish.'

Eagerly they each took a hand and began to press their fervent lips all over it. Emma felt a *frisson* of desire as she imagined their cherry-red mouths pleasuring her in other ways. As if reading her mind, Lily said, 'Lead her onto the bed, dear boys, where she may lie in repose. She's lonely and longs to be attended by her adorable naked cherubim, but where can they be?'

'*We* could be her cherubs,' Michel exclaimed, as if he had thought of it all by himself!

Lily helped them to undress while Emma lay watching, in a state of escalating desire. Soon it was obvious that although they were almost identical in the rest of their physique, by some sport of nature they had been differently endowed in their generative organs. Although both phalluses were now fully erect, Antoine's was a good deal smaller than Michel's, whose lusty glans was bursting impatiently from the end of a thick, seven-inch shaft.

Perhaps sensing that Antoine already had a sense of inferiority in that department, Lily tactfully proceeded to praise his equipment to the skies. 'Oh, what a darling little stalk this sweet cherub has! May I kiss the dear fellow, Antoine? Let me kneel here before you. Your charming organ shall be my God, and I shall pay it homage thus!'

So saying she bent her lips to the minuscule prick which responded by swelling up even more with pride.

Envious of all the attention his twin was getting, Michel climbed onto the bed and began to kiss and fondle Emma's breasts. 'That's the way,' she murmured. 'No part of my body is out of bounds to you. Feel free to play with me, dear boy. Explore me thoroughly.'

Soon he was lying at her side, cramming as much of her generous bosom into his mouth as he could manage. It didn't take him long to find the wet chasm between her thighs, into which his unskilled fingers poked and prodded mercilessly. Fortunately Emma was already sufficiently lubricated to find his rough handling of her parts stimulating. She reached down and felt his strong member, warm and solid in her hand, making her moan with the sudden sharp increase in her longing.

'Won't you plant your nice big carrot in my garden?' she suggested, coyly, imitating Lily's nursery talk.

'You mean my pee-pee?'

'Yes, sweetheart. It will fit very nicely into the hole already prepared for it down there.'

'But Mamma said that was a naughty thing to do.'

'It is naughty, for little boys. But you're a great big man now, aren't you, so there's nothing wrong with it. In fact, it will prove what a manly fellow you are if you can get it in.'

'Really?' His naive young face gleamed with joy at being given permission to do what he secretly desired. 'How do I do it . . . like this?'

He was on his knees between her legs now, the meaty prong pointing straight at her vulva. Emma parted her labia with the fingers of one hand, using the other to guide him in. 'That's right, now push! Oh yes, you're in now all right. Hole in one! That feels so good, doesn't it?'

He made an incoherent sound, lying there quite still, like a beached whale. Emma gave his cock a reassuring squeeze, but when it remained inert she realised she must give him further instructions. 'You may move it in and out if you like. It will make both of us feel even better.'

He began to rise and fall in an ungainly fashion as if he were doing press-up exercises. Emma told him to bend his knees and move from the hips which he did, but in a very jerky and uncoordinated fashion. All the while she could hear his brother whimpering with delight as Lily played on his tiny pipe, bringing him closer to orgasm. Her own was approaching too, despite the clumsiness of her young lover's actions. However inexpertly he might be wielding it his stout organ was

173

filling her hungry quim most satisfyingly, and by clenching and releasing it in rhythmic fashion she was heightening both Michel's arousal and her own.

At last the two lads reached their climax, almost simultaneously, and Emma found their cries and whimpers sufficiently stimulating to trigger her, too. She moaned quietly as the warm and throbbing flood engulfed her with pleasant, though not extreme, sensation and her more discreet sighs were drowned by the brothers' ecstatic moans as they enjoyed their first heterosexual experience.

The twins finally collapsed in a fraternal heap on the bed and Emma, temporarily exhausted, moved over to make room for them. Soon the room was reverberating to heavy snores. Emma became aware that Lily was gathering up her clothes from where she had hidden them beneath the bed. Her friend looked up with a finger on her lips, then beckoned her out of the curtained boudoir.

'Get dressed quickly, Emma. I think we should leave now,' she whispered. 'Those two are in their cups and will be no more use to man, woman or beast till morning!'

'Are you sure?'

'Quite sure. Here, let me help you with your dress. I shall tip the wink to the patron and he will look after them. I can promise you that Duval is used to coping with such situations!'

They tiptoed out of the room and were soon covering the few hundred yards back to Lily's apartment. When they arrived she led Emma straight into her bedroom and lit the lamp.

She sat down on the bed smiling. 'Well, that was fun, was it not? Come here, my dear, you look too ravishing to be keeping your distance. Now tell me, were you satisfied by young Michel's amorous technique?'

'Oh I came off, if that's what you mean, but it wasn't particularly wonderful. Of course there was no time to teach him properly.'

'I was by no means satisfied either, although I enjoyed it all immensely. It gave me a thrill to feel I could still attract young men. Oh, having you here has done me so much good, my dearest. May I kiss you?'

Her lips were warm and full, pressing gently against Emma's until they opened and their tongues met in passionate accord as at their last intimate encounter, years ago. Now Emma felt much more ready to reciprocate those feminine kisses and caresses. Eagerly they undressed each other down to their chemise. Then, her face glowing with joyous desire, Lily slowly raised the hem of Emma's garment and began to kiss her way up her body.

Emma felt her thighs tingle in response to those soft wet lips, starting a chain reaction of fierce longing that spiralled up her spine. She stroked Lily's flowing hair and gasped as the short curls of her own pubic hair were nuzzled by her friend's questing mouth, followed by a brief lick of her tumid clitoris. Slightly disappointed, Emma felt her move on, but knew that it would not be long before she returned to that most sensitive spot. Her bosom was enticing her upward, over the smooth mound of her stomach, pushing up the thin cotton until her breasts were fully revealed with their red peaks already taut with desire.

'Oh, I have dreamed of these!' Lily sighed, seizing the firm flesh with both hands and taking one stiff nipple into her mouth. She suckled gently at first, filling Emma with sweet thrills and making her utter small grunts of satisfaction. One hand dropped to her belly, then to her thigh, rousing her below until she moved restlessly, seeking more direct stimulation. Sensing her need, Lily switched to the other nipple and her fingers found the wet chasm of Emma's sex open and ready for her, the petal-like surfaces coated with dewy liquid.

Now it was Lily's turn to groan with sudden lust as she made her way back down to the vibrant source of Emma's pleasure. She reached up and continued to stroke her demanding breasts while her lips and tongue

175

gave her equally voracious pussy the attention it was craving.

'Oh, Lily!' Emma sighed, as the delicious throbbing intensified. 'You make me feel so good!'

The active tongue was probing now, as far inside her as it could go, making Emma squirm with growing eagerness for satisfaction. She was aware of Lily reaching under the bed and bringing something out. Looking down in curiosity, she was astonished to see a rosary dangling from her friend's fingers. Was she about to become involved in some peculiar religious observance?

Lily withdrew her mouth and knelt between Emma's thighs, looking down on her with a secretive smile. Emma asked what she was doing. 'You'll see!' Lily replied, her smile widening.

She reached under the bed again and brought out a small pot of scented cream which she smeared over her hands. 'Just relax, my darling. You are going to love this!'

Emma lay back, confident that she was about to experience something novel and exciting. She watched as Lily gently stroked her clitoris with one hand while her other fingers slowly insinuated themselves into her anus. She could feel herself becoming loosened, voluptuously enjoying the sensations that were simultaneously flooding through her front and back portals. Then, when she felt wide open, Lily picked up the rosary and began to press it into her crack, gradually pushing it further in until the hard beads were inside her and the ebony cross dangled against her outside cheeks.

Once again, Lily bent her mouth to lick and suck at the sweet fruit of her vulva with renewed vigour while her left hand pulled at one nipple then the other. Emma felt her final ascent begin, taking her to new heights of tingling pleasure as she squeezed the muscles of her anus and quim, feeling her chest grow tight as she rapidly approached the climax. Then, as the first blissful contractions spasmed through her, she felt Lily pull on the cross of the rosary and the knobbly beads massaged the walls of her back passage, bringing her to an earthy, sensual fulfilment. She heard herself scream and cry out in the last extremity of ecstasy, only half conscious as the rip-tide of passionate fire swept her out into a mindless sea.

In the quiet that followed the cataclysm, Emma was vaguely aware of Lily's arms around her, holding her against a warm, soft body whose contours fitted her own perfectly. She snuggled close, feeling safe and mothered. After a while her fingers began to outline the generous curve of her friend's breast, and her lips grew hungry for kissing. Lily responded at first, but when Emma's hand strayed down past her stomach to the tangled bush beneath she gently stopped it.

'You have given me such pleasure,' Emma murmured. 'Now it is your turn, Lily.'

To her surprise, Lily chuckled. 'No, my dear, I have already had my reward. When I make love to a woman I prefer to be active, it is just my way. Now sleep a little, sweetheart. You have a long journey in the morning and must be up early.'

'Dear Lily, you are so good to me. If ever I should leave Daniel, and you were still living alone, I should like to come and stay with you.'

'Hush, darling. I never make plans. Just enjoy the moment and try to live each as if it were your last.'

'You are a truly extraordinary woman,' Emma sighed as her heavy lids closed again.

Chapter Twelve

As the Renault automobile made its stately way through the village of Morville, with the deep shine of its immaculate navy coachwork reflecting the brass fittings, Emma sat high in the back seat behind the uniformed chauffeur, feeling like a Duchess. Every villager they passed saluted her, and by the time they swung into the long drive leading to the fairy-tale chateau in the middle of the park Emma had come to realise why Henrietta Northrop had good reason to be grateful to the woman who had made it all possible – herself.

Recalling that debauched evening she had spent with Hetty's father and his friend, Emma smiled to herself as she pictured the scene in Compton's with Sir James begging Emma to educate his wife, as well as his daughter, in the ways of love. Should she tell Hetty that she had seduced her father? Perhaps not. On the whole she preferred to leave it to others to disclose such details if they so wished, and to keep her own counsel.

Hetty had appeared at the imposing front door as soon as she heard the motor arrive, and now she was rushing excitedly from the porch. 'Darling Emma, I am so happy to see you!' she enthused, embracing her warmly. 'I apologise for not being at the station to meet you, but I had promised to go riding with Jules this afternoon. He wanted me to try a new filly.'

'Ah! So all those riding lessons in Rotten Row were not wasted!' Emma smiled.

Hetty took her arm affectionately and walked her up to the house. 'Since leaving the Academy I have made good use of all the skills we acquired – riding, skating, dancing, music, art appreciation. I admit that I found Madame Berthier's French conversation classes tedious, but now I am reaping the benefits. I never imagined that I would be marrying a Frenchman!'

The imposing entrance hall was filled with Empire Style furniture and a sweeping staircase led up to the first floor where, Hetty informed her, her husband Jules was awaiting them in the drawing-room. Emma had already met the Marquis of Morville at Hetty's wedding but there had been no time to do more than exchange pleasantries on that occasion. Now he welcomed her courteously to his beautiful home, kissing her on both cheeks and inviting her to join him in a glass of the claret produced on his estate.

While he carefully poured three glasses from a crystal decanter Emma studied his face and figure, coming to the conclusion that Hetty was a very fortunate young woman indeed. In addition to his wealth and title Jules was blessed with a strong, manly body and boyish good looks, with a certain gleam in his brown eyes that revealed a natural lust for the good things of life. His hair was black and glossy, curling appealingly round his ears, and his lips were full and sensually curved, revealing well-shaped teeth when he smiled, as he did frequently. Emma also smiled to think of all the pretty French noses that must have been put out of joint by his marrying an English girl!

She took the wine glass and waved it under her nose appreciatively. 'This is very good!' she smiled, taking a mouthful. 'Soft fruit in abundance, with a touch of the cigar-box and a good deal of tannin. Perhaps a little young?'

Jules gazed at her in wonder. 'You speak like a *connoiseuse*, madame! Where did you learn about wine?'

'Oh, I just picked up a little knowledge along the way,' she replied nonchalantly. 'Your wine is classified as a *Deuxième Cru*, I believe?'

'Yes, though Papa thought it should have been a *Premier*. He was a young man when the classification was made for the Médoc region. But we do very well and, yes, you are right about this vintage. It has at least another five years to go before it reaches its peak. Perhaps you would like to see the *chai* and vineyards?'

'Oh, Jules, she has only just arrived!' Hetty protested, placing an arm around him and kissing his cheek. 'I'm dying to show you round the chateau, Emma. Jules let me have a free hand with decorating and furnishing some rooms, including the one you will be staying in.'

Emma smiled to see her looking so happy and fulfilled. In the smart peach voile gown trimmed with guipure lace she was looking very attractive, and marriage to Jules seemed to have given her a new poise and confidence. She congratulated Hetty as they walked from room to room of the chateau, ending up in the charming guest bedroom with a view out over the vineyards, where Emma was left alone to prepare for dinner.

They dined by candlelight amidst heirlooms and portraits of the Morvilles, with huge gilt-framed mirrors reflecting the glowing candelabras. Emma had put on her most glamorous gown, a creation by Worth in emerald taffeta with ecru lace around the low *décolletage*, and she wore the emerald necklace, bracelet and earrings that Daniel had given her, long ago. When she entered the splendid setting Jules complimented her on her appearance and bent to kiss her hand, and Emma felt a thrill of erotic response pass through her. She blushed a little, mindful that his wife was standing close by, but when she glanced at Hetty the young woman was smiling broadly, quite unconcerned that her husband was showing their guest so much gallant attention.

Hetty herself was looking particularly lovely in a

loose-fitting flounced evening gown of cream silk, decorated with shimmering beads. With her pale skin and fair hair she looked almost angelic, yet there was a voluptuousness to her figure that Emma had not noticed before. It suddenly dawned on her that Hetty might be expecting her first child.

As the meal progressed, Emma became more and more convinced of it. She saw Jules throw his wife many a fond, solicitous glance, and when she pushed away a plate of sickly sweet *Crème à la Valois* he did not comment. There was also a special bloom about her skin, a kind of translucent glow that Emma had often noticed amongst women in a certain condition. Perhaps later, when they were alone, her friend might confide in her.

When Jules began to talk about the vineyards, however, Emma's attention was diverted and she became fascinated by the passion and enthusiasm with which he described his own wines and compared them with others. He insisted that they should end the meal with a glass or two of *Chateau d'Yquem*, the most expensive wine in the world, and Emma could not help expressing her amazement at its honeyed richness and exquisite nose, that inspired you to sip again and again from the glass in a mood of increasing rapture.

'Ah!' sighed the Marquis at last, leaning back in his chair and eyeing the two women with great satisfaction as he drained his glass. 'What a delightful experience! The beauty of the wine outclassed only by the sight of you two gorgeous ladies!'

'I told you she was beautiful,' Hetty said, proudly. 'And wise and clever, too. She taught us how to win a man, and how to keep him happy – especially in bed! It is to Emma that we owe our marital bliss, dear Jules.'

'Yet you are not married yourself, Emma,' Jules said, thoughtfully. 'Do you have a lover?'

The question did not seem so direct when expressed in such a seductive French accent. Emma replied, rather wistfully, 'Yes, we came to Paris together. But he has business to do, so I came to see Hetty for a night.'

'You must be missing him.'

Jules' dark eyes were regarding her penetratingly, and Emma felt her heart flutter a little. There was an intense atmosphere in the room, an air of suspense that filled her with thrilling anticipation, and yet she did not know what she was expecting to happen.

'When you took Emma round the house, did you show her the master bedroom?' the Marquis asked his wife, suddenly.

'No, Jules. Only my own.'

'Then we shall visit it now. I would like our guest to see my oriental miniatures. She is obviously a woman of taste and refinement who has the great virtue of also being a woman of the world.'

'Oh, yes!' Hetty rose from her chair with enthusiasm. 'You should see them, Emma. They are quite extraordinary.'

Filled with curiosity, Emma followed the pair up the stairs to the bedroom in the front of the house overlooking the park. Jules lit the oil lamps and the room was revealed in all its baroque splendour. The bed caught Emma's eye immediately, being canopied in velvet borne by two gilded cherubs and displaying the Morville coat of arms. Hetty went at once to lie down on it, leaning upon her elbow so that she could watch the other two from a distance. Jules went to a cupboard and brought out a locked box, which he placed on a round table then drew up chairs for Emma and himself.

'I shall give you these to examine one by one,' he announced. 'They are very precious, but they benefit from being handled as the ivory gains a fine patina from contact with human skin.'

He handed Emma a small carved object that on close examination proved to be two figures locked together in sexual intercourse. The pair were facing each other with their organs joined and their backs rounded, giving a pleasant curvature to the whole. Both the man and the woman had Japanese features and were smiling blissfully.

'How sweet!' Emma exclaimed. 'Do you have more of these dear little carvings?'

'About fifty.' He took the object back and gave her another. 'They are called *netsuke*. The Japanese use them as toggles on their kimonos. My father acquired them from a travelling merchant in exchange for a dozen cases of our best vintage. Some of them are very old and quite priceless.'

Emma loved the warm, knobbly feel of them, and the way they fitted so neatly into her palm. She could see that the craftsmanship was of a very high quality, and their *risqué* nature would doubtless add to their value for a collector of such items. The one she was examining now had a man entering a woman from behind while he fondled her breasts.

Jules showed her many more, some with solitary figures masturbating, others with couples in the most elaborate intertwining postures, but all with an explicitly erotic theme. The effect of seeing so many suggestive images in succession was very arousing. Emma was reminded of the early days of her marriage to Sir Henry Longmore, when she would spend long hours studying his vast library of erotic literature. The same secret agitation was stirring her veins, filling her with insistent longing. The only difference was that now there was no willing husband nearby to satisfy her desires – none of her own, anyway.

'This one is the *pièce de résistance* of the collection,' Jules said at last, bringing out something wrapped in black velvet. 'It is larger than the others. Here!'

Emma gasped with surprise as he handed her a long, slightly curved tusk of ivory with four figures carved around the sides, two male and two female, each caressing the genitals of their neighbour, forming a kind of masturbatory chain. Although each had a distinct face they shared the same domed skull, formed from the rounded end of the tusk.

'That is my favourite,' she heard Jules say, his voice husky with emotion. 'It is not a *netsuke* but a dildo. I like to think it has acquired a very special kind of patina down the ages, formed from the sweet love juices of the *geisha* girls as they waited impatiently for their lovers in the tea-houses of Tokyo and Yokohama.'

Emma handled it reverently, wondering how it would feel inside her. As if reading her thoughts, Jules added, 'I do not know how effective it would be in use.'

'But I do!' came Hetty's amused voice from the bed. 'I tried it out one night, dearest, when you were away. I forgot to tell you.'

'And how did it feel? Was it a good fit in your dear little cunt, sweetheart?'

Emma's discomfort grew as she realised she was eavesdropping on an intimate conversation between husband and wife, but neither seemed to mind her presence. 'Oh yes!' Hetty murmured, throatily. 'It gave me great satisfaction.'

'Then I should like to observe you using it again, right now.'

The pair seemed completely oblivious of Emma's presence. She watched Jules help to remove his wife's dress and petticoats, then her silken shift and drawers. Once she was quite naked Emma saw that she had guessed right: Hetty's stomach and bosom were definitely enlarged. Her breasts looked heavy and pendulous, dark-nippled and veined with blue. She gazed in fascination, never having seen a pregnant woman in the altogether before. It evoked mixed feelings of awe and envy that she found uncomfortable, but suddenly Hetty noticed her and smiled.

'I am expecting in the autumn, Emma.' She gave her husband a proud smile. 'Jules is sure it will be a boy because he kicks so vigorously. Oh, he is starting now. Do come and feel him!'

'Are you sure?' Emma rose uncertainly, but Jules added his encouragement and soon she was sitting on the bed with her hand on Hetty's mountainous belly, feeling the fluttery little movements within.

'How strange!' she breathed, softly. Her eyes locked

in wonder with those of Jules, and the feeling of intimacy deepened. They were sitting on either side of his wife and a subtle mood of complicity seemed to be developing between them. 'Hetty finds it uncomfortable to make love in the usual positions now she is in this condition,' he said, conversationally. 'But her sexual urges have not diminished.'

'On the contrary, they have increased!' Hetty smiled, adding, in a mock reproving tone, 'You never warned us that we might become nymphomaniacs when we were pregnant, Emma!'

'I have had no experience of it myself, so how could I know? I believe when many women are *enceinte* they cannot bear their husbands near them, but perhaps others are more like you.'

Jules had begun to stroke his wife's thighs, pushing them apart until the pouting pink lips of her vulva could be seen. Emma knew that something very titillating was about to happen, and her heart began to race. Should she leave the happy couple to their love-play or did they want her to stay? It was already obvious that neither felt inhibited by her presence, yet if she were to remain on the sidelines as a mere spectator she would be most frustrated.

'Hetty still loves to have her breasts caressed, even though they are swollen and tender,' Jules said, producing the ivory dildo. 'Perhaps you would oblige, Emma *chérie*?'

Realising that she was to be included, Emma felt both relief and excitement flood through her. She reached out and gently stroked the enlarged mammaries, feeling the soft flesh slowly growing firm beneath her fingertips. Hetty lay back and purred in feline bliss, letting her thighs flop wide open. Her nipples stiffened and Emma bent to touch them with her lips, receiving an encouraging moan that led her to take one into her mouth and lick it thoroughly.

'That's right,' she heard Jules murmur. 'Open your sweet little pussy wide, my darling.'

His fingers were dabbling between her labia now, making it easy for the hard nose of the dildo to find its way in. Emma could tell from the squelching noises that her quim was brimming with secretions and she felt her own juices running in sympathy. She saw the ivory tusk make its way inside, guided by Jules' careful hand, and felt her cunt start to throb with empty longing. She squeezed Hetty's ample mounds harder, making her moan with mingled pleasure and pain, while Jules inserted the dildo to its full extent, filling his wife up completely.

'Oh, my darlings, this feels wonderful!' Hetty sighed, wriggling sensually. 'Push it slowly in and out, sweetheart, the way I like it. Ah yes, that's better!'

'This instrument is all the more effective for being curved,' Jules explained in a matter-of-fact tone as Emma continued to stroke the yearning breasts. 'If I place it in curving upwards, like so, then contact is maintained with her clitoris throughout.'

Emma found the sight of that artificial phallus moving in and out almost too much to bear. She craved similar stimulation but was obliged to remain an observer. It was too frustrating!

'A little faster, Jules, I am on the verge!' Hetty gasped.

Suddenly there was a long series of low moans, and Emma felt Hetty's great breasts throbbing and shaking with extreme emotion, thrusting upwards against her palms in time with her gyrating pelvis. She placed her lips on the crest of her belly and blessed the child within, wondering what it was making of this great cataclysm that was shaking its temporary home.

Eventually Hetty sank back in repose, her breathing gradually returning to normal, and Jules withdrew the substitute organ, slick with her juices. 'Thank you, Emma,' he said, gravely.

Hetty opened her eyes, surveying them both. She smiled in sleepy gratitude and beckoned them to lie beside her. Emma snuggled into the crook of her arm, her cheek against the smooth side of her right breast, while Jules did the same on the other side and all three fell into a doze.

In the middle of a dream, Emma felt warm lips pressed to her cleavage and thought that Daniel was making love to her. Awakening, she realised that the delicious sensations were actually happening but it was not Dan who was kissing her but Hetty's husband. He had changed places with his wife and now she was smiling down at Emma over his shoulder.

'I have been selfish, making the pair of you give me what I wanted,' Hetty declared. 'So I thought you might like to borrow Jules for a while, Emma. He has been well trained, for I taught him everything you taught me.'

'Hetty, you wicked woman!' Emma laughed.

But her friend just smiled and came round the bed to divest her of her garments while Jules removed his own. In a few minutes all three of them were lying naked on the bed again, only this time it was Hetty's turn to play 'gooseberry'. She did so with evident joy, watching closely as her husband mounted Emma, his sturdy prong rearing impatiently.

There was, by now, no need of lengthy preliminaries. Emma, her blood previously stirred by witnessing Hetty's climax, had been brought even nearer to her own by her erotic dream. Eagerly she touched the Marquis' thick shaft, so much more warm and velvet-smooth than the ivory fake, and her loins shuddered. Jules smiled as he knelt between her legs and surveyed her body, his foreign eyes smouldering a silent message that needed no translation.

'Oh, you look so fine together!' Hetty exclaimed, as she watched him plunge straight into the streaming vagina of her former teacher. 'Ride her good and hard, darling, the way we used to when we were first wed. Let her feel your great knob inside her, and show her what a wonderfully virile man I've married!'

Emma grunted out her satisfaction as every inch of her slippery quim was invaded by hard, sleek flesh. He set up a rhythm of alternate strokes, a long slow plunge that filled her up to her complete satisfaction, then three shorter ones that gave her jutting clitoris the friction it desired. While he shafted her Jules reached out for her breasts and gathered them up, rolling the erect nipples with his thumbs until Emma could feel the first unmistakable flutters of her approaching orgasm.

'Oh, where's that dildo?' she heard Hetty say as Jules altered his rhythm, keeping her hovering in suspense with tiny strokes against her engorged vulva and delaying the satisfaction of that final long thrust.

'Ah! That's better!' Hetty's sigh of contentment hovered on the edge of Emma's consciousness as all her attention was concentrated on her own hotly pulsating pussy. While she relished the ever-increasing arousal of her clitoris, wallowing in the keen sensations that were flushing through her body, Emma remained in suspense, awaiting that one act of full penetration that she knew would bring her ultimate relief.

Yet Jules seemed determined to deny her. The persistent hovering on the brink went on and on, sending her on a seemingly infinite upward spiral of arousal. Her own words echoed mockingly, words uttered to the select group of students to which Hetty had belonged: 'Remember, ladies, the longer you both wait for it, the more it will be worth waiting for!'

Then, just as Emma was beginning to fear that her clitoris could not take much more of this endless friction without chafing, Jules delivered the *coup de grâce*. His rampant prick came sliding swiftly into her, massaging the walls of her quim and giving her a wonderful feeling of completion as it reached her womb. She squeezed it hard with her inner muscles and felt the first tremulous quivers of her climax. It gathered force then raged through her like a forest inferno, setting all her nerve-endings alight with blissful fire.

Jules thrust into her one last time and triggered his own orgasm, sending a fierce jet deep within her that only increased her satisfaction. She was moaning continually, first with rapture and relief, then with disappointment as the spasms grew weaker and the beautiful feelings faded into a softly melting afterglow.

'Oh God!' she heard Hetty exclaim, evidently arriving at the same ecstatic state just as hers was waning. She opened her eyes and giggled to see the ivory prick sticking out from below her friend's rotund belly, giving her the appearance of that bloated little *Baccino*, the fountain in the Boboli gardens in Florence.

Her laughter broke the ice. Suddenly all three of them were rolling around on that stately bed in hysterical glee, not sure why they were laughing but somehow aware that the situation was farcical. They were like three naughty children who had broken the rules and got away with it.

For the rest of the night they remained together, sometimes playing silly games, sometimes making love, sometimes feasting on champagne and caviar that they stole from the pantry and cellar. In the morning Emma felt quite exhausted, but very happy. She rose early and, before she left, was given a conducted tour of the vineyard and winery.

'I am sorry to be leaving so soon,' she told a tearful Hetty on the station platform. 'But I will come again, next time I am in France. And you must be sure to visit me when you're next in London.'

'I shall, dear Emma. And I shall send news of the birth, when it happens. I am sure that my night with you will help to produce a lusty boy!'

Laughing and crying at once, the two women parted as the train steamed into the station. On the way to Paris, Emma was in a more sober mood. She had left a note for Daniel telling him she would not be back at the hotel until late afternoon and she couldn't help wondering what mood she would find her lover in. It disturbed her that, while she was frolicking with Jules and Hetty, she had not once thought of him. Was he starting to mean less to her?

Yet when she saw him awaiting her in the hotel lounge, his dark head with flashes of grey at the temples bent over a copy of Huysmans' *A Rebours*, her heart fluttered painfully in her chest with the old, nostalgic longing for him. She felt guiltily ashamed of her urge to pay him back for abandoning her. Rushing up to his chair, she seized his hand and said, breathlessly, 'Dearest, I am back!'

'Oh, Emma! I have been so worried about you.'

His dark eyes were regarding her soulfully, with reproach, but she just laughed. 'I was in Bordeaux with my ex-pupil Hetty, who married a French marquis. We had a marvellous time.'

Daniel closed his book and rose, smiling, to his feet. 'I am so glad you were not lonely while I was gone. Shall we go upstairs and discuss where we should dine on our last night in Paris?'

Happily Emma took his arm and they left the room. It was always like this, she reflected. As soon as she was with him again she felt as if they had never been apart.

Once she returned to London Emma did her best to forget about Daniel, who had gone straight back to Yorkshire after all. But the familiar routine of the Academy was suddenly interrupted one day. The housekeeper knocked at the door of the room where she was addressing her morning class. 'Excuse me, ma'am, but there is someone asking to see you. A young woman.'

Emma nodded to Mrs Perkins, her face drawn. 'Very well. I had better come.' She turned back to her class. 'Please get out your 'Guides to the Observances of Good Society' and read chapter three, on "What is a Lady"? We shall discuss it on my return.'

Following Perkins' bustling figure to the drawing-room, Emma was filled with trepidation. Kitty had not come home last night, and she feared the worst. The young woman who stood wringing her hands by the window was wearing a faded dress and patched jacket, her hair coming out of its loose bun in untidy wisps. When she turned, her agitated face only confirmed Emma's fears. 'Lady Longmore, I'm sorry to disturb you like this, but Kitty said I was to come. She said you'd be worried.'

'What has happened to her?'

'There was a demonstration at Mr Asquith's house in Cavendish Square. It was awful, ma'am! I was there, but I didn't get into trouble. But Kitty was with Annie, you see. Annie Kenney, that is . . .'

Emma stopped her gabbling flow and made her sit down. Then she sent Perkins for some tea. 'Now, my dear. Take a deep breath and tell me your name, and where you are from.'

'My name's Effie Barnes, ma'am. I came up west with a group from the East End. We're all suffragettes down 'ackney way,' she added, proudly.

'Tell me about it from the beginning. Why were you demonstrating at the home of the Chancellor?'

'Well, last week there was this meeting in Northampton where Mr Asquith was declared "an enemy of women and workers". So we go to protest on 'is doorstep. Course 'e wouldn't let us in. So Annie starts ringin' the doorbell and she won't stop. All the servants are peerin' through the windows and cheerin' her on – it was a right carry-on.'

'Did they call the police?'

'Yes, ma'am. They arrested Annie and some others along with 'er, includin' Kitty. Annie's been given two months, and the rest six weeks.'

'Prison! Oh, my God!'

'And it ain't no good offerin' to pay 'er fine, ma'am, 'cause she won't let nobody.'

'But that's preposterous! She must let me get her out. Where do I have to go?'

"olloway, ma'am. I'll come with you.'

Emma ordered a cab and dismissed her class, telling Mrs Perkins where she was going. If only Daniel were here, Emma sighed, as she got herself ready. But he was far away in Yorkshire with his wife, who was fretting over her health during her pregnancy.

The grim entrance of Holloway Jail for Women made

Emma's heart sink as they approached. In answer to her request to visit Mrs Kitty Belfort the porter showed them in to the office and explained the position. 'She's been classed as third division, so she ain't allowed no visitors. If you want to pay her fine I'll 'ave to send a warder to bring back her reply.'

Emma sighed. 'Very well, if that is your rule. But please tell her to think of her daughter and come home, I beg of you.'

'We'll give her the message, ma'am.'

The two women were left alone in the cell-like room. For a while there was silence, then Emma said, 'What does "Third Division" mean, Effie?'

'They don't get no privileges, like visitors or writin' letters, and they 'ave to wear prison dress. Some of our sympathisers want us classed as first division prisoners when we go to jail. They say it's a scandal that the likes of Mrs Pethick-Lawrence and Lady Harberton should be in danger of being put in with common prostitutes and the like.'

Emma nodded, profoundly moved by what this earnest little East-End factory girl was telling her. The Suffragettes seemed more determined and organised than she had imagined, with women from all ranks of society prepared to go to prison, if necessary, for the Cause.

The porter returned, shaking his head. 'She won't budge,' he announced. 'Says look after the girl for her, she'll be out in six weeks.'

Heavy-hearted, the women returned to Brunswick Square. Emma provided a splendid tea for Effie, but the poor girl was so nervous and upset that she could not manage more than half a scone. As she left she asked, 'If you really want to help Kitty, ma'am, you'll join the Union. We could do with more ladies like you.'

'I'll think about it,' Emma promised, but she could not imagine herself demonstrating in the streets. It was not cowardice. Much as she sympathised with the movement she still disapproved of their tactics, especially when they resulted in mothers of young children being sent to jail.

Later on Emma wrote to Daniel, needing to confide in someone, and then made up a story for Jane to tell Milly, about her mother having to go away in a hurry to visit a sick relative. She was sitting in the drawing-room reading an account of the fracas in the *Daily Mirror* when Mrs Perkins announced another visitor. 'It is Mr Charles Purchase, ma'am.'

Chapter Thirteen

'Charles! Yes, do send him in,' Emma smiled, pleased at the prospect of seeing an old admirer. She had great need of company that evening.

He had come because he'd seen Kitty's name in a newspaper as being amongst those arrested. Quickly Emma explained what had happened and they spent some time discussing their mutual friend's plight.

'I am still fond of her you know, Emma, even though things went badly between us.'

'That is because you are a sweet and generous man.' Emma kissed his cheek. 'Anyway, all that was my fault. My dalliance with you cost me dear. All three of us were losers in the end.'

'I miss you, too,' Charles sighed. 'Tell me what you have been doing since I last saw you. It seems a very long time ago.'

Emma had a great deal to tell him, especially about their other mutual friend, Lily Merchant. He chuckled as she related how they had spent their night together in Paris.

'I can see the two of you growing old disgracefully together!' he chortled. 'Not two old maids but two bold jades, a danger to every lusty young man in the vicinity!'

'I shall take that as a compliment.'

'But tell me, what became of that young woman whose lover was being blackmailed?'

'Sybil? Oh she has gone to Florence for the summer with her new lover, Rupert Heaven.'

'You mean Angel?' Charles frowned. 'Last I heard he was divinely in love with you, my dear. Don't tell me the angel has fallen from grace!'

'I was glad to let him go to her,' Emma sighed. 'He was rather ... wearing. But I have not seen Daniel since we returned from Paris and there is no-one new in my life. Sometimes the prospect of seducing someone new seems just too fatiguing.'

'Then why not try someone old?' Charles advanced towards her with a twinkle in his eye. 'I have an enduring fire for you, Emma dearest, you know that. And since there is no-one important in my life either at the moment, why should we not indulge ourselves? I see no harm. Kitty is no longer interested in me, and even if she were ...'

'You mean she is safely locked up in prison and therefore need not know?' Emma said, tartly. 'Shame on you, Charles!'

'My philosophy of life has but two principles: pragmatism and opportunism. It works particularly well where beautiful ladies are concerned. I ask myself what will be the result of my taking any opportunity that presents itself, and if the answer comes back, "Pleasure for both parties with harm to none other" I feel an irresistible force moving me in that direction.'

'Then you are a hedonist, too!' Emma laughed. 'Oh, Charles, you are quite incorrigible!'

'But if anyone knows how to correct my deficiencies, it is you. Why, you have known me practically from the cradle. I was a virgin youth when you snatched me from my mother's bosom and made a man of me, for which I am eternally grateful.' He gave her a sly smile. 'Will you not let me prove how grateful?'

Emma opened her mouth to protest but found it swiftly covered by Charles' red lips. The overwhelming feelings that his kiss produced in her were a timely reminder of how much sexual joy she had been deprived of since returning from Paris. Now she revelled in the sensual thrill as his tongue played cat-and-mouse with hers, one hand holding her close while the other stroked and clutched her buttocks beneath the layers of her clothes.

'Oh Emma, there is no woman to match you!' he breathed, his voice guttural with lust.

While his lips nibbled softly at her ear and neck, Charles began to undo the buttons of her blouse until the top of her chest was exposed. His mouth travelled down to the deep vee between her breasts, nuzzling the sensitive skin and sending electric impulses shooting up and down her spine. Emma could feel her legs weakening and, unwilling to let the love scene proceed where they might be interrupted by a servant, she pulled away from him and suggested they should move upstairs.

'Tell me you want me!' Charles demanded, his eyes red-rimmed with passion. 'I need to know that you really desire me, Emma, and are not just giving in out of pity.'

Emma was shocked. 'I *never* make love out of pity. Really, Charles, what an idea!'

'I am sorry. Sometimes I forget what a truly remarkable woman you are. One meets so many young women who are not at all like you.'

'That is the whole *raison d'être* of my Academy. But do you really wish to discuss the female condition right now? I rather think not!'

'No, let us proceed upstairs, my dear.'

At the door she paused, turning with a solemn expression. 'One moment. Do you undertake to let me do with you whatever I want?'

Charles said, with a mock bow, 'You may take complete charge of me, Emma. I am at your disposal.'

Laughingly she led him from the room and upstairs to her own bedroom. Emma had not forgotten that he was partial to a good thrashing. Neither had she forgotten that he and Kitty had had the temerity to mete out such punishment to *her*, when they were all three together in that same room. Well, she would make him pay now.

Emma made him strip and lie face down on her bed. Then she found two tasselled cords and tied first his ankles, then his hands behind his back just above his buttocks.

'There you are, trussed like a bird for the oven!' she chuckled.

'Whatever is your pleasure, Madame!'

'Oh, you'll pleasure me soon enough. Now be a good boy and lie there nice and quiet.'

Quickly Emma undressed and, sitting on the end of the bed, began to tickle the soles of his feet. Every time he squirmed and squealed she slapped the fat cheeks of his behind, making them wobble and blush, then returned to torment him saying, 'Lie still, you naughty boy, or I'll smack you again!'

Charles wriggled all the more, evidently enjoying the excruciating sensations of being first tickled then slapped. Emma knew, from the way he was groaning, that his libido was high and her own desires were being increased in the process. She began to pinch his buttocks, then dipped her hand between his tightly clenched thighs and felt the hairy balls beneath, making him writhe and giggle all the more. It excited her to see him getting so worked up. There was something of the concupiscent glee of the boys' dorm about it, the tussles and teasings, the masturbatory games after lights out. Mature as he was in years, she knew that Charles had never quite outgrown such pubescent pranks and she was happy to indulge him.

At last she managed to push him over onto his back, noting with satisfaction that he was displaying a fine erection. For the time being she ignored it, coming to sit on his chest with her knees level with his ears. She plumped up the pillows so that his head was at the right angle, then slid down until her vulva could be reached by his mouth.

197

'Now it's time to play licky-licky!' she smiled. 'Put that tongue to work and if you behave yourself we might play an even more exciting game afterwards.'

There was something very relaxing about having a man half immobilised, so that his mouth could do its work on her overheated pussy in isolation. Sometimes Emma grew tired of wandering hands and probing fingers. Sometimes all she wanted was this, the interaction of soft, wet flesh and the mingling of cool secretions. His tongue moved lazily around the delicate folds of her vulva, catlike and sensual, making her sigh with contentment as she entered a state of dreamy voluptuousness.

Emma leaned back supporting herself on her arms, thrusting her breasts into the air and tilting her pelvis upwards to allow him to penetrate her with the tip of his tongue. She felt her juices flow more freely in response to his ministrations and knew that she would soon be ready for something more stimulating, more focused. She could feel the prominent nub of her desire growing hard and demanding, knew that soon his gentle tonguing of her flesh would not be enough. But she could wait. For the time being she revelled in the pure satisfaction of putting his mouth to service, of having him rouse her without satisfying her so that she floated on a cloud of warm bliss without striving for more.

Dreamlike, Emma remained in that state for as long as it pleased her. She only became aware of the strain she was putting on herself, and on poor Charles' willing mouth, when her legs suddenly succumbed to an attack of pins and needles, obliging her to change position. She rose abruptly and rubbed her calves until the pains vanished.

'That will teach you!' Charles giggled from the bed. 'And my tongue has cramp, too!'

Emma still felt the warm throbbing between her legs, but now it was more insistent. She clambered up, this time over his thighs, and prepared to lower her thoroughly moistened quim over his turgid penis. Charles sighed with relief as their organs made contact, thrusting upward to facilitate her entry, and soon the pair were locked in joyous conjunction. Again, Emma found the restriction of his hands somehow freed her to enjoy their copulation even more, enabling her to do just as she liked with his eager phallus.

She rode it like a willing horse, now at a gentle amble, now rising to a trot, now at full gallop. Charles was evidently finding his restriction very arousing, the manacled wrists and ankles adding to his frustration so that his release, when it finally came, would be all the greater. He strained and heaved, groaning and sighing as she brought him achingly near the brink then, sensing that he was about to come, slowed right down again and dampened his ardour enough to keep him, and herself, going longer. Only when the destination began to seem more compelling than the journey did she let her homing instinct take over. Riding him hard until the first exquisite ripples of her climax became a seismic force, Emma felt the orgasm ripping through her with the strength of a cataclysm, turning the pair of them into one heaving, sweating animal and leaving her limp and exhausted.

She freed her lover from his bonds and they lay quietly, Charles with his arms and legs luxuriously outstretched. Emma felt satiated, but also sad. Why was it that Charles could not satisfy her as completely as Daniel? He was certainly the younger man. And in many ways he was the perfect lover: enthusiastic, experienced, sensual. Their affair had a past, although nowhere near as extensive as the sexual history she shared with Daniel, and at the moment it seemed to have a more promising future. Yet there was a certain vital dimension missing to their relationship. Try as she might, Emma could not put her finger on it. It was like trying to explain why a rose was more 'romantic' than, say, a hyacinth. When you had exhausted all the obvious factors of colour, shape and scent you were still left with a mystery.

Nevertheless, he was the best that was available to her for the time being and Emma was determined to make the most of her opportunities. She picked up the threads of her old acquaintance with the literary and artistic set, using Charles as her entrée, and attended some of the stimulating lectures that Virginia Stephen, Vanessa's intellectual sister, was giving at Morley College. Her affair with Charles was settling into a kind of routine. He would take her home after meetings and soirées, usually staying the night, and they had begun to see each other about three times a week.

One Saturday morning in July, Charles and Emma were making love with lazy insouciance after a late night, taking their time with each other and enjoying the fact that neither had any other pressing business to attend to, when there came an urgent hammering on the bedroom door. Emma sat bolt upright in alarm, pulling the sheets about her instinctively. Then a voice called, 'Emma, it's me, Kitty! Please open the door.'

'Oh, my God!'

She leapt from the bed and drew on a dressing-gown. Cautiously opening the door an inch or so, she peered out. Kitty looked pale and wan, her eyes peering out from her bleached face like two dark holes in a sheet. 'Kitty! What are you doing here? I thought you were still in Holloway!'

'They let me out on health grounds. I was taken bad with the 'flu.' She gave a hacking cough. 'It's gone to my chest, and I was keeping everyone awake with my coughing.'

Quickly Emma slid through the door, but not quickly enough. Kitty had managed to get a glimpse of the room beyond and its occupant. 'I'm sorry, Emma, I thought you were alone.' She became suddenly suspicious and pushed the door a little wider. 'I see!' she scowled, as Charles failed to dive beneath the bedclothes in time. Her tone became bitingly acerbic. 'You two wasted no time, did you? Thought I'd be safely locked up for another fortnight, I suppose. Well I shan't bother you any more. I'll go straight to my room and stay there.'

'Kitty, please don't think too badly of me . . .' Emma called, forlornly, after her retreating figure. But then, realising that apologies and explanations would seem fatuous, she went back into her bedroom and closed the door behind her.

'Oh Lord, we've done it now!' Charles exclaimed. 'I don't suppose she'll ever forgive us. She was in high dudgeon last time.'

'I must get Perkins to send up some beef tea or mutton broth.' Emma's feelings of shame and guilt were temporarily submerged beneath her concern for the invalid. 'Oh, and Doctor Moran must be summoned. Poor Kitty may have suffered badly under prison conditions or even contracted some dreadful ailment. If only she'd let me pay her fine!'

For the next few weeks Emma did her best to ensure that Kitty regained her health and strength, but relations were very strained between them. Whenever Emma entered the sick-room she felt unwelcome and, in the end, decided to stay away. Instead she would ask Milly, who had been given permission by Dr Moran to see her mother every day, for progress reports.

'Mamma is much better today, thank you Aunt Em,' came the response one day. 'She ate all of her jelly and took all her medicine, just as I did when I had the gripe. And when I read to her out of *Little Women* she said that Louisa May Alcott was a suffer-something, just like her. Aunty Em, what did she mean?'

Emma chuckled to herself. 'I suppose she meant "suffragette", dear. Your mother believes that women should have the right to vote, and I suppose Miss Alcott did too.'

'Are you a suffer ... one of those women, Aunt Emma?'

'Not really.'

'Don't you think women should be able to vote, like men?'

'Yes, I do.'

'Then you must be a suffer-gette, like Mamma!'

The child's remorseless logic was irrefutable. Emma

felt shamed. If only the issue were that simple. And yet for Kitty, just as for her young daughter, it *was*!

After a while Kitty began to leave the house and was often away overnight. Any approach from Emma was brusquely rebuffed, so she had no idea what was going on in her friend's life. Then, just as the summer vacation was beginning at the Academy, Kitty announced that she would be moving out. 'There is a flat with a room available, and I shall be sharing it with three fellow suffragettes. I need to be with them, Emma. There is so much work to be done.'

'What about Milly?' Emma said, coldly. 'I suppose you want me to go on looking after her here for you.'

'It will only be for a few more weeks. In September she will be starting at Cheltenham Ladies College. Vincent has agreed to pay her fees.'

Emma was horrified. The casual way in which Kitty had delivered the news, as if it were of no consequence to either of them, wounded her deeply. Although she had expected something of the sort to happen one day, she had not expected to be informed so brutally.

Even so, Emma strove to appear calm and rational. 'I am glad to hear she will have a good education,' she said, forcing a smile. 'Perhaps when she is finished at Cheltenham you would consider allowing her to attend the Academy.'

The look of disdain that contorted Kitty's features spoke volumes. 'I would not dream of it! If she does well at school I would expect her to go on to Oxford or Cambridge so that she can make something useful of her life, not learn how to become some rich man's whore!'

Her stinging remarks made Emma realise how deep the gulf had grown between them. Seeing there was no point in arguing, she shrugged and went on to speak of practicalities: did Kitty need help in transporting her possessions? Would she be visiting Milly on a regular basis? How could she be contacted in case of emergency? But beneath her calm exterior her heart was near to breaking.

Determined to make the most of her god-daughter's last weeks with her, Emma took her on visits in and around London. Charles had just bought himself a new automobile and drove them down to Brighton one day, much to Milly's delight. Yet, as they bowled along the country lanes Emma found it hard to explain, in answer to the girl's innocent enquiry, why they might not re-visit 'that big house in Yorkshire where that nice man with the other motor car lives.' As the date of Caroline Forbes' confinement drew nearer Emma found all her old jealousies and insecurities surfacing. It did not help that Daniel had been silent for ages.

At last the day of Milly's departure came. She looked so smart in her white blouse and navy serge skirt, her lovely auburn hair tied back with a large black bow instead of tumbling free in its usual profuse ringlets. Emma had paid for her to be photographed, and the photographer's boy arrived with the prints just as the girl was setting off for the station.

'Now I shall have something to remember you by,' Emma smiled, hiding her tears as she kissed her smooth cheek.

'May I have a photograph of you as well, Aunt Em?' Milly asked.

So Emma had to run upstairs and find one. She chose a wistful portrait of herself in an evening gown that she had posed for one Christmas at Daniel's request, and of which she had several prints. Milly was thrilled. 'I shall get a frame for it and place it by my bed, alongside Mamma's,' she smiled. 'And I promise to write to you at least once a month.'

Emma smiled bravely, waving as the girl and her mother went off in the cab, but as soon as they were out of sight she hurried back into the house with tears streaming down her face.

Mrs Perkins brought her a cup of tea. 'The house won't seem the same without that little madam!' the house-keeper observed. 'Never mind. They'll turn her into a proper lady in that posh school, won't they?'

I hope not! Emma thought, with a wry smile.

To fill this third great gap in her daily life, Emma turned to Charles and his 'Bloomsbury Set'. She began to read more, enjoying *Where Angels Fear to Tread*, the first novel of Morgan Forster who frequented Gordon Square, subscribing to the *Athanaeum* magazine, and even tackling the *Principia Ethica* of George Moore, who stressed the 'pleasures of human intercourse and the enjoyment of beautiful objects' – a philosophy which Emma found most congenial. Soon, instead of sitting on the sidelines during the intellectual discussions, she felt increasingly confident about contributing to them.

One evening, when a group was gathered in Vanessa's study in the Gordon Square house, someone brought up the topic of Women's Suffrage. An argument ensued about the word 'suffrage'.

'Surely it comes from "suffer" in the sense of "to allow", doesn't it?' Clive Bell said, as if there could be no further dispute.

'As in "Suffer little children", you mean?' Vanessa smiled.

'I rather think not,' said someone called Bertrand – or was it Bernard? – with an air of authority. 'There are two possible Latin derivations for *suffragium*. One is from *suffrago*, ankle-bone, the other is from *suffringere*, to break, as in a potsherd. Both were used as tokens for voting.'

'But what of *women's* suffrage, as a concept?' Virginia insisted. 'People seem to have conveniently forgotten that many men are deprived of the franchise too.'

'*Hodie mihi, cras tibi*,' laughed Charles. 'Where the women lead today, the men will follow tomorrow!'

'What do you think, Emma?' Vanessa asked, suddenly. 'More precisely, what do your young ladies think on this issue?'

'I am sure they have varying opinions, but I try to instil a spirit of independence in them. I believe women can influence events, but that their power is best employed behind the scenes rather than in public. A woman who struts and rants like a politician is, I believe, abhorrent to both sexes.'

'Well said!' laughed the Latin scholar adding, tongue in cheek, 'Women reign supreme only where they are most appreciated – in the bedroom!'

'Since "bed" and "board" go together, perhaps women also have a place in the boardroom!' Virginia joked, to much applause.

Emma felt exhilarated, as she always did, by the conversation of these people. They seemed to bounce words and ideas off each other like a hectic game of verbal tennis. Sometimes she wondered if they were more interested in playing with words than in finding the truth, but they were entertaining company and a general air of benevolence prevailed at their gatherings. Their rarefied world offered a welcome respite from the humdrum and an escape from the loneliness she felt whenever she thought about Kitty, Milly or Daniel. But as the Academy's term proceeded she had less time to spend with them.

Nevertheless Emma was keen to return their hospitality by inviting them to tea at Brunswick Square. She asked Virginia when they met by chance in the British Museum.

'Oh, your invitation is timely, Emma! Just lately, having exhausted all other topics of conversation, we have begun to talk about sex. Unfortunately, given the predilections of several of our number, all we ever seem to discuss the ins and outs of, so to speak, is buggery. Poor Vanessa and I have to endure all the ups and downs of the buggers' love affairs until we long for some plain "boy meets girl" romance. I have even been tempted to write the "Great Romantic Novel" as an antidote to Sods' Lore! It will be enormously refreshing to hear how you educate your young ladies in the amorous arts, for a change!'

They arrived *en masse* one wet Sunday afternoon in October and the house was soon filled with pleasant chat and warm laughter, lifting Emma's spirits. After she had described the purpose of her Academy and the more specific instruction she gave to her select few, Virginia insisted on seeing a copy of her 'special syllabus', the details of which she read out to the others amidst hoots of laughter.

'*How to tell if a man is interested in you*. Well, I suppose you keep an eye on his trousers! *How to keep a man interested in you: The Art of Flirting without seeming to.* Hm! This is dangerous stuff, Emma. If this document were to turn up in the Carlton Club or Brooks's your girls would be sunk!'

'I think not,' Emma smiled. 'One may know the rules of tennis inside out and still play an interesting game.'

'But only if you keep your eye on the ball!' Vanessa giggled.

Her sister came in on cue. 'Or shuttlecock, if one plays with a battledore! Mind you, the mating game is all a racket!'

'Enough of your cock and ball story!' giggled one of the 'buggers', and the conversation degenerated into a dreadful series of puns that had them all groaning. Emma was always surprised by the ease with which they could be discussing matters of grave import or philosophical complexity one minute, and be rolling around in adolescent glee at their own silliness the next.

After tea, the tone grew more serious since the topic under discussion was the latest exploit of the suffragettes. They had been arrested at Central Hall and classed as second division prisoners, and their plight had caused much public debate. The latest news was that they had finally been granted 'first division' status.

Emma did not know whether Kitty was amongst those imprisoned or not. She had almost completely lost touch with her, and it was very painful, but somehow she could not bring herself to make the first move and regain contact. Yet she did not believe that it was her affair with Charles that had really caused the rift. It was politics, rather than love, that had come between them.

Throughout the afternoon Emma was aware of

Charles' eyes upon her, knew that he was waiting for the others to leave so that he could have her all to himself. Just lately Emma had felt herself beginning to tire of him, although she could not bring herself to tell him so. She had sometimes pretended to be otherwise engaged when he had called, or not answered his letters, and when they were together she often felt detached and distanced from him. The strange thing was that her air of indifference seemed to encourage him all the more, as if he preferred to find her unapproachable. It had occurred to her that she was only maintaining their affair because it gave her access to the company of others, but with no other lover in prospect she felt lazily inclined to maintain the status quo.

Almost as soon as the last guest was out of the house, Charles took her roughly in his arms in the drawing-room. 'Emma, you look wonderful in that tea-gown!' he declared, running his hands over the sea-green silk that swathed her breasts. 'I have wanted to kiss you all afternoon. I don't remember a word anyone said, I only had thoughts of you!'

'What a shame!' Emma mocked, turning the handle of the Victrola. Soon the strains of 'The Last Rose of Summer' filled the room. 'I was reflecting on the nature of progress and the importance of equality between the sexes in bringing about true social reform.'

'I'll show you who's equal!' Charles declared, pressing his lips firmly to hers and thrusting his tongue between them.

Emma weakened, letting him guide her over to the chaise longue where they collapsed together. His head was soon delving beneath her underskirt and she felt the softness of his lips upon the sensitive skin of her inner thighs, making her melt and sigh. She lay back in a languid pose, aware of his slow progress up her legs and towards her crotch, confident that soon he would be giving her the satisfaction she craved.

At last his fingers undid the buttons that secured her knickers and Emma felt them being eased down over her hips exposing the damp bush within. He gasped out his gratification as his fingers found her moist and receptive to his touch, the folded flesh already hot and swollen with desire. Yet she herself lay passive, indifferent. He had told her before that he found the contrast between her listless state of mind and the wanton readiness of her pussy incredibly arousing. It didn't seem to matter how she was feeling – bored, irritated, tired – Charles continued to find her irresistibly appealing. It was almost as if her sex organs had a life and identity of their own as far as he was concerned.

Now he was referring to her pudendum in the third person. 'I know what little pussikin wants,' he cooed. 'A good licking, that's what. She'll feel much better soon.'

Emma looked down at the absurd spectacle of a man's head disappearing up her skirt and wanted to giggle. As soon as his mouth found her projecting clitoris, however, she settled back with a comfortable sigh and let him get on with it.

The slow ascent towards orgasm begun, Emma was listening to the last chorus of the song that issued from the Victrola when the door was suddenly opened. Startled, she turned her head towards it and was horrified to see Daniel entering the room. 'I knocked, Emma, but the gramophone was on so you . . .'

His voice faltered and his eyes started almost out of his head. Suddenly realising there was a third party present, Charles popped up from beneath her skirt with a scarlet face and the two men confronted each other, both of them too shocked to speak. Emma smoothed down her skirt and rose from the sofa with as much dignity as she could muster, trying hard to remain in control of the situation. 'I think you had better leave, Charles,' she said, unable to look either of them in the eye.

When the two of them were alone, Daniel exploded. 'I thought I told you not to entertain your arty-crafty friends here, Emma! I don't want them in my house. I detest that type!'

'You are being unreasonable,' she said, coldly.

'I think not. If you wish to see those people you can meet them on their own ground. Perkins told me you had a whole crowd of them here this afternoon. I won't have it!'

Emma stared at him, near to tears. She had longed so ardently to see him again, but now that he was standing before her his face was contorted with anger. Although all her instincts were telling her to appease him, she could not allow him to rule her so completely.

'We shall talk about it when you have calmed down, Dan. Shall I send for some tea?'

His answer was to stride over and grasp her brutally round the waist. She saw the glittering hardness in his dark eyes, smelt the alcohol on his breath, sensed the primitive energy flowing through him, and flinched. Surely he would not hurt her?

'I can think of something I would rather drink,' he muttered, his voice thick with some cruel distortion of lust. 'Are your juices still running where that toad was kissing you? Are you still hot and wet down there, Emma?'

She was shocked by the naked jealousy in his gaze, the blatant hunger for her. Seldom had she seen him in this state, and her instinct was to ring for help from below stairs. Yet Emma was fascinated by his aggressive manner and, while she hesitated, he struck. Pushing her back onto the chaise longue he pulled up her skirt and petticoat and pulled off her knickers so violently that the buttons were scattered. Then, ignoring her feeble cries, his mouth fastened onto her still-throbbing vulva and he began to suck vigorously, as if to obliterate all traces of his predecessor's saliva.

Daniel was attacking her tender parts with his mouth as if she were a fruit to be sucked dry. Emma felt his mouth covering the entire area, his tongue stabbing insistently into the opening at the centre and his teeth grazing her swollen clitoris, making her moan with a sensuality that was perilously close to pain. His hands were gripping her thighs hard, keeping them apart, forcing her to submit to his wilful lust.

Soon she could feel him fumbling with his clothes and knew that he was going to enter her, to take her as abruptly and ruthlessly as he had years ago, in a Florentine cloister. The memory of it made Emma shudder with dark excitement. Yet while Daniel had then been fuelled by pure desire, now she sensed that other emotions had been called into play: jealousy, guilt, and a kind of desperation that had been festering in him since his marriage.

Daniel thrust deep into her with his rigid cock, probing the open, vulnerable core of her being as if he were conducting a primitive investigation of her innermost thoughts and feelings. Even while her body was going through the familiar routine of arousal Emma felt her privacy was being invaded, that he was asserting himself with no regard for her. Resentfully she lay in passive compliance, detached from what was happening to her, indifferent to the way her flesh was responding to the insistent battering.

They had reached some opposite pole in their relationship, a deep antagonism that was destroying their mutual trust, and she could do nothing to stop it. Yet while Daniel appeared to be overpowering her with his fierce virility, Emma knew that, at some more subtle level, victory was hers. She would not come for him. Although she had no control over the swelling and moistening of her tissues, she could hold back from giving him that ultimate satisfaction and the proof of her own.

Daniel was breathing raggedly, staring down at her with a desperate glint in his eye as he rammed his penis home, time after time, willing her to give in to him. Emma stared back impassively, hating him for spoiling the reunion she had longed for. What they were now engaged in seemed like a parody of love, a mocking charade of sexual intercourse. He was striving to wrest her orgasm from her, like a prize, but she held the pent-up energy tight within her and would not let it go.

On and on the pounding went until Emma could feel her clammy stockings sticking to her thighs and her breasts were on fire beneath her stifling clothes. Daniel was snarling at her like a wild beast, cursing her between gasps, but still she would not give in. She wanted him to know what it was like to hunger for something, or someone, he could not have. She wanted to punish him for all those lonely days and lonelier nights, when she'd longed for him to uplift her with his presence and fill her empty heart with loving bliss.

The exertion was telling on him. Looking up, Emma could see the distorted tendons in his neck, the straining jaw and look of desperation in his eye. He resembled a warrior more than a lover. A part of her wanted to laugh at him, he seemed so ridiculous in his striving for male supremacy, and yet she dared not ridicule him openly, acknowledging that he had real physical power over her. Her tender parts felt raw and bruised but still she endured his relentless onslaught, determined to win in this terrible battle of wills.

Then, to her intense relief, she heard him give an explosive gasp and felt the potent gushing spray her insides. Her vagina closed over him like a vice, squeezing the life-force out of his deflating penis as if it were her due, and making him squirm and cry out. For a while she continued to hold him, feeling his organ grown soft and useless yet unable to move out of her grip. Daniel lay to one side of her, exhausted, grim-faced. He seemed oblivious to the fact that she still had him in her clutches, but when she at last let him flop out he gave a loud sigh.

Emma knew that if she continued to lie beside him her tender instincts would return and she would want to be reconciled with him, but he had hurt her too badly for that. She rose from the chaise longue, smoothing down her skirts and left him there alone while she went to her room. Sooner or later she knew she must confront him again, but just then she needed to be alone with her feelings.

Emma stripped to her chemise and cleaned herself at the wash-stand in her bedroom. Despite the fact that Daniel was still in the house she felt desolate and alone. Paris now seemed a faded memory; since then she had felt alternately neglected and abused by him. Marriage had changed him in a way she couldn't understand. The old trust had gone, to be replaced by hostility and suspicion. Emma felt he was punishing her – but for what?

Scarcely had she finished her toilet than there came a peremptory knock at her door, followed by Daniel's coldly polite request. 'Emma, please let me in. I wish to talk to you.'

At least he is observing the proprieties, she thought bleakly. She went over and opened the door. He regarded her impassively, his eyes blank, unreadable. Emma retreated to the bed, where she sat in her dressing-gown waiting for him to speak.

'I make no apology for what happened just now,' he began. 'I was incensed by your disobedience and, on reflection, I realise that I cannot let you go unpunished this time.'

The words were an echo of previous pleasures, when they might have been a cue for some mild flagellation as a prelude to further teasing games. Yet something in his tone told her that this time it was different. Everything seemed altered now, the present a travesty of the past. She waited in trepidation for him to continue.

'So I have decided to terminate your residency in this house. You may have until the end of December to make your plans. After that I shall be selling the property.'

Emma gaped at him, horrified beyond belief. How could he do this to her, and so callously? Then anger took over, propelling her from the bed to stand before him, shaking. 'How dare you?' she growled. 'You said I could stay here until the end of my days!'

'Provided you behaved yourself. But I will not tolerate

that riff-raff. Since I cannot trust you not to invite them here, then you must go.'

'I see, so it's Daniel the Autocrat now, is it? Who have you been practising on, your wife?'

The slap caught her on the side of her nose and made it bleed. Emma rushed, gasping, for a towel to stem the flow but Daniel just stood there. Helplessly she felt the tears begin to roll, mingling with the blood. She knew she was being weak, but she had no defences left against him. He had cut the ground from under her.

'Times change,' she heard him say, his voice almost a monotone. 'People change. I have other responsibilities now. But I will not throw you out without a penny. I recognise that you have been important to me in the past, and deserve some compensation. You may have a lump sum or a small pension, whichever you prefer.'

'I don't want your money!' she snorted.

'Don't be a fool, Emma! When you leave here you will have to pay rent for the first time in your life. And if you wish to continue with your Academy you must find new premises.'

'The Academy!' Emma stared at him in dismay, the bloody towel still in her hand. She had taken the blow personally, not thinking of the full consequences. 'So you would ruin my business too, would you?'

'That is not my intention. Think clearly, and you will see that this could be to your advantage. You could find a building more suited to your purposes. This house was never ideal.'

She knew he was right. Since there were always more applicants for the Academy than she could take, Emma had often wanted to expand. Perhaps a larger building would be the answer. Wearily she returned to the bed and lay down, her head thumping. Daniel relaxed enough to sit in the armchair and a melancholy calm pervaded the room. Emma thought of Lily, and how she had been 'pensioned off' by her rich lover. How naive she had been to imagine that she could never be in the same position!

'By December, you say,' she murmured, forcing herself to think practically as a refuge from the welter of emotions that threatened to overwhelm her.

'I think that is fair. You will be able to give parents of pupils two months' notice. Of course, I am prepared to recompense you for your loss.'

Emma thought, what of my personal loss? There could be no recompense for that. She lay silent, thinking of their past joys and how she would never experience them again. Through the mist of tears she saw him as he now was, grizzled and balding, yet still with something of his old fiery attraction for her, and dared to ask, forlornly, 'Why have you done this to me?'

'You betrayed me, by choosing lovers and companions who are unworthy of you.'

'Nonsense! You have never shown such jealousy or possessiveness before!'

'I told you, people change. I expected you to show more dignity now that you . . .'

'Now I am past it, is that what you are trying to tell me?'

He shrugged. 'We are neither of us young any more, Emma. My life has altered its course, and if you had any sense you would see that yours does too. Why not find yourself a husband, someone who could be a steadying influence on you and give you security in your old age?'

Summoning all her dignity, Emma rose from the bed and stood before him like a battle-weary Boadicea, bloodied but unbowed. 'You want someone to take me off your hands, is that it? Well, you may no longer be the old Daniel but I can assure you I am still the old Emma. Now please leave me alone. I must think about my future plans. I will speak to you about the financial settlement another time.'

Sensing that there was no more to be said for the time being, Daniel did as he was bid. Emma opened the window to give herself some air, looking down onto the green lawns and flower beds below where she had spent so many pleasant summer afternoons, but she did not weep. Instead a great weariness overtook her. Was this really to be the end of everything she had known for the past ten years? Everyone seemed to be deserting her and the Academy, too, was in jeopardy. How could she find the strength to carry on?

Then she remembered Lily's words, on her last visit to Paris: 'When people say you are too old, or too ugly, for love do not heed them, Emma dear. Seek it out for as long as you can, enjoy life and love to the full. Then, if at last you can attract no more lovers, at least you will have a rich harvest of memories to succour you in your old age.'

At the time those words had seemed mere empty philosophising but now, only a few months later, they had begun to ring true.

Chapter Fourteen

*T*he only close friend that Emma seemed to have left over the following weeks was Charles Purchase. When he heard about Daniel's ultimatum he was outraged on her behalf.

'But, damn the man, he cannot turn you out on the street like that after all these years!'

'He can, and will,' Emma sighed. 'At least I have been given some notice. But I've had to inform parents that the Academy will close at Christmas. It is so humiliating!'

'If there is anything I can do to help, my dear . . .'

'Thank you, Charles.' She smiled at him as he sat at the foot of the chaise longue. He took her hand and kissed it, then his lips followed on up her arm, brushing against the downy hairs beneath the loose sleeve of the silk kimono that he had brought her back from Paris.

For Emma there was not even the slightest *frisson* of desire, although she knew that his blood was roused and, if she had consented, he would have taken her right there and then on the sofa. But gone was the eager spirit ever ready to embrace a lover, the heart that sang in response to a kiss, the womb that danced in anticipation of bliss. Emma did not know whether her old enthusiasm for love would ever return, and she would never give in to him out of pity.

'Why do you think he has turned against you?' Charles frowned. 'Surely not simply because he found you with me? He's always known you had other lovers, or so you said.'

'Yes, I've never had any secrets from him.' Emma gave out a long sigh. 'I can only surmise that it has to do with his marriage. You know his wife expects a child soon?'

'You did mention it. But why should that affect you?'

'Sometimes I think it may be that he feels he has betrayed me in settling down to be a husband and father, or that he has vented his anger on me because he feels ashamed of his past. He has become quite respected in Yorkshire society, you know, marrying a local girl and putting a great deal of money into his business and estate. I suppose that having a mistress in London no longer suits his new rôle of gentleman industrialist.'

'There must be more to it than that, Emma. You say he wishes to sell this house? Maybe money is the cause. It generally is.'

Emma shrugged. 'The plain fact is that my life with Daniel is over and my days here are numbered. The sooner I start to make new plans the better.'

She smiled sweetly at him, but inside she felt bleak and alone. Was she going to have to let Charles go, too, just because she could no longer give him what he wanted? If she gave him the slightest encouragement she had the feeling that he would marry her, but that was not on her agenda. Once she had believed that her husband, Sir Henry, would endure a childless marriage for her sake, but she had been wrong. Then she had thought that Daniel was prepared to give up everything for her, but now she found he was not. She would not make that mistake a third time.

Once Emma had announced that the autumn term would be the last for the time being, she became determined to give her current crop of young ladies the best possible guidance before they left. She made a pact with herself to get all six of her favourites matched up by Christmas.

217

The select group was gathered in the drawing-room of the Academy one late October afternoon to read their essays on 'My Ideal Man'. Last to reveal her dreams was Lucy Meyer. Emma had a soft spot for the shy brunette with the look of a wide-eyed gazelle. Under her tuition she had seen the girl flower, become more sensually aware. Yet there was something intensely vulnerable about her, and Emma feared for her future.

Lucy began to describe her perfect beau. 'I truly believe that beauty resides in a man's soul, not just in his body,' she began, introducing a more philosophical note into the proceedings than the previous girls, whose essays had more in common with shopping lists. 'I was orphaned, and when I come of age I shall be a wealthy woman in my own right so I must take care not to become the prey of bounty hunters. I would like a caring and experienced lover, but he must also be a man of artistic sensibility, who is as moved as I am by beautiful paintings or stirring music. Perhaps he will be an artist himself, or at least frequent artistic circles . . .'

Suddenly Emma had a flash of inspiration. She *knew* the perfect man for Lucy, knew him intimately, and would be overjoyed to see him wed this exquisitely sensitive young woman. It would be a love match, she was sure of that. For while many men were able to appreciate Lucy Meyer's type of female beauty, he was also a connoisseur of beauty in the arts.

Furthermore, she was in an ideal position to bring the pair together. While Lucy went on to describe her dream suitor's sunny disposition and ardent nature, almost as if she had that same individual in mind, Emma laid her plans.

The first priority was to make them known to each other, so Emma sent a note to Charles Purchase asking him to call on her at tea-time tomorrow as a matter of urgency. She knew that when he arrived she would be with her girls, but that was all part of her plan. Promptly at four-thirty Mrs Perkins knocked at the door of the

218

library, where Emma was reading extracts from Cleland's *Memoirs of a Woman of Pleasure* to her young ladies.

'So sorry to interrupt, ma'am,' the housekeeper began nervously, since she'd been told not to intrude on that class unless absolutely necessary. 'But Mr Purchase is in the drawing room.'

'Oh dear! I cannot come straight away.' Emma looked around the circle with a feigned air of disquiet before picking out Lucy, apparently at random. 'Lucy, dear, would you be awfully kind and keep my visitor company for a few minutes, while I finish off the discussion?'

Lucy's calm expression grew troubled. 'Oh, Miss Emma, must I?'

Emma raised her brows. 'I thought you would be pleased at the opportunity to put into practice what we discussed last week!'

The reference to 'The Subtle Art of Flirtation' was not lost on the other girls, who giggled.

'Very well, but I have no idea what to say to him.'

'Remember our lesson on 'The Art of Pleasant Conversation', Lucy? Today you may begin with apologies on my behalf.'

'Yes, Miss Emma.' Her doe-like brown eyes still looked worried.

'Now run along, do. You must not keep either Mrs Perkins or my visitor waiting.'

Shepherded by the housekeeper, Lucy left the room. Emma gave the book to Mabel to read, but her mind was elsewhere. In her imagination the door of the drawing-room was opening to reveal that young vision of loveliness in her pale lilac dress and glossy dark tresses, hair that would not submit entirely to the restrictions of pins and clips, *tournure* frames or wavy rolls, but insisted on giving forth creeping tendrils to add a look of enchanting dishevelment to her otherwise immaculate appearance.

Knowing that Charles would instantly be taken with her, she imagined him making conversation while poor, nervous Lucy blushed and cleared her throat, speaking barely above a whisper. Of course that would endear her to him all the more. He would invite her to sit down and watch the coltish grace with which she took her seat, taking in the pretty curves of her high breasts and her slim waist. If he asked what she had just been studying she would blush again and mumble, but he would declare that he had read the work and pronounce it a 'damn fine read' without batting an eyelid.

Gradually, Lucy would lose some of her gaucheness and even smile at one of his feeble jokes, showing her perfect white teeth. Heartened by this Charles would tease her – something about the curriculum at the Academy being more liberal than that of Harrow, perhaps. Emma glanced at the clock on the mantelpiece and decided to make her move. She bade Helen take over when Diana reached the end of the page and left the room.

The scene in the drawing-room was almost exactly as she had pictured it. Charles stood by the window, legs apart and hands behind his back, while Lucy sat on the edge of her chair, flushed and excited, her dark eyes sparkling with amusement at something he had just said.

'I am so sorry, Charles, but I could not leave the girls right away,' she explained as she swept in. 'I hope you have been recompensed by having Lucy's company for a few minutes.'

'Yes, indeed!' he said, emphatically, as Lucy rose awkwardly from her chair. 'Miss Meyer was just telling me about the reading list you gave them. It sounds extremely . . . edifying!'

'I try to widen their horizons a little! You may go now, Lucy. Thank you for your help.'

Was she mistaken, or did she see a flash of disappointment in the girl's dark eyes as she turned to leave?

'You might have left us alone a bit longer, Em,' Charles complained, only half jokingly. 'Charming girl, absolutely charming. Where do you find them, I wonder? Such gems are never to be found at any of the social gatherings I attend these days.'

' "She dwelt among the untrodden ways" . . .'

'What's that?'

'Wordsworth, one of the "Lucy" poems. I thought it appropriate. "A Maid whom there were none to praise, and very few to love".'

'Surely not! A lovely young lady like that must have many admirers.'

Emma sighed. 'I'm afraid not.' Sudden inspiration struck. 'She is a penniless orphan, you see, brought up by a crusty old guardian. Hardly a "catch" in today's mercenary society. But I am doing my best. Since she has been with me her gradual discovery of the secret pleasures of being a woman has been a joy to behold.'

'A man should be teaching her such things, not you Em.' It was how he often chaffed her.

'I agree entirely. However, since no man is available I must prepare her as best I can for eventual marriage, since that is what her guardian expects. Heaven knows what will become of her when the Academy closes in December! Still, enough about Lucy. I have a confession to make. It seems I have summoned you here under false pretences.'

'Any pretence will do for me to come here, you know that.'

'Thank you, Charles, but that is not what I meant. I asked you to come because someone told me that Kitty was amongst those arrested at Central Hall. I wanted you to accompany me to the prison, as I could not bear to go there alone.'

'Of course I would . . .'

'It is all right, thank you Charles, the rumour proved to be false. Since then I have heard that the supporters of the imprisoned women are planning a grand banquet at the Savoy Hotel when they are released. Would you credit it? Mr Bernard Shaw has been invited. I wonder if they will pander to his strange diet or whether he must bring his own nuts!'

Charles laughed heartily, and they resumed their easy familiarity with each other, yet there was still a certain spark missing. It is Lucy who can light his fire now, Emma thought wistfully. Yet she had already sown the seeds and she was determined to see them bear fruit.

It was time to move quickly, while each was still interested in the other. Emma was well aware that since she was denying Charles her sexual favours he might look elsewhere, and she would rather he looked in Lucy's direction. She asked his advice about whether the Pre-Raphaelite exhibition at the Tate Gallery would be suitable for her young ladies and, as she'd hoped, he offered to accompany them and give them the benefit of his knowledge on the subject. Of course Lucy was one of the three chosen to attend.

'What a charming couple they make!' Emma thought, seeing the pair set apart from the others as they viewed a particular painting. She had, of course, been quick to distract the attention of the others so that they might enjoy their few moments of private intercourse.

Afterwards she was rewarded by Charles saying, 'Such a fine appreciation of the Arts young Lucy seems to possess. Much of it instinctive, of course, but none the worse for that.'

'Yes, she is an intuitive creature,' Emma remarked, adding casually, 'I have often found that the more intuitive a woman is, the more sensually aware she turns out to be.'

As for Lucy, she had begun to blush at the very mention of Mr Purchase's name.

More had to be done to bring the would-be lovers together on a more intimate basis. Emma heard that there would be a special 'double bill' showing of the American film, 'The Great Train Robbery', at the Empire Theatre, Leicester Square, together with a new British adventure called 'Rescued by Rover'. Knowing that many of her young ladies had never experienced the wonders of the Cinematograph, Emma invited all who were prepared to pay the shilling entrance fee to attend. Casually she mentioned to Charles that she would be taking a party of five on Saturday afternoon, if he would care to accompany them.

It was a tricky matter to ensure that Lucy sat next to Charles at the end of the row but, somehow, Emma managed it. She had seen film before and was taking a calculated risk that Lucy would be so terrified by the sight of trains puffing and dogs leaping with life-like alacrity all over the screen that she would seek reassurance from his manly presence.

The lights were dimmed, the first fearsome images appeared shakily above them, and Emma saw by the flickering glow that her ruse had worked. While the other girls gasped and screamed, Lucy clung to Charles' arm in terror until she realised that the locomotive was not actually going to smother them with steam, neither were the robbers going to fill them with lead. Soon she relaxed and began to laugh, but Emma noted with great satisfaction that she kept tight hold of Charles' arm throughout and, several times, he patted her hand.

Later, when all her charges had been safely dispatched to their various homes, Emma and Charles sat alone in the drawing room at Brunswick Square. Suddenly she said, 'You are quite smitten with Lucy, aren't you Charles? Don't try to deny it. I have been watching the pair of you all afternoon. I think she feels the same way about you.'

The look on his face was part hang-dog, part relief, part anxiety. 'Forgive me, Emma, but I cannot help admiring that young woman. Of course, I wouldn't dream of taking it further.'

'Why not?'

He gazed at her with incredulity. 'Well because I am sure it would upset you, of course!'

'Charles, it would not upset me in the slightest,' she told him, gravely. 'On the contrary.'

'Emma! What are you saying?'

He was practically at her feet, his eyes searching hers with a strange desperation. This was the moment she had been dreading, the point where she must give him up for the sake of the younger woman. Despite the fact that she no longer wanted him, she could not help feeling nostalgic for their former passion.

Tenderly she took his hand and kissed it. 'Charles, you have been a great help to me in these past trying weeks, but it must have been obvious to you that our love affair, such as it was, is over. Now I wish to be as good a friend to you, and see you find happiness with someone else. I think Lucy would be the ideal young woman to give you that happiness.'

It was a relief to end her painful speech. Her reward was to see grateful tears spring into Charles' grey eyes. 'Oh, Emma, I wish . . .'

She put a finger to his lips. 'Hush, dear, let us not have any regrets. I would rather talk about the future – your future. Tell me, you are not averse to marriage on principle, are you?'

'No, I suppose not. I thought I might wed some day, but I have been in no hurry.'

'Then I think you should act quickly, as far as young Lucy is concerned. She is susceptible to your charms, I know that, but once she leaves the Academy your opportunities to meet her may be restricted. I will do what I can, but you must press your suit if you are to win her.'

'I'm sure you are right. Oh, Emma, what a gem you are to do all this for me!'

She did not tell him what she secretly suspected, that she had taken on this project as a challenge that would distract her from the aching emptiness of a life without Daniel.

A week later, quite out of the blue, Emma had a letter from one of her former pupils, Bella, Lady Sandborn. Thanks to Emma's 'social godmothering' Bella had married Lord Sandborn of Moorvale. They had kept up an intermittent correspondence, but now Emma was invited to attend a Christmas house party at Dulcombe Park, near Exmoor.

'*Do come,*' Bella pleaded in her letter. '*I find all the talk of shooting and fishing so tedious. I would far rather gossip about the guests with you, dear Emma! If you wish to bring any friends we can accommodate two more, but please let me know soon.'*

She realised at once that this would be the perfect opportunity to bring Charles and Lucy together once and for all. Both seemed keen to accompany her when they knew the other was going. And if Emma had any lingering doubts about Lucy's feelings, they were dispelled when she caught the girl sitting in the library one morning with a dreamy look on her face and a writing pad on her knee. Glancing down, Emma realised she'd been composing some poetry.

'May I see, Lucy?' she enquired.

Although she was flushing bright pink, Lucy gave up her poem for scrutiny.

The Thief

> *My Love steals glances from me,*
> *He fills me full of bliss,*
> *How long must this, my song be –*
> *When will 'he' steal a kiss?*
>
> *My Love steals whispers from me,*
> *Wounds me with Cupid's dart,*
> *How long must this, my song, be –*
> *When will 'he' steal my heart?*

Although Lucy would never make the first poetess laureate, her feelings were plainly expressed in the simple verse and Emma had no need to ask who 'he' was.

Soon Emma was speaking equally plainly to Charles. 'You must ask her guardian for permission to propose to her at once,' she declared. 'I will give you his Chelsea address. He is in his dotage now and will be glad to get her off his hands.'

She suspected that the old tyrant would indeed be relieved to see his duty discharged. He had told Emma that he relied on her to see that any suitor had Lucy's best interests at heart and he would accept anyone she recommended, since he did not want to be bothered with the vetting of candidates.

Charles returned triumphant from his visit to Chelsea. He went to Garrards and bought a magnificent diamond ring, which he planned to present to Lucy during the house party. Emma was very pleased, but only part of her goal would be accomplished by their engagement. She needed to be sure that her protégée would be awakened sexually by her lover with tender care, enjoying all those sweet fruits of love that Emma had often described in her classes.

Even so, she found it strangely embarrassing to raise the matter with her former lover. Although she knew his amatory style inside out, and was sure that he would be considerate towards his virgin sweetheart, Emma could not bring herself to speak of it outright. He would take it for granted that Lucy was more knowledgeable than most young women of her age, having had a term at the Academy, but she did hope he would not be expecting too much. She was still a shy, sensitive little thing that needed careful handling.

They travelled down to Exeter by train in bleak weather and were met by an ancient Brougham. The ride across the moor was rough, but when they finally arrived at the large, grey house Bella welcomed them all warmly. Emma was glad to see her old pupil looking so happy.

They were introduced to the tall, gauche figure of David, Lord Sandborn, then Emma and Lucy were given adjoining rooms and offered the services of a lady's maid. While her clothes were being unpacked and Lucy was resting, Emma joined her hostess. When they were alone in the library, Bella confided that she had taken a lover from amongst the local gentry.

'His name is Richard, and he is so passionate! I married David for his wealth and title, but – Oh, Emma! – I am with Richard for love. David is sweet and kind but he is so very . . . English. Public school, and all that.

Of course I would never do anything to hurt him, but I must have my secret pleasure too. David thinks that now he has sired two sons he need not bother with that side of our marriage, which has become completely platonic.'

'I wish you well,' Emma smiled. She was glad that Bella was living out the philosophy she tried to instil into her girls, that they should never compromise on their own happiness.

After dinner that night Emma found time to listen to some of Bella's 'secrets' and also met her lover, dashing Sir Richard Parwell, but her mind kept leaping forward to the Christmas Eve Ball and the aftermath that she had planned for her two love-birds. If all went well, she would also be privy to their first night of passion.

The following day was mostly taken up with preparations for the evening. While the men went off for some shooting, the ladies conserved their energies for the dancing. After tea, Emma offered to help Lucy dress, as the maid was hard pressed. She went next door in her dressing gown and found her young friend just emerging from the bathtub.

'Come, you will catch your death of cold!' Emma warned, picking up a large towel to drape around her slim form. She had a brief glimpse of the girl's body: skin pale and translucent as alabaster, with only two soft pink buds and a neat black delta to break the even whiteness of her skin. Her waist was tiny, no more than a man's handspan, and although her breasts were not large they were beautifully high and round.

Soon she was dry and in her chemise, the rest of her underwear and her pretty cream taffeta ball gown with the diamond jewellery that had been her mother's spread out on her bed. But she seemed nervous and apprehensive.

'What is the matter, Lucy?' Emma asked, softly. 'Aren't you looking forward to tonight?'

'Yes, of course. But I cannot help wondering if Charles

227

will wish to dance with me. There will be so many other pretty young ladies present.'

Emma laughed. 'I can assure you, Lucy, that he will only have eyes for you!'

She was right, of course. As soon as they entered the grand ballroom, lit by a dozen large chandeliers, Charles approached with an air of reverence and offered Lucy his arm.

'Please will you do me the honour of this dance?' he asked, solemnly.

Although Emma danced with a half a dozen local gentry that night her eyes were always upon the happy couple and when she saw them sneak off together into a side room she knew that the great moment had come. They emerged some minutes later with Lucy looking radiant, a diamond glinting on her left hand.

Of course Emma had to feign ignorance, but the minute she sat down near the buffet Lucy came up, her sweet face wreathed in smiles. 'He has asked me to marry him!' she said, breathlessly. 'See my gorgeous ring!'

'Congratulations! I am so happy for you, Lucy dear. And that is a most wonderful gem. May I see? Would you mind if I tried it on?'

Lucy willingly took off the ring and gave it to Emma, who fumbled and exclaimed in mock horror, 'Oh, how clumsy of me, I seem to have dropped it! Did you see where it rolled?'

She lifted up the white cloth that covered the buffet table, and Charles appeared. 'What is the matter, Emma? Have you lost something?'

'Oh, I've been so stupidly careless! I have dropped the lovely ring you gave to Lucy. I could kick myself! What a foolish woman I am to spoil such a happy event.'

'It is no matter,' Charles said, generously. 'I dare say it will surface when they clean the place, but if not I shall go back to Garrards and ask them to make me another, just the same.'

Emma felt mean, seeing Lucy's woebegone face, but it

was all a necessary part of her final plan, to which Charles was privy. She was confident that, later, the girl would be more than recompensed for her anxiety.

When the ball was over and the last strains of Christmas carols had died away, Emma handed Charles the concealed ring with a wink as she said goodnight. When she was in her dressing-gown she knocked at the door of Lucy's room and found her sitting up in bed wearing her pure white nightgown of satin and lace. 'Oh, Emma, I shall not sleep a wink tonight!' she declared, smiling.

'Then you are not too upset about the ring?'

'Of course not! It is only a token, and I shall ensure that Charles is not out of pocket if he buys another. Would you believe, he did not know I was an heiress until my guardian told him? In fact, he had gained the impression that I was impoverished. Well, at least I know that his love for me is true and not based on avarice.' She stretched her slender arms voluptuously above her head. 'Oh, Emma, I love him so much, I can hardly wait for my wedding night!'

You may not have to, Emma thought wryly.

She said goodnight and pretended to leave the room, but instead hid in the closet just by the door. It was a large space, with only a few of Lucy's clothes hanging in it, and with the curtain drawn across a little she could peep out and get a clear view of the bedroom, with Lucy's dark head outlined on the pillow in the glow from the night-light. She looked so small and childlike, as if she had just hung up her stocking and were waiting for Santa to make his visit. Well, she might get more of a Christmas present than she expected!

About ten minutes later, when Emma was beginning to feel stiff and cold, there came a knock at the door. 'Who's there?' Lucy cried in alarm.

'It is I, Charles. May I come in? I have some good news.'

Her face broke into a smile. 'Yes, do. The door is unlocked.'

Emma heard him tell her that the ring had been found and saw the enthusiasm with which she kissed him on the mouth. They were soon so absorbed in each other that she grew bold and pulled back the curtain even further. Their kiss went on and on, growing ever more passionate, until Lucy finally broke away with a sigh. 'This is not proper, Charles. Perhaps you should leave.'

'Do you want me to?'

'No!' she smiled, shyly. 'I suppose if we are engaged . . .'

'Precisely. Throw back the covers, there's a good girl, and let me come in beside you just for a moment. I want to hug you.'

Emma saw him take off his shoes, socks and trousers and get into the bed in his shirt-tails. At once he began to kiss Lucy again, his hand stroking her breast over the nightgown. Emma thought how virginal she looked in that lace-trimmed white garment. With a circlet of lilies on her brow and a veil over her eyes she would have resembled a blushing bride.

'My darling, I love you so much!' Charles whispered. 'May I ask you a special favour?'

'What is that, dearest?'

'I wonder if I might just lift up your nightdress and look at your body. I promise that I will not touch you, unless you want me to. But I have longed to set eyes upon your lovely nakedness ever since I first saw you.'

Lucy gave a shy smile and, without a moment's hesitation, drew the long gown up over her head and threw it onto the floor. 'There, Charles! Gaze your fill!'

He looked at her adoringly then kissed her on the forehead. 'Beautiful, exquisite! I am used to looking at works of art, Lucy, but none can compare with nature in all her glory. You are a lovely child of nature, and I worship at the altar of your being!'

'You may touch me if you wish,' she encouraged him, taking his hand and placing it on her bare breast. He stroked the slowly hardening nipple and gazed down at her bush. Emma detected a brief shudder in the girl's belly and knew it was not from cold.

'You may kiss me there, too,' Lucy continued, beginning to radiate like an exotic bloom in the heat. Emma felt a sympathetic tingling in her own breasts, but the scene she was witnessing seemed somehow too chaste, too sacred almost, to evoke earthy instincts.

Charles bent his head, with the thinning crown visible, and took her soft nipple in his mouth. Lucy gave a little 'Oh!' of surprise at the sensations that accompanied his act. She stroked his head as he grew more ardent, squeezing and stroking the white globe of her breast while he coaxed its pink crest into proud affirmation. Soon he was stroking her other nipple, bringing it into the same pert state, making her sigh and moan with newly-discovered pleasure.

His lips moved to kiss her again, and this time Lucy seemed to yield to him completely, pressing the whole length of her body against his. Inexperienced as she was, the girl was instinctively rubbing her thighs together and preparing herself for greater pleasures to come. As the kiss progressed, Charles' hands roved from breast to stomach and casually brushed against her demure little bush, but he would not go further without permission.

'Charles, my love!' Lucy sighed. 'I feel so warm and wet below. Is that how I should feel?'

'I'm not so sure about that,' Charles smiled, making gentle fun of her. 'Shall I check?'

Understanding the game she grinned, elfishly, her dark hair lying tousled about her shoulders. Slowly she opened her thighs for him to feel between them and, when he found the hot little jewel that lay within the velvet folds of her pussy, she closed her legs again, trapping his fingers within. 'Now I have your hand exactly where I want it,' she told him, teasingly. 'And I shall not let it go.'

'You need not make a prisoner of my poor hand, darling Lucy. It is where it has longed to be for weeks, my dear. Loosen your thighs and let me move my fingers, then you will soon see how happy a man's hand can make you!'

Embarrassed by their innocent play, Emma began to feel like the *voyeuse* she was but she could not tear herself away. The drama that was unfolding before her was as old as time; it was her own story, every woman's story, and she must see it through to the end.

Charles began to stroke his beloved's moist cleft, lubricating her with her own juices. She leaned back onto the pillow and threw back her head, moaning softly. Her thighs were limp and relaxed now, trusting him to treat her gently and willing him to continue sending those extraordinary feelings throughout her yearning body. Emma saw her small breasts grow taut and strained at the first erotic tension of her awakening. She knew Charles would not fail her, but would continue with his tender, rhythmic caresses for as long as she wished.

Every so often he bent his lips towards her body, to alight on a thrusting nipple or the delicate hollow of her navel, or brush against the curly hairs of her pubis and send thrilling shivers up her spine. When he did so Lucy reached out and touched his head, like a benediction. Her pelvis was active now too, bucking and swivelling as his fingers increased their pace, meeting his more urgent friction with a horizontal dance of hips and thighs. Then, as she was clenching her buttocks and lifting her mons to his touch with an almost desperate longing, Charles suddenly withdrew his hand and began to stroke her thighs.

Lucy opened her eyes and looked at him, clearly disappointed – but not for long. Quickly he bent his mouth to her delicate, exposed tissues and bathed the whole of her vulva with his cool saliva. From her vantage point Emma could see his tongue moving rapidly over her engorged clitoris like a hungry cat lapping milk. Lucy gave a series of escalating gasps. Then, placing both hands on his head, she declared in breathless

wonder, 'Oh, Charles my love, that is so exquisite that I
... aaah!'

Emma watched with both envy and pride as the girl's
first ever orgasm tracked its fiery path through her
amazed body. She saw the rippling muscles of her
stomach as the tremors shook her womb, saw the flush
at her pale throat, heard the evocative moans and cries
of a girl being initiated into womanhood and felt a faint,
answering echo inside herself. Although it was Charles
who had made Lucy come she felt a certain pride herself,
knowing she had brought them together. Her last pupil
had been mated with her last lover: there was a kind of
poetic justice about it. Yet Emma hardly knew whether
she would have either pupils or lovers again.

Leaving the happy, satiated pair to their privacy
Emma crept from Lucy's bedroom and into her own.
Lying there in darkness, hearing the whispers from the
other side of the wall, she felt the first, inevitable tears
start to flow.

Chapter Fifteen

*T*he house that Kitty shared with three other suffragettes was in Islington. Emma was grateful when
she was offered temporary accommodation there, but
she missed the elegant Brunswick Square mansion and
although all the women were polite to her she couldn't
help feeling like an outsider. Every day they had some
demonstration to attend, some meeting or recruitment
drive to organise, and there was a constant stream of
visitors to the house.

Since there were no servants the women fended for
themselves, like the East End working women, and
Emma was obliged to live as they did, forsaking her
elegant gowns for more everyday wear that she could
manage herself. They all seemed to subsist on a series of
tea and buns at a café around the corner, supplemented
by endless talk. Emma knew she could not stay there
long, but it gave her some breathing space in which to
plan her future.

Whichever way she looked at it, however, her future
seemed bleak. The thought of building up her Academy
again from scratch was daunting, especially as she no
longer had Daniel's money to fall back on. True to his
word, he had begun to pay her a small monthly pension
and she had some savings, but it was not just a question

of money. Emma had also lost her old enthusiasm. Perhaps it was time to retire gracefully. Her thoughts turned with increasing frequency to Lily Merchant. Should she go and live with her? But at the thought of them living together in that poky apartment she would sink into despondency.

At last Kitty noticed that Emma was no longer her old self and she tried, in her fashion, to help her. 'Why not come along to one of our meetings?' she suggested. 'You might have more in common with us than you think. Some of our number are quite civilised, you know!'

'Maybe I shall,' Emma smiled, but she did nothing about it.

Then, one day in early February, Kitty and her friends returned from a march covered in mud. They had started at Hyde Park and walked to the Strand in torrential rain, but their spirits were still high. While water was heated to fill the tin baths the women stripped off their filthy clothes, laughing and joking. They impressed Emma with their determined talk. One of them called to her as she was filling a tub, 'Better a mud bath than a blood bath eh, Emma?'

A red-headed girl called Joyce said, 'When are you going to join us, then? Remember, if you're not with us you're against us.'

Seeing those mud-caked faces, Emma found her resistance weakening. They were so brave and persevering. Perhaps she was wrong to condemn them for taking a militant stance. Her old objection to Kitty taking part was no longer valid, now that Milly had been sent away to school, so what excuse did she have for not taking them seriously?

'I don't mind coming to hear one of your speakers,' she said at last. 'I'll listen to what they've got to say, and judge for myself whether it makes sense to me.'

Kitty dashed up, bright-eyed. 'Would you, Em? Would you really?' She planted a kiss on Emma's cheek making a dirty mark. Everyone laughed.

'Now you're one of us whether you like it or not!'

Joyce cackled. 'First mud, just like "first blood" in hunting circles. You've been initiated into the clan.'

Emma grinned. 'I said I'd go along to the next meeting, that's all. When is it?'

'Women's Parliament!' Kitty said, eagerly. 'This Tuesday, the same day as the opening of the men's Parliament. If there's no mention of votes for women in the King's speech we intend to march on Westminster.'

'Well I hope it doesn't rain again!'

There was a warm camaraderie amongst the women that night which Emma found infectious. They sat round drinking soup from tin mugs and singing some of the campaign songs and Emma, much to her surprise, found herself joining in. Was she becoming a convinced suffragette? Or was she simply a lonely woman who wanted to find new friends? When Kitty finally kissed her goodnight and said how happy she was that her 'dearest friend' had agreed to attend a meeting, Emma felt a warm glow that was almost sexual in its intensity.

Afterwards, as she lay in her bed listening to female voices still debating below, Emma suspected that politics was beckoning her solely to fill the void that losing Daniel had created. She still felt cheated by him, cast aside for the sake of respectability, and that gave her an affinity with other women who had been abused by their husbands or lovers. But was their cause any less valid just because most of the suffragettes bore some kind of personal grudge against the male sex? She was still debating the issue in her mind when she fell asleep.

Three days later, Emma found herself sitting in Caxton Hall and listening to Mrs Pankhurst open the proceedings. She was a good-looking woman, a widow with a quietly persuasive manner, and her two elder daughters were passionately committed to the Cause. But Emma was more impressed by another widow, Charlotte Despard, whose snow-white hair and regal manner were reinforced by her eccentric garb, a black lace mantilla and sandals. It was she who pointed out, in answer to hecklers, that the property qualification was the real evil, for not only did it bar working-class women from the vote but many men also.

While she was speaking, Emma caught the eye of one of the few male members of the audience. He was nodding and smiling in accord, but when his eyes met Emma's a flash of sudden recognition passed between them that took her completely by surprise. He was a young man of striking appearance, eyes like smouldering black coals and dark curls that tumbled in wild disarray about his shoulders like rays from an ebony sun, and Emma found it hard to believe that what she had seen in his gaze was raw, seething lust for her. Surely she had been mistaken, she reasoned, her eyes still glued to the back of his head. It had been wishful thinking, that was all. The very idea of a thirty-five year-old woman attracting such a handsome lad was ridiculous. He would have young, pretty girls falling over themselves to flirt with him. Yet soon he turned his head again, looked back through the crowd to where she was and then gave a brief, shy smile before facing front once more. Emma felt her heart beating fiercely. She no longer paid attention to what was being said, so that when they turned and began filing out of the hall she was taken by surprise.

Kitty appeared from nowhere. 'Will you march with us?' she asked. Vaguely Emma nodded, her eyes still scanning the teeming crowd for the good-looking stranger. 'Then you may stand behind our banner. Annie and I embroidered it between us,' she added, proudly.

As they filed out of the hall somehow the strange man contrived to move near her until they emerged into the daylight almost side by side. He exuded a sensual, virile energy that made Emma feel faint with longing so that she could hardly bear to look in his direction. When she did he gave her a smile of such dazzling radiance that she was forced to believe the incredible truth, that he really did find her desirable.

Then Kitty noticed him and, to Emma's secret satisfaction, addressed him by name. 'Marco! Come and help

237

us carry the banner. We need a strong man to keep it upright.'

'Of course!' he grinned, his voice wonderfully low and lilting, sending new shivers of excitement down Emma's spine. It was so long since she had felt those sweet pangs of desire, activated by some mysterious chemical attraction to a stranger, that she had forgotten how strong they could be. Now her knees were weakening beneath her, and she began to wonder how she would manage the walk to Westminster.

As Marco sidled through the crowd to take the pole, his hand brushed hers and a jolt of fire passed up her arm. For a second their eyes met at close range, and again there came that dark flash of mutual recognition before he murmured, 'Excuse me, please,' in his liquid Italian accent. Emma gave a faint smile and stepped back, her heart thudding rapidly and her mouth dry. Then she felt a shove from behind and realised that the column had started moving and was sweeping her along with it, pushing her forward whether she wished to go or not.

Emma made a determined effort to place one foot before the other, but her gaze was riveted to the flowing raven curls of the man in front. He wore a white shirt and black trousers, with a jerkin of purple, white and green – the suffragette colours. Apparently oblivious of the cold he held his head high beneath the fluttering banner, marching proudly as if aware that he was helping to make history. Emma felt all parts of her being respond to his powerful young presence: head, heart and womb were dancing dizzily to his tune.

Suddenly Kitty was by her side, linking arms. 'How does it feel to be on the march with this rabble?' she joked. 'Not so bad, is it? Look behind and see how far the column stretches.'

Emma did so, and was amazed at the endless line of faces and banners snaking back to Caxton Hall as they cut a broad swathe down Victoria Street. At the front Emma could see the bobbing white head of Mrs Despard, already likened by the press to a 'Fighting Téméraire'. But she could not resist asking who the young sympathiser with the banner was.

'Oh, that's Marco,' Kitty replied, airily. Her voice dropped. 'He's the illegitimate son of an Italian aristocrat and Nellie Flanagan, one of our followers. Gorgeous, isn't he?'

'He's obviously full of youthful ideals.'

'Don't you mean 'ideal youth'?'

Kitty gave her a mischievous grin but Emma would not be drawn. Whatever attraction there might be between her and the 'gorgeous' Marco was a fragile thing, scarcely acknowledged and certainly not to be exposed to prying eyes or wagging tongues. Yet Emma found herself unable to look away from that noble head, those slim hips and the rotund curves of his buttocks as he strode rhythmically along. She gazed, too, at his hands: strong and brown, they clasped the thin pole almost lovingly, the way she could imagine them caressing a woman's flesh. The sight of him was intoxicating enough but, accompanied by the shouts and chants of the throng and the jeers or cheers of the bystanders, Emma felt her head reeling as her feet carried her along the street towards the Houses of Parliament.

Before they got there, however, a cry went up from the front marchers: police! They were there in force awaiting them, many on horseback. Emma saw them lined up before Westminster Abbey and her blood chilled. They were a fearsome sight, a solid wall of navy serge and black or brown horseflesh, blocking the road ahead. The pace of the march slowed but did not falter, and the horses grew restless as they saw the great tide of people coming towards them. Emma heard one of the officers ordering the leaders to turn back and someone shouted, 'Never! Not until women get the vote!' Then the chant began, 'Votes for Women!'

They continued walking forward, aiming for the House of Commons, but the officer gave the order to charge and, before Emma realised what was happening,

239

there was a terrible confusion of neighing horses, shouting policemen and screaming women. She could hear a clattering of hooves and saw several women fall to the ground, but she couldn't see Kitty anywhere. The march was in disarray, people fleeing in all directions to escape the horses and truncheons, but Emma was rooted to the spot with panic and hardly knew which way to go.

Someone grabbed her hand and pulled her towards the pavement. It was Marco. Dazed, she heard him say, melodramatically, 'Come with me, I will save you!' and she followed him blindly through the mayhem, running as fast as she could, hearing the clamour diminish as he led her up Tothill Street and then through to Birdcage Walk and into the green sanctuary of St James's Park. She held his hand tightly, finding warm reassurance in his grasp, but when their pace finally slowed Emma felt like a giddy girl again, playing 'spinning top' by revolving as fast as she could then standing still while the world went on whirling before her eyes.

'Are you all right?' Marco asked.

'Yes, just a little out of breath, that's all!' Emma gasped, trying to smile. He led her to a park bench and they sat down together. Two curious ducks waddled up, looking for titbits, and Emma couldn't help laughing. 'They don't care, do they? What is it to them what is happening down the road? This park is their universe!'

'And ours too, for the moment.' Marco fixed her with his dark, soulful gaze and Emma felt powerless to resist. 'I am sorry, I do not know your name. Mine is Marco Donelli.'

'I am pleased to meet you,' Emma said, conscious of the rather ridiculous formality as she held out her hand to him. 'My name is Emma Longmore. I'm a friend of Kitty Belfort.'

He took her hand and this time did not let it go. 'You are new to the movement? I have not seen you before.'

'I thought I was only coming to the meeting, in Caxton Hall. I had no idea that all this would happen.' The memory of it all suddenly overwhelmed her. 'Oh God, I hope Kitty is all right! Those dreadful men on horseback.'

'They are growing scared. They can no longer laugh at us, but now we are a force for them to deal with. We are winning, I think!'

'I wish I could share your optimism, Marco.'

'You will. You must!' His eyes gleamed seductively at her, willing her to share his vision. Emma was filled with both adrenalin and passion and was reluctant to let the heady moment of opportunity fade. So when Marco suggested they should walk through the park to Piccadilly and find a café, she readily agreed.

For hours they sat exchanging views and debating issues until the talk became more personal, more intimate. Emma discovered that Marco had lived in Tuscany until the age of sixteen then come to London with Nellie, his mother, whose allegiance had soon transferred from the Italian Anarchists to the English Suffragettes. Now he shared her impassioned devotion to the Cause.

'Aren't you worried about her?' Emma enquired. 'Was she on the march?'

'No, she is still in Holloway after the last time,' he grinned. 'I will visit her tomorrow and tell her I held the banner when the horsemen charged. She will be proud of me!'

'What happened to the banner?'

'It was trampled in the dirt!' They both laughed. 'Never mind,' Marco added, 'You can make us another one.'

He turned on his sultry charm and Emma shuddered with longing. Her body was hot for him, all her secret, dewy folds opening up to him. She *must* have him, and soon. But how?

'It is getting late,' Marco announced eventually, when the table before them was littered with empty cups and plates. 'I shall take you home. Where do you live?'

'In Kitty's house. Do you know it?'

'I have not been there. Is it far?'

'Islington. We could get a cab.'

Emma spoke without enthusiasm. Somehow she knew that once they went back there the house would be overflowing with people, the talk all of the march and its aftermath. Much as she wanted to know what had happened to Kitty and the others, Emma was loath to break the delicate rapport she had built up with Marco over the past few hours.

He sensed her hesitation. 'Maybe the police will be looking for you there,' he said. 'Perhaps you should come home with me, just for tonight. The others in my house are not connected to the suffragettes. You would be more safe there.'

Emma was grateful for the excuse, suspecting that he felt the same way as she did. Outside the café he hailed a cab and told the driver to take them to an address in Finsbury. It was already dark as well as cold, and they huddled close on the leather seat with Emma's cloak spread over them both.

'Why did you not wear a jacket?' she asked him, as he shivered beside her.

'Because it would hide the colours. I am not ashamed to wear the Union colours. I would rather freeze.'

'You are so committed, Marco,' Emma said, with grudging admiration. 'Sometimes I wish I could see things in black and white, as you and the others seem to do.'

'You will, Emma, you will,' he murmured, planting a soft kiss on her cheek whose imprint lingered for a long time afterwards, filling her with rising hope and desire.

The terraced house was dark and dingy inside, and the hallway littered with pamphlets. Marco apologised for the mess with a disarming smile. 'I live upstairs,' he said. 'Come.'

He occupied the front room which was of a decent size, with a large bed and washstand, wardrobe, table and several chairs. Some attempt had been made to make the place seem homely, with a few potted plants and pictures on the walls, but it was clear that Marco did not spend a great deal of time there. 'Would you like

242

some tea?' he asked. 'Oh, there is no milk. But I have lemon. Or there is some wine.'

'A glass of wine would be nice,' Emma smiled, sounding brighter than she felt. The mood of euphoria that had buoyed her up all afternoon had begun to desert her. What am I doing here? she wondered. Surely this boy is merely being kind, and wants no more than friendship.

But when he chinked glasses with her and murmured, 'Cheers!' she felt more at ease. He brought out a photograph album and showed her pictures of his family: his mother, a handsome woman, laughing in a flowery meadow with a man who looked like Marco, and a wizened old lady – his Irish grandmother – sitting in a chair by the sea.

'Do you have any family, Emma?' he asked, seriously.

'Oh I broke away from them, years ago, and now they are almost all dead,' she replied.

'Then you may share mine! I will find you some more photographs later.'

'Oh, Marco!' she giggled.

'No, really. I have a sister in Siena, very pretty. And a brother in Dublin. Also very pretty.'

Emma giggled as the wine began to take effect. 'But not so pretty as you, surely?'

'If you say so.'

He was close now, close enough for her to smell the spicy odours that hung about him, fuelling her lust. Yet, for the first time in her life, she felt unsure. It was not just that she doubted his intentions. Her old confidence had gone, and she no longer felt desirable. Why would he want me, a woman old enough to be his mother? she asked herself. Was he just being friendly? If so, he had no idea what torments he was putting her through.

Emma looked into his eyes, trying to read them. They smiled back at her, warm and ingenuous. He sat on the rug at her feet and rested his head against her knee.

Tentatively she reached out and felt the springiness of his hair, like coiled silk. 'Such lovely thick hair you have,' she murmured. 'Is it from your father? You look like him.'

He turned with his white-toothed grin shining up at her. 'I grow it long, like a gypsy. My mother tells me I am wild, so I decide to look the part. Do you think I am wild, Emma?'

'I don't know you well enough to judge.'

'Would you like to know me well?'

The question threw her off balance. Did he mean they should be friends? She didn't know if she could stand it, seeing more of him but not having him. With some men it might be possible, but not with Marco. 'I . . . I suppose so,' she hedged.

'How well?' His question came low and husky, sending tremors down Emma's spine. Awaiting her answer, he placed his chin on her knee and looked up at her like a fond spaniel.

She reached out and stroked his irresistible hair once again. He continued looking up at her with his soulful eyes on fire, making words seem irrelevant. 'What are you asking me, Marco?' Her voice was heavy with desire.

'You remember in the hall, earlier today, when our eyes met for the first time?' Emma nodded. 'I thought to myself, there is one unhappy woman. But at the same time I knew that I was the one who could make you happy, and that was when I made up my mind.'

Emma was in suspense, unconsciously witholding her breath as she waited to be absolutely sure. Could it really be that what she wanted more than anything right then was what he wanted too?

At last she said, 'Yes?'

His smile brightened. 'Oh, Emma! Please say "yes" like that again, and this time we shall both know what it means!'

She smiled and whispered, 'Yes, my dear Marco,' seeing the light flare in his eyes and feeling a corresponding surge of longing within. Slowly she leaned forward, and at the same time he raised himself up on his knees until their mouths were in contact. He tasted so fresh and sweet, his plump lips soft and yielding to hers. Emma gave out a long sigh as their first kiss began.

Everything about him was so wonderfully soft and tender: his tongue, that entwined with hers in languorous pleasure; his fingers, which stroked her cheek as they kissed; his olive skin, which she stroked with increasing ardour, ranging from his long neck across his bare shoulders and beneath the open-necked shirt to the top of his smooth chest. Soon she was fumbling with the buttons, wanting to experience more of his warm flesh, but he began to laugh in gentle ridicule at her haste.

'Oh, poor Emma! Is it so long since you had a man?' She grinned up at him, ruefully. He removed her hands and took the shirt off himself, revealing a hairless torso adorned with two dark brown studs. She bent her lips to one of the nipples and soon had it stiffening wetly while Marco uttered quiet moans of tortured bliss. Her lips traced a breathless course down his curved chest and flat abdomen to his waist, where a leather belt secured his trousers. Emma undid the buckle and was about to unbutton his fly when he laughingly pulled up her head.

'Why hurry? Let us take our time about it, Emma, and then it will be all the better.'

'Of course you're right, but I am so hungry for you!' she moaned. In her belly she could feel her womb aching for him, with a hollow emptiness that cried out to be filled.

'Do you think I do not hunger for you, too? But love is a feast that must be savoured, or it soon goes sour. Let us discover each other slowly, I beg of you. Tell me you will spend the night here, so I know we shall not be rushed.'

Emma thought of Kitty and the others: would they worry about her? Either they had been arrested themselves or they would presume that she had been. There would be time enough for them all to discover the truth in the morning. 'Yes, I will stay,' she murmured.

'Then I should like to undress you slowly, Emma. May I?'

There was something very erotic about being gradually stripped of her clothes by such gentle hands, gentler than any lady's maid she had known. Each button, each ribbon, was lovingly opened and a kiss planted where each new strip of skin was revealed. All the while Marco spoke to her in Italian, the liquid sounds greatly increasing her enjoyment of the proceedings. Each *carissima* was accompanied by a cascade of kisses; each *amore* brought with it some new adoration of her body; each *bella* came with a loving lick of the tongue.

Soon Emma was down to her underwear, the last layers of silk and lace waiting to be stripped away. Marco was in no hurry, but was paying prolonged attention to the tops of her breasts as they spilled over the broderie anglaise of her camisole, his mouth lingering in the sweet valley between the mounds. The delicacy of his kisses was tantalising Emma almost beyond endurance, and she could feel her rigid nipples tingling expectantly beneath the thin cotton lawn while down below, in a region as yet quite untouched by the young explorer, the damp swamp of her sex was growing hot and steamy as the tiny dynamo at its heart hummed and throbbed away.

'Oh God, Marco, I want you so much!' she moaned, hoping to encourage him to make bolder advances. Yet he seemed immune to her feverish desires, content to cover her chest with light kisses while he stroked her hair.

Much as Emma longed to force the pace she knew that would be unwise. An inexperienced lover like Marco could have his confidence shaken if she tried to make him do things he was not ready to do. The marvel was that he seemed so perfectly in control of himself. Emma could feel the long, hard ridge between his thighs as it brushed against her own, but he seemed in no hurry to sate his own lust. Gradually she began to relax and savour the delicate sensations that his lips and hands were producing in her, wallowing in a sensuality that was so light and free it seemed almost divorced from desire.

At last he pulled the bodice up over her aroused nipples to reveal her naked breasts. For a while he sat observing them, murmuring his appreciation in his native tongue, then he stroked their undersides very tentatively, feeling their taut firmness before he cupped them with both hands and slowly closed his fingers over their protuberant peaks. Emma gasped as ripples of pure joy passed through her, giving her momentarily what she craved. Marco curled up between her spread thighs with his head on her stomach and held her breast to his mouth, then he enclosed her left nipple and began to suckle gently, like a sleepy babe. The rippling pleasure spread through her again, gathering force as her tumid nipple responded to the mild suction with tingling expectancy. She took his other hand and placed it on her right breast which he began to stroke softly, doubling her satisfaction.

The drowsy suckling went on and on, filling Emma with long-buried maternal feelings. She delved into his thick curls with her fingertips and felt the slow build-up to orgasm begin between her cunny lips, so lazy and relaxed in its coming that she could hardly believe it was happening. She continued to caress his silky locks while he circled her nipple with his tongue, lapping around the elongated teat and then drawing it softly between his lips again. Between her labia Emma could feel the hot pulse intensifying, taking her to the brink all by itself. She felt totally calm: the exquisite feelings were reaching their crescendo of their own accord, filling her with a voluptuous delight that was centred on the slow stimulation of her breasts. But her cunt was responding fully. The familiar glowing prelude to her climax was upon her and now, incredibly, it was happening in slow motion, each individual spasm prolonged to deliver the utmost satisfaction before the next began. On and on went the gently overlapping waves until Emma was no

247

longer aware of herself feeling anything, only of a vast and seamless universe swallowing her into an infinity of pure ecstasy.

When she finally emerged from the last ebbing bliss Emma found there were tears in her eyes and Marco was smiling down at her, brushing them away with the corner of the sheet.

'Why so sad, *cara*?'

'I don't know. It was so beautiful. I don't remember feeling quite like that before.'

He gathered her into his arms with a fond chuckle, kissing her brow. She felt safe in his embrace. While he was sucking at her breasts she had experienced strong maternal emotions, but now she felt mothered by him. Emma had believed that she had been through the full gamut of sexuality with Daniel, but now here was a whole new dimension to explore. It was very strange, but immensely satisfying.

So much so that Emma made no objection when Marco said she could have the bed and he would sleep on the couch. They were both exhausted after the stress of fleeing from the mounted police, and while their desire for each other had brought renewed energy for a while once their first appetite was sated neither had the strength to carry on. Emma stretched like a cat between the rough sheets and felt pure joy suffuse her veins. Marco had come into her life as suddenly as a summer storm but now he had become a part of it literally overnight, as central to her being as Daniel had been yet in an entirely different way.

In the morning Emma woke not knowing where she was but, once she remembered, a slow smile spread over her face. Marco was still huddled on the sofa, his tousled hair spread against the cushion and his dark lashes fringing his cheeks. How beautiful he was! She had not even seen the lower half of his body, she recalled. The thought of all the treats to come was thrilling, making her feel like a child anticipating Christmas. Tiptoeing across the room she lit the oil stove and soon had a kettle coming to the boil. By the time she was carrying two enamel mugs of hot coffee across the room Marco was awake.

'Emma!' he smiled at her, drowsily. 'Did last night really happen, or was it a dream?'

She sat down on the couch and took his face between her hands. Bending her head she kissed him gently. 'Remember now?'

He smiled up at her, content. Taking the mug he began to sip the hot drink while Emma did likewise. She wanted to linger but knew she could not. Kitty and the others would be anxious about her, and she must go straight back to their house.

As it turned out, none of them had been arrested although Mrs Despard and several others had. There was a public uproar. The *Daily Chronicle* published a cartoon captioned 'The London Cossacks' with mounted policemen bearing away ladies' hats as trophies from the fray. A new bill giving women equal voting rights was talked out at the second reading.

For a while Emma felt compelled to keep her affair with Marco secret from the others. Their love was such a fragile thing that she felt protective of it. For two whole weeks they made do with furtive meetings in his flat, but he would not let them consummate their love in those sordid surroundings.

'When you give yourself to me entirely I want it to be perfect,' he murmured one evening, after he had pleasured her with his mouth. She had still not persuaded him to take off his trousers and their relationship was becoming a strange inversion of courtship, with Marco playing the blushing virgin and Emma the artful seductress. However, he proved to be strong willed and, although he was prepared to do anything to ensure her satisfaction he seemed strangely indifferent to his own. The effect was to make her want him more and more. Her womb ached for him constantly, as if for the child she had never had.

For some time Emma debated with herself whether to

join the suffragettes whole-heartedly, but she was still dubious about their methods. Marco had no such doubts, however, and soon persuaded her to join in a second march from Caxton Hall to Westminster, on March 22nd. This time Lady Florence Harburton, of the 'Rational Dress Movement', led the march in her divided skirt. There were some boos and catcalls along the route, but on the whole more cheers and shouts of support from the bystanders. When they reached Westminster they were again met by ranks of policemen but this time no horses. Momentarily admitting defeat they returned to Caxton Hall only to rally once more, with Christabel Pankhurst urging them to, 'If possible seize the mace, and you will be the Oliver Cromwells of the Twentieth Century!'

When they returned to Westminster, Marco held Emma's hand tightly as havoc broke out all around. They narrowly escaped arrest when they found themselves suddenly surrounded by navy serge, but then a more serious scuffle broke out elsewhere and the policemen's attention was diverted. It was soon clear what had happened. A party of protesters had managed to get into the Palace Yard in a wagonette, pretending to be sightseers, and the bobbies were called to evict them.

'I think it is time to go, Emma,' Marco grinned. 'What is that fine English saying about fighting and running away?'

'He who fights and runs away, lives to fight another day!' Emma grinned. Still holding his hand she lifted up her skirt with the other and they dashed off, skirting the mob, but found their former escape route blocked by more police.

'This way!' Marco gasped, pulling her towards the Embankment. They hurried along beside the Thames until they came to Vauxhall Bridge then stopped, panting. 'Now, do you feel like a true suffragette at last?' he asked her, teasingly.

She gave a rueful smile. 'Not quite. I still can't believe

it is right to provoke such force. It does the image of women no good.'

'On the contrary, I love to see you when you are flushed from the chase Emma, like now!'

He kissed her fully on the lips, and she tapped him on his nose by way of reproof. Then they walked up to Victoria, where they caught a cab to Marco's flat. In the hallway a small, bright-eyed woman in a tailored jacket was sitting, awaiting his return.

'Mamma, they have released you!' he beamed, hugging her tenderly.

'Yes, but only so as to make room for today's new prisoners,' she grinned ruefully, patting her dark hair in which strands of grey were showing. 'Who is your lady friend, Marco?'

'Forgive me, this is Emma Longmore! Emma, this is my dear mother, Nellie.'

'I am pleased to meet you, Mrs Longmore,' Nellie Flanagan said, looking her up and down. 'Are you one of us?'

For a moment, Emma did not realise what she meant. 'Oh, a suffragette!' she said, at last. 'I'm not quite sure if I qualify. I haven't been arrested yet!'

Nellie laughed, but soon turned back to her son. 'Aren't you going to invite me up, Marco? I've only been out of Holloway an hour and I'm dying for a cup of tea. What's happening up at Westminster? I heard there was another big demonstration today.'

As mother and son fell to chatting, Emma felt left out. 'Perhaps I had better go back to Kitty's,' she said, uncertainly.

'Please don't leave on my account,' Nellie said. 'At least have some tea with us first.'

She agreed, but as they sat drinking tea in Marco's tiny room she felt ill at ease. Then Nellie said, 'Your father has been taken ill, Marco, and there is no-one to take charge of the farm. Perhaps you had better go back to Tuscany for the summer, darling.'

Emma felt her heart somersault. Back to Italy! But she

was only just getting to know him. It seemed too much to bear. She rose unsteadily, placing her mug on the nearby table. 'Excuse me, I really must go now. I want to know if Kitty and the rest are safe. I'll let myself out.'

'No, no! Wait a moment . . .'

He followed her out of the room and down the stairs. 'Mother likes you,' he told her, as they reached the front door. 'I can tell. When can I see you again?'

'I'm not sure. There are things I have to do. I shall send you a note when I am free.'

She let him kiss her on the cheek, but then was gone.

Chapter Sixteen

*I*t was Emma's birthday. She had all but forgotten, and only seeing the date on the big calendar that hung in the kitchen reminded her. This year there would be no celebration. Daniel and Charles were gone, and Kitty was too occupied to think of such trivia. Ah well!

In her darker hours, Emma saw her old way of life coming to an end. The spectre of Lily in her run-down Parisian apartment continued to haunt her. However, she tried not to get too depressed as she set about the business of finding somewhere more convenient to live. She felt she had overstayed her welcome in the suffragettes' house since she was still not whole-heartedly committed to their cause, and if Marco was returning to Italy she must think about her own future more realistically. She had only seen him once since his mother came out of prison two weeks ago and, although he had been friendly she had cut short the contact. Knowing that he would soon be leaving the country had been just too painful, and the idea of continuing their intimacy under such circumstances was torture to her.

She was sitting in her room, scanning the newspaper for rented accommodation, when there came a knock at her door and Kitty entered. 'Emma, there is to be a meeting at a house near Holland Park this afternoon. Please say you will come with me.'

'Well, I am not sure . . .'

Kitty smiled, putting her arm around Emma's shoulders. 'Please!' she wheedled. 'I am sure you would find it worthwhile. I believe Charlotte Despard will be there. She is to talk on 'Constitutional Militancy – the Moderate Way'. There are rumours that she may form another faction amongst the suffragettes, one that believes in withholding taxes rather than demonstrating. Although I disagree with her views, I cannot help admiring her.'

Emma was intrigued. 'Very well, I shall come.'

Kitty kissed her cheek. 'Good! We shall take a cab at three, then.'

The house in Holland Park was very grand, reminding Emma of her former style of life which did nothing to improve her spirits. After a footman had ushered them in and taken their coats, they were shown into a large room on the first floor overlooking the park.

As soon as they entered there was a shout of welcome and cries of 'Happy Birthday!'. Emma stood at the door, astonished. Towards her, smiling broadly, came her old friend Bella and Emma realised at once that this must be Lord Sandborn's London residence.

'Welcome, dear Emma!' Bella said, kissing her on the cheek. 'And many happy returns! See how many of your friends and former pupils we have managed to assemble here today.'

The group of excited women crowded round. Faces she had not seen for years were smiling fondly at her including Yvette, Bella's close friend, and Henrietta, over from France.

'Why, this is more like an Old Girls' Reunion!' Emma laughed, recognising yet more of her former pupils and greeting each with a kiss.

Not all the guests were female, however. Hovering on the sidelines was Charles, with Lucy on his arm and, beside them, Rupert Heaven with Sybil. Emma's eyes began to fill with tears at the sight of so many dear friends gathered together for her benefit.

Then, with a shock, she saw Marco. He was hanging back shyly, as if afraid he might be unwelcome, and Emma's heart plummeted for a moment. She forced a smile and went forward to embrace him but his presence filled her with mixed emotions. As she kissed his cheek a tear rolled from her eye and wetted it. Smiling sadly, she wiped it away with her lace handkerchief.

Someone put a jolly tune on the Victrola and the room was suddenly full of chatter and laughter, lifting Emma's spirits. She noticed the long table, spread with fancy cakes, moulded desserts and a two-tier birthday cake, and thanked Bella warmly for her pains.

'It is our thank you to *you!*' she insisted, with a smile. 'Come and open your presents. I put them all on a table in the corner.'

The afternoon passed in sheer delight, with Emma catching up on the news of affairs and engagements, marriages and births. She could happily have spent a whole afternoon with any one of the guests, and to have them all there at once was overwhelming. Most invited her to visit them, however, and Emma began to envisage a glorious few months travelling from friend to friend. Perhaps she would not need a place to live for a while, after all!

Emma was aware of Marco's presence throughout, but she tried not to look in his direction as he made conversation with one attractive woman after another. Although Kitty had meant well in putting him on the guest list, she did not know that Emma had been trying to avoid him, or the pain that his impending return to Italy was causing her.

The time came for the ceremonial cutting of the cake. Bella made a pretty speech on behalf of them all. 'Emma, we graduates of your wonderful Academy owe you a great debt,' she began. 'You have taught us about an aspect of life that conventional education ignores completely. The skills that you have passed on to us have allowed us to make the most advantageous of marriages and liaisons. But above all, and I am sure I speak for all of us here, you have taught us to value ourselves most highly as women, to prize our sexuality instead of being ashamed of it, to glory in our ability to please both our menfolk and ourselves. Dear Emma, may your Academy continue to flourish, along with your good self!'

Then they toasted Emma, bringing tears to her eyes again. 'I cannot let my Academy go,' she told herself firmly, as she looked around the semi-circle of happy faces. Somehow she must find the strength to carry on. She had certainly been given the inspiration.

Looking again from one dear, familiar countenance to the next Emma realised that there was one face conspicuous by its absence, that of Daniel Forbes. Strangely enough she had not thought of him until now and it struck her, with a faint pang of guilt, that she did not miss him in the slightest. Her glance fell on Marco, his expression one of sweet adoration, and her pangs deepened. Must she lose him too?

After the food and champagne had been consumed, one by one the guests made their departure until only Kitty, Bella and Marco remained. Emma turned to her friend and chided her, playfully. 'So this is the "meeting" you invited me to attend, little minx! How can I ever trust you again?'

'There is a meeting actually, but it is tomorrow,' she smiled back. 'Anyhow, I had to get you here somehow. Heaven knows what I'd have had to invent if you had declined to come.'

'Shall we walk in the garden?' Bella suggested. 'It has been such a fine day, and I feel the need of some air.'

Somehow, when they were strolling over the lawn, Bella and Kitty contrived to separate themselves from Marco and Emma. On purpose, she suspected, but now there was nothing for it but to confront her lover directly. When they were under cover of some tall rhododendron bushes Marco suddenly seized her hand. 'You have been avoiding me, Emma. Why is that?'

'Because you will soon be going back to Italy. Oh Marco, I have been through such heartache this year, I do not feel I can bear any more.'

He regarded her searchingly. 'And I do not feel I can bear to go either. Oh Emma, what can we do? Just tell me you want me to stay and I shall ask Mamma to engage a man to sort out the family affairs. She will grumble, of course, but she will do it.'

'I would not wish that,' Emma sighed. 'You should not put off going on my account.'

'There is nothing I would not do for you, my dearest,' Marco declared, fiercely. 'I hope you know that.'

Before she could protest his mouth was crushing hers, taking the breath from her lungs, filling her heart with new hope despite herself. Emma yielded to the onslaught of his lips, let his passion temper into a warm sensuality that was like balm to her soul. His tongue tasted both sweet and sour, the way she felt.

At last the long kiss ended and the pair regarded each other candidly. 'Come back with me tonight,' he pleaded. 'It is your birthday. I wish to give you a present that you will always remember, no matter what may happen.'

Emma could not resist his impassioned rhetoric. Smiling, she nodded. Then Bella and Kitty appeared from behind a tree talking loudly. 'You must visit us in summer, when the roses are in bloom,' Bella was saying. 'That pergola is a sight to behold covered in the American Pillar rose. I saw it a few years ago at Chelsea ... Ah, there is Emma! It is a little chilly now. I think we should go in.'

As they walked back to the house Emma hardly noticed the chill in the air. Her blood was heated with longing for Marco and the champagne she had drunk was fuelling her desire. Again she thanked Bella effusively for the wonderful birthday surprise, and told Kitty that Marco would be taking her out for the evening.

'Do not wait up for me,' she said, and saw the knowing look that the women exchanged.

In fact, the lovers had no intention of going out that night. Recklessly, Emma suggested they should book into a hotel. If this was to be their last night together they would do as he had said and make it memorable. Wickedly she hit on a plan: they would go to the hotel in Kensington that Daniel sometimes used, and charge their night of love to his account. That would teach him to forget her birthday!

Thankfully, her ruse worked. The clerk did not flinch as she explained that she was a 'friend' of Lord Merton, and one glance at Daniel's signature on the cheque he had recently sent her was enough to convince him. However, she felt obliged to claim that Marco was her brother and to ask for separate rooms. It was no great inconvenience. She knew that the single beds in such a luxurious establishment would be almost as ample as the doubles.

For a few minutes Emma was alone in the sumptuous bedroom, enjoying the pleasurable prospect of soon being joined by Marco. She washed herself and perfumed her body, taking off her earrings and necklace so that she would be unencumbered but keeping her clothes on. She had a suspicion that Marco might be disappointed if she undressed herself, that he might wish to do it himself. Either way, she certainly would not be needing the hotel's personal maid service that night.

There came a polite rap on the door and Emma called 'Come in!' with an imperious tone, as if to a servant. When Marco appeared, she giggled. 'I thought you might be a lackey bearing champagne. Shall we order some?' She rang the bell before awaiting his reply.

They filled in the time with a long lingering kiss, fuelling their already burning desire for each other, but as soon as the champagne had arrived and Emma's birthday had been toasted they gravitated towards the bed. There they kissed again, this time letting their hands explore where bare flesh could be felt, at neck and wrist. Gently Marco undid the hooks that secured Emma's

258

dress until the bodice could be prised free and the tops of her breasts caressed as they reared provocatively from her corset. She shivered with the tickling touch of his lips upon her cleavage, her flesh become more sensitised the further down into the cleft he ventured.

'Oh Marco, I never thought to see this night!' she sighed. 'How wonderful to know that you shall be mine at last!'

He looked at her with devouring eyes. 'I feel the same, my dearest. Oh, I have dreamed of you every night since we were together, and every morning, when I awoke to an empty bed, my tears fell.'

'No need for tears now,' she assured him, kissing his soft cheek. 'Let me undress you please, sweetheart. I long to see you completely naked.'

He lay there, compliant, while she unbuttoned his shirt and exposed the smooth, beige flesh. With trembling fingers she undid his belt and felt the thin line of hair that ran from his navel towards his pubis. How boyishly slim his hips were! Soon she was easing his trousers over them, and his cream worsted drawers plainly showed how well aroused were their contents. Emma could not resist the urge to squeeze him there, just a little, enjoying the feel of solid flesh within the soft woollen pouch.

'Wait!' he whispered. 'We are unevenly matched. Let me remove some of your garments too, Emma, before you go further.'

She smilingly agreed and soon Marco had removed her dress and petticoats. He took his time about rolling down her stockings, kissing the silky skin of her thighs as he went and sending urgent signals up to the swelling folds between them. Emma wriggled sensually, her moist cleft opening in sweet anticipation of the delights to come. She sat up for him to unfasten the last of her stays and then the constricting corset was levered off, allowing her breasts to expand into their natural shape. His hands enclosed them for a second, giving the mounds a reassuring squeeze and making her nipples stiffen with acute hunger for more stimulation. All too soon the brief caress was over, but Emma knew those fingers would return before long.

Now that she was down to her shift and drawers, Marco was content to let her remove the last refuge of his modesty. He lay stroking her thighs as she slowly pulled the covering over his bulging erection. His penis thrust eagerly upward as it was freed, and Emma could not resist taking it by the sturdy root and examining it with a smile. It was so elegantly shaped, long and straight, tapering to a head that called to mind the *Duomo* of Florence cathedral. The shaft was a dusky olive hue and contrasted sharply with the delicate shell pink of the glans, from whose tiny eye a pearlescent drop was already escaping.

In its tumescent state the phallus seemed less a thing of flesh and blood and more like a work of art – fashioned out of bronze and rose-quartz, perhaps. 'Oh, he is so beautiful!' Emma breathed, bending to kiss it.

'He has been saving himself for you!' Marco declared, shyly.

'You mean, you have never . . . ?'

He nodded, modestly averting his dark eyes. Emma's heart was full to bursting with joy. She took the pink glans between her fingers and slowly passed the tip of her tongue over its slit, tasting the first, slightly bitter fruit of his loins. His hand travelled up beneath her shift and found her mound, hot and damp beneath the silken knickers. He had felt her there before, tasted her love juice even, but now the gesture seemed all the more significant. Now she understood his previous reluctance to consummate their love, knew too what trust he had placed in her by offering himself to her as a birthday gift. Emma felt a shuddering deep within her as she contemplated the thrill of initiating him fully into the female mysteries.

Slowly she lifted her chemise over her head, exposing her breasts in all their burgeoning glory, but she left the white silk drawers for him to remove. His hand strayed to the pearl button at her hip and a gush of fluid soaked her gusset. How she wanted him! In some long-gone *affaire du cœur* she might have desired a man more keenly, but somehow she doubted it. The gift of Marco's sex was all the more poignant, all the more meaningful, because some kind of fatal cord linked their two souls. Yet they were bound to love and leave each other, perhaps forever.

Brushing the thought from her mind, Emma helped to push down the silken veil that hid her mons from view. Her lover's penis leapt when he saw the dark golden fleece on her belly and he bent to make obeisance. His lips brushed the curly hairs with electric effect, making her squirm, but then she felt his tongue slide down between her labia, parting them so that he could lap at her fresh juices. 'Turn around,' she whispered, as the cool tip of his tongue found her clitoris and soothed its fevered heat. 'Let me taste you too.'

His glans was smooth as a cherry between her lips. When she licked it Marco let out a sigh that blew warm air around her parts, filling her with heightened feeling. Emma enclosed the whole of the pink bulb with her mouth and moved her lips over the rolled foreskin, making him thrust impatiently. She pressed at the strong root of his penis, holding him back. He was working his tongue in and out of her cunny now, teasing the soft tissues of her vulva and making her own miniature glans throb and harden with the friction.

There was a heat spreading throughout her lower region, bringing her close to a climax, yet Emma did not want it yet. She knew that Marco would like to make her come with his prick inside her, for the first time. His mouth was lubricating her for their intercourse but she would not let him take her over the edge. Equally, she would restrict her stimulation of his eager penis so that he would not ejaculate too soon. Withdrawing her lips she contented herself with tiny kisses, alighting like butterflies on the exotic flower of his phallus then moving on before the contact became too sensual.

When she was swimming with a mixture of her musk and his saliva, Emma stroked his dark curls and murmured, 'I think we should put your poor penis out of his misery, Marco dear. Let him venture where he longs to go. He knows the way!'

For an instant Marco smiled up at her but then his eyes darkened with desire and his mouth came crushing down on hers. His kiss grew fervent as he seized her breasts and felt the lengthening nipples with his fingers, then he replaced them with his lips. At the same time he moved astride her, letting her hands guide his twitching organ between her thighs and nose its way between her labia.

'Oh Emma!' he sighed, as his weeping glans found her entrance and thrust straight in. 'If you only knew how I have longed for this moment!'

She clasped him in a vaginal embrace, her muscles working to caress his long shaft and enhance his wonder at being inside a woman for the very first time. His brown eyes were already clouded with ecstasy, and Emma knew it would not be long before he experienced his first vaginal orgasm. Well, she would make sure it was mutual. That would not be difficult for she was having to hold herself back, awaiting the first climactic spasms from his cock before she let herself go completely. He was thrusting more rhythmically now, getting the hang of it as she gently guided him in and out with her hands on his hips.

Arching down, he fastened upon her left nipple with his lips and pulled it upwards, making her squirm with excruciating pleasure. She lifted her hips to let him penetrate her more deeply then wriggled her mons against his hard belly and felt her clitoris pulsating wildly. If he did not come soon she would have to follow the convention of 'Ladies First', hoping he would be a gentleman and not leave her in the lurch!

But then she felt a new urgency in his actions, his pelvis riding her hard and his mouth sucking on her nipple with hungry abandon. 'Oh, Emma, my senses are overwhelming me!' he gasped. 'I cannot help myself . . .'

As she felt the first shuddering expulsion of his seed, Emma gave herself up to the swirling currents of energy that were enveloping them both and her own climax burst upon her with pent-up force. His phallus seemed to fill the whole of her sex, womb and all, bathing all her womanly parts in a delicious, molten fire. Again and again she clasped his penis as it plunged and spurted, eliciting further moans of incredulous joy as the novel sensations invaded his consciousness. While she fully enjoyed her own orgasm, Emma was also aware of the impact that the experience was having on her young lover, and feelings of the most exquisite tenderness filled her heart: a tantalising mixture of protectiveness, sensuality and pride that she had never felt before. Was this what it was like to have maternal feelings? she wondered, as the mood impressed itself upon her more forcefully.

Playing his part to perfection Marco collapsed with his head on her bosom, letting her stroke his damp curls and croon softly, 'There, my love! Now you know what love is all about, sweet boy.' He was still inside her but she could feel his erection diminishing, becoming limp and soft. Utterly spent, he lay like a dead weight on her body and she had to shift position to get comfortable. Then, embracing him, she joined him in a long, contented doze.

Emma woke first, and managed to get up from the bed without waking him. She stood looking down on his boyish form. In repose his face was classically beautiful: the dark lashes sweeping his cheek below the aristocratically arched brows; the nose long and slender; the lips full and slightly parted to show his small white teeth. Her gaze swept down over his quietly undulating chest and flat stomach to where his flaccid penis lay, casually spread over the black mat of pubic curls. How perfect he is, she thought.

But did she love him? Wearily Emma contemplated

the state of her soul as she tiptoed into the adjoining bathroom. She decided to risk waking him with noisy plumbing and turned on the copper tap from the gas boiler over the bath. It ignited and was soon pouring forth scalding hot water and clouds of steam. Soon she was immersed in water softened with scented salts, luxuriating in the warmth that was soothing her aching limbs. But no amount of hydrotherapy could ease her aching heart.

Her birthday had been wonderful but its aftermath, there in the lap of luxury, was proving bitter-sweet. She was filled with the mean suspicion that Marco had wanted an experienced woman to deflower him but that he would forget all about her once he returned to Italy, and was surrounded by doe-eyed Latin beauties of tender age. Perhaps, she concluded with a sigh, that was just how it should be.

Yet her own future was still undecided. There seemed little point in her remaining in London unless she wished to re-open her Academy, and somehow she had no energy for the task. Perhaps a round of visits would see her through the summer nicely, take her mind off both past and future and allow her to live wholly in the present, without a care in the world. That, she thought ruefully, would be an achievement in itself.

Suddenly there was a noise and Marco was there at the door, brushing the sleep from his eyes. 'Emma! I woke to find you gone and thought, for one terrible moment, that you had deserted me!' He came forward, with a smile. 'How lovely you look, all pink and shiny in that splendid bathtub.'

'Like a boiled lobster, you mean?' she smiled, forcing herself to be gay.

He laughed and came to pick up the soap. Kneeling beside her he began to work up a lather between his hands. She did not have the heart to tell him she had already washed herself, but let him do it all again and lay back, revelling in the renewal of her erotic appetite as his hands slid over her breasts and stomach then slipped down between her thighs. She heard a distant church clock chime midnight and some superstitious streak in her expected the enchantment to come to a sudden end and everything to melt away, but it did not. Her Prince Charming remained by her side, ready to do her bidding, and already she was thinking of quite a few things she would like to have done to and for her.

They went back into the bedroom and this time Marco took control of the proceedings. As he invented new ways of pleasuring her with his lips and fingers, Emma thought, 'He is like a child that I have helped to walk, and now he is learning to run by himself.' Marco continued to caress her compliant body with bold assurance, bringing her swiftly to that state of sweet lubricity which allowed his penis to glide smoothly into her and then riding high and hard until her tumid clitoris finally reached its climax, precipitating them both into harmonious bliss.

Again, once the glory had faded Emma was consumed by sadness but this time, although she turned away from her lover, she didn't manage to hide the tears that trickled down. Marco took her in a fierce embrace, dismayed. 'Please do not weep, Emma. I cannot bear to see you unhappy. What is the matter?'

'You know,' she sniffed. 'Soon you will be returning to Italy and I shall be left alone. Oh Marco, I cannot bear it!'

He kissed her wet eyelids, smiling tenderly. 'Then come with me!'

'What?' Emma stared up at him incredulously.

His dark eyes regarded her solemnly. 'I intended to ask you, but you have forestalled me. I have been thinking about it constantly, and I have decided that if you will not come with me I shall remain here. I cannot live without you either, *carissima*.'

'Do you mean that?' Hope and excitement were bubbling in her breast. 'I should not want you to neglect your family duties on my account, but how could I go to Tuscany? What on earth should I do?'

'My father's villa is not far from Florence. You could set up your *Accademia* there. Many English girls visit that city in the course of their education. I am sure it would be possible.'

Emma's mind was buzzing with new thoughts. Of course it would be possible. And the cost of living was cheaper in Italy, too. She could offer short courses, say of a month's duration, for those whose time was limited. Perhaps they could be linked to Italian lessons and include visits to the monuments and galleries. She had heard that many rich American girls did the Grand Tour these days, and Florence was on all their itineraries. The more she thought about it the more likely it seemed that she could make a success of it.

'It is a wonderful idea!' she said at last, kissing him. 'We could live like the Medicis of old, carrying out our business in the city during the week and retreating to our country villa at the weekend or on holidays.'

'Oh Emma! Then you will come?'

'Yes, oh yes!' Then she had a thought. 'But what of the Women's Movement, Marco?' she reminded him, teasingly. 'How will they ever manage without you?'

He laughed. 'Perhaps it is best if victory is achieved without us mere men. Besides, the ladies will be clamouring for the vote in Italy, too. It will probably take longer there, but I am sure that women will be the equal of men all over Europe soon.'

'You dare to suggest that I am not your equal already, Marco? Shame on you!'

'Of course you are not my equal, Emma. You are my superior, far superior!'

They began laughing and teasing each other like playful children. Predictably their joy triggered another round of rapturous love-making but this time, when their ecstasy diminished, Emma lay contentedly, dreaming of her new future. After a while, however, her thoughts returned to the past, and she couldn't help contrasting her present lover with the shadowy memory of Daniel. How different the two men were! And how differently she felt about them both. Her former lover had maintained a hold over her that now seemed like some feverish disease that intermittently broke out, rendering her helpless to resist him. Their attraction for each other had been a perverse force, leading them into paths unknown to ordinary mortals, persuading them to worship some dark god of sensuality.

With Marco, on the other hand, she revelled in the fresh naivety of their love-making. Through him she was discovering anew the simple pleasures of the flesh, his youthful innocence imbuing everything they did with a sense of wonder. She felt redeemed, like a figure from some dark medieval fresco transported into a scene by Botticelli, all light and air. It seemed fitting that she should return to the city that had been the birthplace of the great European Renaissance. For Emma, too, it would be a rebirth.

THE HOUSE IN NEW ORLEANS – Fleur Reynolds
ISBN 0 352 32951 3

ELENA'S CONQUEST – Lisette Allen
ISBN 0 352 32950 5

CASSANDRA'S CHATEAU – Fredrica Alleyn
ISBN 0 352 32955 6

WICKED WORK – Pamela Kyle
ISBN 0 352 32958 0

DREAM LOVER – Katrina Vincenzi
ISBN 0 352 32956 4

PATH OF THE TIGER – Cleo Cordell
ISBN 0 352 32959 9

BELLA'S BLADE – Georgia Angelis
ISBN 0 352 32965 3

THE DEVIL AND THE DEEP BLUE SEA – Cheryl
Mildenhall
ISBN 0 352 32966 1

WESTERN STAR – Roxanne Carr
ISBN 0 352 32969 6

A PRIVATE COLLECTION – Sarah Fisher
ISBN 0 352 32970 X

NICOLE'S REVENGE – Lisette Allen
ISBN 0 352 32984 X

UNFINISHED BUSINESS – Sarah Hope-Walker
ISBN 0 352 32983 1

CRIMSON BUCCANEER – Cleo Cordell
ISBN 0 352 32987 4

RUDE AWAKENING – Pamela Kyle
ISBN 0 352 33036 8

GOLD FEVER – Louisa Francis
ISBN 0 352 33043 0

EYE OF THE STORM – Georgina Brown
ISBN 0 352 330044 9

Published in January

WHITE ROSE ENSNARED
Juliet Hastings

When the elderly Lionel, Lord de Verney, is killed in battle, his beautiful widow Rosamund finds herself at the mercy of Sir Ralph Aycliffe, a dark knight, who will stop at nothing to humiliate her and seize her property. Set against the Wars of the Roses, only the young squire Geoffrey Lymington will risk all he owns to save the woman he has loved for a single night. Who will prevail in the struggle for her body?

ISBN 0 352 33052 X

A SENSE OF ENTITLEMENT
Cheryl Mildenhall

When 24-year-old Angelique is summoned to the reading of her late father's will, there are a few surprises in store for her. Not only was her late father not her real father, but he's left her a large sum of money and a half share in a Buckinghamshire hotel. The trouble is, Angelique is going to have to learn to share the running of this particularly strange hotel with the enigmatic Jordan; a man who knew her as a child and now wants to know her as a woman.

ISBN 0 352 33053 8

Published in February

ARIA APPASSIONATA
Juliet Hastings

Tess Challoner had landed the part of Carmen in a production of the opera which promises to be as raunchy as it is intelligent. But to play Carmen convincingly, she needs to learn a lot more about passion and erotic expression. Tony Varguez, the handsome but jealous tenor, takes on the role of her education. The scene is set for some sizzling performances and life begins to imitate art with dramatic consequences.

ISBN 0 352 33056 2

THE MISTRESS
Vivienne LaFay

It's the beginning of the twentieth century and Emma Longmore is making the most of her role as mistress to the dashing Daniel Forbes. Having returned from the Grand Tour and taken up residence in Daniel's Bloomsbury abode, she is now educating the daughters of forward-thinking people in the art of love. No stranger to fleshly pleasure herself, Emma's fancy soon turns to a young painter whom she is keen to give some very private tuition. Will Daniel accept her wanton behaviour or does he have his own agenda?

ISBN 0 352 33057 0

To be published in March

ACE OF HEARTS
Lisette Allen

Fencing, card-sharping and seduction are the favoured pastimes of Marisa Brooke, a young lady who lives by her wits amongst the wealthy hedonistic elite of Regency England. But love and fortune are more easily lost than won, and Marisa will have to use all her skill and cunning if she wants to hold on to her winnings and her lovers.

ISBN 0 352 33059 7

DREAMERS IN TIME
Sarah Copeland

Four millenia from now, two thousand people remain suspended in endless slumber, while others toil beneath a hostile sun for the means to wake them. Physical pleasure and desire are long forgotten, until Ehlana, a historian and time traveller, discovers that her own primal memories are the key which unlocks the door to another world – and her own sexual awakening.

ISBN 0 352 33064 3

If you would like a complete list of plot summaries of Black Lace titles, please fill out the questionnaire overleaf or send a stamped addressed envelope to:-

Black Lace
332 Ladbroke Grove
London W10 5AH

WE NEED YOUR HELP . . .
to plan the future of women's erotic fiction –

– and no stamp required!

Yours are the only opinions that matter.

Black Lace is the first series of books devoted to erotic fiction by women for women.

We intend to keep providing the best-written, sexiest books you can buy. And we'd appreciate your help and valued opinion of the books so far. Tell us what you want to read.

THE BLACK LACE QUESTIONNAIRE

SECTION ONE: ABOUT YOU

1.1 Sex (*we presume you are female, but so as not to discriminate*)
Are you?

Male   ☐
Female   ☐

1.2 Age

under 21   ☐   21–30   ☐
31–40   ☐   41–50   ☐
51–60   ☐   over 60   ☐

1.3 At what age did you leave full-time education?

still in education   ☐   16 or younger   ☐
17–19   ☐   20 or older   ☐

1.4 Occupation _____

1.5 Annual household income
   under £10,000 ☐   £10–£20,000 ☐
   £20–£30,000 ☐   £30–£40,000 ☐
   over £40,000 ☐

1.6 We are perfectly happy for you to remain anonymous;
   but if you would like to receive information on other
   publications available, please insert your name and
   address

   _____

   _____

   _____

   _____

SECTION TWO: ABOUT BUYING BLACK LACE BOOKS

2.1 How did you acquire this copy of *The Mistress*?
   I bought it myself ☐   My partner bought it ☐
   I borrowed/found it ☐

2.2 How did you find out about Black Lace books?
   I saw them in a shop ☐
   I saw them advertised in a magazine ☐
   I saw the London Underground posters ☐
   I read about them in _____
   Other _____

2.3 Please tick the following statements you agree with:
   I would be less embarrassed about buying Black
   Lace books if the cover pictures were less explicit ☐
   I think that in general the pictures on Black
   Lace books are about right ☐
   I think Black Lace cover pictures should be as
   explicit as possible ☐

2.4 Would you read a Black Lace book in a public place – on
   a train for instance?
   Yes ☐   No ☐

SECTION THREE: ABOUT THIS BLACK LACE BOOK

3.1 Do you think the sex content in this book is:
    Too much ☐   About right ☐
    Not enough ☐

3.2 Do you think the writing style in this book is:
    Too unreal/escapist ☐   About right ☐
    Too down to earth ☐

3.3 Do you think the story in this book is:
    Too complicated ☐   About right ☐
    Too boring/simple ☐

3.4 Do you think the cover of this book is:
    Too explicit ☐   About right ☐
    Not explicit enough ☐

Here's a space for any other comments:

SECTION FOUR: ABOUT OTHER BLACK LACE BOOKS

4.1 How many Black Lace books have you read? ☐

4.2 If more than one, which one did you prefer?

4.3 Why?

SECTION FIVE: ABOUT YOUR IDEAL EROTIC NOVEL

We want to publish the books you want to read – so this is
your chance to tell us exactly what your ideal erotic novel
would be like.

5.1 Using a scale of 1 to 5 (1 = no interest at all, 5 = your
     ideal), please rate the following possible settings for an
     erotic novel:

      Medieval/barbarian/sword 'n' sorcery   ☐
      Renaissance/Elizabethan/Restoration   ☐
      Victorian/Edwardian   ☐
      1920s & 1930s – the Jazz Age   ☐
      Present day   ☐
      Future/Science Fiction   ☐

5.2 Using the same scale of 1 to 5, please rate the following
     themes you may find in an erotic novel:

      Submissive male/dominant female   ☐
      Submissive female/dominant male   ☐
      Lesbianism   ☐
      Bondage/fetishism   ☐
      Romantic love   ☐
      Experimental sex e.g. anal/watersports/sex toys ☐
      Gay male sex   ☐
      Group sex   ☐

     Using the same scale of 1 to 5, please rate the following
     styles in which an erotic novel could be written:

      Realistic, down to earth, set in real life ☐
      Escapist fantasy, but just about believable ☐
      Completely unreal, impressionistic, dreamlike ☐

5.3 Would you prefer your ideal erotic novel to be written
     from the viewpoint of the main male characters or the
     main female characters?

      Male   ☐   Female   ☐
      Both   ☐

5.4 What would your ideal Black Lace heroine be like? Tick as many as you like:

Dominant	☐	Glamorous	☐
Extroverted	☐	Contemporary	☐
Independent	☐	Bisexual	☐
Adventurous	☐	Naive	☐
Intellectual	☐	Introverted	☐
Professional	☐	Kinky	☐
Submissive	☐	Anything else?	☐
Ordinary	☐	_____	

5.5 What would your ideal male lead character be like? Again, tick as many as you like:

Rugged	☐		
Athletic	☐	Caring	☐
Sophisticated	☐	Cruel	☐
Retiring	☐	Debonair	☐
Outdoor-type	☐	Naive	☐
Executive-type	☐	Intellectual	☐
Ordinary	☐	Professional	☐
Kinky	☐	Romantic	☐
Hunky	☐		
Sexually dominant	☐	Anything else?	☐
Sexually submissive	☐	_____	

5.6 Is there one particular setting or subject matter that your ideal erotic novel would contain?

_____

SECTION SIX: LAST WORDS

6.1 What do you like best about Black Lace books?

_____

6.2 What do you most dislike about Black Lace books?

_____

6.3 In what way, if any, would you like to change Black Lace covers?

_____

6.4 Here's a space for any other comments:

_____

_____

_____

_____

_____

*Thank you for completing this questionnaire. Now tear it out of the
book – carefully! – put it in an envelope and send it to:*

Black Lace
FREEPOST
London
W10 5BR

No stamp is required if you are resident in the U.K.